PRAISE FOR ALLISON BRENNAN'S

NOTORIOUS

"Brennan's *Notorious* introduces readers to a new and fascinating heroine worth rooting for. She's an investigative reporter who's not afraid to kick butt, climb a tree, or go to jail in pursuit of her story. She's savvy and smart and takes no prisoners. Buckle up and brace yourself for Maxine Revere."   —Sandra Brown

"Fast-paced fun! *Notorious* packs in the thrills as investigative reporter Max confronts new murders and old family secrets in a suspense novel guaranteed to keep you up late at night."   —Lisa Gardner

"A high-octane thriller . . . Max Revere is a smart, savvy, and irrepressible modern hero."   —Andrew Gross

"I've been a fan of Allison Brennan's novels from the beginning, but *Notorious* blew me away. Explosive suspense ratchets up with every turn of the page as murders—both past and present—twist into a story that demands to be read in one sitting."   —James Rollins

"Brennan is guaranteed to excite fans with the launch of [this] new suspense series . . . With Maxine Revere, Brennan has created a complicated and compelling new protagonist."   —*RT Book Reviews* (4½ stars)

MORE . . .

"The novels featuring Lucy Kincaid and her cohorts are marked with deep characterizations and details of the workings of investigations by private eyes, the police, and the FBI . . . Catch the latest in this series as Lucy continues to evolve in strength and wisdom."

—*Romance Reviews Today*

SILENCED

"Brennan throws a lot of story lines into the air and juggles them like a master. The mystery proves to be both compelling and complex . . . [A] chilling and twisty romantic suspense gem."

—Associated Press

"The evolution of Lucy Kincaid from former victim to instinctive and talented agent continues in Brennan's new heart-stopping thriller . . . From first to last, this story grabs hold and never lets go."

—*RT Book Reviews* (Top Pick)

"An excellent addition to the Lucy Kincaid series. Lucy and Sean continue to develop as complex, imperfect characters with a passion for justice . . . The suspense was can't-put-it-down exciting."

—*Fresh Fiction*

Compulsion

ALLISON BRENNAN

St. Martin's Paperbacks

This is a work of fiction. All of the characters, organizations, and events portrayed in this novel are either products of the author's imagination or are used fictitiously.

COMPULSION

Copyright © 2015 by Allison Brennan.
Excerpt from *Poisonous* copyright © 2016 by Allison Brennan.

For information address St. Martin's Press, 175 Fifth Avenue, New York, NY 10010.

Library of Congress Catalog Card Number: 2015002540

ISBN: 978-1-250-03803-6

Printed in the United States of America

St. Martin's Press hardcover edition / April 2015
St. Martin's Paperbacks edition / February 2016

St. Martin's Paperbacks are published by St. Martin's Press, 175 Fifth Avenue, New York, NY 10010.

10 9 8 7 6 5 4 3 2 1

For my father-in-law, Larry Brennan (1925–2014), who passed away last year while I was writing this book. Larry lived a wonderful life, raising five children, enjoying eleven grandchildren, and befriending all. But what I'll remember most about Larry is how every dog he met became his best friend. It's as if dogs sensed his kind heart—and the treats he carried with him everywhere! God bless you, Larry. I'll bet every dog you've ever owned—and all the strays—are following you around in Heaven.

Acknowledgments

Many people assist in the creation of a book. The author creates the story and the characters over hundreds of hours of writing and rewriting. The editor reads the draft, asking the hard questions and pointing out weak spots in both the writing and the story. Then the author goes back, armed with the editorial notes, and spends another hundred hours or so rewriting the story to make it the best it can be.

I have been truly blessed to have found a fantastic editor in Kelley Ragland at Minotaur. Or, rather, I should thank my agent, Dan Conaway, for putting us together. Our process may look messy to outsiders, but it works for us, and I'm grateful that Kelley understands my chaotic writing method. Or maybe she's just humoring me!

There are many others at Minotaur/St. Martin's Press who are instrumental in the publication process, and I want to thank especially Andy Martin, Jennifer Enderlin, Elizabeth Lacks, Sarah Melnyk, and the amazing art department. Plus, the brilliant copy editors who find all those pesky mistakes I miss even after proofreading the book a dozen times.

As always, there are people I call upon to help me with

my research. If I get something wrong, it's not their fault, it's all mine. A special thanks to Dr. Doug Lyle, FBI Special Agent Steven Dupre, and fellow author Alafair Burke. Alafair probably forgot she let me pick her brain about the New York courthouse and legal process, but I'll never forget her generosity of time and patience.

There are a real Jim and Sandy Palazzolo, friends of the family who were so kind and generous during the time my father-in-law passed. So when Sandy said she wanted to be a character, I asked would she mind being dead? She didn't, and I thank Jim and Sandy for lending their names to my missing persons (who are much, much older than the real-life Palazzolos!).

The Sacramento Public Library Foundation hosts a fund-raising dinner every year to benefit the children's reading program, a cause near and dear to my heart. I was thrilled that Sally O'Hara generously donated to the program and allowed me to use her name. Originally, she was going to be a murder victim, but I loved her name so much that she became an NYPD detective and, I hope, a continuing character.

And finally, I must always acknowledge my family—my husband, Dan; my children, Katie, Kelly, Luke, Mary, and Mark; and my mom, Claudia. Without them I would get a lot more writing done—but I'd have no one to love and play with. You make my life complete.

Compulsion

Prologue

Sweat beaded on Adam Bachman's forehead. He told himself the lights up ahead were just emergency vehicles because of the accident. No one cared about him or this car.

But it wasn't his car.

He had another problem. The girl was starting to move in the trunk.

Everything had gone wrong from the beginning, but he didn't see it right away. Because he was focused on *her,* the pretty blonde. The way she looked at him and he *knew* she was worthy. When she looked over at him at the bar, she smiled a little smile as if they shared a secret.

Maybe he'd imagined it. Maybe he'd made a mistake picking her. Why had the drug worn off so quickly?

Except it wasn't quickly. He'd been stuck in this traffic jam for thirty minutes. Only one lane was open, and cars were backed up. It was summer, people wanted to get out of town, but it was *Tuesday,* not the weekend, and so the accident must be pretty bad for them to only allow a couple of cars through at a time.

The girl kicked the trunk as the car rolled closer to

the emergency vehicles. Then Adam noticed the two cop cars. They must be here for the accident.

If it was just a terrible accident, why was his heart pounding?

Be quiet, girl. Just. Be. Quiet.

The drugs usually kept them out for two hours. Enough time to drive to his secret spot. To revive them. To watch them die. Sometimes, it took hours. Preparation and practice to get everything *just right*. There was a fine line between life and death. Uncovering that exact moment, right before their very last breath, wasn't science. It was art. Every person was unique. It's what made his process so interesting, so provoking. If he made movies, he'd win awards for his precision and care.

He'd made mistakes, but he'd cleaned up his mistakes. The last two had been perfect. First the boy, then the girl. And he'd thought this girl would be just as satisfying. *More* perfect.

He rolled closer to the police cars. They waved cars through, barely glancing inside.

Okay. Good. Stop sweating.

Why would they be looking inside at all? Did they suspect something? Habit because they were cops and all cops were suspicious by nature?

There was no way these cops knew anything about the girl in the trunk. He'd only grabbed her forty-five minutes ago. No one even knew she was missing. His process was perfect; no one had ever been reported missing until they were already dead.

This girl had been very chatty at the bar. She lived in Baltimore. She'd come to the city—alone—to visit her boyfriend. She stayed with him one night, but nothing was the same between them.

"People aren't who you think they are," she'd said.

He had agreed. She'd read his mind.

She stayed in a hotel on her daddy's credit card for a few days while she figured out what she wanted to do with her life. Enjoy the city. Visit a couple of museums. Eat good food.

He couldn't lose. Not after five perfect murders.

The trunk was silent, but he still didn't relax. Three cars remained in front of his. They each slowed to a roll, were waved through, and then disappeared onto the bridge.

He rolled, slowed, and one of the cops waved him through. He pressed the gas pedal.

A piercing scream came from the trunk.

He froze. He wanted to press the gas to the floor, find a hole to drive through, keep going until he drove off the bridge. Ending his life, and the life of the girl in the trunk.

Maybe they hadn't heard her.

He glanced at the two cops. They were walking quickly toward him. Their guns were already in their hands.

"Sir! Keep your hands where we can see them!"

Instead of fleeing, Adam put his hands on the steering wheel and forced himself not to cry.

Chapter One

"Tenacious bitch!"

Maxine Revere stood in the doorway of Ben's office while he finished his conversation with the New York City district attorney.

Max took the D.A.'s verbal attack as a compliment. After all, she had a love-hate relationship with him. In fact, she had a love hate relationship with most of the people in her life.

"Yes, she is." Ben caught her eye and put his finger to his lips as he leaned over his speakerphone. "I'll give her the good news. Thank you, Richard."

He pressed the off button before the D.A. could change his mind—or Max could give him a piece of *her* mind.

Ben's huge grin threatened to swallow him. He jumped out of his chair and squeezed her arm as he grabbed his blazer off the coatrack.

"I don't know what you said to him, Max, but it worked."

"It was as much you as me," she told her producer. She'd played hardball with Richard and Ben played Mr. Nice Guy; between them, they got exactly what she wanted. An interview with Adam Bachman, the twenty-seven-year-old bartender on trial for five murders.

"You'll have twenty minutes," he said as they walked to the elevator. The *Maximum Exposure* offices occupied half of the eighteenth floor of a Seventh Avenue skyscraper, south of Times Square. "Make them count."

She didn't respond to his comment, too energized about this interview to be irritated over Ben's habitual lecture. She'd been maneuvering for time with Bachman ever since she figured out that the missing person's case she'd been investigating since last summer followed the same pattern as Bachman's killing spree.

Max was covering the trial for the station's news programming. She'd been NET's on-site reporter for several high-profile trials. NET wasn't CNN or Fox, but it was making a name for itself. It had exclusively been an Internet news show until three years ago, one year before Max joined the team. Now, while 75 percent of its schedule related directly to up-to-the-minute news, it featured several original daily, weekly, and monthly programs including Max's true crime show *Maximum Exposure,* which Ben produced. She liked that NET was independent and run by a close-knit family with good business sense.

"No cameras," Ben said as he pounded the down button several times, as if the repeated motion would make the door open faster. "But you can record it."

"And that makes you mad," Max said. Max didn't care half as much about the visual, not with this case. She'd been fighting for this interview for too long to quibble over the details. Months of talking—with the D.A., the defense lawyer, cops, the victims' families, everyone she could get access to, but not the killer himself.

Until now. Exclusive. One-on-one. Pen, paper, and an

audio recorder. An old-fashioned interview. Because, as the D.A. had said, she was a tenacious bitch.

"Get him to agree to go on camera after the trial," Ben said. He peered at his reflection in the shiny metal elevator doors and adjusted his tie. Such a yuppie, she thought. "A follow-up after he's convicted."

Max glanced at Ben as the doors opened and interrupted his preening. "Innocent until proven guilty," she said as they stepped inside the empty elevator. The doors swished closed behind them.

"You don't for a minute believe that bastard didn't kill those people."

She'd seen some of the evidence, enough to believe the prosecution had a solid case. But she was a reporter first; she wanted the truth out, no matter what. And while her instincts told her New York's Finest had caught the right guy, anything could happen.

"He's not going to admit his guilt to me the morning his trial begins," she said. "I'll push for the follow-up, but these twenty minutes were hard-fought."

"If you wanted it you could get it," Ben mumbled.

She laughed. "I love that you have such confidence in me."

"NET will be set up to do a live interview with you during the court's lunch break," Ben said. "What happened the first morning of the Bachman trial, yada yada, then again when court recesses for the evening. They'd like you to post comments on your Twitter feed."

"No can do—I told you the judge's rules." Judge Tarkoff had met with lawyers and reporters Friday afternoon about trial conduct. While court was in session, there would be no social media posts from inside the courtroom or the reporter would be banned for the duration of the trial. Commentary would be allowed only during official court breaks. "No electronics inside at all. If you need me, call David or Riley."

"Where *is* Riley?" Ben asked. He sounded irritated, but it was his usual demeanor when he couldn't immediately order someone to do something. Though he hadn't liked Riley Butler when Max first hired her last month, the Columbia grad quickly earned her way into his good graces. Ben cared about two things: competence and speed. He expected the job to be done well, and to be done fast. Riley had picked up on that immediately and ingratiated herself with Ben in less than a week. A new record.

Max just wished her right-hand man David felt the same.

"I sent her on an errand. I'm picking her up on the way to the courthouse."

He glanced at his watch. "Isn't that cutting it close?"

"It's important." She had Riley doing a bit of undercover work with Bachman's former friends and neighbors. She didn't want to share details with Ben because he didn't like that she'd been sending Riley out into the field. Ben felt an office assistant should be in the *office* assisting. Max countered that an office assistant should be *assisting* in whatever needed to be done. If said assistant could take care of basic footwork that gave Max more time with research and interviews—and more time to write.

The elevator doors opened. They stepped out and headed toward the exit. Voices echoed in the cavernous lobby, so Ben lowered his voice. "Are you going to ask him about the partner?"

"Of course." She caught Ben's eye. "Why?"

"I kind of told Richard that you weren't pursuing that line of inquiry," he said as he cleared his throat.

"Why the hell would you say that? You *know* that's the primary reason I wanted this interview."

"I thought you wanted to find out if he killed the Palazzolos."

"I know Bachman was involved; I want proof. And you damn well know that I've been working on this killing pair theory for months."

"When you're not flying down to Miami to annoy your ex, or flying off to California to screw your lover."

"Screw you," she said. Sometimes, Ben acted like the little brother she never had. "You had no *right* telling Rich I'd dropped that theory. I'll ask Bachman whatever I damn well please."

Ex–Army Ranger, personal assistant, and sometime bodyguard David Kane approached them. She had never wanted a bodyguard or a personal assistant, but after threats during a trial nearly two years ago, Ben had insisted. Now David was not only indispensable, he was her closest friend and the only person she trusted explicitly. He'd earned it. Largely because he hadn't quit on her, though she'd given him ample opportunity. And he seemed to be the diffuser of wars waged between Ben and Max.

Truth was, she wasn't the easiest person to work for.

"David, I e-mailed you a revised schedule," Ben said, ignoring Max's glare. She was *not* dropping it. And he knew it. So why would he tell the D.A.—her friend (sort of)—that she would?

David nodded once. "We have to go, Max. I'm parked illegally."

"Ben will pay for the ticket," Max said. She patted him on the cheek, still angry that he was playing games with her interview. "Won't you, Benji?"

He reddened. "Just—watch yourself."

"*I* didn't make that ridiculous promise."

"The D.A. is an asset to NET. Don't blow it."

"Let me handle Richard Milligan. And never make a promise for me that you know damn well I won't keep."

"Max, this is a great case for you."

"Meaning, don't blow it?"

"Stop trying to piss me off. Your interview is going to be picked up everywhere. Just—well, do what you do best."

She arched an eyebrow. "Antagonize people?"

"Find the truth."

She relaxed. She and Ben butted heads often, but she respected him. "That I can do."

"You always do."

She strode through the lobby, David at her side.

"Ben never liked your theory," he said. David was one of the smartest people Max knew, and she rarely had to explain anything to him.

"He's playing games with my reputation. I can make or break my own reputation."

David tipped the security guard who'd ensured his car didn't get towed, then opened the passenger door for Max before she could reach it. "You're not my chauffeur," she grumbled.

He shut the door without a response, then slipped into the driver's seat, and pulled away from the curb. "I drive because you're the definition of a distracted driver," he said.

"He jokes," Max said.

David smiled, as much as his half smiles were.

"I'm right about this," she continued.

"I don't doubt you."

She glanced at him. "But you aren't convinced."

"I'm convinced that if Bachman has a partner, you'll prove it." He stopped at a light. "You rarely surprise me, but I didn't think this was going to happen."

"I can't believe you doubted me," Max said with mock hurt. Then, "I knew Bachman wanted to talk to me—I have his letters to prove it—but his attorney *and* the prosecutor were two stubborn roadblocks. So I went around both and talked to Milligan directly."

David grunted.

"The important thing is that it's happening. I've been planning for this interview for months—I have a number of directions I can go, depending on his answers, but he's going to slip up and I'm going to confirm my theory."

"I don't have to tell you to be careful with him," David said.

"He's in custody. He can't hurt me."

"Don't be cocky, Max. If you *are* right, that means there's another killer still walking free. And you know that."

"And that's why I have *you*, dear David, by my side." She smiled, trying to lighten the conversation, but David stared straight ahead, expertly weaving through traffic.

Bachman had no close friends, no roommate, no siblings. His mother lived in Hartford, Connecticut, and his father wasn't in the picture. His closest childhood friend had enlisted in the army when he turned eighteen and was currently deployed overseas. Bachman's only known friend from college, his former Boston University roommate Chris Gibson, was a social animal whom Max had already dissected; she could find no violent tendencies. What's more, Gibson couldn't have assisted with at least two of the crimes as he was out of town.

So who was Bachman's partner in these murders?

She changed the subject. "Did you tag Riley?"

"She's waiting for us."

He didn't say anything more, and Max let it go. David wasn't sold on Riley. David would come around, because Max trusted her gut, and her gut told her Riley had the chops. Max wanted to train her. She just wished she understood why David didn't like her.

Max had sent Riley Butler to befriend Chris Gibson.

Max wanted information about Bachman—insight that would help her write a three-dimensional story of a man who by all accounts was average, with a steady job as a bartender at a popular club and a loving mother in Connecticut. He fit the profile of a Ted Bundy—charming, attractive, polite—the last person anyone expected to brutally kill strangers.

Max had sent Riley because she was closer to Gibson's age. Gibson worked as a waiter while trying to break into theater. He was sociable and Riley was cute—it worked well. Riley was born to be an undercover reporter. That she came from a long line of Boston cops and had sharp instincts made her even more valuable to Max. She graduated from Columbia with a major in psychology and a minor in journalism, and Max, hands down, thought Riley was smarter than all of her previous assistants combined.

She wasn't perfect. In the six weeks she'd worked for Max, she'd once pursued an inquiry without first clearing it with Max—something Max could appreciate, but not when Riley was still in training, so to speak, so Max had to be much clearer about the rules and her expectations. Riley also didn't care much for the paperwork that went with her job and cut corners, which could be a problem in the future or just a sign of immaturity. Yet Riley was tech-savvy, which streamlined much of the mundane part of her job.

David pulled over in front of a Starbucks in SoHo and Riley slipped into the backseat. She was a petite bundle of energy. A twenty-three-year-old workaholic. Her dad was an Irish cop from Boston. Her mother was a half-black, half-Hispanic pediatric surgeon at the Children's Hospital. Riley was a beautiful blend of the two—skin the color of latte with an added shot of espresso, curly light brown hair, and huge green eyes. She looked like a teenager and had an aura of innocence and trustworthiness that put people at ease. She had two older brothers, one a fire-fighter and one a cop, who'd taught her to defend herself. She leaned forward and handed Max a drink, and another to David. "Latte, black coffee." She grinned.

"Thanks," Max said and sipped.

"I got something," Riley said, unable to contain her excitement.

"Spill it. We have seven minutes until we get to the courthouse."

"I brought Chris over a bottle of wine last night after he missed out on a part he wanted Off-Broadway. Which sucked, because he was called back, so he thought it was a sure thing, and—"

"Faster, Riley," Max interrupted.

"We played the 'who you know' game, back and forth, and *he* said he knew the most notorious serial killer in New York City, Adam Bachman. We drank, talked, and I learned something that seems important. Chris thinks Bachman is obsessive-compulsive."

"And he has a psychiatry degree to back this up?"

"No, but—"

"What else?"

Riley frowned, but continued. "He said Bachman was moody and absolutely anal about his stuff—very meticulous, everything had its place, a place-for-everything kind of OCD. He was gone for a semester his sophomore year. Bachman told Chris that he just needed a break from school, but Chris thinks he was in a mental hospital. Just like you suspected."

"Why?"

"But you said—"

"I *said* I had a hunch, but I had no proof. Did he see meds? Bachman say anything about talking to a shrink? Does Chris know where he went?"

"No, but—"

Max turned in her seat and caught Riley's eye. She could see the girl was fuming, but Max needed her to understand that conjecture was bullshit without something tangible to back it up. Max had a lot of theories, but she didn't flap her mouth until she had a thread she could pull.

"Riley, what you think means nothing. It means you should follow up on your theory, but it's not tangible." She didn't want to demoralize the novice, but she also needed her to understand that rumors and theories weren't printable without evidence. "How can you prove Chris's theory?"

"Talk to Bachman's family. Friends."

"No one is going to talk to you. I worked that angle hard, and couldn't get inside. His mother is completely devoted to him, will not talk to reporters *or* the police. He has few friends—even Gibson hasn't seen Bachman since college." Max softened her tone, just a bit. "I can tell you there's nothing in the files about Bachman being committed. Medical records are practically sacrosanct and if the police don't know something exists, they aren't going to know to ask. His mother, if she knew, didn't tell the police, so she's not going to tell a reporter. And everything Gibson told you might just be a horny guy bragging in the hopes of getting you horizontal, so take everything he said with a grain of salt."

Riley looked down at her hands, which were clenched into fists. She was angry, and Max didn't blame her—Max had articulated her theory that Bachman had spent time in a psych ward, and Riley thought she had proved it. Max had done some preliminary research, but didn't have enough information to narrow down where he might have stayed. Plus, medical records were next to impossible to come by and without a specific location, she'd have to spend months of legwork on a hunch that might not pan out—especially after one of the *Maximum Exposure* researchers had spent two weeks in Boston last fall looking into Max's theory with zero results. Ben was still fuming over the expenses.

Riley needed more direction. "If I had that lead, I'd make a list of all the private, live-in, mental health facilities within a hundred-mile radius of Bachman's home and college that existed during the year in question. That information is already in the files from when we first looked at that angle, so half your work is done for you. Next, I'd find out who ran the facilities and check into disgruntled staff who left *after* the year in question. Disgruntled employees are the most apt to talk. If I could get someone to confirm that Bachman was a patient, I'd pull as much information as I could from that person, and then use it to put the pieces together and follow up on each claim. The *why* being the important thing here. Having a time frame helps."

Riley was taking notes. Good.

"But," Max said, "this is a long shot. I might know in my gut that there's something here, but proving it is the hard part." She planned on tugging that thread with Bachman, however. Now that she had a partial confirmation of her theory—even if it was just the opinion of a former roommate—she felt more comfortable pressing it.

"So I wasted all that time?" Riley's voice was almost a whine.

"No. You're not going to get a big information win here, Riley. Investigative reporting means taking small pieces of information and seeing where they lead. Proving or disproving suspicions. It's a lot like being a detective, only we don't have to follow the same rules. Investigation is as much proving something *isn't* as proving something *is*."

"Okay," Riley said. "I get that." She paused, glanced

first at David, then at Max. "Can I sit in the courtroom with you?"

"I need you outside."

"But—"

David glanced at Max and she knew what he was thinking. She ignored the veiled glare. "I need you in the halls. Observe. Listen. Be accessible for me to send you to follow up on any number of things. Answer Ben's calls. I guarantee, he'll call you at least twice an hour, if only to make sure you'll answer your phone and know where I am."

"Fine," she said with a sigh. David cleared his throat. So Riley was a little dramatic; he needed to cut her some slack.

"And because you can use your phone and I can't, start researching those facilities. You can get the list from my cloud files. Go through it, narrow it, be smart. The notes from the staffer we sent to Boston should be there. My guess? He used a facility closer to home than to college. Someplace where he felt comfortable and safe. Being an investigative reporter is not all glitz and glamour. It's legwork. Paperwork. Research." Honestly, that was the most fun for Max. She much preferred being in the background to being on camera.

Max slipped David a note. "Can you follow up on this for me?"

He glanced at it while stopped at a red light, nodded.

Riley leaned forward. "What? Can I do it?"

Max shook her head. "Boundaries, Riley."

The paper crumpled in David's hand. He'd been a soldier. He was used to taking and giving orders, and he didn't like subordinates to question. He was also both smart and fearsome and Max depended on him. If he really wanted her to drop Riley, she would—because she couldn't lose the only person she could truly count on. She prayed it never came to that, so she diffused the tension by giving a brief commentary on Bachman's defense team and the prosecution and describing who Riley needed to keep an eye on in the halls.

As soon as David pulled up in front of the courthouse in a drop-off zone, Max turned to Riley and handed her a twenty-dollar bill. "The bailiff for Judge Tarkoff is deputy Frank Knolls. He likes his coffee black with a dollop of honey. Go introduce yourself as my assistant, give him the coffee, be nice, smile. Don't ask questions and just walk away."

"Okay. But why?"

"Because making friends with the bailiff, the clerk, and anyone else in support is how we get ahead in this business."

"What about the clerk? Bridget Davis, right?"

"Good memory. She already hates me, attempted to stab me in the back during the last trial I covered. I wouldn't give her water on the hottest day in August, let alone the mochas she likes."

Max waited until Riley exited, then turned to David.

"She's young and inexperienced. But she has good instincts."

"You would never have tolerated insubordination with any of the others."

"They weren't as sharp or dedicated as she is."

"Intelligent, maybe—but she has no common sense."

"Give her time. I've gone through a half-dozen assistants. I don't want to search for another one." And none of her previous assistants had half Riley's drive.

"You're giving her too much freedom."

"Following up on mental health facilities is a good lead. It confirms what I suspected, even if we can't prove it yet."

Time wasn't on their side—the trial would last four days, according to the court clerk. Tarkoff kept his court moving, so Max suspected that estimate was accurate—especially since the defense lost a series of pretrial motions that could have extended testimony. "It might lead us to his partner or give us insight into his motivation."

If Riley found something to the theory, it might put another spin on Max's report from the human interest side. Could someone have predicted Bachman would become a killer? If there was truth to him admitting himself to a facility, she could follow up about the viability of these places. Do they really help? Do they have a moral or ethical obligation to share a psychopathic diagnosis with law enforcement if they suspect someone is a danger to others? What flaws are there in the system that so many people who need mental health services fall through the cracks? Was Bachman one of those people?

She put her hand on David's. "What is it? Tell me what's really bothering you about Riley. You ran the background check yourself, you said she was clean. You even said you admired her family."

"This is a game to her."

"She's eager. Ben said I like her because I'm a narcissist and she's a mini-me."

Max was trying to be light, but David couldn't keep the anger out of his voice.

"That little girl will never be you."

"I'm keeping my eye on her. But if you want me to cut her loose, I will. Just say it."

David's eyebrow shot up. "You'd do it, too."

"For you I would."

"I just want you to be careful with her. You've given her a lot of freedom, freedom that she hasn't earned."

"What are you concerned about, David?"

"Her safety. Your safety. And honestly? She's overeager. She's going to make mistakes that will come back and bite you in the ass."

Max opened her mouth to argue, but David had touched on something she'd wondered herself. "Point taken."

She put her hand on the door handle. "She *is* a lot like I used to be," she told David. "She works her ass off and isn't afraid to get her hands dirty."

"She may share your work ethic, but she's nothing like you."

David didn't know the old Max. The wild college girl who'd made far more mistakes than she wanted to talk about. Even if he'd read her book about the murder of her best friend while they'd been on spring break in Miami, it had been written through the lens of history, and while Max had been honest and forthcoming about her mistakes, David might not see them as such because he didn't know her then.

One of the courthouse guards approached their car since they were in a no parking zone, and Max couldn't continue the conversation. She made a mental note to cook dinner for David one night and get him to open up more about this. He was more forthcoming when he'd been well fed. "You okay with talking to the cops up in Queens?"

"Of course. They didn't ban *me* from their precinct." He smiled, his hard, scarred face bemused. "I'll be back before your live report at noon, but if I'm not, don't leave the courthouse until I return."

"I wouldn't think of it," Max said, her voice edged with sarcasm.

David put a hand on her arm before she got out of the car. "Max, since I've been working for you, you've covered five major trials, and each one of them yielded serious threats. There's no reason to think the Bachman trial is any different—especially since you're pursuing the idea that he wasn't working alone."

"I haven't printed a word about that theory."

"But you're about to ask him."

"Good point. I'll be good." She blew him a kiss and got out of the car. "You have my word."

Chapter Two

"I've advised my client not to speak with the media."

Gregory Warren, Bachman's defense attorney, puffed out his chest as if that would make him look important. It only made him look silly.

Max didn't respond. Warren was a blowhard. Bachman couldn't afford a high-priced lawyer who might have been able to kill this interview, but had just enough scratch to bring on a slimy ambulance chaser. Warren was probably making more from the ancillary gigs. A case like this could yield lecture fees at law schools. A friend of hers in publishing said Warren was already working on a book deal.

They stood in a corridor on the third floor, adjacent to rooms used primarily for lawyers to consult with their clients between court proceedings. Max looked at her watch. Time was ticking, and Tarkoff ran a tight courtroom. If Richard was playing around with her, giving her this promise then creating delays, she'd skewer him. She and D.A. Richard Milligan had a long friendship—one that Rich might deny if asked. Didn't matter to Max—she didn't kiss (or not kiss) and tell—but it certainly helped when she needed something. Like access to Adam Bachman.

She heard the *click click click* of sensible heels before she saw the petite A.D.A., Charlene Golden, turn the corner and approach them.

"Maxine."

"Counselor."

"Richard sent me to babysit you. I have a shitload of work on my desk, not to mention a trial starting in ninety minutes, so I'm holding you to the agreed-upon twenty minutes."

"I object to this entire interview," Warren interjected.

Charlene dismissed him with a sidelong glance that would have melted ice, but ice had more self-awareness than Warren.

Rich had brought Charlene on shortly after he was elected as D.A. She was smart and loyal to her boss. Word had it that Charlene would replace Rich when he moved on—he was eyeing attorney general as a stopover to governor or senator. And he'd get it—he was blunt and forthcoming and didn't bullshit. It's why she liked him, even if he had called her a bitch on more than one occasion.

Tenacious bitch.

If the shoe fit.

"Here's what's going to happen," Charlene said. "Mr. Warren and I will be watching through the observation room. There's a guard outside the door. There will be no physical contact. Mr. Bachman is dressed for court, but will be handcuffed to the table. You'll leave your phone, briefcase, purse—everything except for one notepad, a pen, and your recorder—at the guard station. You are not to give Bachman anything, nor take anything from him. Understood?"

"Yes."

"I'll tap on the window when you have two minutes remaining. When the twenty minutes is up, the guard will escort Bachman to the holding room. If Bachman wants to end the interview early, he'll say so. If you want to end it early, call for the guard."

"I understand." This wasn't the first time Max had interviewed a prisoner. She'd met with those on trial and those who'd been convicted. She'd gone into maximum security prisons to interview violent predators in the hopes of getting answers.

Out of the two dozen such interviews she'd conducted over the last decade, she'd often become frustrated. Convicts lied. Or they attempted to manipulate her into printing an article showing them in a convincing light. Others wanted to "set the record straight" either by claiming their innocence or accusing the police of bullying.

But Max had learned early on that most prisoners simply wanted a forum to talk. They saw her as a conduit to the public, as a way to give them a voice. Once she deciphered their endgame, she learned tricks to get them to tell her anything she wanted to know.

Of course, if the letters she received after the interviews were any indication of her skill, they were rarely happy with her articles. She'd been accused of lying, manipulating, and cheating, but she didn't care. What else were criminals going to say? In the same breath they said they were innocent, they thought she put words in their mouth. She did not. She usually got exactly what she wanted— and they said the words that she recorded to back her up.

Though she always felt tainted when she finished an interview with a killer and craved a hot bath and several glasses of wine.

Charlene left to talk to the guard, and Warren said to Maxine, "I told him not to do this."

"So you said." Max assessed the defense counsel. He was in his fifties, wide, with watery blue eyes and thick glasses. She'd done her homework—he'd won a couple high-profile cases early in his career, but nothing of significance in the past decade. He had a high plea rate with the D.A.'s office, who thought he was competent but not much more. He specialized of late in taking appeals for convicts who'd been represented by public defenders—not lucrative, but it kept the lights on in his one-room Manhattan office. The Adam Bachman trial was definitely the most high-profile case he'd had in a long time.

"If you'd like to interview me after the trial, I would be happy to have a sit-down." He smiled broadly, revealing impossibly white teeth.

Big, bad wolf.

"We might have to do that," she said, though she had no intention of interviewing Warren unless there was a compelling public interest reason to do so, if Bachman was acquitted for instance. Then it might be interesting to her viewers. Still, keeping Bachman's defense counsel on her goodish side could be important.

Charlene returned. "They're getting Mr. Bachman ready now. Two minutes."

"I need a minute with my client first, Counselor," Warren said.

Charlene nodded to the guard, and Warren followed. Max said to the A.D.A., "I appreciate your time."

Charlene waved off the comment. "Don't mess with my case, Max."

"I have no intention."

"I don't have to tell you that when the judge denied my motion to sequester the jury that makes the media far more dangerous."

"Or helpful."

"I know you. Excuse me." Charlene pulled out her phone and walked twenty feet down the hall, effectively ending the conversation before it even started.

Fine by Max. If she wanted to interview Charlene for the show, she'd go through Richard anyway.

But the A.D.A.'s attitude annoyed her. Max had always been fair to Richard and his staff. From what Max had seen and heard from her sources, Charlene had a solid case.

So why was she so intimidated by Max?

Adam Bachman was twenty-seven but looked younger in the too-large dark gray suit and slim navy tie. Max suspected his attorney had intentionally brought him a suit that didn't fit, to make the young man appear more vulnerable and less threatening to the jury. His brown hair had been neatly trimmed, and his hands—which were cuffed in front of him—immaculate and soft. He was neither fat nor thin, attractive nor ugly. He was, in fact, average and pleasant-looking. On the surface, he looked trustworthy— the kind of guy people would immediately be comfortable with. The kind of guy people are surprised when he's not what he seems. He looked *nice*. If ever there was a person that fit that boring word, it was Adam Bachman. Every interview Max had done leading up to today confirmed that no one thought *nice* Adam Bachman could have done anything so violent.

Max smiled and sat down across from Bachman. It was a wide table—she wouldn't be able to touch him unless she reached all the way forward—but she had no intention of getting that close. He'd suffocated five people.

Seven if you're right, Maxine.

But she wasn't going to lead with her theory.

"Thank you for agreeing to this interview, Mr. Bachman. Per your request, there are no cameras here, just a tape recorder. That's to protect you as much as me. But also as you requested, the tape will not be publicly aired."

He didn't say anything, simply stared at her with a half

smile. It was the smile of someone with a secret, but she suspected his expression meant nothing. He might want to get under her skin, or he might just not know how to start. He might intend to play games—it wouldn't be the first time a killer tried to manipulate her.

She said, "Because we only have twenty minutes, I'd like to get right to my questions."

He nodded again. *Great.* If he didn't talk she'd have nothing to write. She could see the headline now: MUTE MAN ON TRIAL FOR MURDER.

She knew her questions by heart, but glanced at her notes to ground herself. Her goal in this meeting was to find a thread that she could pull on the disappearance of Jim and Sandy Palazzolo. The couple, in their midfifties, had been on their second honeymoon. They'd checked out of their hotel a year ago and had not been heard from since.

Their disappearance coincided with Adam Bachman's killing spree. There were many similarities. Just like the other five victims, the Palazzolos disappeared on a Tuesday (Bachman had Tuesdays and Wednesdays off from his bartending job); they were tourists from out of state staying at a hotel in Times Square; they had at one point during their vacation gone to the bar where Bachman worked.

The police focused only on the *differences*: that the other victims were kidnapped while alone; they were under forty years of age; their bodies had been found within a week of their disappearance, dumped in various empty buildings in Queens.

It was partly because of the Palazzolos that Max had been banned (she would argue temporarily) from every NYPD precinct in Queens. She'd been detained for trespassing twice while searching abandoned buildings, looking for their bodies. That the assistant chief in Queens already hadn't liked her contributed to her temporary banishment. But there were hundreds of places and thousands of nooks and crannies to search. The police argued that the other victims had been relatively easy to find— discovered by people who worked or lived in the area or, in one case, teenagers who went into an abandoned cannery to get stoned.

The other key difference was that the Palazzolos had checked out of their hotel room and had been seen on security cameras driving out of the parking garage. They weren't reported missing until one of their kids started looking for them when they didn't arrive home on schedule.

But Max's gut told her there was something here. It was a series of events and comments after Adam Bachman was arrested that convinced her. She'd interviewed his former neighbors, his professors, one of his college roommates, and his best friend from childhood who was in the army. She wanted to understand him better, because that would help her convey the true Adam Bachman to her viewers. And, in the back of her mind, she thought this case might be right for her next true crime book.

One of her sources at the crime lab who'd processed Bachman's apartment told her he kept his place immaculate, almost obsessively clean, which confirmed what Max had learned from others and what Riley learned from his former roommate. The guy was fastidious. Bachman also had many books, mostly biographies, and appeared to be an avid reader. In addition to his job as a bartender, he was taking online classes in pursuit of a masters in history.

"I'm not going to go through all the preliminaries I usually do on an interview—I have your background pretty well documented. I've already talked to people who know you. Anything out in the public that you wish to correct?"

He shook his head, that secretive smile still curving his lips.

"Until your arrest last July, you had never been in trouble with the law. Correct?"

"Not even a speeding ticket," he said.

His voice was quiet and clear. He maintained eye contact, almost to the point where it was creepy. Likely an intimidation technique.

"You pled not guilty to all charges. How optimistic are you that the jury will acquit you?"

He shrugged.

"Do you think there's enough reasonable doubt that the jury won't issue a guilty verdict?"

"You'll have watch the trial. I have no idea."

He continued to stare at her, and while Max had faced far more violent predators than Adam Bachman, this focus was unnerving. He was pale, to the point of appearing gaunt. But his dark eyes were sharp. Assessing her.

Max had read and analyzed all information that had been released to the public, and picked up a few details that hadn't been released through eavesdropping and talking with key contacts. While the deaths were tragic, they weren't particularly brutal—he didn't sexually assault his victims, for example. Based on what had been revealed, Bachman kidnapped the victims—drugging them to the point of unconsciousness—and took them to an unknown location where he kept them alive up to twenty-four hours before suffocating them. His "killing ground," as Charlene said a bit too grandiosely at a press conference, had never been located, and Bachman hadn't talked. Bachman disposed of each body in different abandoned buildings in Queens. According to the forensics report Max had bribed a CSI to show her, Bachman had moved their bodies immediately after death. To Max, that told her that when they were dead he was completely done with them, wanted them out of his sight. Perhaps to make way for the next victim.

Bachman had been apprehended because of a series of unfortunate events—the drugs he'd given what would have been his sixth known victim had worn off because he hadn't dosed her right; he was stuck in traffic because of an accident on the Queensboro Bridge. Because of the accident, police were managing traffic. The victim, twenty-four-year-old Ava Raines, had been tied up in the trunk. She screamed, the police opened the trunk, then arrested Bachman. He didn't resist and had since been a model prisoner.

Max needed to push him. She'd initially thought that he'd agreed to the interview because he wanted to talk—so she asked open-ended questions in the hopes that he would ramble. But he wasn't talking. He was just staring at her with that know-it-all smile.

"Mr. Bachman, you agreed to this interview. Is there anything you want to say?"

"I've seen your show. The camera loves you."

She ignored the comment. "So you know what I discuss on *Maximum Exposure*."

"Yes. I've seen every show. Multiple times."

It was his tone, as if he was trying for seductive. Or possibly admiring. But it failed. It was almost sneering. She kept her expression blank.

"Your mother has been supportive of you from the moment you were arrested and told the press that this is all a misunderstanding. Have you seen her recently?"

"My mom visits me every week."

"She's expected to be in the courtroom for the duration of the trial. How does that make you feel?"

He laughed. Odd response, and he didn't comment further.

"According to your neighbors in Hartford, your childhood wasn't all cake and parties. Your father left when you were a toddler, and your mother's second husband was abusive. She filed and won a restraining order against him when you were thirteen."

"I've already talked to the government psychiatrist. I have no interest in talking about my childhood. It's irrelevant."

"Some people believe that the past shapes the future." He tilted his head. "Do you think that?"

She couldn't allow him to ask questions.

"Maybe," she said vaguely. "Some people find solace in getting help from the outside. A teacher, a friend, a therapist. What about you? According to a friend of yours from college, you left to get psychiatric help because of problems adjusting to living on campus." She had totally made that up, but wanted to give him something to refute. "What was that like?"

He reddened. "Who said that? They're lying!"

His first real reaction was a big one.

"People want answers," she said. "It drives human nature to seek explanations for the unexplainable. Did you battle violent tendencies even back then? In high school? College?"

His jaw clenched. "I'm. Not. Violent." He swallowed, gathering his composure.

Not *I haven't killed anyone* or *I'm innocent.*

I'm not violent.

Max had interviewed killers who enjoyed bragging about their crimes. She'd interviewed killers who'd denied their guilt even when faced with overwhelming evidence. When she covered the trial of a city manager who'd been accused of embezzling millions of dollars from the city pension fund, he'd tried to justify his actions—essentially he was trying to make the city *more* money through his high-risk investments that, ultimately, ended up with him getting rich and hundreds of employees losing their retirement.

But Adam Bachman was different. She couldn't put her finger on why.

"Did you admit yourself into a private psychiatric facility while you were in college?" she asked bluntly.

"I don't have to answer that."

"You don't have to answer anything. You agreed to talk to me, but right now, you're not saying anything that's of interest to me or my viewers." She closed her notebook to emphasize her point.

He reddened again, and that's when she saw it. The ego underneath the calm. She used that.

"You'll be a mere footnote in criminal justice classes, if that, because you're letting everyone else define you. Define yourself. Tell me why you're here. Why you wanted to talk to me."

He didn't answer right away. He rolled his head and shoulders, a technique she used when tense and trying to relax. He leaned forward and overenunciated, "Do you think that anyone is capable of taking a human life?"

"Mr. Bachman, why—"

"Call me Adam," he interrupted. "I mean, you're *older* than me. Why call me *mister*?" He smiled, a hint of his charm coming out in his expression, but his eyes were cold and shrewd.

"If you're going to play games, I'll leave. I have more than enough background information to write ten articles. I don't need your input." She was trying to make him angry, push him into giving her something quotable.

"But you want it," he said with a shrug. "*You* want to know the truth."

She didn't react, but his comment hit her dead-on. She always sought the truth. It defined her, it drove her. It wasn't a big secret—if he'd seen even one episode of *Maximum Exposure* as he claimed, he'd know that the truth was more than a little important to her. But the way he said it sent a chill up her spine.

"Yes," she said, keeping her voice even. She couldn't let him know he'd gotten under her skin. "I want to know the truth. I want to know if you killed those five people all by yourself, or if someone helped you."

He shifted, just a bit. It wasn't a physical movement so much as a tightening of his muscles. A slight twitch in his jawline. She was right. She knew it.

Another killer was still out there.

Then he said, "I see what you're trying to do. If I say I didn't have help, you'll write that I admitted to killing those people. If I say I did have help, I'm admitting to killing those people."

"People who know you describe you as 'sweet,' 'considerate,' 'clean,' and 'meticulous.' Those are the people who like you, who were surprised at your arrest for murder. The people who don't like you? They call you 'anal-retentive,' 'obsessively neat,' and 'fastidious.' One woman you worked with said you washed your hands after touching money every single time without fail. That you have a phobia about germs. That you kept a gallon-sized bottle of hand sanitizer in your locker."

"Melinda," he said, looking behind her, as if picturing his chatty co-bartender. Melinda Sanchez had been one of the few people who told Max that, hands down, she thought Adam was creepy from the minute she started working at Fringe, six months before Adam was arrested.

"Adam, right now I have a piece running on the wire that will be printed in every major newspaper and Web site. I can choose to quote your colleague or your childhood best friend who said you helped him graduate high school by tutoring him in math. What's your spin on this trial? What do you think will happen this week? Tell me what you wanted to tell me. Tell me why you agreed to talk."

He refocused his attention on her and leaned forward. That damn smile returned.

"Have you ever gone fishing?" She didn't answer, but tilted her chin up in a sign to continue. There was a light tap on the window; she prayed time wasn't up.

"You hook a fish. It's not supposed to hurt them, but who knows because fish can't talk. You put them down and they flop around, their gills trying to get air, but they can't. *Flop, flop, flop.* Slower and slower. Until they are lying there, unmoving, except for those little flaps on the side of their head. If you throw them back into the water, they're disorientated for a minute, then they swim away. Only to be hooked again. They don't learn from their mistakes. They still see the bait, they want the bait, in the back of their little pea brains they might even recognize there's a danger, but they dismiss it. They get hooked every time.

"Eventually, if you leave them out of water long enough, they die. But I was always mesmerized by that time between, from panic to resignation. And I always wondered why they didn't learn.

"Like you."

He stared at her, his eyes darker than they were at the beginning of the interview, as if he were excited. He whispered, so low she didn't think her tape recorder would pick it up.

"You'll never find them. And it'll eat you up forever."

"You're talking about the Palazzolos."

"I'm not the violent one," he whispered.

She wasn't certain she'd heard that right. "Excuse me?"

He smiled. "Five, four, three, two, one."

There was a knock on the door and the guard came in. "Time's up."

"I *will* find them," she said, her voice hitching just a bit.

He smiled wider as if he had a victory. Her stomach flipped. She'd screwed up. She'd reacted to his story, to his near-confession. He'd reeled her in like the damn fish he was talking about. He'd told her he'd seen her show, how she craved the truth. Then he dangled the truth out there and snatched it back, giving her nothing. And her reaction let him know he'd hit her button.

She picked up the recorder and notepad and walked out without looking back.

Damn, she was usually better than that.

Chapter Three

David Kane walked into the 115th Precinct in Queens. Though the cop shop was swept and cleaned by janitorial crews at night, a gray pallor hung over the old building, accented by the deep scent of unwashed criminals and burnt coffee. He approached the desk sergeant. Her badge read DUNN. The woman was fifty and plump around the middle, but had the sharp eyes of someone who'd seen it all and was never surprised.

He said, "I'd like to speak with Detective O'Hara."

"ID, please."

"I'm carrying, and have a license to carry," he said before reaching into his coat pocket and removing his identification. His New York State driver's license, his veteran's card (because with cops, being a veteran often granted access or courtesy), and his concealed carry permit. Even with David's background and high-level security clearances from his time in the army, a CCP was next to impossible to get in New York City. After threats against Max when David first started working for the show, and obtaining his private security license, it had finally come through. David suspected either Max or Ben had been involved, but he'd decided he didn't need to know.

David also had *Maximum Exposure* press credentials, but he'd found that in a police station, those particular credentials would get him tossed on his ass.

Sergeant Dunn scrutinized his identification. "Which O'Hara? We have three cops named O'Hara."

He didn't know.

Dunn sighed. "What's it about?"

"A cold case. Palazzolo."

"Sally O'Hara. Have a seat."

David stood, his back against the wall, and surveyed the room. A kid high on something was mouthing off to two uniformed officers as they wrestled the brat into booking. A young black couple, the woman with a tear-stained face, was reporting a break-in. "They took my mama's wedding ring."

A teenage girl smacking her lips with a thick wad of gum glanced over at David and winked. He didn't react. But if his daughter ever wore a skirt that short or dyed her hair an impossible color, she'd be in a convent.

As if you have any say.

Brittney made his life miserable, but Emma had grown up surprisingly normal for a girl with a selfish, conceited, childish mother and a gay father who only saw her a few weeks of the year. She was twelve, and David supposed the worst years were to come, but he cherished the limited time he could spend with her. She'd be flying to New York City to spend six weeks with him this summer. Max had already bought tickets to two of the hottest musicals, and then planned on sending him and Emma to her house in the Hamptons for three weeks. Because, as Max said, New York in August was hell on earth.

David Kane had considered law enforcement when he was honorably discharged from the army, but he'd had enough run-ins with MPs during his ten years in the service that he decided it wasn't the place for him. He liked rules, he liked structure, but he sometimes had issues with authority. Specifically, authority that abused its power.

He'd considered reupping, but the last year he'd been in had been hell. Everything that could go wrong, did. David wasn't political, but the actions of politicians and people who had no business running military ops had put him and his team at great risk, repeatedly.

And then he'd lost his closest friend.

Sometimes he missed the life. The Ranger motto— "Rangers lead the way"—meant something to him. Especially as part of a special reconnaissance unit, where he was used to gathering information in dangerous situations.

Working for *Maximum Exposure* hardly qualified as dangerous, but he was good at it. And, surprisingly, he liked his job. Especially now that Max had adjusted to most of his security changes. Working for Max wasn't always easy, but he respected her in ways he didn't most people.

A plainclothes cop approached the desk sergeant, then glanced at him. When he caught her eye, she bypassed the sergeant and made a beeline toward him. She looked like the girl-next-door type with a mess of white-blond curls that touched her shoulders and big blue eyes. If it wasn't for her gun and badge clipped to her faded jeans, David wouldn't have pegged O'Hara for a cop. He would have thought she was barely old enough to drink, until she got closer and saw the faint crow's-feet framing her eyes.

"Let's walk." Without waiting for an answer, O'Hara led the way outside.

David followed. He didn't have to ask—O'Hara knew who he was and why he was here.

She glanced over her shoulder, but wasn't looking at

him. "Good," she said and slowed her pace. "You can buy me coffee. But no way in hell I'm going there." She jerked her finger to a coffee shop across the street from the precinct. "We're walking three blocks so O'Malley doesn't hear I was talking to you."

"You must know Max."

"I really didn't believe she'd send anyone out here. I told her she was getting her panties in a wad, but she doesn't take no for an answer."

David suppressed a smile. He could just imagine how that conversation went over with Max. "She asked me to follow up on the Palazzolo investigation and gave me your name."

"Yeah, she found out it was passed over to me and thought she could use our friendship to push her crazy-ass theory. Last time I helped her I got my hand slapped. If O'Malley finds out I'm giving her anything after he banned her from the precinct, I'll be demoted to manning the drunk tank."

David had known Max for nearly two years, but hadn't heard of O'Hara. That probably shouldn't come as a surprise; Max knew a lot of people.

"Then maybe it's better that she sent me."

"You're not exactly Mr. Incognito. I totally knew who you were."

"Really?"

She shot him a narrow glance. "Who else is going to be here asking about the Palazzolos? And I recognized your name when Dunn called me."

"Give me the story and I'll get out of your hair."

"There *is* no story. We're just following through on some things."

"Like?"

She didn't say anything for an entire block. Then she turned in to a Starbucks. It was a short line for nine thirty in the morning. David paid and they took their drinks to a small table outside. The table and chairs were chained together. Didn't make them impossible to steal, only more of a challenge.

"How much has Max told you?" O'Hara asked.

"I know about her theory that Bachman killed the Palazzolos."

O'Hara glanced around. "Shh! Dammit, there *could* be cops here. Or reporters."

"All the reporters are at the courthouse."

"Right. Every damn one of them in all of New York City," she snapped sarcastically. "Look, I want to find these people as much as Max. More. It's my damn *job*. I work missing persons. All of Queens, not just in the one-one-five. There are two of us in each borough, and six in Manhattan. We're pretty tight so I knew about the Palazzolos from the get-go. But who does Max call? *Me*. Just because she helped me once, I feel like I've sold my soul to the devil and I'll never get out of debt."

Max had that way with people.

"So," O'Hara continued, "she's been nagging me on and off, but truthfully, there was nothing there. We all thought they'd left like they were supposed to and got jumped at a rest stop on their way back to Ohio. But there were a few things that bugged me. None of their cards were used after they filled up with gas near the I-95 interchange. We checked the surveillance cameras in the area and saw their car leave the station, but we can't see who was driving the car and there's no surveillance of the car crossing any bridge or entering the tunnel within twenty-four hours of that last charge."

"So something happened to them in Manhattan."

"We walked, talked, harassed everyone in the area and nada. No one remembers them, no one claimed to see anything. It was a dead end."

"If they disappeared in Manhattan, why do you have the case?"

"That's what Max asked me, and I avoided the answer like the plague, but she bribes cops with baseball tickets and Scotch. There has *got* to be something illegal in that," she said under her breath. She sipped her coffee, silently fuming, but David had her pegged. She wanted Max's help—because Max's help meant Max's resources—but Sally didn't want to make it seem like she was easy.

"Somehow," Sally continued, "Max figured out the case had been sent over to me. We had a witness, about a week after the Palazzolos disappeared, who claimed to have seen the Palazzolos' car in the area surrounding the old Long Island rails. There's an abandoned strip in southern Queens. So because the case *might* have had a Queens connection, Manhattan slid it over to me a few weeks ago so their clearance record would look better. *Assholes*."

"That's a largely abandoned area," David said. "Similar to where Bachman dumped the bodies of his other victims."

"There was nothing there a year ago. But when I got the case, I decided to retrace everyone's footsteps, even though we have no hard evidence that the couple were anywhere near that area. Their car *may* have been seen, but we only have a partial number and mention of the colorful Ohio plate. The witness is eighty if he's a day, and the call came in a year ago. Now he doesn't remember any of it. Frankly, it's like they just vanished. Poof! Into thin air." She sipped her quad-shot latte. "I can see why Max is so obsessed with the case."

Sally O'Hara didn't know the half of it. The disappearance of Jim and Sandy Palazzolo hit all of Max's buttons: they were an older couple, they vanished without a trace, and they had a family who wanted answers.

"Detective, Max wouldn't have asked me to come out

here if she thought she was going to have her own theory regurgitated back at her."

"I don't know how she knew," O'Hara mumbled.

David didn't say anything. He just stared at Sally until the cop talked.

"We found something, okay? Shit, one of my cops must have flapped his chops." She shook her head. "No proof of anything, and it probably isn't connected to the Palazzolos *at all*, but it's weird. You know Max was almost arrested two weeks ago for trespassing."

Of course David knew. Ben had to do some fast talking to keep Max from getting more than a slap on the wrist.

"Fortunately, my team had already gone through the rail station and removed potential evidence, so she came down to the precinct and raised hell like she does, and O'Malley kicked her out and swore none of us would tell her."

"He's suppressing evidence?"

"No, it's all in the files, he just doesn't want Max to have them. She vilified him three years ago when those girls went missing from the airport. Just skewered him. And while he made a mistake, he didn't deserve to have his reputation tarnished like that."

David didn't know what case she was referring to, but nodded just the same. He'd have to ask Max about it later.

He steered Sally back toward the case at hand. "What did you find?"

"I swear, if she ever tells anyone I told you this, I'll never speak to her again."

"Understood."

"I go through cold cases at home, reading through trying to look at things from a different perspective. I started thinking about that witness who called, and realized no one had been back to the area since. Not for a comprehensive search. So a couple of weeks ago I got a pair of uniforms who owed me a favor to help. It took us three days, but we covered every abandoned building in a four-block radius.

"In one of the abandoned train stations, a block from where the witness had *possibly* seen the Palazzolos' car, we found an empty container marked sodium hydroxide. Lye."

"I'm familiar with the chemical."

"It was just sitting there, in the middle of the tracks, sort of hidden from sight because of the angle of the structure and debris that had piled up around it. It had been there a long time. It seemed so odd that I ran the serial numbers and it came back as having been sold to a business in Brooklyn—along with two other twenty-five pound containers. We followed up, but there was no such business and the address belonged to an old lady who didn't speak English and had no idea what we were talking about."

"Someone used her as a mail drop."

Sally nodded. "We brought in a translator and pushed, talked to neighbors, but we didn't even know what to *ask*. And there's not like a doorman at the building who could tell us about a shipment that arrived nearly a year ago."

"Nearly a year?"

She hesitated, then nodded. "The sodium hydroxide was ordered the day after the Palazzolos disappeared. It was delivered the day before the call came in about their car in Queens."

"And you haven't found the other two containers."

She shook her head. "There is absolutely nothing to connect the empty container to the Palazzolos. Nothing. I can come up with a dozen plausible scenarios. And even *if* someone had killed them and destroyed their bodies with sodium hydroxide, why leave only one empty container? Where did they do it? Why? They weren't poor or rich. They had some credit cards and maybe five hundred in cash on them. Their cards haven't been used since they disappeared. I only ran the numbers on the container because Max got into my head and I could practically hear her telling me to do it." She stared at her cup. David recognized the expression.

"You think it's suspicious."

"Damn straight I do. I had forensics analyze the container to see if there was anything else odd, and they came back with bleach residue. No prints. Someone wiped it down with bleach? Why on earth would they do that except that they didn't want their prints on it. So, it may have something to do with the Palazzolos' disappearance."

She looked him in the eye, her expression determined. "I'm a good cop, Kane. I know when something is wrong, and this is wrong. And if I thought for one second that Bachman was involved, I would be all over his case. But it doesn't fit, and nothing Max Revere says or does can force a square peg into a round hole. Even if the lye was involved in their disappearance or murder, that doesn't mean Bachman was involved. He didn't use lye on any of his other victims, and I went through each case—no containers or even a hint of the chemical was found at any of the crime scenes."

"I have a favor to ask."

She closed her eyes and sighed. "Of course you do."

"Take me to where you found the container."

"I have work to do, Mr. Kane."

"Then tell me where you found it and I'll go on my own." He smiled at her. He liked O'Hara, and he could see why Max liked her, too.

"Shit." She glared at him. "Fine, I'll do it."

"May I look at the file?"

"Don't push it." She got up and walked out. He followed.

He'd get a look at the file before they were done.

Chapter Four

Max had a terrific seat in the courtroom with a great view of the jury box and prosecution in particular. She was on the defendant's side of the room, but from her angle next to the center aisle, she also had a good look at Bachman's profile, especially when his attention was on the jury or a witness.

Charlene's cocounsel was a doofus named Roger Hayes. He was older than Charlene and thought he should always be first chair, but in one of Richard's more relaxed moods when he and Max had gone to a charity event together (as friends, but Page Six made more of it than it was), he'd told her how Roger was a screwup. Out of respect for the D.A., Max had never printed anything he'd said, but she itched to see Roger Hayes screw up firsthand so she could shine a light on his incompetence.

The opening statements were standard fare—the prosecution outlined what they were going to prove, using lots of adjectives like "evil" and "cunning" and "premeditated" and "brutal." Max ignored most of those because they didn't tell her anything about their actual case. It was when Charlene explained to the jury how the victims died that

Max's ears perked up. Most of the specific details had been kept from the press during the investigation, and she'd only heard bits and pieces.

"The state will prove that Mr. Bachman not only suffocated his victims with a clear plastic bag, but we'll prove that first he tortured them for more than twenty-four hours."

Now *that* was news. No one had leaked anything about torture.

Charlene continued. "The coroner will testify that each victim was suffocated to the point of losing consciousness, then brought back from the brink of death only to be suffocated again. The evidence will prove that the victims fought against their restraints to the point of cutting their wrists and ankles raw from the rope Mr. Bachman used to restrain them. And we will prove that Mr. Bachman, after torturing and killing each victim, callously and without remorse dumped their bodies amid garbage and filth in abandoned buildings all over the city."

Bachman's words came back to her.

"You put them down and they flop around, their gills trying to get air, but they can't. Flop, flop, flop. Slower and slower. Until they are lying there, unmoving, except for those little flaps on the side of their head. If you throw them back into the water, they're disorientated for a minute, then they swim away. Only to be hooked again."

The bastard. It was a confession.

She glanced at Bachman. Almost did a double take. He was looking at her.

He gave her that half smile he'd worn during most of their interview.

She refused to look away. He turned first. She breathed easier.

"We will be calling to the stand Ava Raines," Charlene said, "who was kidnapped, drugged, and locked in the trunk of her own car and, only through a chance accident on the Queensboro Bridge, was able to alert police. The police officer who arrested Mr. Bachman will tell you what he found in the trunk of Ava's car. And the head of our criminal investigation unit will share what his team found in Mr. Bachman's apartment—personal effects from each of the victims, including car keys from two of the victims."

That, too, was news to Max. The police had never revealed that detail. She needed to see those records. If Bachman was a trophy killer, he would have taken something from the Palazzolos. But if the police didn't know what they were looking for, they might not recognize the "trophy."

After Charlene's monologue, it was Warren's turn.

He began, "It is the obligation of the state to prove beyond a reasonable doubt that my client—who has never been in trouble with the police, who has a good job, and a college degree—is guilty. Beyond a reasonable doubt. What does that mean? It means that if you believe, based on the actual evidence presented and not what the A.D.A. says in her opening statement, that my client is guilty, you must convict. But if the state doesn't have evidence, if they can't prove to you, the distinguished jury, you must acquit. And I will show you, with each and every witness, that every piece of evidence against my client is circumstantial. There is no physical evidence linking Adam Bachman to any of these murders. No DNA evidence on the bodies or at the crime scene. No witness who can place Mr. Bachman at any of the crime scenes. In fact, the police don't even know where these poor people were killed. Moreover, even the star witness for the prosecution, Ava Raines, could not pick Mr. Bachman out of a lineup. She doesn't know how she got into the trunk of her car, and she doesn't remember seeing Mr. Bachman the night she was abducted.

"I must remind you—the state must prove its case. My client does not have to say a word; it is strictly up to Ms. Golden to produce solid evidence that Adam Bachman committed these crimes. And I will argue that the evidence is so weak, so circumstantial, that it means nothing. Once again, I will prove that the police rushed to judgment and didn't consider other possible suspects. In fact, they had no suspects because there is no physical evidence against anyone—including my client.

"Ladies and gentlemen of the jury, the state will fail to prove—beyond a reasonable doubt—that Adam Bachman is guilty. And therefore, I am certain, when you see that the state has built a case on weak, circumstantial evidence, you will render a verdict of not guilty."

Riley Butler's earliest clear memory was at her first ballet recital when she was four.

After having two boys, Riley's mom wanted a girly girl. Her dad had won on the gender-neutral first name, but her mom painted her room pink, gave her dolls and tea sets, and started her in gymnastics and ballet from the minute she could walk.

Riley loved gymnastics—who wouldn't love jumping on the trampoline and doing somersaults across the floor?—but she hated ballet.

Wearing tutus, dumb shoes they called *slippers*, and tights that made her legs itch was bad, but worse, it hurt her head to put her mass of curly hair up into a tight bun and the gunk on her lips tasted repulsive. And her brothers teased her *all* the time.

But the hardest part for Riley was the *waiting*. Waiting, waiting, waiting. Waiting for everyone else to have their turn. Waiting to go on stage. Whatever it was she was supposed to do, Riley did it wrong. Her teacher chastised her *all* the time.

Riley, wait your turn.

Riley, that's not your cue.

Riley, please wait.

That recital when she was four, she'd lost out on the privilege of performing the lead dance to a brat named Tiffany Dolan. *Tiffany.* What a stupid name. Riley was in the same preschool class as Tiffany and she was just as bratty at school as she was in ballet. Worse, teachers loved her. Tiffany could do no wrong. Tiffany got to hand out the cookies. Tiffany got to take the roll call to the office with whomever *she* chose, and she never chose Riley. And Tiffany got to be the lead in the recital even though *Riley* was better. Riley heard her teacher tell her mother, "Riley doesn't take direction well."

So she was fuming in the wings, watching Tiffany twirl and twirl, having to wait to go out with all the other butterflies.

Riley moved out onto the stage before she was supposed to.

"Wait, Riley!" her teacher said.

Riley glared at her. She ran out onto the stage and did cartwheels around Tiffany. Literally. She got applause and laughs and she loved those three minutes of fame.

Her brothers thought she was cool. Her father frowned disapprovingly, but his blue eyes sparkled. Her mother was mortified and stuttered when apologizing to the teacher.

Riley never went back to ballet. She learned to follow the rules, she learned to listen to her elders, but the one thing she'd never learned to do well was *wait.*

She did exactly what Max had told her to do, but that took all of eighteen minutes *and* Riley had dragged her feet. Then she sat on the bench with reporters and other people who hadn't been granted access to the courtroom. Everyone spoke in hushed tones, if they talked at all.

Riley sat. And paced. And *waited.* She used her phone

to research the mental health facilities, and she had a couple of ideas on how to narrow it down, but it would be a lot easier if she had her computer. And the help of a certain Columbia grad school friend who was far better with computers than she was. Meaning, he knew how to hack without getting caught. But what she wanted to know might not even require breaking the law. Maybe just skirting it.

The problem was, she couldn't figure out how to identify disgruntled employees from eight years ago out of the dozens of facilities that Adam Bachman *might* have admitted himself to.

And she *really* wanted to watch the trial.

She wanted to be in the middle of the action. She didn't know why Max had her waiting out here babysitting Ben Lawson. The producer was high-strung. He'd called her *three times* the first hour after the trial started, and she had nothing to tell him because there was no information coming from the courtroom.

Riley had been curious since she was a little kid, she loved writing, and she'd first heard about Maxine Revere three years ago when she was a junior at Columbia. Maxine came to speak to her journalism seminar and then Riley knew exactly what she wanted to do. She wanted to be an investigative reporter. This was before Max had the television show, and her third book had just been released. It was about human trafficking in Mexico and Max had been detained in a Mexican jail while researching the case. It had started as an investigation into kidnapped Americans held for ransom, but turned into a horrific human trafficking conspiracy. It was terrifying and exciting at the same time, Riley thought, and she wanted to do something equally important. She read everything Max had ever written and focused on improving her own skills.

So when Riley had the opportunity to work for *the*

Maxine Revere, she jumped. She wanted the job so bad she almost panicked. Then, after her interview with Ben Lawson, she knew she wouldn't get the job. He hated her. She'd been overeager and talked too fast and came off as a hyperactive know-it-all. After a couple of drinks with her best friend, she convinced herself Ben Lawson was an idiot who was intimidated by smart, strong women.

That she'd been called back for a second interview with Max herself had stunned her. It was clear Ben didn't like her at first, but Max hired her, and Ben capitulated. And for a while she thought that her second assessment was accurate.

Except, it was clear that Ben wasn't intimidated by Max. They fought bitterly, but at the end of the day they were friends, on some level that Riley didn't understand. Riley had proven herself to Ben and now he seemed to like her.

Then there was David Kane. He hated her, she saw it as clear as day. Hated her with a passion. As if he could be passionate about *anything*. Again, her gut assessment about him had been wrong. Initially she thought he was just dumb muscle—she'd met a lot of them who'd worked for her dad or were friends with her brothers, cops who had brawn but lacked it upstairs. She quickly learned— fortunately before she screwed it up with Max—that David was the only person Max deferred to. And he had a brain to go with all that muscle.

Riley didn't get it. She tried to figure out what it was between them, but couldn't. She figured they were doing the horizontal bop, but she didn't see even a hint of it when they were together—and she was looking *hard*. If they were having an affair, they were keeping it supersecret. And there was the cop in California that Max was seeing. Riley hadn't met him, but Ben had mentioned it half a dozen times, usually in the context of *Max, you'd better not even think of flying off to California until after this trial.*

Riley had impressed Ben with her dedication. She'd already pegged him as someone who would tolerate most anything if you did a good job. That meant meeting deadlines, doing grunt work, and getting information—especially if you went over and above in the information department. He'd even given her a couple of assignments and she made sure she did them not only well, but fast.

But *nothing* Riley did made David Kane happy. The harder she tried, the more he hated her.

Riley looked at the time again. Eleven forty-five. When were they going to break for lunch? Noon? One? *Never?* Riley felt like she'd been here for three days instead of three hours. She didn't know how much work she'd have to do back at the office—her job seemed to change daily, which she liked. She typed a message to her computer guru friend, asking if he had time to see her.

She hit send and accidentally brushed by someone in the hall. "Sorry," she said, sheepish, glancing up at the person she'd run into.

"Isn't there a law against walking and texting?" the older guy in a suit said. At first she thought he was mad, but then he winked.

"Should be." She grinned. "Sorry."

He waved off her apology and went down the stairs. Her phone rang. David.

"I'm here." She added, "still waiting."

"Tell Max I'm in Queens. I'll be back before the trial ends for the day, but if I'm not, I'll send a car for her."

"I can grab her a taxi," Riley began, though she suspected Max could get a taxi faster than anyone.

"Relay my message, Riley." He hung up.

It wasn't her imagination, he hated her.

Spectators began to file out of the courtroom down the hall, where Bachman was on trial. Max was easy to spot— she was tall *and* wore heels *and* had dark red hair. Plus, she wore a colorful scarf that Riley had coveted from the minute she'd seen it. Tall women always looked good in scarves. They made Riley look more like a dwarf.

Riley raised her hand and waved.

Max looked around for Riley, irritated that she wasn't waiting right outside the courtroom doors. If she'd left the building, Max was going to flip.

Then she saw Riley near the rotunda, and Max realized that she was overreacting. She'd let Adam Bachman get in her head during the interview and that made the entire three hours she'd sat in the courtroom excruciating. If he *was* giving her undue attention it was because he'd sat across from her for twenty minutes and believed he had some psychological connection with her. She'd seen that with others she'd interviewed, both perpetrators and victims. Like she was a lifeboat in an uncertain world.

Max wove her way through the reporters and spectators to where Riley stood waiting. "Where are we running the interview?"

"North entrance. Tommy staked out a place there, and Ace is doing his person on the street thing."

"Good. David here?"

"He said he was stuck in Queens and will be back before the end of the day or he'd call you a car."

Why was David still in Queens? Had Sally tossed him some juicy tidbit? Why wouldn't he tap her for input?

She rubbed her temples. He'd tell her when he had something. Though she'd been working for *Maximum Exposure* for two years, and David had been with her almost that long, she was still used to working cases on her own.

Having a team of people was great in many ways . . . except that she was used to being in control.

"Are you okay?" Riley asked.

"Fine. Just need to eat. You can watch the interview, get a better sense for how we do it, and then we'll get a hot dog."

"Hot dog?"

"The best hot dog cart in the city is on the corner. And he has sauerkraut."

They took the stairs instead of the crowded elevators. "Why is Ace interviewing you? Why don't you just give a report?"

"Because the report is for NET, not my show. I'm not a NET reporter, and I don't want to be." Though she was doing more and more for the station and had begun to wonder if that had been Ben's plan all along. "I'm covering the trial because I'm doing a show on Bachman's victims. Ace and I have done this before. Catherine and Rob like the format, it gives a different perspective, adds depth and continuity."

"What was sitting across from Bachman like? Did he give you anything?"

"Not enough," she said.

You'll never find them. How would he know unless he was the one who killed them?

"Was it a waste of time?" Riley asked.

"No." She didn't want to talk about it, not until she could listen to the tape again and fully process the interview.

"Do you think I could go see a friend of mine this afternoon? While you're in the courthouse? He's a computer god, I think he can help me narrow down the list of facilities and—"

"No. I need you here." She stopped walking just inside the doors. "Look, Riley, being a reporter isn't glamorous or fun. It's often grueling work, a lot of waiting, a lot of boredom. But you still have to keep your eyes and ears open. You never know when something is important. It's learning to put together all those disparate clues into a viable picture that separates you from everyone else. You need to learn that."

"I'm sorry, I didn't mean—"

"And stop apologizing. I hired you because you're eager, your writing is solid, and you have good instincts. But you don't have experience, and if you'll just watch and listen and learn, you'll gain enough experience to land anywhere you want in two years. Got it?"

Max didn't wait for Riley to answer, because she'd spotted Ace on the other side of the door. He didn't look happy.

She left the building and approached Ace Burley, the lead reporter for NET who covered all things crime-related, except her show. She and Ace didn't always see eye-to-eye, but they had a good working relationship—after the initial bumps. He looked good on camera, with a square jaw and gray eyes and chiseled cheekbones and impossibly straight, white teeth (which Catherine had once told her, after a few drinks, were all capped). He also had a great voice, and recorded a news summary podcast every evening that surpassed expectations. It was a subscription-based podcast, one of the first of its kind. But he had a temper and was cocky, and his wife Nadine was a bitch who Max avoided at all costs. Catherine often called them Ken and Barbie, if Ken had a mean streak and Barbie was a ball-breaker.

Ace approached her as soon as he saw her emerge from the building. "You interviewed Bachman without telling me?"

"It happened last minute. You knew I was pushing for it."

"My contacts said it would never happen."

He should have had more faith in her, but she didn't say it. "Ben should have told you."

"He did—as I was leaving the studio to come here. I would have prepared. I'm going to look like a fool."

"You could never look like a fool, Ace." Stroking his ego usually calmed him. "And don't ask me about it. I'm using it for my show."

"People know. It's out there. Two stations said you were interviewing him."

"Why would they promote another program?"

He sighed loudly. "It's *news*. He hasn't talked to *any-one* and he picks *you?*"

"Is that an insult?"

He looked perplexed. "No. No, of course not. It's that you're not exactly known for coddling killers. I have to ask you about it. NET gets the exclusive. You don't have to give everything away, just a taste."

"There's nothing to give away. He didn't give me shit." Nothing she could use to find the Palazzolos, at any rate. "But be general, and I'll share a teaser. Fair?"

Tommy was waving for them and tapping his watch.

"It'll have to be," he said, still angry. "Let's do this."

Tommy had set up two tall director's chairs so they could sit—Max never thought the trick would work, but when she'd seen clips of similar shots, she liked how intimate and friendly the outdoor sit-down looked. They were running a live four-minute spot, then they'd tape an extended interview, which would be edited for the expanded Internet release and a special for *NET News at Night*.

Ace led with a brief on Adam Bachman, then his "People on the Street" quotes—what the average person thought about the trial and if they felt safe in light of the murders.

"You can watch the clips now on NET." He smiled, turned to Max. "Our viewers are pleased that NET's own Maxine Revere is sitting in the courtroom for the duration of the trial, one of fourteen reporters approved by Judge Tarkoff to claim a coveted spectator seat. Because the courtroom is closed to most of the public and all electronic devices banned, this report is the first coming from day one of the trial. Maxine, what was your first impression after listening to opening statements?"

"Good question, Ace," Max said, giving him the verbal pat on the back that his ego needed. "It's the first impression that often sticks with the jury after a weeklong trial. What struck me is that the defense is relying on the tactic of attempting to prove that the evidence is wholly circumstantial and that, in fact, there is reasonable doubt as to Mr. Bachman's guilt. The prosecution is focusing on evidence more than emotions. They told the jury what they would prove, claiming to have sufficient evidence to prove that no one except Mr. Bachman could have killed these five tourists."

"Sounds very cut-and-dried."

"In many ways it is. Though Judge Tarkoff is known to be a tough judge—hence the banning of electronics, even among the media—he set out a tight calendar. He expects to have the trial wrapped up in four days. That means the jury could get the case as early as Thursday afternoon."

"What's the jury pool like?"

"A cross section of age and race. Eight women and four men."

"Any surprises this morning?"

"None. It was very routine."

"But you had some good news. Adam Bachman has kept a low profile since his arrest, but he agreed to grant you an exclusive interview. What was that like?"

"I'll be reporting more in depth on my interview with Mr. Bachman on the next *Maximum Exposure,* but two things struck me. First, his appearance is that of a young, neat, articulate man. People who know him have called him 'fastidious.' As you and I both know, Ace, killers often don't look like they could commit violence. Mr. Bachman has that pleasant guy-next-door appearance, which will be something the prosecution is going to have to deal with."

"Sort of like Ted Bundy?"

Though Max was tired of the Ted Bundy comparison, which seemed so outdated and cliché, she smiled and nodded. "Exactly. The second thing that struck me was his complete lack of fear for the process. He didn't seem to be nervous about what faced him in court. He smiled at me, almost as if he was looking forward to the proceedings."

"Because he's innocent?"

"He made no claims of innocence or guilt to me," Max said. "I asked him what he thought the outcome would be and he shrugged and said he had no idea what the jury was going to decide. He made a point of saying he wasn't violent."

"He's accused of killing five people. He doesn't consider that violent?"

That was a good segue back to the trial. "As the prosecutor revealed in her opening statement, the five victims were suffocated. A.D.A. Golden said she would prove that Mr. Bachman put a clear plastic bag over their heads and watched them suffocate. I would call that violent. But the jury will have to make the final decision as to whether Adam Bachman committed these murders."

"Maxine, based on the opening statements, what do you think will happen?"

"Honestly, Ace, if the prosecution proves what they claim to be able to prove, I don't see how the jury can come back with anything but a guilty verdict. However, that's the key, right? The State has to prove the facts, and as you and I both know sometimes the State fails."

Chapter Five

After eating a hot dog with Riley, Max sent her assistant on a quick errand and took the opportunity to call James Palazzolo, Jr. J. J. was the oldest of Jim and Sandy's three children. Married with two kids of his own, he had resented his youngest sister contacting Max about their parents' disappearance, but after Max flew to Ohio last fall to meet with the three Palazzolo children, all animosity disappeared. J. J., Rachel, and Cindy were grieving. They knew in their hearts that their parents were dead, but not knowing what happened was sucking the life out of them.

Max understood how they felt better than most people, and though she hadn't particularly wanted to look into the case after Cindy contacted her, once she met the family she knew she had no choice. Max had written an article for a women's magazine called "An American Family" that detailed the quiet middle-class life of Jim and Sandy and how they bought a home, raised their kids, and put them through college. Jim had been an electrician and Sandy was an elementary schoolteacher. The three kids were grown and creating their own middle-class families in a quiet community in an uncertain world.

For all of Max's wealth, for all her property and family connections, she envied the Palazzolos. Love, affection, and respect flowed freely. J. J. told her about how every night the family had dinner together and talked, sometimes for hours after the meal. How they went to church on Sunday and had afternoon barbecues and went to Friday night high school football games even after J. J. graduated. There was so much history, so many memories in the family house that J. J. had decided they would never sell it.

But they needed to know what had happened to their parents. They needed to bury their bodies and have funerals. Answers. Closure.

Max slipped into an empty interview room for privacy. The rooms were off-limits to reporters, but Max knew enough people in the courthouse that they usually turned a blind eye.

She logged on to Skype from her iPad and waited for the call to go through to J. J.'s work computer. He answered, and she saw him sitting behind his cluttered desk. He was a veterinarian and she could hear yelping in the background.

"Hello, J. J. I'm glad I caught you."

"I cleared my lunch hour, since I thought you might call."

"I had my interview with Bachman this morning."

"You got it." He smiled, but there was no humor. "I knew you would. What did he say?"

"He didn't admit to anything."

"But?"

"He made some cryptic remarks. I'm going to follow through on them. My colleague, David Kane, is working with a detective in Queens following up on a lead. I promise, J. J., I will call the minute I know anything definitive."

He sighed heavily, his head sinking into his hands. Then

he looked back at her and said, "Knowing that you care about my parents means a lot. It's been nearly a year since they disappeared. Two more weeks—if we still don't know what happened to them, we're going to have a memorial service. My sisters and I want you to be here, if possible."

"E-mail me the details. I hope to learn something before then, but I can't make promises. Just know that I am doing everything I can to find out what happened."

"Thank you. I'll tell Rach and Cindy you called."

"I'll check in later this week." She disconnected the call and stared at the blank screen.

It wasn't fair in any sense of the word that J. J. and his sisters had to suffer like this. Even a memorial service like they planned wouldn't give them the closure they needed, only diminish their hope. They believed their parents were dead, because in no world they lived in would their parents walk away from them and their family and home.

Believing they were dead and *knowing* it were two different things. They would learn to accept, learn to live again, but that niggle of doubt and worry in the back of their minds that they *could have, should have, would have* found the truth if only . . .

That's where Max came in. She wanted the truth as much as they did. The truth was tangible. Adam Bachman knew the truth and she would find a way to get it out of him, to find some thread to give her and the Palazzolos the closure they needed.

After the lunch break, the prosecution began to build their case. Charlene first called the officer who'd initially arrested Bachman, which Max thought was a smart move. The key was to walk the jury through the case as it unfolded so that they couldn't come to any conclusion other than what the prosecution intended.

The officer went through his credentials—a twelve-year veteran of NYPD, several commendations—and then Charlene asked him about the night he stopped Adam Bachman's car.

"Why were you stopping cars on the Queensboro Bridge?"

"There was a serious, nonfatal accident on the bridge. Four cars were involved, so we had an extensive backup and only one lane open. We were managing the traffic flow so the cleanup crew could get the damaged vehicles off the bridge while investigators processed the scene. We stopped cars when we needed to, then waved them forward. Basic traffic management. I had just waved Mr. Bachman's car through but I heard a female scream. My partner and I pulled out our weapons and ordered Mr. Bachman to stop and keep his hands on the steering wheel. I called in the other unit and they kept an eye on Bachman while my partner and I opened the trunk."

"So to clarify, you had probable cause to open the trunk."

"Yes, ma'am. Both my partner and I heard the scream."

"What did you find when you opened the trunk?"

"A white female later identified as Ava Raines. Her feet were bound and she had duct tape hanging from her cheek. She had duct tape on her hands, but she had managed to cut the tape off on the inside of the trunk lid."

"Objection," Warren said. "Speculation."

"Sustained," the judge said.

Charlene nodded and said, "Did you see remnants of duct tape on her wrists?"

"Yes, ma'am."

"Did Ms. Raines say anything at that time?"

"She said, 'Help me. Thank God you're here. Please help me.'"

"And then what did you do?"

"We removed the woman from the trunk, called for an ambulance, and took her statement."

"The official statement is Exhibit Four," Golden told the jury. "Continue."

"Ms. Raines informed us that she woke up in the trunk of the car, which she realized was her car because her things were in the trunk, and her hands and feet were bound. She kicked and tried to signal for help."

"Thank you, Officer."

Max wrote her impressions in her own unique shorthand. Clear and straightforward, Max noted. Established the facts and a time line, plus probable cause, which was important for the jury. Very typical of an experienced officer. He'd probably testified in a hundred trials during his tenure. Score one for the prosecution.

Warren's cross-examination was brief, but he asked the one question Max knew he would.

"Did you ask Ms. Raines who abducted her?"

"Yes."

"And what did she say?"

"She said she didn't know."

"Did you ask her if she recognized the man driving her car?"

"Yes, I did. She said he looked familiar, but she didn't know why."

"And did Mr. Bachman comply with your orders?"

"Yes, sir."

"Mr. Bachman in no way resisted arrest?"

"No, sir."

"And you read Mr. Bachman his rights?"

"Yes, sir."

"Did Mr. Bachman say anything before you read him his rights?"

The officer looked confused and glanced at Charlene. Max agreed—the question was odd. She put a star in her notepad then wrote down the question and waited for the answer.

The judge said, "Answer the question, Officer."

"He repeated several times, 'I don't understand.'"

"Did you think that he didn't understand why you were arresting him?"

"No, sir. He understood his rights and verbally acknowledged such."

"Meaning, did he seem surprised that there was a woman bound in the trunk of the car?"

"Objection," Charlene said.

"It goes to my client's emotional state of mind, Your Honor."

"You may answer the question, Officer. But, Counselor, please tread carefully in this area."

"Thank you, Your Honor. Officer, did Mr. Bachman seem in any way surprised that there was a woman bound in the trunk of the car?"

"I really can't say, sir. The only thing he said was, 'I don't understand.' He didn't say anything after we read him his rights, except to affirm that he understood them."

"Thank you."

I don't understand.

Max underlined the comment. It was odd for Bachman to have said it to the police, and equally odd in how the defense brought it up to the officer. What was his purpose? To attempt to show confusion on Bachman's part? To cast doubt on his knowledge of Ava Raines being in the trunk? He was driving her car, after all.

"Redirect," Charlene said and rose from her chair. "Officer, were you aware that Mr. Bachman was driving a car registered to Ms. Raines?"

Max smiled. Charlene could have pulled the question right out of Max's head.

"Not until after we placed him under arrest. We then

ran the plates on the car and determined that it was registered to Ava Raines of Long Island. That coincided with the registration we found in the glove compartment box."

Bachman shifted in his seat and whispered something to his lawyer. Max wished she was a fly on the table in front of them. What was he saying? He looked agitated, as if he wanted to say something to the court. His lawyer put his hand on Bachman's, whispered something into his ear. Whatever he said didn't seem to appease Bachman. He slouched in his chair and frowned like a reprimanded child.

Warren didn't ask any more questions and Charlene called the second officer, who corroborated his partner's testimony. Then the paramedic who was first on scene, who reported his observations about Ms. Raines's wounds, followed by the doctor who confirmed she'd been drugged with a depressant that caused memory loss.

During the twenty-minute recess, Max quickly wrote up a summary for the *Maximum Exposure* Web page. She sent it to Ben just as the bailiff was about to close the doors. He let her slip back in.

As soon as Judge Tarkoff was seated, he called for the next witness. Charlene called Ava Raines to the stand.

Max had great interest in the next witness. Not only because Ava's testimony could make or break the case, but because Ava had agreed to let Max interview her once the trial was over. Her statements—here in court and then in a personal one-on-one interview—would add even more depth to this tragic story.

Ava was of average height, on the slender side, with long straight blond hair and large brown eyes. She wore a modest dress, a bit casual for court, but not inappropriate. She wore only a little makeup, which made her look younger than her twenty-four years. She shifted nervously.

Charlene did a great job of putting Ava at ease. She asked a few easy questions. Her name, where she lived, then what she was doing staying in a hotel in Manhattan that weekend when she lived on Long Island.

"It was supposed to be a girls' weekend," Ava said, "with my two best friends, Mandy and Ginger. We were all recently single and thought why not just go to some shows, go shopping, pretend we're tourists?"

"You stayed in the same hotel room?"

"Yes, Saturday night. And we had fun—but then Mandy's boyfriend called her Sunday morning and wanted to talk." Ava rolled her eyes, then quickly glanced around as if that were inappropriate. "I'm sorry."

"That's okay, Ava. Mandy's boyfriend called and . . . ?"

"I had driven us, and I was mad and didn't want to leave. I'm training to be a paramedic, and I'd just taken my certification test. I'd worked sixty-hour weeks for hardly any pay for so long, and studying—I deserved to have fun, you know? And I was nervous, because it takes two weeks before they give you the results. And Trevor called, begging Mandy to come back so they could talk."

"You and Mandy both live in Medford, correct?"

Ava nodded.

"You need to answer out loud, Ms. Raines."

"Sorry. Yes. We all live in Medford. We went to high school together and stayed friends."

"Did you drive Mandy back to Medford?"

"No. I was mad and I didn't want to leave. My dad gave me some money when I reached my required EMT hours, and I wanted to have fun because I knew when I got my certification, I would have to find a job and be the rookie and work longer hours. I wanted to stay and enjoy myself. We fought—it was awful. And Ginger got mad at me and went back on the train with Mandy."

"And you stayed."

"I had tickets to see *Rock of Ages* Sunday night." She frowned and glanced down.

"Are you all right, Ms. Raines?"

She nodded. "Yes."

"Let's go back to the afternoon you were abducted. Can you tell the court what you remember?"

"I . . . that day has always been fuzzy. Because he drugged me."

"Objection!" Warren called.

"Sustained," the judge said.

Ava frowned, and Charlene nodded. "Ava, let's go through that night step by step, okay? What do you remember about Tuesday? Start with when you woke up."

"I woke up about eight in the morning. I went to the hotel gym, then came back to my room and showered and packed. I didn't really want to go home, but three nights in a Manhattan hotel is expensive, especially since Mandy and Ginger left and only split Saturday night with me. I checked out, but left my car in the garage so I could go shopping."

"What time did you check out?"

"Around eleven in the morning."

"Where did you shop?"

"Um, first I went to H and M, then the Nike store for new running shoes because they were having a sale, then I had a late lunch at Fringe."

Fringe. Bingo. Max wrote rapidly. Fringe was the bar that Bachman worked at, though he had Tuesdays off.

"Had you been to Fringe before?"

"Yes—on Sunday, after I saw *Rock of Ages.*"

Max looked at Bachman. He was staring straight ahead, not looking at Ava or at the judge.

Charlene said, "Let the record show that Exhibits Nine through Twelve are receipts from Ms. Raines's hotel and shopping that day, confirming the time line."

"So noted," the judge said.

"When did you leave the restaurant?"

"About two thirty."

Charlene said, "Let the record reflect that Ms. Raines paid for her meal at two twenty-one, per the time stamp on the receipt."

Ava said, "I hung around another few minutes, texting Ginger."

Charlene introduced those texts into evidence. "Did you make plans?"

"I told Ginger I was leaving the city and maybe we could get together later. I was still mad, and wanted her to apologize, but I also needed to apologize because I said some mean things."

Charlene said, "Let the record show the exchange of text messages between Ms. Raines and her friend Ginger."

"So noted," the judge said.

"What did you do when you left Fringe?" Charlene asked Ava.

"I wanted to get out of the city before traffic. I walked back to the hotel, but stopped at this little gift shop first—I can't remember the name. But they had these apple earrings in the window. They were so touristy, but I loved them, and I think I bought them." She frowned.

Charlene said, "Let the record reflect that Exhibit Fifteen is a receipt for a pair of apple stud earrings from Big Apple Gift Shoppe, time-stamped two forty-eight P.M."

She prompted, "Then you went back to the hotel?"

"I think so."

"Objection," Warren said.

Charlene said, "We have testimony from Ms. Raines' medical team as to why she has a memory loss at the time she was drugged. I would ask for leniency here, as we're trying to determine exactly what Ms. Raines remembers and what we'll be able to prove with other witnesses."

"Overruled," the judge told Warren.

Good, Max thought. Tarkoff was tough but fair. So far Max didn't have any problems with the way he'd run the trial. She didn't even have a problem with the no electronics rule—iPads and computers and cell phones could be distracting. Even the sounds from the pens on paper from the reporters around her were annoying.

"You say you think you went back to the hotel," Golden prompted.

"I remember looking at the earrings and wanting them. And I see myself walking down the street and turning the corner. I thought someone was following me, but there's always so many people in Times Square. I didn't want to be paranoid. I've lived on Long Island my entire life. I come to the city all the time. I turned around and saw a blur and a hand and my neck hurt. The next thing I remember I woke up with my feet and hands and mouth tied up and I was in a car. A trunk."

"Just to clarify, you don't remember who was behind you on the street outside the Big Apple Gift Shoppe?"

"No, I don't. It's fuzzy."

"You woke up in the trunk. Then what did you do?"

"The car was moving, slowly. I heard lots of noise from cars, and knew I was in traffic. It was dark in the trunk, but I saw a little light coming in from a seam or crack or something. At first I didn't realize it was my car, but then I felt my shopping bags, the ones I'd been carrying around, I just kind of knew. And there's this screw on the trunk lid. I rubbed my wrists against it trying to break the duct tape. I kicked the trunk lid a couple times, hoping someone could hear me. Once I got my wrists free, I pulled off the tape on my mouth. When the car stopped, I screamed. I just screamed as loud as I could and then the trunk opened and for a minute I thought it was whoever took me and he was going to tape me up again, but it was the police and I had never felt so happy to see anyone."

There were tears in her eyes, but she kept herself together. *Brave girl,* Max thought. *Smart and resourceful.* She made a note to follow up on the post-trial interview. Ava would do well on camera. She would give other young women the inspiration to fight back when they found themselves in dangerous situations.

"You told the officer that you thought the man driving your car was familiar, but you didn't know his name. Do you know why he was familiar?"

"Yes," Ava said. "From Fringe."

"Objection," Warren said.

"Overruled, Mr. Warren. I told you in chambers that this line of questioning was admissible; please don't make me warn you again."

"Sorry, Your Honor."

Max leaned forward. She glanced at Bachman. He seemed to have shrunk even more into his seat, his too large suit now looking enormous on him.

Charlene said, "Did you see Mr. Bachman when you were at lunch?"

"No, I don't remember seeing him that Tuesday. But I was at Fringe on Sunday night, after the musical. I came in for a late dinner and a couple glasses of wine. The tables were full, so I sat at the bar. He was the bartender. I didn't know his name, but he came over to talk to me a couple of times. I was there for nearly two hours, then walked back to the hotel."

"Do you remember what you talked about?"

"Mostly theater. I told him about *Rock of Ages* and how much I loved it. I told him about Mandy and Ginger and probably said something stupid like guys are jerks. He asked if I had a boyfriend, I said not now, I had a breakup last year and then just focused on studying."

Max kept her eyes on Bachman. He'd deflated from between their interview until now. It was as if every sentence Ava Raines spoke made him smaller. Had he truly not believed the State had enough evidence against him? Had his attorney not properly prepared him for the testimony? He looked defeated, and the trial wasn't even one day done.

Charlene asked, "Did he ask for your phone number? Where you were staying?"

"No. But since I had three glasses of wine, he offered to call me a cab. I said no need, my hotel was less than two blocks away. I might have mentioned which hotel, but I don't honestly remember."

"What time did you leave?"

"Midnight."

Charlene said, "Let the record show Exhibits Nineteen and Twenty, the ticket stub from the seven thirty P.M. show of *Rock of Ages* and the Fringe receipt time-stamped twelve oh five that night. Let the record also show that the server on the time stamp was listed as Server 414. Exhibit Twenty-one are the employee records from Fringe. They list all employees by employee number, and Server 414 is known to Fringe as Adam Bachman."

"So noted," the judge said.

"Ms. Raines, did you see the bartender from Fringe at any other time on Monday or Tuesday?"

"No, not until the police officer asked me if I knew who was driving my car. He looked familiar, but my head hurt and I didn't know why he looked familiar. And I was scared and relieved and shaking and my hands were bleeding. I was confused then. I'm sorry."

"There's no need to apologize, Ms. Raines. Your witness, Mr. Warren."

Warren stood. "No questions at this time, but I reserve the right to recall Ms. Raines."

"So noted," the judge said. "You may step down, Ms. Raines."

Ava got down. She looked over at Adam and as Max watched, Adam looked down. Guilt? Remorse? Far more emotion than he'd shown in their interview.

As Max watched, she realized that Bachman looked *angry*. Perplexed. His attorney leaned over and whispered something, but Adam turned his head away as if he didn't want to hear it.

But it was clear to Max that Ava had hammered in the first nail on Adam Bachman's conviction.

Chapter Six

Max stood in the middle of her home office sipping a glass of wine and reviewing the facts.

When she first bought her apartment, Max had done extensive remodeling. The previous owner had been an eccentric artist. While the light and windows of her penthouse were amazing, he'd destroyed the floors with paint and chemicals, never updated the kitchen or bathrooms, and in a fit of rage he'd demolished his bedroom wall.

She'd completely gutted and refinished the apartment. It was largely open with a two-story great room as the focal point. Her bedroom was at the top of an open, freestanding staircase that curved nearly 360 degrees. Off her bedroom and up a half flight of stairs was her office—an opening looked down into her bedroom and the two-story wall of windows that showcased the river and part of the city.

She'd taken the largest wall in her office and covered it with magnetic whiteboards where she could both pin things up and write on. Her current project always took up most of the board, including a time line across the top, newspaper clippings, photos, questions, and facts. The first time David had walked in he'd dubbed it "the Wall" and the generic nickname had stuck.

Her office also had a functional desk, a reading chair, and a small couch. A bookshelf had been built into one wall and held most of her research books, plus extra copies of her own four true crime books. She had a file cabinet with articles and other research papers and an oversized closet designed for storage. But her wall always had her attention.

She'd never have been interested in the Bachman investigation under normal circumstances. There were hundreds—thousands—of murder trials in New York. Her focus was missing persons, and while there was a human interest angle in how Ava Raines had survived, justice was being served, as far as Max was concerned. The killer had been arrested, the victims had been recovered, their families had closure, and that was that.

The Palazzolos, however, were a different matter.

When the Palazzolo children contacted her, several months after their parents' disappearance, Max was interested immediately. She'd visited the family in Ohio, wrote an article about them, and pushed law enforcement in New York and the neighboring states as much as she could with the limited information she had.

However, when the family sent her phone and credit records of their parents' last week in New York—several months after Bachman had been arrested—she immediately became interested in the Bachman investigation.

The Palazzolos had disappeared on a Tuesday after having dinner in the bar at Fringe Sunday night. Fringe is always crowded before and after Broadway shows because of its location and reputation. Max had even eaten there a few times, though she usually steered clear of Times Square.

Max felt in her gut that Bachman killed the Palazzolos

and they, in fact, were his first victims. That their bodies hadn't been recovered told her that he'd hidden them on purpose, perhaps because there was physical evidence tying him to the crimes. There were too many commonalities between their disappearance and Bachman's known victims.

Fringe wasn't in the heart of Times Square, but it was close. Police cameras were everywhere in the Square, but they thinned out the farther one walked from the touristy areas. And there was always the issue of broken cameras and unclear shots and the lack of manpower to scour footage. That was why most security footage was pulled after the fact—police knew what happened, so they pull tapes from the area to see if they had evidence for an arrest. Definitely not as fast or easy as television, but the information was there—if the crime happened on camera.

Max had already checked with her sources and there were no police cameras on the block where Ava Raines was abducted, so there was no visual proof that Bachman had abducted her. The only evidence she'd heard about was that a white male was seen on camera driving Raines's car out of the hotel garage. There was no positive identification that it was Bachman, though the image was certainly not petite, blond Ava Raines.

What stumped Max—and she hoped the prosecution addressed this tomorrow—was how Bachman maneuvered the unconscious Ava Raines a full block to the garage, up the staircase (the elevator had a working camera inside), and into her trunk during daylight hours with no one being suspicious. Max supposed he could have pretended Ava was his drunk or sick girlfriend, but no one had come forward as a witness. With the canvass that the police must have done, coupled with the publicity, they would have found one.

Max's theory that Bachman had a partner had also

developed over time, not just because of the Palazzolos, but because of how smooth and seemingly easy it was for Bachman to kidnap five strangers. Six, including Ava Raines.

What if, she considered, his partner retrieved the car while Bachman tracked Ava? He could have dropped his partner off before heading toward the bridge.

Or maybe Bachman retrieved her car first? But . . . how did he know when she would return to the garage after shopping? Someone must have followed her.

It could be that his partner drugged her, Bachman came by with the car, they dumped her in, and Bachman drove off.

There just *had* to be a partner. Not only because it made sense given the evidence of these abductions, but after interviewing Bachman's friends and family, she didn't see how a man so completely clean to the point of being a germophobe could physically handle a dead body. Max had seen enough crime scene photos to know that people in death, even if it wasn't a bloody death, weren't pretty. Their bodies often purged fluids, leaving a mess. It made sense that he used their own cars to transport, but getting the dead body into the car and moving it to another location wouldn't have been easy. Did he have one killing spot, but dumped the bodies in different locations in order not to be tracked? That made sense, because killing them in different places meant a greater chance of being seen.

A girl the size of Ava Raines would be manageable, dead or alive. But Bachman wasn't large. He was six feet tall and slender. He didn't regularly work out, so didn't have muscle mass built up. Two of the victims were men bigger and heavier than Bachman. Yet the autopsy reports—which Max had bribed a pathologist to look at— showed minimal postmortem bruising. Which meant that the bodies weren't excessively jostled around or dragged.

The only explanation was that Bachman had help. Maybe not with killing his victims, but definitely help in transporting the bodies from his killing spot to Queens.

When she'd broached the subject with Richard a few months back, he'd flipped.

Max and Richard were having drinks at an exclusive club where no one would reveal that they ever had a conversation, let alone were members.

"Don't you understand what you'll do to our entire case if you leak that unproven theory to our potential jury pool?" he'd said.

She tilted her chin up and stared at him. She was angry, but she recognized that Rich was the D.A. and he had other concerns. She tried to understand them. "Rich, I won't write anything I can't prove."

"Don't even go there—just asking the questions could get back to his defense and then they may come up with some complicated game to confuse the jury."

"You should know me better than that."

"That's the problem. I do know you. You get these ideas and don't think about the damage they can cause."

"And I don't voice my theories publicly without backing them up."

"He's guilty, Max."

"Have you ever thought a man you tried for murder was innocent?"

"That's not fair."

"I've seen enough to believe you have the right person. But I still don't think he worked alone. I will prove it."

"I'm begging you—"

"Don't beg, Richie, it won't get you anywhere. But I promise you this: if I find proof, something tangible, I'll take it to you first."

He closed his eyes and sighed. "You're impossible."

"I'll take that as a compliment, because you really shouldn't insult a reporter who's putting friendship ahead of a scoop."

"So we're friends?"

That had stung, just a bit. *"Of course we are. What did you think?"*

"With you I don't know."

"Sweetheart, if we weren't friends you would have heard about my theory along with everyone else in New York: on television, not privately over a glass of wine."

Her cell phone rang, interrupting her thoughts. It was David.

"I have information."

"I can't wait."

"I'll be up in a minute."

Max hung up and glanced one more time at the wall. The Palazzolos were the outlier only in that they had gone missing as a couple and their bodies haven't yet been found. Max knew all the arguments as to why Bachman wasn't involved. But the parallel to Ava Raines was too close. The Palazzolos and Ava went to Fringe after a Sunday night show. They ate at the bar because of the crowd. Adam Bachman served them. They disappeared the following Tuesday afternoon, a day Adam had no alibi.

But the police never asked him about his alibi for the Palazzolos because the police didn't think he had anything to do with their disappearance. If they had only worked the case differently Max might not be so frustrated, but because Richard Milligan didn't want to risk a conviction on the murders of five people, he would never approve that line of inquiry. And while Max understood that intellectually, emotionally she wanted answers.

No one should have to live without the truth. No one understood that better than Max. Her mother, her best friend, both gone—presumed dead—but with no proof either way, no truth. No justice.

Max filled the void in her heart with work. It drove her to do what she did, it drove her to push, to prod, to find answers for others because she couldn't find them for herself.

David buzzed her door. Max didn't own a car so there was no need for her to use her parking spot, so David had unhindered access and didn't have to go through the doorman. At first he was uncomfortable with that, but he'd grown used to it.

He held a bag of Chinese food. "In case you haven't eaten."

"Yum." She took the bag and David followed her to her kitchen.

She loved her apartment in TriBeCa, off Greenwich with a view of the Hudson River. Her little corner of the world. Bigger than she needed, but considering she traveled more than half the year living out of hotel rooms, she wanted her own space. She'd bought it after her college roommate was murdered nine years ago. She'd still been in a battle with her family over her great-grandmother giving her one-fifth of her estate in her will, but Max knew she'd win and had no qualms about spending some of that money on this two-story apartment.

She hadn't furnished it right away. Even after the remodeling, she didn't know exactly what she wanted to do with the space. She bought a small desk and put it in the corner of her living room, where she could see the river and watch sunsets and write. The rest of the living room had been bare after she came back from Miami and wrote the book about Karen's disappearance. It had taken her years to turn the place into her home, but now it was the only place that truly felt hers. Her sanctuary.

After she took gourmet cooking classes, she'd had her

kitchen redesigned in a chic Tuscany style. High brick walls and wood-beamed ceilings, a large natural stone island with pots hanging from the rack above, double ovens, and a custom tile backsplash. It opened into the gathering room because she liked having the open space. She preferred eating at the bar or the island or in her office, but she had a dining table that could seat ten if she wanted. She just rarely wanted.

She brought out her everyday plates that she'd found at a pottery shop on an excursion to Vermont. Simple and functional. Max knew she was attached to her things because she'd never had anything she was allowed to keep for the first ten years of her life. And even when she moved in with her grandparents, it had never felt like her home. Everything inside was theirs. This was the first place Max knew, in her heart, was all hers.

Max poured herself a second glass of wine while David dished up.

"Beer?" she offered.

"Thanks."

She was mildly surprised. David wasn't much of a drinker. She pulled out a bottle of Harp. She didn't care much for beer, but Harp Lager was David's favorite so she always had some around.

She sat down and took a couple of bites, forgetting how hungry she'd been. "I haven't eaten since a hot dog at the courthouse," she said.

"I figured. Where's Riley?"

"Not here. She doesn't work twenty-four hours a day."

"Hmm."

"Did she do something?"

"Not yet."

She caught his eye. "Cut her some slack."

"I don't cut anyone slack. You should know that by now."

She laughed. "Okay, you win. Besides, your blatant animosity toward her will keep her on her toes. Now, what happened that kept you in Queens all day? I knew O'Hara would talk to you, I just didn't expect her to keep you so long."

"She wanted me to tell you that after this she owes you nothing and, in fact, you owe her."

"Now you've got me very curious."

"You already knew half of what she told me."

"You mean that she was searching for the Palazzolos in the area where the witness spotted their car."

He nodded. He drank half his beer, put it down. "O'Hara made it clear that she thinks that the Palazzolos are dead, that they were murdered in a robbery, and their bodies hidden with their car. She also found an empty twenty-five gallon container that had once contained sodium hydroxide, a chemical used to make soap."

"Lye." Her heart skipped a beat. Bachman's voice came back to her.

You'll never find them.

"She traced the lot numbers and learned that the container was shipped with two other identical containers to an address in Brooklyn where the resident knew nothing about the shipment, nor did she speak English. She went back to the original witness, who doesn't remember calling the police, but he's elderly. I asked—very nicely—for her to take me to where she found the container and to let me look at the records."

"I knew she'd let you."

"She let me because I am persuasive and diplomatic. When she learned what army unit I was in, she opened up." He sipped his beer, caught her eye. "Why do I think you planned this all along?"

Max smiled, though her mind was still partly back at the interview with Bachman. "I've known Sally for years.

Her dad was career military. She trusts you more because so were you."

"Ten years doesn't make a career."

"Long enough."

"I got her to consider other possibilities. *Not* that Bachman killed them, but that maybe whoever did made that call about their car. The sodium hydroxide was ordered the day after the Palazzolos disappeared, and it was delivered the day before the witness call."

"Both were Wednesdays," Max said from memory. "Bachman always took Tuesday and Wednesday off. Did they record the witness call? Have a phone number?"

"No on the recording, yes on the phone number. After a lot of persuasion, Sally let me trace it. It was a burn phone. The name and address of the person is real, only we don't think he made the call."

"Why?" Max asked, mostly to herself. "Why make the call in the first place? Did they want the bodies to be found? But if they did, the police would have found them. The search was competent."

"Competent?" David almost smiled. "High praise from you."

"Meaning, the police did due diligence—until they refused to consider that Bachman was responsible. Why would Bachman—or his partner—call the police with a false witness sighting?"

No longer hungry, she put her fork down and sipped her wine.

"The car was tagged in every police system from the minute their kids filed the missing persons report," she said. "If it had been abandoned on a street, it would have been found. That means a private garage or the bottom of a lake."

"The lye container had been there for a while, but there were no prints, nothing to help us ID when it was left or who left it. We searched the abandoned train station, found nothing. Sally had already been through it. But we have an idea, and she's going to follow up on it."

"What idea?"

"That the bodies are in the car, and the car is in a place that wouldn't have been searched."

"You're sounding cryptic, dear David."

"Two ideas. The first is that the car is parked inside an abandoned building."

"For nearly a year."

"It's possible. We identified the abandoned buildings within a one-mile radius of where the car was allegedly spotted and Sally is going to tag some cops to help with the search."

"And the second idea?"

"That the car is deeper down one of the underground tunnels, many of which were sealed off by the city after the last major hurricane flooded them and created a bigger hazard."

"How well sealed?"

"I don't know."

"Is it possible to hide a car down there?"

"Yes."

"If the bodies were destroyed with sodium hydroxide, we won't find anything. That's exactly what he meant."

David put down his fork and looked her in the eye. "What do you mean?" he said in a far too serious tone.

"Bachman didn't admit to killing the Palazzolos, but he said I would never find them."

"*Exactly* what did he say?"

" 'You'll never find them. And it'll eat you up forever.' " She shook her head.

"Max—"

She cut him off. "And you know something else? This all connects."

She got up and motioned for David to follow her upstairs to her office. She climbed up her footstool and added to her time line when the lye was ordered and when it was picked up. She then got down, moved the footstool to the end of the time line, climbed back up and added the day Sally found the lye.

"Shit," David muttered.

Sally had found the lye the day before Adam Bachman sent the letter agreeing to interview with Max.

"This is it," Max said. "This proves that Bachman is working with someone. He watched that area and saw the police return."

She paced. "Except, it's not going to prove anything to the D.A.," she argued with herself. "If I take this to Richard, he'll make Sally's life hell for talking to me, and he won't do anything." He would table it until after the trial. And then would he pursue it? If it could give Bachman grounds for an appeal?

"Can you blame him?" David said. "He wants Bachman in prison for killing five people."

"And I want to find the Palazzolos."

"Bachman might tell you the truth after the trial is over. When he's convicted and sentenced."

She doubted it. "Do you think Sally can find them?"

"Your call two weeks ago jump-started her into action. She's motivated, and she has a plan. But it's going to take her time to search all the places she has in mind."

"I can—"

He put up his hand. "She said if you offer to help, in person or by hiring anyone, to respectfully decline."

She wasn't upset by Sally's comment. There was a chain of evidence issue, and while Max didn't always abide by law enforcement rules, with this one—where evidence was tenuous at best—she would. Because she knew and trusted Sally.

For the first time she thought they would finally get answers as to what had happened to the Palazzolos.

"Will there be any evidence of their bodies left?" she asked.

"Depending on the environment, the chances are that there will be some remains. Unless the killer kept the chemical reaction going over a day or two, or stored them in a small, airtight space, there's going to be something to test. Bone will dissolve, but not completely. Teeth are especially durable. DNA can be extracted from teeth."

"How do you know all that?"

He tilted his head. "I'm well-read, dear Max."

She smiled, then sobered up when she looked back at her time line. At the photos of the Palazzolos and the other five victims.

"Maybe something in their car will point to Bachman as the killer."

"Maybe he didn't do it."

"He did." Max was certain. Bachman and his unknown partner.

"If the police can't prove it, at least the family will know for certain what happened to their parents."

"That might be all we can get." Max sat on her couch, staring just beyond David at her wall.

"You don't say that like you mean it."

"I'm not going to let it go that easily."

He leaned back against her desk and crossed his arms. "I didn't think you would."

"When we find the car, I'll find a way to twist Bachman around until he spills it."

David said, "Play me the tape of your interview with Bachman."

Max got up and walked over to her desk. She'd downloaded the file earlier to her computer. She enhanced the sound, hoping David could catch all Bachman's whispers. But without his facial expressions, his voice was flat.

Still, David didn't say anything as he listened.

When the interview was over, Max had the same impression she had while she'd listened to Bachman in person: he was smart, manipulative, and hadn't acted alone.

"Max," David said, "promise me you won't go anywhere alone."

"For the rest of my life?" she said flippantly.

"If that's what it takes. You're right about this."

"I usually am," she teased. She didn't like the dark look on David's already hardened face.

"Dammit, Maxine, I'm serious. We've gone round and round about whether Bachman had a partner, and while your theory made sense, there was no evidence. None. But he knew the sodium hydroxide container had been found, and the only way he could know is if he had someone on the outside who saw the police in the area. He knew when to call you for the interview. That makes him a lot smarter than I gave him credit for."

"If it makes you feel any better, I never underestimated him. Had he not been slowed down by the accident on the Queensboro Bridge, Ava Raines would be dead today, and no one would have suspected Adam Bachman."

"But the police don't believe he worked with anyone, and unless I can convince Sally O'Hara—who seems to be the only person in the NYPD who doesn't hate you— that he has a partner, the partner gets off scot-free. He could see you as a threat, especially after you air the show on the murders."

"I'm sure I have one or two other friends in NYPD."

"For shit's sake, Maxine!" He slapped his hand on her desk. "Take me seriously!"

She opened her mouth to argue, then closed it. Finally she said, "David, I do take you seriously."

"They drew you in."

"What do you mean?"

"I mean that if that time line is accurate, and Bachman called you *because* the sodium hydroxide had been found, that means they intentionally drew you into whatever game they're playing."

"I was already invested in the Palazzolos. Long before I sat down with Bachman. Before I even suspected he was responsible."

David's face was still firm, so she added, "The good news is I'll be safe at the courthouse all week and Sally will be searching for the Palazzolos, and maybe by Friday we'll have answers."

David didn't comment. He stared at her board. She didn't know exactly what he was thinking.

"I have a change of plans for tomorrow," Max said.

"No."

"You can come with me."

"Oh, I can?"

She ignored his sarcasm. "I scheduled a meeting with Dr. Arthur Ullman here at two in the afternoon. I'll bail on court, let Riley have my credentials. It'll be good for her, and I saw the docket. Tomorrow afternoon it's the forensics reports, which I've read and much of the information is dry and boring. So right after my noon report with Ace outside the courthouse, we'll grab lunch and head back here."

"That's a change I can live with," David said. "What do you make of his comment about not being violent?"

"You're getting really good at this," Max said. "Soon you'll be the investigative reporter."

David shot her a nasty look as they walked back downstairs to finish dinner.

"He said it twice," she said. " 'I'm not violent.' He's a

hands-off killer. He likes watching his victims die, almost passive. I think Arthur will steer us in the right direction."

"I'm serious about your security measures,"

"I know you are. And I promise, I'll be just as serious."

"Don't pursue his partner without me."

"I wouldn't think of it."

Chapter Seven

When the door opened, Riley held up the six-pack of Blue Point Summer Ale from the local brewery on Long Island.

"Oh, God, Riley, you want something." Kyle groaned. "It's ten o'clock. I have class in the morning. At *nine.*"

"Nine? That's *early?* Wuss." Riley walked in before Kyle could shut the door on her.

He grabbed the six-pack and frowned. "I'm not sharing."

"I got them all for you," she said. "Besides, I have to be up at *six* to meet my boss at *seven.* So don't complain about a nine A.M. class."

"I'll give you an hour."

"If you're good, that's all it'll take."

He rolled his eyes and put the six-pack in the refrigerator. He pulled two out, grabbed the bottle opener that was attached to the refrigerator, and opened them up. He handed one to Riley. "You know I always share."

She clicked her bottle to his and sipped. "Thank you, sir. I'm hoping this will be easy, but I'm kind of stumped on where to start."

Riley had met Kyle Callahan at Columbia when she was a senior and he was a junior. He started dating her roommate and the first time they met, Riley had seen far more of Kyle than she wanted when she walked into a romantic tryst in the dorm. Kyle and her roommate had broken up after a semester, but Riley and Kyle remained friends. He'd graduated last month, but was taking summer classes toward his masters in communication. He was a computer genius, as far as Riley was concerned, and she didn't know why he hadn't gone into the field. She'd asked—often— but he'd never given her a straight answer.

"One hour," Kyle said. "I need my beauty sleep."

She snorted a laugh, then explained what she wanted. "I have a list of all mental health facilities, public and private, within a seventy-mile radius of Hartford, Connecticut." She'd narrowed the list down by putting herself in Bachman's shoes—if he was truly having difficulty adjusting to college, then he would want to be closer to home. That was her guess. According to all of Max's notes, he was still close to his mother. There would be a comfort there, she thought. If her idea didn't pan out, she had a second list of facilities closer to Boston.

"I need to find out if someone was a patient there, but patient records are confidential. So the best thing is to narrow down to the type of facility, and then when I get a workable list—under ten—to run a search for disgruntled employees or someone on the staff who might talk."

"Is this about Adam Bachman?"

"That's confidential."

"It's just you and me here."

"I'm not supposed to talk about the case."

"This is *me,* Riley." He pouted. "We've been friends for three years. You've seen me naked."

"God, don't remind me."

He snorted. "You're blushing!"

"Am not."

"Are too."

"Fine, it's about Bachman. But that's totally confidential, okay? It's a small little thread I'm following up on. Can you help me?"

He sighed, reached for his laptop, and started typing. Riley was fast on the keyboard, but Kyle could type circles around her.

"Basically," he said, "we need to find out exactly what records are available online. They won't have patient records, but each of these facilities will be licensed, public or private."

"I want to narrow it down to a facility that doesn't take criminal cases."

"What do you mean?"

"You know, where people are sent because of a court case or trial or something. Max thinks he wouldn't have gone to a criminal facility. Also, it needs to be both in- and outpatient."

Kyle continued typing, running different types of searches. He dismissed a variety of leads faster than Riley could see what had come up. "Okay," he said after a few minutes. He drained half his beer. "Basically, each of the facilities is licensed by the state. I can easily cull a list of all facilities by when they were first licensed and whether they're still operating today. The hard part will be if a facility is no longer operating—if I have the name, I can look it up that way, but it won't be on the active list."

"I'm going to have to assume that it's a facility that's still around. This would be only six to eight years ago."

"Probably a safe assumption. And you said no criminal?"

Riley hoped she was right about that. "Yes," she said. "And his family didn't have a lot of money, so it would need to be a place that takes insurance."

He frowned. "Hmm. That might help. Do you know what kind of insurance he had then?"

"No, but his mother worked for the City of Hartford."

"Hmm."

He opened another search window and typed rapidly. "Bingo," he said. "All city employees have the same provider. But wouldn't Bachman have insurance through the college? I got that, because it was cheaper than being on my dad's plan, since my dad's self-employed and pays through the nose."

"I didn't think of that."

"Because your dad is a cop, and he probably could cover you cheaper than if you got it through Columbia." Again, Kyle typed. "Okay, the college plan at BU would only cover services through campus health."

"He wouldn't have gone there," she said, fairly confident based on everything Max had shared with her. "He would want to be away from college. He told his roommate he needed a break from school."

"Then we'll stick to the City of Hartford plan. Let's see what I can find out about it." He was quiet for a long while. He held up his empty beer bottle without a word. Riley sighed, grabbed it, and returned with another for him. He took it, guzzled a third of it down, and put the bottle aside. He typed, read, typed, read, and Riley paced. She stared out the narrow windows into the lights that were New York City. Kyle lived in a one-room studio only a few blocks from campus. It was a great location, but the building was old and the studio small. She tried not to think that his couch was also his bed. She didn't think that way about Kyle. Much.

"I got you a list," Kyle said, excitement in his voice. "Unless he paid out-of-pocket, the City of Hartford insurance plan would only cover expenses for these three facilities."

Three! She grabbed the list. "How did you narrow it down? There must be hundreds in the state."

"No—not with the parameters you have. Many are for drug and alcohol addiction, so I took those out because almost all of them are used by courts for DWI convictions. There's several that are inpatient only, and many that are outpatient only. There's only three that fit the noncriminal, in- and outpatient criteria."

"So," Kyle said, "what are you going to do now?"

"Convince my boss to let me go to Connecticut."

David had left at nine thirty, and Max had promised herself that she would give her mind a rest and read a book or watch television. And she did—for an hour. But she was compelled to go back and simply look at her information, to see if anything else came to her.

Then she made the mistake of listening to the interview again.

She called Sally O'Hara. It was late, nearly eleven, but Sally would still be up, Max was sure. Like Max, Sally was a workaholic. And when she wasn't working, she was with family.

Max knew that she was putting her friendship with the cop at risk, but she needed someone on the inside who could get her information about Bachman.

"Why did I know you'd be calling me?" Sally said when she answered.

"You didn't have to pick up the phone."

"With you, that never works. You'd probably end up on my doorstep."

"Thank you for working with David."

"I didn't do anything," she said. "Certainly did *not* help anyone in the media gather information."

"Bachman had a partner."

"I don't want to hear this."

"Milligan won't listen to me—"

"Now *that*'s a huge surprise, that he doesn't want the

biggest trial of the year to blow up in his face when he's on the verge of running for attorney general."

"Sally—"

"I can't help you. I appreciate the information you've passed my way in the past, and with the Palazzolos. I get it, Max. You care about them, you always do. But last time I stuck my neck out for you, I was transferred to Queens. I actually like my new digs here, I don't want O'Malley to toss me to Brooklyn or, God forbid, the Bronx. When he heard we were still talking, he threatened to take me off missing persons. I like missing persons, even when it's depressing. The wins make up for the losses. This is all I want to do."

"You're good at it. O'Malley's an ass."

"See? That's why I'm your only friend on the force."

"You're not my only friend."

"The only one who'll admit it."

That might be true.

"Can I just bounce some ideas off you? You think like a cop."

"I *am* a cop." Sally sighed dramatically. "What about Kane? He's a sharp guy."

"He is. And I have. But I need a different perspective."

"I don't want to hear about your stupid-ass theory that Bachman has a partner. I'm more inclined to believe he killed the Palazzolos—and I don't believe he did—than I am to believe that someone is helping him."

Max hesitated. She had to bring Sally over to her way of thinking, but she didn't know how to convince her. "Have you seen the forensic reports of Bachman's five victims?"

"La-la-la, I'm not listening, la-la-la."

Max spoke over Sally's chant. "There was minimal postmortem bruising."

"So?"

"How could one person move a body without damaging it?"

"I can think of a half-dozen ways. Wheelbarrow. Lift. Strong guy. Wrapping the body with a tarp. I see what you're getting at, Max, and if you even breathe a word of this, Bachman's attorney is going to get his damn reasonable doubt."

"If there's another killer out there, the police have an obligation to pursue the theory," she said, increasingly irritated that no one in law enforcement was taking her seriously.

"There's no proof that Bachman had anyone helping him. He had no close friends. No one claimed to see him with anyone regularly. The people he worked with said he was a pleasant loner. And I know you know all this. So what the fuck do you want from me, Max?" Sally was losing her patience. Max knew she was abusing their friendship, but for this case she had to. Maybe that's why Max didn't have many friends. She pushed and pushed until they stopped talking to her.

Sally sighed, then said, slightly calmer, "I'm already allocating resources searching for the Palazzolos' car."

"You're doing that because you want to find them as much as I do," Max said.

"Dammit, you're not making this easy for me."

"Life isn't a bed of roses."

"Please."

"I want access to the files."

Sally laughed. "No way in *hell* am I doing that. I'd be fired, Max. I already risked too much just showing your guy Friday the Palazzolo files. Bachman isn't even my case."

"The bodies were found in Queens. I know you have access."

"It's in the D.A.'s office, sweetheart. You want them,

you either kiss up to Charlene Golden or Milligan himself. Because I couldn't get them if I wanted."

"But you can get the witness statements. I know they're in the database."

"The witnesses will be part of the record once they testify at trial."

Max stared at her wall. What did she really want from Sally? From anyone? She couldn't prove her theory, and she had no way of knowing where to start unless she had *something* to go on. A picture. A name.

"Max, I know this is hard for you, but you have to let this one go." Sally had lost her anger. Her voice was soothing, because she really did understand Max. That's why they'd been friends for so long—even when they butted heads. "If we find the Palazzolos' car, I suspect we'll find their bodies, and it's because you've been nagging me for so long that I think we have a chance. I'm looking at the case from a different perspective than I did before. You care about finding them as much as I do. If I thought you had an ulterior motive, I wouldn't be talking to you. I promise—if I find them, I'll let you know. And if there's *anything* connecting them to Bachman, I will do everything in my power to not only give you something for your show, but make sure the D.A. looks at the evidence.

"But listen to me when I tell you this: nothing good will come from you pursuing this ridiculous theory that Bachman has a partner. No one believes it. And if anyone did? They wouldn't breathe a word. There have been no like crimes in the five boroughs since Bachman was arrested. No similar patterns of missing people. If he had a partner, that guy isn't doing anything, and that means you're searching for a ghost. I know how you get when you're obsessed, Max. It ain't pretty."

Sally paused, but Max didn't have anything to say.

"Max? Take a breather. Cover his trial. Run your interview. Do what you do, just don't fuck with the case."

"Thanks for going back to the Palazzolos," Max said and hung up.

Sally had given her an idea.

There are no other like crimes in the five boroughs.

If Bachman had a killing partner, what if he had a different fetish? Bachman used the victim's own cars, suffocated them at an unknown location, and dumped their bodies where they would be found; what if there were actual *missing* people who his partner was responsible for? What if there was another common denominator?

She rubbed her eyes. Where could she possibly start? There were hundreds of missing people from New York City. Bachman's partner could be working out of New Jersey or Connecticut or upstate New York or even farther away. But serial killers had a common methodology. What she needed to do was tap into the FBI database and find unsolved serial crimes, then compare the timing.

And, in fact, she already had something. The Palazzolos. What if the *partner*'s methodology was to destroy the bodies? Or to kidnap in pairs? Or target people over fifty?

It might not get her anywhere, but it was a place to start. And that was all Max needed.

She didn't realize that two hours had passed until after one in the morning when her computer beeped at her. She had an incoming Skype call from Nick. A jolt of anticipation hit her, and a tinge of regret. She missed him.

Detective Nick Santini. How had they gotten so comfortable with this long-distance relationship so quickly? They'd only met six weeks ago in California. They'd worked a case together—she was pretty certain he didn't consider her involvement as "working together," but she did. Max had a thing for smart cops and Nick was both smart and hot. After he arrested the killer, they'd spent the weekend together. Most of it in bed.

They were more than compatible. Max found herself thinking about Nick when she had downtime, and they talked via Skype several times a week. She'd flown to California for an overnight two weeks ago, which was somewhat foolish because of the long distance. She hadn't told Ben because he would have had a fit that she'd left while they were preparing for the Bachman trial. The whirlwind day and night of being a tourist in San Francisco, eating at Fisherman's Wharf, taking in a show, and making love past dawn in a suite with a view of the Golden Gate Bridge had left her satiated, satisfied . . . and lonely. Because she had to leave him and return to her world and her work.

She put her notes aside and shut down the computer search engine. She'd already sent messages to her researchers at *Maximum Exposure* and asked Riley to tap her resources—namely her family—to help with the missing persons database.

She clicked answer on the computer and smiled when she saw Nick's face on her monitor.

"I hope I didn't wake you up," he said. Then he really looked at her. "You're working."

"Was working. I need a few hours' sleep. Perfect timing."

"You look tired."

"It's been a long day."

"I read your article online. You didn't tell me you had an interview with that killer."

"It happened last minute."

"I have a feeling you left something out of the report. It seemed very—standard. And you don't write standard."

Keen observation, but she expected no less from the detective.

She hadn't shared with Nick her theories about Bachman working with a partner. She had, of course, talked about the Palazzolos, but the partner—that was a topic she'd already received too much grief about, and she didn't want to be mad at Nick. Especially since he was three thousand miles away and couldn't help.

"Bachman didn't admit to killing the Palazzolos, but he came close. Nothing I could actually put in print."

"And?"

"He said I'd never find them."

"That's personal."

"Excuse me?"

"He said that *you'd* never find them. Not that the police would never find them or that they'd never be found. I'm sure David thinks it's unwise to put yourself on a killer's radar."

"He's in jail." Another good reason not to tell Nick about the partner theory. He'd worry, and telling him he didn't need to worry because David had her back would irritate him.

"They have a solid case?" Nick asked.

"Yes. Unless something completely unexpected happens, he'll be in prison for a long time." She smiled. "I don't really want to talk about the case."

"That's a first." Nick leaned back in his chair and grinned. "What do you want to talk about?"

"What are your plans for this weekend?"

"This weekend?"

"If the trial is over on Thursday like the judge expects, what if I come and visit for the weekend? Are you working?"

"I have Sunday and Monday off. I could probably switch with someone for Saturday."

"I need a break. Maybe a weekend in bed will do me good."

He raised an eyebrow. "You plan to sleep the entire time?"

She laughed. "Yes. Every minute I'm not using your body for my own personal pleasure, I'll be asleep."

"You won't hear me complaining." He leaned forward. "Seriously, Max, you look exhausted. Get some sleep and we'll talk before Friday, okay?"

"Yes, Detective. Whatever you say."

He snorted. "I wish you were this easy all the time."

"No, you don't." She blew him a kiss and disconnected.

Without looking at her notes again, she shut everything off and went down the half staircase to her bedroom. With a button she rolled down the privacy shades—she could still see out, but no one could see in—went into her bathroom to brush her teeth, stripped naked, and fell into her plush bed.

Sleep came easy, especially when it started with a dream about her favorite detective from California, as naked as she.

Chapter Eight

"What the hell are you doing, Maxine?"

That was Ben's greeting when she stepped off the elevator Tuesday morning. She didn't need his attitude. Her dreams had started out fabulous with a naked Nick in her bed, but they'd turned dark and cloudy as they inevitably did, waking her before dawn and leaving her with less than four hours of sleep.

"Good morning, Benji," she said, irritated that he had obviously been waiting for her to arrive. "What were you doing, watching the security monitors?"

"I don't believe you! I came in with assignments on the next case you're covering and the entire research team tells me you've already given them work? On *Bachman?* We're done. We're covering the trial; then it's over. All you have to do is the live cut when the verdict comes down and tape your monologue from the interview for the June show."

She put up her hand. "Stop." She strode past him, down the hall and into her office. He followed and slammed the door. "God, Ben, I haven't had enough coffee for this."

"You're impossible."

"You knew that before you brought me on board." She

walked over to her Keurig, grateful that the early morning receptionist always turned it on for her when she arrived at six. She popped out the old coffee pod and put in a new one, then pressed brew.

"Max," Ben said, forcing his voice down two decibels, "we have three cases for July, none are in the bag, and you're working on old news."

"All cold cases are old news."

"Dammit!" His voice went up again.

She took her time to prepare her coffee—a dollop of cream, a single sugar-free sweetener—and sipped. Better.

She sat at her desk. "I'm meeting with Arthur Ullman this afternoon."

"Why?"

"I want his insight."

"Will he come on the show?"

"I'll see what I can do."

"Okay," Ben said, calming down. Max had interviewed Arthur before, and his interviews had always gone very well. He had a gravitas that drew in an audience, and just enough charm to be attractive. "You're not just placating me?"

"I'll ask him." Maybe. Depending on how their meeting went this afternoon.

"The research staff told me you have them looking into cases outside of New York and it's too broad. Missing persons, victims over fifty years old, on the entire East Coast? Really? Do you know how many that is?"

"Not the *entire* East Coast."

"Shit, Max—"

"That's why we have a research staff, right?"

Ben was boiling again, so Max said calmly, "Ben, I talked to Sally O'Hara and she said some things that got me thinking about this from a different angle. I know I'm right about the partner. Richard isn't going to listen, now or after the trial. Not unless someone else dies, and proving it's connected to Bachman? Next to impossible. There are no like crimes to the Palazzolos'. Not in the area. We need to think bigger."

"Why can't you have Riley do this? She's your assistant."

"She's covering the trial for me this afternoon."

His eyes got the squinty look when he suspected she was up to something. "What?"

"I told you, I'm meeting with Ullman. This afternoon was his only free time because he's teaching at NYU."

"You can't have the entire research staff. Pick one."

"*One?*"

"Don't push me on this right now, Max. We have deadlines and commitments and I'm setting up interviews with the parents of the missing boys in Oregon—or did you forget about that case?"

She tensed. "Of course I didn't." Three young teenagers had disappeared without a trace two months ago. The police had no leads. She'd been contacted by the father of one of the boys who said he didn't know who else to turn to.

"We shift focus in two weeks to Oregon, and you already have the research team digging in there, how do they have time to run down this tenuous—at best—theory of yours?"

"I'm only asking for this week." And maybe next, but she wisely didn't say anything.

"*Please.*"

"Sit."

He did, fidgeting. "I need the research staff."

"So do I."

"You can't—"

She raised an eyebrow.

He corrected, "You should consult with me before you assign major projects."

"This was last minute. I'm serious, Ben, you need to see

the potential in this story. Sally O'Hara is actively searching for the Palazzolos after months of inaction. Because of a lead *I* generated. She's narrowed the search area, and I really believe she'll learn what happened. If our team can pull down information that might give us a pattern . . ."

"You can have one."

"I need—"

"You have Riley, your own dedicated assistant. Why do you need six more?"

"Two."

"*One.* You can pick."

Dammit. "C. J.," she said without hesitation.

"Fuck."

"You said I can pick."

"Fine, you get C. J. None of the others."

"Fair enough."

"More than fair." He rose, went over to make himself a cup of coffee, and Riley burst in.

She looked from Max to Ben. "Sorry."

"It's fine, we're done," Ben said and left with his coffee.

Max brewed herself a second cup. "What did you learn?"

"Excuse me?"

"You know something, spill it."

"I'm really excited."

"Don't keep me in suspense," Max said, glancing at her watch. "David will be here in ten minutes to take us to the courthouse."

"I, um, think I figured out where Adam Bachman spent his semester off."

Max smiled, leaned forward. "You did?"

"One of three places."

"How did you narrow it down?"

"My computer friend, Kyle, helped. I didn't give him

details, just asked how I could narrow down mental health facilities near Hartford."

Max wasn't certain she believed that Riley hadn't shared details with Kyle—but she let it slide for now. This inquiry wasn't supersecret, but some of Max's research angles were, and she hoped Riley understood the difference.

"Since the previous research into Boston area facilities was a bust," Riley continued, "and with your idea that he would keep it close to home because of his relationship with his mother, I focused on Bachman's hometown and places nearby. That narrowed them down, but there were still too many. Kyle asked me what insurance he would have used. That reminded me that his mother worked for the City of Hartford, and as a college student he could have been covered under her insurance. There are only three facilities that accept that particular insurance."

"He could have paid out of pocket."

"Yes, but unlikely. He didn't have a job at the time, and I don't think he would have asked his mother for cash. I think it's one of these."

She slipped over the list to Max. Max looked at it, nodded. It was a good lead.

"We'll go up to Hartford tomorrow, first thing in the morning."

"We? But I can go up right now—"

"*We.* You're still new at this, I want to train you, for lack of a better word."

"But—"

"No buts. I need you in the courthouse this afternoon. You'll take my credentials and take good notes on the trial. Then write up a report for me."

"Where are you going?"

"I have a meeting."

"Can I—"

Max stepped out of the elevator into the lobby, then turned and admonished Riley. "No. I've given you far too much leeway already. I think you're forgetting that you're my assistant."

"I haven't."

"I'm not sending you to Hartford alone. We'll go together. Or you can stay here."

She shook her head. "I'll go with you."

"Good. Now prioritize this list. Checking into all three will be an overnight excursion. I want one. Your best, educated guess."

Riley looked concerned. "I already made assumptions—and what if I'm wrong?"

"Talk to C. J. He's good to brainstorm with. Go through your methodology. Between the two of you, I'm confident you'll identify the right facility."

"I appreciate your faith in me."

"It has nothing to do with faith. I'll see you at noon at the courthouse. Don't be late."

Max spotted David watching her five-minute interview with Ace Burley. He had on his sunglasses and she honestly couldn't tell if he was looking at them, or watching the modest crowd that had gathered. Probably the crowd. When she was done and thanked Ace and the crew, he came over to her and led the way to where he'd parked a block away. He always seemed to have the best luck with parking places.

When he pulled away from the curb, he asked, "What happened in court?"

"The next logical step—how the D.A. got a warrant for Adam Bachman's apartment and what they found in their search. Jewelry or other personal items from all five victims, things that were known to be missing. One of the victim's driver's license because he didn't wear any jewelry."

"And you're thinking about the Palazzolos."

"If the police don't know what's missing from their bodies, they might not know what to look for. The good news is that everything from his apartment is in evidence, so if we can find a way to get photos of the evidence to their kids, maybe they'll see something familiar that the police may not realize is important."

"Good idea."

"The testimony was tedious, so I'm glad they did it in the morning. The big selling point from the prosecution's standpoint is that the earrings that Ava Raines bought before she was abducted were found in Bachman's pocket during the initial search."

David pulled into Max's parking garage under her building, but they didn't go upstairs. They walked a block and a half to the Tribeca Grill for lunch. It was crowded, per usual, but Max had made reservations and they were immediately seated. She ate here at least twice a week when she was in town; it was one of her favorite places.

Max told David about her conversation with Sally O'Hara the night before.

"She's determined to find them. Maybe as determined as I am."

"How did you and O'Hara become so chummy?"

"I wouldn't say we're *chummy*."

"She answered your call."

"It's a long story."

"We have an hour and ten minutes."

Max didn't know why she hesitated. Maybe because she never talked about it. She still had so many emotions about what had happened, and she'd been much younger, much less experienced. She'd often wondered if she had the case now rather than seven years ago if she would have solved it faster, or with less bloodshed.

She said, "Seven years ago there was a missing child. Thirteen-year-old girl. Jane O'Hara."

"Sally's . . . ?"

"Little sister. Most of the authorities believed she was a runaway. There was no evidence of an abduction, family or stranger. Sally had been in law school. Her family was torn apart, she dropped out of law school, helped with her other siblings. Sally's the oldest of four children, Jane the youngest. On the one-year anniversary of Jane's disappearance, another girl went missing—the same age and same basic look. White, female, thirteen, blond. Sally had read my book about Karen's disappearance, and contacted me. The police didn't think there was a connection because the second girl was abducted from Virginia, hundreds of miles from here. Marco and I were still involved, and I convinced him to run like crimes in the FBI database." Marco—why had he turned out to be such a macho control freak? There were times when they worked so well together she thought she'd found her soul mate—and then other times she couldn't stand being in the same room with him.

She said, "We found a pattern. Jane had been the first, but there were two other missing girls who fit the same description who'd disappeared in the Northeast *before* the girl from Virginia. That meant four girls within sixteen months. Marco helped get the New York FBI office involved, but there was no solid evidence, only that weak pattern. They did a little work on it, but it grew cold. So I convinced Marco to access the records so I could see what they knew, and I took it from there."

"Marco? That surprises me."

Max smiled slyly. "Marco wasn't always an ass. He used to bend the rules a lot more."

"Before he got promoted?" David suggested.

Max couldn't disagree. Two years ago, right before she started *Maximum Exposure,* Marco had been promoted to Supervisory Special Agent in Miami and everything changed. Maybe that was truly the beginning of the end of them—though she could hardly say they'd ever had a smooth relationship. "It took Sally and me six more months, and the abduction of a fifth thirteen-year-old girl, before we found a witness who gave us a partial license plate taken off a security camera near where the last girl was abducted. We followed it through. A bunch of shit ensued, largely making it near impossible for me to drive through West Virginia without being arrested. But we found them.

"The kidnappers were a couple—common-law marriage—building some sort of psycho cult of 'purebloods'—white, blond hair, blue eyes, whatever. Pseudo-Nazis, I suppose, though there was nothing overtly political about their cult. They had two teenage sons who were involved. I don't need to go into the nasty details. Jane was pregnant when we found them. There was a standoff and hostage situation and one of the boys and one of the victims in the throes of Stockholm syndrome were killed in a suicide-by-cop ploy. The other three culprits, and those who helped them, are in prison. The four surviving girls, including Jane, were returned to their families."

David stared at her. "Why didn't I hear about this?"

"It was in West Virginia."

"You know what I mean."

She did. "I didn't write a book."

"That's not like you."

"Sally asked me to keep it quiet. Jane kept the baby. She's twenty-one now. The child is seven. He's being raised by Sally's parents because Jane is a mess. Not to mention that the family had two other children between Sally and Jane." She paused. "In my third book, the one about the abductions for ransom in Mexico, I wrote about the impact of missing persons on the people left behind. I wrote about their family and the cult, I just changed the names."

"And that's why Sally listens to you."

"I don't know that she listens, but she's not going to shut me out. She trusts my instincts, usually. She was going to be a lawyer. She finished law school, passed the bar, but decided to enroll in the police academy. We can't help but be changed by what happens to us. Sally would have made a great lawyer, but honestly? What difference would she have made? But she makes a big difference, a positive difference, as a cop."

Chapter Nine

In Max's job, she had dozens of contacts in law enforcement. One of her favorite people to consult was Dr. Arthur Ullman, a brilliant, retired forensic psychiatrist who had been one of the original FBI profilers way back when— before psychological profiling became a recognized tool in criminal investigation.

The first time Max met Arthur was his last year working for the FBI. He'd been assigned to the disappearance of her best friend Karen Richardson. She'd butted heads with him—at twenty-two she butted heads with nearly everyone she met—but he was the only person who'd been honest with her from the beginning. He told her that yes, he believed Karen was dead, and that yes, he thought she knew her attacker. He also had insight into the type of killer who would befriend, kill, and disappear his victim. And if it wasn't for Arthur, Max knew the FBI would never have been able to put a name to Karen's killer.

That he'd been right hadn't settled the case. Karen's body had never been found, and her killer—the playboy bastard Max knew was responsible—left the country, snubbing his nose at not only Max and the FBI, but the justice system as a whole. He'd gotten away with murder because no physical evidence and no witnesses tied him to the crime.

Max learned a valuable lesson that year. Psychology and forensics could only get you so far.

But if it weren't for Arthur, she'd never have the pieces of Karen's final day, never would have known who was responsible. And if Karen's killer ever came back to the United States, Max would be there to make his life miserable.

Arthur now had a teaching position at NYU and consulted with law enforcement. Max had consulted with him on any number of investigations, but she hadn't spoken to him in nearly a year, when he was her expert consultant on *Maximum Exposure*. She'd offered to meet him at his office, but he said he'd prefer to meet at her apartment, where he knew she'd have set up a wall of information.

"You took the best parts of my system and made it work for you," he'd said. "I'd like to see your visual representation of the crimes."

Arthur was punctual, as usual. Max gave him a warm hug when she answered her door. "Arthur, it is so good to see you. You remember David Kane, my right hand?"

"Of course. And it's always good to see you, Max. You know you don't have to call only when you need help."

"I have no excuse."

"There's never a dull moment with you. I took the liberty of reading up about the Adam Bachman case."

"I'm surprised you haven't before now."

"Oh, I have, but only what the average person might read about the case. I took a deeper look last night. Let's go see the wall."

Arthur was in his sixties, gray, his hair thinning on top. He was still physically active, and teaching kept him intellectually engaged. He was a widower, losing his wife to cancer long before Max met him. He'd never remarried and once told Max that Beth was the love of his life and no one could replace her.

Max wondered if she'd ever feel that way about anyone. Maybe she didn't have it in her. Unconditional love didn't come easy to her. If at all.

They walked upstairs and Max turned on the lights. She and David stood to the side, to give Arthur time to read and absorb what was in front of him. He didn't speak for fifteen minutes, putting Max on edge. She stopped herself—twice—from scraping the polish off her fingernails. A bad habit she couldn't seem to break.

"Can I listen to your interview?"

"Of course," she said. She walked over to her computer. "I think—"

"I want to hear your theory, but let me listen to him without your bias." He sat on the couch and closed his eyes in concentration.

Bias? She was *biased?* What did he mean by that?

She pressed play. They all listened to the twenty-minute interview again. His description of the fish still unnerved her, but she was more angry about the comment that she'd never find "them." The Palazzolos.

When the recording ended, Arthur said, "I had a friend send me the video of Bachman's original interrogation, so I have some information that you don't have, which I think will answer some of your questions.

"First, Bachman didn't kill the Palazzolos."

Her stomach flipped. She wanted to argue with Arthur. He wasn't psychic, how could he just know that?

He said, with a touch of humor, "I know you want to tell me to go to hell, so I'll quickly get to my point."

"I wouldn't," she said.

David grunted and she ignored him.

Arthur said, "He didn't kill them because their bodies weren't found."

He stood and walked over to her wall. He picked up her pointer as if he were the teacher and she the student.

"Bachman is a nonsexual sadist sociopath. He is not a narcissist in how you and I would define a narcissist, both clinically or casually. He may be a malignant narcissist, which is a term rarely used and doesn't quite fit here—they usually associate with a group or cause and kill as a means to a political or social end. However, without meeting with him I couldn't commit to any responsible diagnosis.

"He is definitely obsessive-compulsive, as you've noted in your research. He works in a bar, yet for the two years he's worked there he's *always* had Tuesdays and Wednesdays off. Why? Because changes in his schedule would rub him raw, like fingernails on a chalkboard. I wouldn't be surprised, for example, that he gets up at the exact same time every day, eats at the same time, goes to bed at the same time.

"His apartment was immaculate, but more than being neat, it was sanitized. He obsesses about germs, per your interview with his colleagues and even his lone childhood friend, but it's clear also in how he lives. Yet he's able to function in a social environment, to communicate and be perceived as being an articulate, friendly person. He's managed to tame his obsessions, at least publicly."

Arthur walked to the beginning of the board. "There were no indications in his early childhood of classic sociopathy—meaning, no abusing animals, no fights, no antisocial behavior. His father left at an early age, and his mother's second husband was abusive—so much so that his mother had to get a restraining order. If his mother lived in fear, Adam could have absorbed those feelings. That's shown through his early childhood—you only found the one close friend, who enlisted in the army when they were eighteen. Essentially, abandoning him even though the friend was following his own dream of being a soldier."

"You really did read all my articles."

Arthur smiled. "I always do, Max. You were my best student."

She laughed. She'd once teased him that he was her personal tutor in all things crazy.

"Adam went to college because it was expected of him. He left his second semester sophomore year. He was quiet and withdrawn—again, pleasant, but not social. He was considered anxious. I could see how living with someone else, in a dorm room setting, would interrupt his balance—his need for rigid order and cleanliness. Outside in the world, he can handle the mess, but in his own domain, he must have perfection. This isn't a sociopathy—it's borderline, but being meticulous and hyperclean isn't necessarily a mental disorder. It's to what extreme the individual goes, and how it affects his day-to-day functioning in society. And I would argue that Adam doesn't have this type of sociopathy."

Max was used to Arthur's long explanations—he always came to his point—but she was getting antsy. "Arthur, I appreciate the history lesson, but nothing you say points to him killing those five people—and you already said he didn't kill the Palazzolos."

"Impatient, dear."

"Yes, I am," she admitted.

"Your theory is that Bachman went to see a therapist, possibly self-committing himself," Arthur said.

"Yes."

"I think you're right. Because at home, his mother wouldn't have seen his fastidious behavior as being odd. His best friend came from a long line of military, and his house was orderly and neat. That's likely why the two were friends. They connected through order."

David interrupted for the first time. "If Bachman likes order and rules, why didn't he follow his friend into the army?"

Arthur smiled as if David was his new favorite student. "I thought the same thing. And the answer comes more from his actions of late than from his past. I would suggest that Bachman likes *order*, not *rules*. It's why he left college for a semester. It's why he works as a bartender in a club— where there is order to the bottles, the business— but few rules. Drinking in many ways breaks rules, or loosens them. He has *his* rules, but he doesn't like *other* rules.

"Do you know what his father did for a living?"

"He worked for the City of Hartford, like his mother," Max said.

"He was the city planner. He made rules. He left with his secretary—abandoning Adam and his mother for another woman."

"I didn't know that."

"Nor did I, until I saw the original interrogation. It was a flip comment by Adam, but I think telling. His step-father was a high school vice principal. Again, someone who makes rules for others to follow.

"The other key point is something that showed as a thread through all your articles and the notes you sent me last night. Bachman had no friends. None, except for the one childhood friend. He didn't socialize or date. He had no girlfriends in high school or college or here in New York. He kept to himself, he functioned well, but he didn't do what normal twenty-seven-year-old men do.

"But I'd argue that he *did* have one person he bonded with. Someone he shared secrets with. Someone who's stronger and more aggressive, but without the social grace that Adam has. Someone who doesn't have a regular job and—"

"Time out," Max said. "You lost me. We know he doesn't socialize, you agreed with me, then you say he *does* have a friend?"

Arthur smiled sheepishly. "Let me connect my thoughts. Growing up, Adam had his mother. Then he had his one friend. When his friend abandoned him for the army, Adam went to college but didn't find anyone to fill that void in his life. But he needs someone. For all his oddities, what he's been searching for—through college, through work, through how he communicates—is one person who understands him. Not sexual—this is more like a buddy, a kindred spirit. In fact, I wouldn't be surprised if Adam was asexual. Meaning, he doesn't like men or women. But he needs a companion."

"Okay," Max said. She thought she understood what Arthur was getting at. "He lost his buddy, he wants a replacement."

"Exactly. And it makes him vulnerable, because he doesn't have the same moral compass others have. Based on his interrogation and how he spoke to you, he's a sociopath in that he doesn't empathize with others. If someone with a stronger personality, with a similar disorder—someone violent—befriended him, Adam would do anything for him. They likely share a fascination with death."

"Him," David said. "You're sure his partner is male."

"Oh, yes, I'm positive. To Adam, women are weaker, incidental humans."

"But he killed two men."

"Because he's not a sexual killer. I can't tell you why he picked those particular five victims without digging deeper into their lives and Bachman himself, but it wasn't based on their gender or their appearance."

"So his partner is a guy," Max said.

"Yes, and this male unsub—unknown subject—will have a record, most likely assault or another violent crime. He's the one who killed the Palazzolos. Probably with his hands, but possibly with a knife where he may have left behind DNA evidence. He's concerned about that because he's in the system; Adam Bachman was never concerned because he wasn't in the system."

"So if Bachman left evidence on the bodies, there was nothing for law enforcement to match it up with."

"Exactly." Arthur helped himself to a water bottle in the minifridge Max had in her bookshelf. "I suspect that the murder of the Palazzolos was Adam's trigger. He helped his friend clean up—Adam is smart, above average intelligence. He majored in biology. He would know about the properties of sodium hydroxide. He would help his friend, because that's what friends do. And he wouldn't think there was anything strange about the request. But I agree with your assessment—he wouldn't touch the dead bodies. It would repel him. Think of this is a quid pro quo arrangement. Adam helps his friend dispose of his victims; his friend helps Adam dispose of his own victims. It could well be that Adam had homicidal fantasies for years, but his fear of germs kept him from enacting them."

Arthur's analysis made sense. She didn't quite see how he got to that conclusion, however, and by the expression on David's face, he didn't see the connection, either.

"You're skeptical." Arthur sat down. "Because Adam is smart and organized, his partner has learned to be more careful, but initially, they made mistakes. They were seen together many times before the Palazzolos disappeared, but not often thereafter. They didn't use phones, but likely had a regularly meeting place."

"Could he have worked in the bar?"

"Unlikely. The Palazzolos' killer is antisocial, angry, doesn't take orders well, and has a problem with authority.

If he has a regular job, it would be where he didn't interact with people, like working in a warehouse or in a stockroom or construction. Possibly skilled labor. I can pretty much guarantee that he was in that bar the Sunday night when the Palazzolos came in." He frowned. "I'm extrapolating here a bit more than I feel comfortable with. Without the bodies, without knowing how they were killed, I can't say for certain that the unsub has issues with one or both of his parents, but it's rare for a killer to target an older couple. My gut, from my experience, suggests it was personal *to him* and the Palazzolos were stand-ins to satisfy his rage."

David said, "Your theory sounds plausible, it makes a good story, but why is it a better theory than Max's? They're both just educated guesses."

"Mine is an educated guess born after forty years of experience in criminal psychology and profiling hundreds of killers. I'm not pulling the profile out of my ass, so to speak." He grinned. "Though, I would certainly need to refine it after meeting Mr. Bachman one-on-one. That recording, Max, tells me a lot. It tells me he's been studying you."

"He admitted to watching my show. I'm an open book."

"Not as much as you think, but to someone who studies human nature, yes. And because he's an introvert and distances himself from people, he's acutely observant. So be careful with him."

Max asked, "Why would he commit himself in the first place?"

"He recognized he had dark impulses to kill and at first, those impulses disturbed him. He probably had them since puberty—which is when most male serial killers start fantasizing about murder. Because there is no overt sexual component—he likely gets a sexual-like release from watching his victims die, but it's a chemical reaction of adrenaline and endorphins, not a physical ejaculation—he probably didn't think he was mentally impaired. But something happened in college that made him question these impulses. I suspect he went into therapy under false pretenses, such as to get help with his OCD, and then he talked about these darker urges—which he would have explained away as dreams. He would never admit to *thinking* about killing anyone, so he would use benign language, maybe calling them nightmares. He may never have even acted on his impulses, until he met this unsub.

"And that is why he started to kill," Arthur concluded.

David asked, "We've been digging into similar crimes to the Palazzolos and have found squat. If this unknown killer is out there, why hasn't he killed before? Or since?"

"They weren't his first, which is why he's in the system—my guess, again. He may not have killed before, but he's on record for a minimum of assault and battery. He may have done some time, but if the crime was in his youth it will have been juvenile hall or probation. After Bachman's arrest, the unsub went into hiding. He'll certainly kill again, but he may have a longer cooling-off period than his partner."

"I need you to convince the D.A.," Max said.

"Maxine, I love you dearly, but you know I won't do that unless he calls me. I still consult with the FBI and local agencies; I'm not going anywhere I'm not invited. But if you can convince Mr. Milligan to call me, and he's willing to share the rest of the case files and let me speak with Adam Bachman, then I will of course help."

Max knew it was fruitless to push Arthur. He was professional, sometimes to a fault, but there was a reason people in law enforcement respected him.

"I'll talk to Richard," she said. It was certainly worth a shot. "Thank you, Arthur. I mean it. This insight is invaluable."

"One bit of advice, Max—not that you're going to take

it, because you tend to be impatient—is that I think Richard Milligan would be far more open to the idea that Bachman didn't work alone *after* the trial is over. There's really no doubt in my mind that the police got the right man for these five murders."

"What's two more days?" Max asked.

Arthur smiled broadly. "You've really grown up since you were twenty-two."

Max walked Arthur downstairs, and David followed. "The sad thing is," Arthur said, "this type of sociopathy could have been cured if he went to the right psychiatrist and worked hard to end these impulses. As Adam himself said twice in your interview, and showed in some of his actions, he doesn't consider himself physically violent. But the person he originally talked to was probably way over his head and didn't realize what was at the core of Adam Bachman's problems."

"Which is?" David asked.

"His inability to bond with people. His entire life he wanted someone who loved him for who he was. Instead, he got a father who left, a stepfather who abused his mother, a mother, likely weak and timid, wrapped up in her own problems, and his best friend who left for the army. Even as a child, he never bonded with anyone. He felt one step removed from society. Lost, introverted, no one saw the signs. That's why he kills without touching his victims. He's removing himself from the process of dying, while observing it like he observes everything in his life—from a distance. And honestly? If he had never met the unsub, I don't think he would have killed. It's a truly sad twist of fate."

When Arthur left, Max turned to David. "Let's go out for drinks."

"Let me guess. Fringe."

She smiled. "You know me so well."

Chapter Ten

David parked two blocks from Fringe and he and Max walked with the hordes of tourists and locals into the trendy restaurant and bar.

The restaurant was on the main floor with intimate booths along the back wall and big party tables in the center. The staff constantly moved, balancing drinks and trays with seeming fluidity. Neon lights, swirling and contemporary, decorated the walls and ceiling in waves of color, which could have been garish, but worked well against the white tablecloths and black wood floor.

Upstairs, the bar boasted first-come seating. People congregated at tables near the floor-to-ceiling windows because of the view looking down at Times Square. The bar itself took up two walls and boasted two dozen comfortable stools. High-top tables dotted the interior, comfortable armchairs were grouped in one corner. Max spotted Melinda Sanchez behind the bar and caught her eye, then crossed over to the armchairs. She took a seat where she could watch Melinda. David took a chair where he could watch the room.

A cocktail waitress approached. "What can I get you?"

"Your fruit and cheese plate appetizer," Max said without looking at the menu, "and a glass of pinot grigio."

"Sir?" she said to David.

"Bottled water."

Max glanced at her name badge. "Shelly, I need to speak with Melinda. If you could please send her over?"

"Um, sure," Shelly said. "I'll see when her next break is."

The girl left, and Max pulled out her iPad to review the notes from her original conversation with Melinda.

Melinda Sanchez had started working at Fringe six months before Bachman was arrested. What had struck Max at the time was that she hadn't had to push Melinda or lead her into saying that Adam Bachman was creepy. Melinda flat out said she didn't like him from the minute she met him. The young woman was rough around the edges, grew up in the Bronx, and currently lived in a small New Jersey apartment with her boyfriend, a sound tech for a major theater company. She clearly had people reading skills—she was sharp and street-smart.

While Melinda had stood out to Max as being both blunt and honest, Max had been so focused on the Palazzolos that she hadn't thought to ask Melinda about Bachman's friends.

Max recognized that one of the problems with the way her career had unfolded, particularly since she started hosting *Maximum Exposure,* was that she couldn't spend as much time in the field working one investigation. Each of her books took her at least nine months to research: interviews, reading, reinterviews, exploring, pouring over forensic reports. Even the freelance work she did for newspapers and magazines took weeks or months to pull together. She used to devote all her time to one project, immersing herself in the crime and the lives of everyone involved.

She hadn't been able to give the Palazzolos her undivided attention; likewise, she hadn't been able to devote enough time to the Bachman trial, either. Every month she had new cases to review, letting the research staff give her information that she used to get for herself. The staff was good—but she relied on nuances that simply couldn't find their way into a written report.

She *should* have followed up with Melinda. Once she had the idea that Bachman had a partner, she should have been here asking *again* about who he might have been seen with. Now? Nine months had passed since Bachman's arrest and Melinda might not remember anything that would help. Max had covered a half-dozen big cases and many smaller investigations in between. The realization that she was spreading herself too thin began to suffocate her.

Melinda brought over their drinks. "I saw you come in," she said and took a seat.

"This is my colleague, David Kane," Max said. "Do you have a few minutes?"

"I got someone to cover for me. What's going on? Is this about the trial? I've been following it. He's not going to get off, is he?"

"I doubt it," Max said. "But I have some follow-up questions."

"Whatever, but I don't know that I'll be of help."

"I have my notes to refresh your memory." Max sipped her wine, put it down, and waited until the waitress left the fruit and cheese platter. "You were the most emphatic that Adam Bachman was odd."

"I called him a creep. And I was right."

"Not everyone thought he was creepy. In fact, most people thought he was reserved, but pleasant. When I pressed, they pointed out his oddities—like he washed his hands repeatedly and that he never socialized with anyone from work."

"That's all true."

"But you said right off you weren't surprised when you heard he had been arrested for murder."

"I wasn't."

"Why?"

"I told you. He gave me the creeps."

"You might not know why, but there's a reason. You started working here six months before he was arrested. That would be about three months before his first known murder. Correct?"

She shivered visibly, but nodded. "Yes. We generally only worked two nights together, Saturday and Sunday. My schedule bounced around, but he insisted on having the same two days off a week. Because he'd been here two years, the manager just let him. He would never switch or cover for anyone."

"Go back to the first day you met him. Why did you think he was a creep?"

She closed her eyes. "I thought he was preoccupied that day. Standoffish. It was something that happened a week later that made me think creep."

She looked from David to Max. "We get busy and it's steady even when we're not superbusy. Management likes the interaction between the bartenders and customers, chatting, being friendly, that kind of stuff. It was a Friday afternoon, before the pretheater crowd. I was working on the floor, Adam was behind the bar. There was this couple sitting right here, where we are, a little too much PDA, but nothing that was off-limits. I went to Adam and said, 'Romeo and Juliet want another round.' He was staring at them, and anyone else would have made a crack, either about getting a room, or how hot they were, whatever. He just stared. Didn't comment or smile. Didn't even acknowledge that I had spoken. But he heard me, because he filled their order. When they left, he called the busboy over and said someone spilled on the chairs and they needed to be cleaned. We have extras in the back, so the busboy swapped them out for two clean chairs. Thing was, they hadn't spilled. They'd just been making out. And he had watched them the entire time. I thought maybe he was getting horny, but then I realized he was just disgusted."

Max wrote it all down. Then she said, "Most people I spoke with said that Adam had no friends, but I have a source who tells me he had a male friend who may have visited him here at work."

Melinda considered, then nodded. "Yeah, I guess he did. A big guy. Not fat, just tall with broad shoulders like he worked out a lot."

David said, "You have a good memory."

"I do," she said. "You have a problem with good memories?"

"No, but it's odd that you remember this now."

"No one asked me before. I didn't think of it."

Melinda sounded defensive. Max smoothed it over with, "That's why I wanted to follow up. Sometimes I don't ask the right questions the first time around. When did this guy come in?"

"Every once in a while. Always sat at the bar. I never saw him when Adam wasn't here." She paused, glanced down for a moment, then looked at Max. "In fact, I haven't seen him in months."

"This is a busy club. Maybe you didn't notice."

"I'm the bartender. I notice everyone. He could have come in when I was off. The guy wouldn't be hard to spot. He has tat sleeves. Nice work, too. Not bad-looking, until you really look at him, then he was scary as hell. The way he looks at you. And that's why I remember him. Adam was one of the most clean-cut guys in the joint. Immaculate. And he hung out with this guy covered in tats? It made *no sense* to me. But they were chummy. I thought they might be gay, asked Jesse what he thought—he's gay, he can usually tell. He said no way."

"Did Adam ever introduce you?"

"No. But once I said something like, 'Is your friend from out of town?' because it was obvious they had known each other for a long time. And Adam said, 'He just moved here from New Haven.' And, like, nothing else. You know—he was much better as a bartender, chatting people up, but he never talked about himself. It was like a show, you know? He acted like a great bartender, but it didn't translate when he was offstage, so to speak." She glanced at the bar. "I gotta get back to work. But let me know if you have more questions. I want to help."

The bartender rose, then said, "You told me back then that I was the only one who flat out didn't like Adam, and I guess that bugged me for a while because some people think I'm judgmental. But my entire life, I've watched people. My neighborhood was tough, I learned to assess situations real quick. Like, I can tell you that the couple at table thirty-three are about to break up and the big, loud guy at table nineteen is harmless, but I'm keeping my eye on the prep at table twenty-four because I think he's planning on having sex with the girl he's with, whether she says yes or not. I read people. And the minute I met Adam Bachman, the hair rose on my skin and I can't for the life of me explain why. But to everyone else? He was a nice guy. Kept to himself. Clean, did a good job, punctual. And that's why no one has anything bad to say about him. He blended into the background, and that's where he wanted to be."

"I like her," David said when Melinda left.

"I should have followed up earlier," Max said. "David, what am I doing?"

He simply looked at her and sipped his water.

"All this"—she tapped her notepad—"I should have known months ago. I should have talked to Arthur earlier about my theory. I should have followed up with Melinda before now. I should have been the one to go to Adam's hometown and talk to his former neighbors, not my staff. I should have talked to Chris Gibson myself, rather than send in Riley. I screwed this up."

"In the last year, you've investigated or reported on more than thirty different cold cases for the show and for the Web site. With what time would you have done all these things?"

"That's the thing—none of those cases have received my undivided attention. I'm losing control." Max nibbled on a grape. "I'm letting people down."

"Ben is happy—as happy as someone like him can be. Ratings are steadily increasing. You've resolved more of those cases than not. You let yourself down because you expect more from yourself than anyone can give."

"I used to remember everything about a case I worked. Not only what to do and who to talk to, but I remembered the names and faces of the victims and family and suspects. Now? I have to really think about the last case I reported on. I don't want to forget anything." *Or anyone.*

"Take a break."

"Really. Wasn't that what I did in California?"

"You call your trip to California a break?" David smiled. He was a handsome guy when he smiled, which was rare. Not that he was bad-looking, just that he had that hard edge and deep scar that made him unapproachable to anyone who didn't know him.

"I spent three extra days doing nothing but relaxing." And handling the fallout from her investigation into the murder of her high school best friend. "I'm planning on visiting Nick if the trial ends on Thursday. He'll be a nice weekend distraction."

"Hardly relaxing with two cross-country flights."

She smiled. "He's worth it." She paid the bill and drained her wine. "Let's go. I'm better now. I just needed to wallow in self-pity for a minute."

David followed her as she got up and headed away from the table. Max did feel better, but she still hadn't solved the fundamental problem that she needed more time with each investigation she committed to. She didn't know how that was going to go over with Ben. Because as soon as this trial was over, she was going to have a heart-to-heart with him about what she would—and would not—be doing for the show.

"Isn't that Ava Raines?" David said as they walked through the restaurant.

Petite blond kidnapping victim Ava Raines was having dinner with another young woman in one of the booths against the wall.

Max strode over and said, "Hello, Ava."

The girl looked up at her, at first confused, then recognition crossed her face. "Ms. Revere. Hi." She glanced at her friend. "This is Ginger. She's my moral support this week."

Max nodded to the girl, then said to Ava, "I'm surprised to see you here."

"I don't want to be scared all the time, you know? This whole thing was a fluke. It doesn't even feel real anymore."

Ginger said, "Ava, remember?"

Ava bit her lip and looked at Max. "The prosecutor told me I'm not supposed to talk to anyone about the trial until after it's over. I'm sorry."

Max handed Ava her business card. "Remember, we're going to talk after the trial."

"Right." The way she said it made Max think she had no intention of calling. Maybe she wanted this all to end. Maybe she was planning on selling her story, like Bachman's lawyer—it wouldn't be the first time a major player in a trial sold an article, a story to the tabloids, or even a book deal.

"Call me after the trial, I'll make the time. I'm glad you're doing well, Ava. Truly."

"Thanks, Ms. Revere."

Chapter Eleven

"No, no, no," Ben said early Wednesday morning after Max told him she was driving to Hartford with Riley. David sat in her guest chair, watching the conversation as if it were a sporting event.

"Ace is happy to sit in the courtroom for NET today. He wanted it from the beginning. Really, Benji, you're the one who told me to work harder to get along with Ace, and now that I'm his new best friend you're giving me grief?"

"You—argh!" He paced her small office. "You know that's not what I meant. Ace doesn't pick up on the nuances."

"This is important. Riley found a good lead—"

"How do you know?"

She hated being interrupted, especially when Ben wasn't looking at the bigger picture.

"Ben, get over it. I'm going. I already have an appointment with the facility director."

"I can't believe you're doing this," Ben said, shaking his head.

"Dammit, I've been pushing this angle from the very

beginning, ever since I learned Bachman skipped a semester in college. What did he do those four months? We know he wasn't living with his mother—we talked to the neighbors. We know he didn't leave the country. We know he didn't have a girlfriend he was shacking up with. One facility. Riley and C. J. narrowed the list to *one*. It's worth my time."

"If you think Riley is the next Maxine Revere, send her up alone!"

"If I thought that Bachman was going to take the stand, I might just do that. But he's not. Riley is still new at this, I need to go with her."

Ben turned to David who had, wisely, stayed out of the conversation.

"I can't believe you're letting her do this."

"*Letting* me?"

David winced. "You're not helping your case, Lawson."

Max was on the verge of losing her temper. When she was in New York, Ben tried his hardest to direct and control her. "I'm an investigative reporter. That is what I do. Riley uncovered something that needs looking into, and I'm going to be the one to do it."

"It can wait until the trial is over."

"Can it? If I'm right and Bachman has a partner, *this* is the lead that will get us the name. My gut tells me there's something here because Bachman has done such a great job of hiding this part of his life."

"Maybe because it doesn't exist!"

"There's still a missing couple out there!"

"They're not going to get any less dead."

She stared at him, mouth open, unable to speak after that comment.

"Max—" he began, softer.

"If you don't like the way I do this job, fire me."

She grabbed her bag and walked out.

Riley was sitting in her cubicle. It was obvious she had heard everything, but she smartly said nothing.

"Did you pick up the car?" Max asked.

"Yes. But it's costing more because I'm not twenty-five—"

"Trust me, if I was driving it would cost twice as much. Let's go."

"Why isn't David driving?"

"Because he's working another angle." That had been another tough conversation. David wanted to go with her for security reasons. Now that Arthur Ullman had convinced him her theory was right and Bachman *did* have a partner, he didn't want to leave her side. But she argued that this trip was spontaneous, she'd make sure they weren't followed out of town, and she would keep in contact. He wasn't happy, but he also knew that his plan to help Sally O'Hara today was just as important.

Riley's brows creased inward. "But I thought he was your bodyguard."

The elevator doors closed, leaving them alone. "Yes and no." Max was irritated, but figured it was the residual anger over her conversation with Ben. Riley was simply curious. "He's my right hand. When he needs to be a bodyguard, he steps up and does it. When I travel, he handles security. If there's a threat, he takes care of it. But he's not just muscle."

"I guess I'm still trying to figure out how things work here."

"Ben is constantly trying to make me into something I'm not and sometimes we argue."

"Well, I think he's wrong. You don't need to be in the courthouse. You should be able to do whatever you want. You're the star of the show."

The doors opened into the basement parking. Max stepped out, but stopped walking until Riley looked at her.

"I know what you're thinking and you're not even close, Riley," Max said. "Ben is your boss just like I am. He is damn good at his job, it's his passion, and I respect that. Just because I disagree with him on occasion doesn't mean he's wrong. He's one of the smartest people I know—I just don't always want to do what he wants me to do."

Riley was obviously confused. Max didn't know how to explain it. "You have two brothers," she finally said. "Do you agree with them all the time?"

"No, but—"

"And I'll bet around the dinner table you give them shit and argue?"

"Sometimes."

"But if anyone outside of the family says a disparaging word about either of them, you'd bite their head off."

Riley twisted her lips together and nodded.

"Consider your head bitten off. You're new, you're a rookie. Ben is my brother, metaphorically. We argue, sometimes passionately, but I will never say an inappropriate word about him in public, understood?"

"Understood."

It took nearly two hours for them to drive to Hartford from Manhattan. Max took the opportunity to review her notes and finish reading the research Riley and C. J. had pulled together on Greenhaven, the mental health facility where Bachman had almost certainly had himself committed.

Greenhaven was founded forty years ago primarily as a drug and alcohol rehab center—one of the first of its kind. Situated on fifty acres on the outskirts of the city in the suburb of Farmington, it had expanded to include treatment of all kinds of addictions, phobias, and social disorders like anxiety. Though it apparently prided itself on its discretion, the tabloids had printed the names of famous people who had used the services—the daughter of a U.S. senator, several actors, and one prominent New York politician who had been outed as a sex addict.

C. J. and Riley had put together a list of the individuals who were outed in the press as being patients at Greenhaven by date. The attached articles didn't name names of *who* spoke to the press, but the time frame would work well if Max could access Greenhaven records, or find someone currently on staff who worked during those windows of time.

Max used a variety of tricks to get people to open up. She could be friendly and understanding; she could also bully. But in a situation like this, she needed someone who was willing to talk off the record. Finding that person wouldn't be easy. Max often spent days getting the lay of the land, researching staff, finding the weak link. Sometimes she'd work that person for a while to get the information she needed. Even more often she'd get some information, then parlay it with someone else for better information, and so on until she could see the complete picture.

She only had one day.

Truth be told, she could take more time. Ben had been right—she didn't have to jump on this today. But now was her best chance at getting the whole story so she could talk to Bachman before he was sentenced and sent to state prison. Once he was in prison, it would be more difficult to set up an interview. She'd have to jump through hoops with the state prison authorities and her friendship with D.A. Richard Milligan wouldn't help.

Would Bachman even meet with her again? All she had to trade was how she portrayed him on *Maximum Expo-*

sure. Wouldn't he rather be known as someone who made mistakes, but in the end did the right thing by turning in his more violent partner? She could play on that theme— his mother, how it would make her feel to know that her son had helped the police put away a violent predator. Forgiveness, redemption, whatever it took to get Adam Bachman to give her a name.

Also, time *was* an issue. The Palazzolos were still missing. Sally O'Hara had a lead, but if it dried up, she had dozens of other cases to focus on. Max had the cop's interest now, but if she lost it, she lost, period. If Bachman ID'd his partner, the police would have a viable lead and could in turn get search warrants, track his whereabouts, interview him. Stop him before he destroyed another family.

She rubbed her temples. She hadn't gotten enough sleep in the last couple of weeks. In fact, since returning from California six weeks ago, Max had survived on roughly four hours of sleep a night. She could easily do it in the short term, but in the long term it crushed her.

Sleep had always been difficult for her. She fell to sleep easily enough, but if she woke up at 2:00 or 3:00 A.M. after only a couple of hours, she was up for good. She suspected that the emotional toll of solving her high school friend's murder six weeks ago was still disquieting. Knowing who was guilty, and how the truth had torn apart not only her family but others, made sleep that much more elusive.

She said to Riley, "We need an established goal for today. I may have jumped the gun on thinking we'd find all the answers."

"But you thought it was a good lead."

"It is," she said. "But usually, if I needed to get information out of a place like this, I would commit myself or have someone undercover." She'd done it once in a nursing home in Florida where an eighty-two-year-old spitfire had helped her end a decade-long case of elder abuse by living at the home and reporting to Max on the outside. The only good that came from one of the most depressing cases in Max's career was that she shut down the facility and had earned a new best friend, Lois Kershaw, who was now eighty-five and living it up in an assisted living condo in Miami, enjoying her notoriety as the "inside man" for a Maxine Revere exposé.

"I'll do it," Riley said. "You trusted me with Bachman's college roommate. I can *do* this."

"We don't have it set up. To go undercover, we need solid documentation and a set plan. When I did it in Miami, I pretended to be Lois's granddaughter, so I had access. I can't use a fake name anymore."

"I can."

"I don't have documents for you. And while you have potential, you haven't even been with me for two months. No way am I sending you into an unknown situation. We stick with the plan. Real names, real problem."

In high school, Riley had a problem with drugs—specifically oxycodone and other painkillers. She'd cleaned herself up, and had been drug-free since she was seventeen, but the backstory was true and would help Max sell their appointment with the Greenhaven director, Nanette Jackson.

"Do you remember the story?"

"It's easy."

"Tell me," Max said. "You have to believe it to make it real."

"I started working for you six weeks ago and because I was so stressed about doing a good job, I started popping pills again. You caught me, and you're giving me this one chance."

"And?"

"And because my dad is a cop I don't want to go to back to Boston where people might know me and tell him. We're looking into a couple of thirty-day facilities to get me clean."

"Good."

"You can still admit me," Riley continued. "And I can be working here while—"

"No," Max said. "I told you, we're not prepared for that level of involvement. I'll tell the director that we're looking at three facilities and will get back to them. If we decide to pursue this, we'll do it next week when I can get an apartment set up here, equipment I can smuggle in, the works." Max was getting excited. She missed working undercover. Ever since she started working the cable show, she could no longer go undercover. It wasn't that everyone recognized her, it was that people *could* learn who she was very quickly. If she went undercover now, she'd have to do a complete makeover—cut and dye her hair, colored contacts, change her style, take on a different persona. She and Ben had talked about it, and when they found the right cold case she would do it.

"Nothing unreal, Riley," Max said. "My name, your name. Same backstory. Don't start making shit up, it'll screw us in the end. Understood?"

"And then what?"

"We're going to wing it, take advantage of opportunities. Do not mention the name Adam Bachman to anyone." She looked out the window. They'd gotten off the freeway, but Max didn't know where they were. "How far?"

"Twenty more minutes, according to the GPS."

"I hate those things."

"They're useful."

"I had a rental car once with a GPS that sent me to hell and couldn't tell me how to get back."

Riley frowned, but didn't comment.

"Can I ask you a question?" Riley said a moment later.

"Anytime."

"Are you nervous about me going undercover because of what happened to you in Mexico?"

Talk about a zinger that came out of left field. "Why on earth would you think that?"

Riley stuttered. "I-um-I read all your books. I read that book a few times. Remember, you gave a seminar at Columbia about human trafficking and foreign travel and—"

"I remember," Max snapped. She hadn't wanted to write that book. It had been an intensely emotional and difficult book to write. She knew her problem with it came from not only what she'd learned, but also what had happened to her.

She'd gone to Mexico to research kidnappings for ransom, but uncovered a far more insidious operation of human trafficking. It was one of those things she knew existed, but had never thought about much. But once she had seen the results—the young women and children and how they suffered—she couldn't sit by and the wrong people ignore it. She pushed and ended up being arrested.

The Mexican jail was far worse than she had imagined. Had she not been a reporter with press credentials, they would likely have killed her or let her die—not the police themselves, but they would have turned her over to others. If it wasn't for her then-boyfriend, FBI Agent Marco Lopez, she'd probably have spent far more than eight days in jail.

She'd thought writing the book would give her peace as well as shine a much-needed light on the problem. While it stimulated debate for a short time in media circles, little had changed in the big picture. It was that book, more than any other, that taught Max that what she did really didn't matter to anyone except the individuals she helped. It didn't matter how much money she had or who she talked to or what she said. She couldn't change the world; she couldn't change public policy.

She could, however, help individual families. She had helped a mother find her son's body in the Rocky Mountains, so she could bury him and have closure. She'd helped identify the killer of a young architect in her hometown so his family could have justice.

And dammit, she *would* find out what happened to the Palazzolos so that their three children could have closure *and* justice.

"I'm sorry," Riley said. "I didn't realize it was a sore point."

She sighed and tried to push back her frustration. She wasn't used to being the one questioned. "What's your question?"

Riley hesitated, then said, "In all your articles, you are really open. You share a lot of yourself. But in that book, when you wrote about the eight days you were in the jail, it was very unemotional. Like you were reciting facts. And it was a short chapter. I can't imagine it didn't affect you more."

It was an astute observation, and Max wasn't certain how she should respond.

Finally, she said, " 'Eight Days of Hell.' That's what I called the chapter. But the book wasn't about me; it was about a truckload of women and children who had been left to die in the middle of the desert, and why. Because they had no value to the people who bought and sold them. It was easier to let them die and find replacements than to rescue them. *That* was the story I wanted to tell. As Major Strasser says in *Casablanca*, 'human life is cheap.' "

Max had given a grant to a university to identify their remains because each one of those girls had families, and their families should know the truth. To date, nine of the sixty-three young women had yet to be identified. But they'd made great progress over the last five years. Her imprisonment was a mere footnote. She refused to give it any more play than what was necessary to get the real story out in the world.

A footnote she had never forgotten, and suspected she never would.

Chapter Twelve

Greenhaven sounded cliché to Max, but what did she know about psychiatric facilities? The grounds were certainly green—a long, wide expanse of lawn, flower gardens all around, and healthy trees marking the perimeter. Riley turned the car up the long driveway that led to a parking lot and a roundabout. There was no gate, no guards, no check-in at parking. Spaces were marked for STAFF and VISITORS, with several slots headed by a personalized sign. There were three doctors—N. Abrams, R. Schakowsky, and C. Duvall. One was identified for Chief Administrative Officer, N. Jackson.

From their Web site, Max knew that "N. Jackson" was Nanette Jackson, an older, attractive woman who had a cultured, moneyed appearance in her photo. And Nanette Jackson was the person Max had the appointment with.

One of the benefits of having money and contacts was getting in to see the head of any facility. Nanette Jackson had been at Greenhaven for more than a decade. She would have been here when Adam Bachman was here. If she was at all good at her job, as soon as Bachman was arrested, she'd have closed ranks, followed the case, made sure that

Greenhaven's name was protected. It wouldn't matter if there wasn't anything untoward about Bachman's admission into the facility, they wouldn't want a notorious serial killer synonymous with Greenhaven.

Max couldn't come in asking questions unless she already had some of the answers.

"You ready?" Max asked Riley who, for the first time, looked a little nervous.

"Yes," Riley said.

"Follow my lead."

They walked up the wide brick steps to the building that was designed to look two hundred years old but was, in fact, erected in 1975. The wide veranda was reminiscent of the South with many chairs and couches in clusters. Two people quietly conversed in one corner; a small group sat in another corner.

Max was greeted by a wall of cool air when she entered the building. The interior was just as reserved as the front. Large, dark furniture juxtaposed against light floors and walls. Everything looked rich and inviting, but the furniture was mass-produced, inexpensive, and modern. Still, Max couldn't find fault with her initial impression of Greenhaven as quiet, restful, and clean.

A small, open office to the left had one desk and a fast-typing receptionist.

"Hello, welcome to Greenhaven. Are you here to visit a guest?"

Guest, not patient or resident.

"I have an appointment with Ms. Jackson." Max handed the woman her card.

She eyed the card. "Of course, Ms. Revere." She opened a drawer and pulled out a clipboard. "You must be Ms. Butler?"

Riley nodded.

"If you can fill these out we can get started."

Max said, "We haven't decided if Riley will be staying."

"It's standard."

"We'll fill out any paperwork when and if we decide to use your services." Max made a point of glancing at her watch. "Our appointment is at ten; it's ten now."

The receptionist looked momentarily flustered, but recovered quickly. She smiled, picked up her phone, and pressed four buttons. Then, "Ms. Jackson, Maxine Revere is here with Ms. Butler for their appointment?"

She hung up and said, "She'll be right out. You're welcome to sit in the gathering room—it's right through those doors."

Riley followed Max out. The ballroom-sized gathering room had enough seating for half the residents. The maximum live-in capacity was one hundred and eighty, but according to the Web site, they also had meetings for "drop-ins" and outpatient counseling services.

"Why weren't you nicer to her?" Riley asked quietly. "I thought you said to always be nice to support staff."

"Authority. If we need her, she'll now respond to you— she sympathized with you."

"Psychology."

"I didn't get a degree in it, but I know people."

It didn't take Nanette Jackson long to greet them.

"Thank you for waiting," she said as she extended her hand to first Max, then Riley. Jackson was fifty, born and raised in New Haven, a graduate from Syracuse in business with a minor in psychology. She was neither attractive nor unattractive, very average even though she made every attempt to put herself above them, including standing one step up.

Max had a bad habit of making instant judgments of people. However, she was rarely wrong. When she looked at Jackson's picture on the Web site and read her bio, she thought *wealthy, cultured, and privileged*—someone you could trust with an expensive and costly facility. Seeing her in person, that impression wasn't accurate—which made Max wonder what else about Nanette Jackson was fake. She wore classic pearls—except they were too perfect, too white, and based on the clasp, cheap. Her earrings matched the necklace. Her suit was off-the-rack—good quality, but not tailored, and it hung too big on her lean frame. Her shoes were new, but also cheap.

Fraud.

Perhaps that assessment wasn't fair, but there was a contradiction to Nanette Jackson. She presented herself well and wanted the world to believe she was cultured, but she wasn't. That duality intrigued Max and made her wonder if there was more this woman was hiding about herself or about Greenhaven.

"Would you like to talk in my office or see the grounds first?"

"How about if we walk and talk?" Max suggested.

"Of course," she said, conciliatorily. Jackson was hospitable, she wanted Max to be comfortable, to make decisions. From a business standpoint, it was smart. You want your clients to feel like they are in control.

They left through wide doors in the back. Framing a large, elaborate garden were four identical two-story buildings, which were functional and matched the old design of the main building. "The dormitories are on the right. Every client gets their own private room and shares an adjoining bath. They're small, but well-appointed. Bed, desk, couch. There's a small kitchen and dining room in each building open twenty-four-seven for snacks and drinks, but three meals a day are provided in the main building for our live-in clients.

"On the left are offices and classrooms. Many of our clients are older teens and college age and because they sign on for thirty, sixty, or ninety days we want to make sure they keep up with their work. We also offer classes on nutrition, time management, stress reduction—issues that are ancillary to addiction problems. Every client is assigned a counselor who specializes in their particular problem."

Max said, "I noticed on your Web site that you have three doctors on staff. Psychiatrists?"

"Yes," Jackson said. "All three are board-certified and combined have more than fifty years of experience in the field. When you sign in to our program, you first spend time with one of our doctors. He or she will evaluate you, run both psychological tests and blood tests. We have random drug testing for all patients, even those not here for drug or alcohol abuse."

"But this is open rehab, right?" Riley asked.

"Yes, Ms. Butler, it is. You're not a prisoner. We don't lock the dorms, though everyone needs a card key to enter, all except for the main building, which is locked at ten each night."

Jackson continued. "Everyone has a personalized schedule, but there's also free time built in. Mornings are individual counseling sessions and classes. Afternoons are group sessions and activities. We have a gym and develop individual exercise routines."

"What sort of tests do you run?" Max asked. "We know what Riley's issue is—why subject her to tests?"

Ms. Jackson smiled as if it was a common but misguided question. "Riley has struggled with drug addiction for many years—"

Riley cut her off. "I've been clean most of the time. It's only been recently that I had a couple problems."

"Well, as you might remember from previous therapy, just because you're not currently using doesn't mean the underlying issue disappears. Our tests are designed to identify the underlying problem that's causing the addiction or phobia or anxiety and solve *that* problem so the addiction or phobia is fixed. Then we teach you tools to avoid relapses."

"Hmm," Riley muttered.

"Ms. Jackson, I'm particularly concerned about privacy issues," Max said.

"Greenhaven is a completely private facility adhering to all HIPAA laws. All clients are required to sign a confidentiality statement. We can and will take anyone to court who violates our policy."

"That may be true, but the information is still out there."

"We have had very few cases where information has been leaked. In the one instance that a staff member was involved, we immediately terminated employment."

"Was this recent?"

"No, three years ago. It wasn't a counselor who would be privy to personal information, it was a support staff member, our activities director. We haven't had an incident since."

"That's good to know."

"Would you like to see the dorms?" she asked.

Max glanced at Riley. "I think Riley should—this is ultimately her decision."

Jackson frowned. "I was under the impression this was an employment issue."

"It is," Max said. "Again, it's her decision about which facility she feels will best help her resolve her issues. I'd like to talk to you about the finances and review your privacy documents. Riley doesn't need to be involved with the mundane details."

"Let's go back to the main building and I'll find someone to give Ms. Butler a tour of the dorms and answer her questions, and we can talk paperwork."

Max glanced at Riley and mouthed, *"Eyes and ears, no questions."*

Riley nodded. Jackson called in a counselor to give Riley a more extensive tour, then Max followed Jackson into her office. The office was more well-appointed than Jackson herself, Max noted—real wood furnishings, plush carpet, a large picture window looking out at the wide expanse of lawn.

Jackson chatted while handing Max papers. She was a nervous talker, Max realized, and she didn't know if it was because Max herself was intimidating, or if she was simply a nervous person.

"You're welcome to take the packet back to New York to review, but it's standard for a facility like this."

"Tell me about your counselors. What type of training do they receive?"

"They're all certified, I can assure you. They work closely with our staff psychiatrists."

"And those three—Abrams, Schakowsky, and Duvall. How long have they been here?"

"Dr. Schakowsky is our newest staff member. She's a recent graduate, but spent her residency in Washington, D.C., working with teenagers suffering from substance abuse. She came highly recommended."

"And the others?"

"Dr. Abrams has been here for more than twenty years. His father founded Greenhaven, and Dr. Abrams has maintained the vision. He teaches part time at the university and is well-respected among his peers. His full bio is on our Web site. Dr. Duvall has been here for eleven years. He's published many articles in industry journals, plus a best-selling book about childhood phobias."

"You indicated that each client is assigned a counselor and a psychiatrist?"

"Our doctors meet with the client, talk to them, determine what underlying issues there may be to their addiction or phobia. Often, addictions start with a fear that the client has never addressed. Counseling is usually sufficient, but if there needs to be a medical intervention of some sort—a prescription for anxiety or depression, for example—our doctors can take care of those needs. All clients meet with our doctors at least twice during their time here, and weekly if they are on medication. Our counselors are fully trained and licensed as well."

"I'd like to meet the doctors."

She frowned. "I don't know that it's possible."

"Excuse me?"

"They're in a staff meeting right now."

"I'd like to get a sense of who they are and how they communicate before I can give Riley a recommendation. And since I'm paying for her treatment, I don't see why that should be a problem."

She hesitated, then said, "If you can wait a moment."

"Of course."

Jackson left, closing the door behind her.

Max pulled out her iPad and immediately brought up the notes C. J. had prepared. Jackson had said the activities director had been fired three years ago.

Bingo.

Three years ago was the time the local politician had been outed as a sex addict. She sent a quick note to C. J. to pull the contact information of the reporter who'd written the piece, but Max didn't know if she would cooperate and give her a name. Sometimes reporters helped each other out, but if it was a potentially juicy story, they were far less likely to talk.

Max went over to the file cabinet. It had a simple lock on it, one that Max easily picked with a small tool she kept in her purse. She'd never forget learning to pick locks with one of her old boyfriends who'd been helping her research her second book. That had been fun—and more than a little bit dangerous.

There were no patient records in the cabinet, but Max hadn't been expecting to hit the jackpot and get immediate access to Adam Bachman's files. But there *were* employment files.

As fast as she could, she scanned the folders. Quickly, she determined that the bottom drawer was for former staff and that Nanette Jackson was extremely organized. They were sorted by year of termination, then alphabetical order. There were several employees who resigned three years ago, but only one activities director who was fired.

She typed the woman's name and last known address into her tablet, but didn't have time to pull up anything more because she heard faint heels outside the door.

As quietly as possible she closed the cabinet, then crossed the room and stared at Jackson's wall of diplomas and certifications.

Jackson walked in. "Ms. Revere, my assistant says they've already wrapped up. If you can come this way?"

"Thank you."

She followed Jackson down the stairs to the main gathering room. The three doctors were talking together. Jackson said, "Thank you, Doctors, for giving me a minute of your time. This is Maxine Revere, whose employee may become a client of ours."

Max put out her hand. "Hello, Dr. Abrams?" she said to the oldest in the group.

"Yes," he smiled warmly. Her snap judgment was that he was the grandfatherly type, though he was only in his fifties. He had a soft handshake, dry and too hot, and wore an expensive, tailored suit, without the jacket and tie. "Very good to meet you, Ms. Revere. When Nanette said you were wanting to meet us, I feared you'd be writing an exposé. I should hope we haven't been brought to your attention for anything but our fine services."

He was much sharper than he looked. He spoke cordially and softly, but his eyes were intelligent.

"No, Doctor, I'm simply here as a potential patron."

"Very good. I hope the facility meets with your approval?"

"It's very clean, very organized, and I read about your success rates."

"My father, he's retired now, believed in treating the whole person. Too often society puts Band-Aids on the problem without curing the ailment, so to speak."

"I agree," she said. Abrams sounded like a true believer.

The young female—not more than thirty—introduced herself. "Rachel Schakowsky," she said.

Her handshake was cold, her hands small and narrow. Schakowsky herself was petite and very pretty.

"Doctor Schakowsky, good to meet you."

"Nanette told us your employee is battling a recurring addition. It's most likely I would be working with her. I specialize in stress-related addictions and stress management. We've found through extensive research and clinical studies that many stress-related addictions stem from early childhood feelings of failure. There is a lot of pressure on young people today to do well in school, perform well on tests, be the best athlete. High achievers often turn to drugs and alcohol to cope with the pressure."

There was a lot of truth to that, Max thought. She'd never turned to drugs, but she drank more than she should when she was working a particularly difficult case. Especially when it involved missing persons. She was self-aware enough to understand her obsession about missing persons cases came directly from her own past.

"I'm sure you would be qualified to help Riley," Max said. She turned to Doctor Duvall. "Doctor Duvall."

"Yes," he said. He, too, extended his hand and Max took it. Duvall was in his forties, attractive, with small glasses and intelligent blue eyes. "It is a pleasure to meet you, Ms. Revere. I read one of your books a while back." He was soft-spoken, the kind of person that you had to really pay attention to because their words could be lost. The kind of voice that always sounded like it harbored a secret.

"Ms. Jackson said you've written extensively about early childhood phobia. Sounds intriguing."

He smiled self-deprecatingly and said, "It's an interest of mine, understanding how the fears from our youth shape who we become. Why some children, even with similar backgrounds and upbringing, have darker fears than others."

Max thanked them for their time, then followed Jackson to the front door. Riley was already there holding a manila envelope. "Paperwork," Riley told her.

Jackson said, "If you have any questions, please call me. I hope you choose Greenhaven, but it's most important that you find a facility where you feel comfortable and protected."

"It's a real nice place," Riley said. She glanced at Max as if maybe she shouldn't have said anything.

"I concur," Max said. "Thank you for your time and the tour. I'll be in touch soon."

They walked back to the car and Max smiled as she slipped into the passenger seat.

"You have something," Riley said as she turned the ignition. "What?"

"A potentially disgruntled employee. And if she lives where she did three years ago, we'll be meeting her this afternoon."

Chapter Thirteen

C. J. always came through. An hour later he sent Max the name, current address, and occupation of Janice Brody, the former Greenhaven staff member who'd been fired three years ago. She was a second grade teacher in nearby New Haven. School was out and Max was able to convince her to meet at a Starbucks near her home.

While they were waiting for Janice, Riley said, "How'd you find out who was fired?"

"Remember when Nanette Jackson told us about the activities director being fired three years ago? That gave me a place to look. Then, I found a way to be left alone in her office." Getting the information wasn't the hard part; convincing Janice Brody to talk would be. And there still was no proof that Bachman had been at Greenhaven.

"Nothing might come from the lead," Max continued. "Our job isn't always a straight path. But this one, I feel good about. What did you learn?"

"Nothing," Riley said, obviously disappointed.

"Yes, you did. You observed, right? What did you *see?*"

Riley sipped her iced mocha. "It was clean. Well-maintained. Quiet."

"Why do you think it was so quiet?"

"I don't know. Maybe everyone was inside. I only saw maybe fifteen or twenty people total, and several of them were staff."

Riley snapped her fingers. "Oh! Betty, the counselor who showed me around, said if I went there, I would have my own bathroom because they didn't have to double up yet. If they have a one hundred and eighty inpatient capacity, that means they had less than ninety staying there now."

"Good deduction. Does that tell us anything about the place?"

"Maybe it's struggling?"

"Could be. It might mean that they'll take in anyone, because they need people. Or the leaks have kept people away. I plan to ask Brody about it." She'd agreed to meet, but that didn't mean she'd talk—or even that she knew anything.

"Good job, Riley," Max continued. "You found Greenhaven. That's a major win."

"But we don't even know if Bachman really stayed there."

"My gut tells me he did. I don't think Janice Brody would have agreed to meet with us if he hadn't. I think she was expecting the call." Maybe not from a reporter, but from someone, like the police.

Janice Brody was fifteen minutes late, and she sat down and apologized. "I wasn't sure I should come," she explained.

Janice was girl-next-door cute with dimples and an engaging smile, which showed through her obvious nerves. Though she was older than Max, she looked Riley's age. She glanced from Riley to Max. "I don't know how I can help you."

Max was looking for confirmation, so she immediately

got to the point. "I have a source who tells me that Adam Bachman was a patient of Greenhaven while you worked there. Of course Greenhaven will neither confirm nor deny."

Her eyes widened. "I can't. I can't talk about anything there. They'll sue me. I don't really know anything."

Bingo. Max's gut won this time.

"I'm not asking for on-the-record confirmation. I won't repeat your name."

She glanced again at Riley, then looked at Max. "I really can't say anything. You don't understand. I made a mistake three years ago and they nearly destroyed me. I said something to my roommate, who talked to a reporter. That tabloid didn't even mention my name, but I got burned all the same."

Max turned to Riley. "Give us a minute alone."

Riley opened her mouth, then closed it and left. Max had assessed Janice immediately and she was nervous and scared—that wasn't an act. The more people who were witness to her comments, the greater the risk.

Max waited until Riley had left the coffee shop before she leaned forward and said, "I've been working on a report about Adam Bachman and the likelihood that he had someone else who helped him commit the crimes he's been charged with. I know he was at Greenhaven the second semester of his sophomore year at college—that was seven years ago. I've already put a time line together on his life, and this is the only blind spot I have. Adam was born and raised in Hartford and went to college in Boston, but a source tells me he has a friend from New Haven. He may have met this friend at Greenhaven." She paused. "This friend may have been involved in the murders with Adam."

"I haven't been following the trial," she said, but didn't look Max in the eye.

"But you know who he is."

"I can't say anything." Her voice cracked.

"Then don't. Nod if Adam Bachman was a patient at Greenhaven seven years ago."

She hesitated, then she nodded.

Max knew it. She knew it in her gut, but this confirmed it. "Did he have a friend there, taller, bigger than Adam, who had tattoos on his arms?"

"I don't know. He never participated in group projects, and I was in charge of group activities."

"Is that unusual?"

"Not really. We had a lot of people there with social anxiety—extreme cases, where they couldn't leave their house, couldn't talk to people without stuttering, even one girl who would faint in public if someone asked her a question as simple as 'How's your day going?' Everyone had a different treatment plan." She paused, frowned as if realizing how easy it was to talk. "I've already said too much."

"Who was his doctor?"

"I'm not sure—I didn't keep track of that. But—"

She stopped, looked down.

"I have no intention of revealing your name to anyone. As far as I'm concerned, you are a confidential source. I've never revealed the name of any of my sources."

She said quietly, "I was friends with a counselor, Anna Hudson. She worked with Adam, and left because of him. I don't know why. She never came back, never returned my calls. I was worried about her, but no one would talk about why she left. I had a warning in my file for asking too many questions. They don't say that's what it is, but that's what it was. I tracked down Anna's mother, who only told me that she moved out of state and wanted nothing to do with anyone from Greenhaven, and to never call again."

"How do you know that she left because of Adam Bachman?"

"The day before she quit, we had lunch together by the fountain. It was the first real spring day. Adam walked by and she got all tense. I asked her what was wrong. She said she couldn't talk about it, but that she thought Adam had far worse problems than mysophobia."

"Mysophobia?"

"Basically, fear of germs. You know, excessive hand washing, cleanliness, fear of dirt, et cetera."

"He still has it to a degree, but he worked at a bar for several years."

"He wouldn't have been able to do that seven years ago, if he was a true mysophobe."

"Anna thought he was misdiagnosed?"

"No, he was obsessively neat—but she thought that he had other things going on. She didn't go into specifics, other than he had said something that disturbed her. The next day, I saw her running across the courtyard and into the main building. I thought someone was chasing her. I turned and looked. But Adam Bachman was standing there, in the doorway of the activities building, just watching her. She left without saying good-bye, and like I said, I didn't see her again.

"The only reason I remember this," she continued, "is because I saw the news reports about Adam Bachman when he was arrested. Anna came to mind, and I hadn't thought of her in years."

"Do you have any idea where Anna is now?"

She shook her head. "All I know is that her mom lived in Stamford when I contacted her."

Max tried to get Janice to tell her more about Greenhaven, but it was clear she wouldn't talk about anything else. "I wouldn't have even told you about Anna, except I've always wondered where she went, how she's doing. If she's okay."

"Tell me more about Anna. How old was she? Do you know where she went to college?"

"She's my age, maybe a year or two older. She went to Southern Connecticut—I only remember that because she started working at Greenhaven as part of their internship program when she graduated. She then left to work at a hospital somewhere, but budget cuts got rid of the substance abuse program, so she came back to Greenhaven the year I started there."

"Which was?"

"Ten years ago. She has an older brother, but I don't know anything about him. I don't think they were close."

Max asked a few more questions, but Janice had nothing else that helped and was getting shorter with her responses. Max reiterated that no one would know that Janice had said anything, then Max thanked her and left. She glanced back once and saw Janice staring at her hands on the table. Bad memories? Worries? Did she think that something had happened to Anna after she'd quit Greenhaven?

Riley was in the car, upset.

"Why did you kick me out?"

"Because she wasn't going to talk with you there."

"What did I do?"

"Nothing—but she was reluctant, and sometimes reluctant witnesses need coddling." Max then said, "You know, Riley, you have to stop questioning me. I know what I'm doing. If you have doubts, write them up and send them after you've thought about it. I want to listen to your concerns and ideas, but I can't have you questioning my every decision. Sometimes I don't even know exactly what my game plan is, but I follow my instincts. This time, I sensed that Janice was nervous because two people were asking her questions—even though you were silent. It made her squeamish. So I booted you. It wasn't personal, so stop thinking that it was."

Riley didn't say anything. She backed out the car and headed toward the city.

Max would have felt sorry for her, but Riley was going to have to learn, and the sooner the better.

She pulled out her cell phone and called C. J.

"I have a person I need you to find. Anna Hudson. She's between the ages of thirty-five and forty. Seven years ago she worked at Greenhaven as a counselor. Her mother lived in Stamford at that time. She left the state shortly thereafter."

C. J. didn't say anything.

"What?" she asked.

"Do you have anything else?"

"She graduated from Southern Connecticut State University, has an older brother, interned at Greenhaven the year after she graduated, then worked for a hospital—likely in Connecticut—in a substance abuse program, which was cut because of budget problems ten years ago, when she went back to Greenhaven."

"That's marginally better. I'll see what I can do."

"I need it quickly."

"Of course you do," he muttered, then hung up on her.

While C. J. was the best in the research department, he was also temperamental. But she smiled.

Riley said, "Well?"

"This is good. I'm going to figure out how and when Adam Bachman met his partner, and I will find him. My gut tells me that Anna Hudson is the key."

Chapter Fourteen

From Monday morning when Max interviewed Adam Bachman until now, Thursday afternoon, the accused had physically changed.

She and the other spectators had just been let into the courtroom after lunch for the defense's closing statement. There was a sense of excitement, almost—the jury knew that the case was almost over, the reporters were chatty, the witnesses relieved. But Max was antsy. She had nothing more than her original theories. She wanted so desperately to learn what happened to the Palazzolos, that the closing statements seemed anticlimactic.

She had some clues, but wasn't much further along than she'd been on Monday.

Max watched Bachman be led into the courtroom by a corrections officer. He wasn't cuffed or chained—he'd been a model prisoner and restraints would be seen as prejudicial to the jury.

But he seemed smaller, as if he'd lost weight in only three days. She wanted to talk to him again, but when she'd crossed Charlene's path in the hall that morning and broached the idea, the A.D.A. intentionally ignored her and walked away.

Max watched the members of the jury listening to each side sum up its case. They were impassive, as they'd been during most of the testimony. Had she been on the jury, she would have voted to convict based on the evidence, though perhaps that wasn't fair because she hadn't been here yesterday during the defense testimony. She'd read Ace's notes, which were far less detailed than hers would have been, but from the important points, the defense seemed to be relying on the lack of physical evidence. Nothing tied Bachman to the victims except for the victims' personal effects in his apartment. Everything else was circumstantial, including the fact that he had no alibi at the time of each disappearance. To Max, that might not have been conclusive, but Ava Raines's testimony and that of the police officer who arrested him in Ava's car with Ava in the trunk had sealed his fate. Without him taking the stand to explain something *other* than what the prosecution said, the prosecution argument that Ava would have been his sixth victim was allowed to stand unanswered.

Reasonable doubt could be a tricky area, though, because some of it was subjective. Max thought Charlene did a competent job laying out the murders and building her case that Adam Bachman was the only person who could have committed the crimes. At a minimum, the jury would have to find Bachman guilty of assault and kidnapping; but the forensics team was good enough to be able to state that the drug used on Ava Raines was the same formula as the drugs used on the other five victims. Though it was tenuous, it did establish a clear connection between the Ava Raines kidnapping and the other five victims.

Max thought it was enough.

She settled in to listen to Gregory Warren list off the weaknesses in the prosecution's case. And by the end of the closing statements, Max was confident that Bachman would be convicted.

As the prosecution closed, she turned her attention back to Adam Bachman.

Hunched over in his chair, his head was swallowed up by the gaping neck of his suit, the same suit he'd worn on Monday. His hair wasn't perfect, as it had been every other day. Did he sense his pending conviction? New York wasn't a death penalty state, but if convicted, he'd be spending the rest of his life behind bars. The prosecution was asking for five consecutive life sentences. He would never be eligible for parole. Was he seeing his life end? Did he fear prison? Did he have regrets?

She would get in to see him again. Richard would allow it, she was fairly confident. Monday, after the jury came down with a verdict. She didn't think it would take them longer, just long enough to prove to the court they'd done due diligence.

He wouldn't be transported to prison until after sentencing. She could get in, talk to Adam, convince him to tell her about his partner. She'd come up with a strategy this weekend, while she was enjoying her time alone with Nick.

It was odd, she thought, that she was looking forward to the break with Nick Santini when generally she resented any time away from an active investigation. Did that mean she had deeper feelings for him than she'd admitted to herself? Why him, and not the other men who'd come in and out of her life?

Stop overthinking, Maxine. Enjoy it while you can.

Detective Sally O'Hara had spent the last two days searching for the Palazzolos' car, going on the assumption that it was in a location near where it had been spotted. But she had limited resources and wanted to be completely thorough, so she called in a favor from crime scene guru Frank

Morelli to search deeper into the abandoned rail yard near where the empty lye container had been found. She was risking a reprimand because her chief had already told her, *"Finding garbage in Queens is not a clue."*

She stood on a broken cement platform waiting for Morelli's team to return from their excursion deep into the tunnels. She would only get in their way, and Morelli knew what he was doing. The trees and shrubs here were overgrown, haunting even in the daylight. Traffic could be heard, but not seen. Graffiti marred the crumbling walls, and she wondered what this place had been like in its heyday. Now, it was a perfect place for murder.

A chill ran up her spine when she remembered what Max had said to her the other night.

Adam Bachman agreed to the interview the day after you found the lye container.

Sally had dismissed it as coincidence, but she wasn't fooling herself, or Max. And Sally owed Max. She'd *said* that this would make them even, but nothing could. How could she put a limit on the value of her sister's life? Jane was messed up, she might never get her life together, but Joey was perfect. Their parents were now in their fifties, but they were caring for Jane and raising Joey. And Sally loved that kid. He was seven now, about to start second grade, and he knew nothing about what happened to his mother, who'd been fourteen when she had him. As far as Joey knew, Jane was his sister just like Sally. Maybe it was wrong to lie to him, but what were the alternatives? The truth was not an option. It would mess him up when he should be a happy kid without the crap world he'd been conceived in.

Max and Sally had become close during the time they were looking for Jane, and remained friends, but they had one huge fight shortly after Joey was born and hadn't completely mended fences.

* * *

Max had come to visit Jane in the hospital. The baby was small, a month premature, but perfect and healthy in every way. Jane treated him like a precious doll, looking every bit a child even though she'd just given birth.

Sally was with her parents. They'd been crying, with happiness and sorrow and fear for the future. They'd talked about giving the baby up for adoption—but the O'Haras loved family, and Joey was their grandson. He was family, as much as Jane, and they could and would love and care for him. It wasn't an easy decision, but once made the dark veil that had covered the family for nearly two years lifted. It was the right decision for them.

Max walked in, stood in the doorway, and waited until Sally came over. Sally hugged her tightly. Max wasn't huggy like the O'Haras, but Sally didn't care—she'd saved their family. "Thank you."

"He's beautiful," Max said. "I heard Jane is recovering well."

"Physically," Sally said. "But she's not all there. Last week she asked my mom when was she going back 'home.' That 'they' would be mad that she had the baby without them." Sally's hands fisted. She was so angry all the time about what the Butcher family had done to her sister and the other girls. How they'd brainwashed them. Even Jane, who'd willingly come to Sally when she saw her, kept having flashbacks to her "real family." Jane was confused and sullen and though she was in therapy, it hadn't seemed to work. At least not as fast as Sally wanted.

"Time," Max said. "She has family."

"That's what her therapist says, but I don't know."

"Have you decided about adoption?"

"We're keeping the baby. I have an attorney friend of mine drawing up the papers. My parents are legally adopting Joey. His birth records will be sealed, but we're telling

him that my parents are his. That he's my brother, Jane's brother."

Max frowned. "I don't understand. What about Jane?"

"She agrees that she's too young and too damaged to be a mother. She's not always confused. And we don't want to confuse Joey. He's going to have questions. What do we tell him? That his mother was kidnapped and raped and was seven months pregnant when we found her? He'll think we would have wanted him to be aborted. And God, I've thought that. That if we'd found her sooner, if she was only a month or two pregnant, it would have been so much easier to start with a clean slate. But seven months—we couldn't even think about it."

"First, don't think about what might have been. That thinking will drive you crazy. Second, you need to be honest with Joey. He's going to figure it out."

"No, he won't. Everybody's on board."

"Even Jane?"

"Yes." But Sally wasn't certain of anything. "She's so confused right now. We're doing everything we can."

"It'll be worse if he finds out the truth on his own. No child wants to learn that they've been lied to their entire life."

"He won't."

"Sally—I know this is hard, but I think you and your parents need to reconsider—"

"What the fuck do you know about how hard this is? You're not part of this family, you don't have any right to judge us or our decisions. But I swear, if you write one word about what happened to my sister—"

"I promised I wouldn't."

Sally was crying. She didn't want to take her anger out on Max. "I'm sorry. I didn't mean to scream at you. Just—please—just respect our decision. This wasn't easy. But it's for the best."

Max said, "Lies are never for the best. But no one will hear about Joey from me."

Over the years, they'd bonded again and put the argument behind them, but Sally knew in the back of her mind that Max still judged her family's decision about telling Joey that his grandparents were really his parents.

He called her parents Mom and Dad. Jane treated him like a little brother, and Sally and her two brothers doted on him. None of this had been Joey's fault.

How do you repay someone who saved your family? Who believed you when you knew, in your heart, that your sister was alive? When no one else, not the police, not the D.A., not the FBI, wanted to listen to your wild theories? Max did. Max not only listened, she helped and never asked for anything in return. She even did the one thing Sally never thought she'd do—kept the O'Hara name out of all the stories about the Butcher family and how they kidnapped girls to use as breeders.

So even though Sally had said they were even, they weren't. Every time Max asked for help, she had a reason that had nothing to do with *her* and everything to do with helping the families of missing persons. Sally wouldn't shut her out. Finding the Palazzolos would give their three children closure, and that meant more than anything except finding them alive. If you've never lost someone—a child, a sibling, a parent—you didn't understand how the not knowing shredded you inside. Knowing, even the bad, was the first step toward peace.

Frank Morelli appeared in the tunnel opening, shielded his eyes against the light, and looked around. "Morelli," she called and walked toward him.

He approached her. "We found something. But I need to bring in more lights."

Her heart skipped a beat. "A car?"

He nodded. "We can't get to it. Debris from the storms last fall washed down into the tunnel, and because the tunnel's not in use, it hasn't been cleared." He talked into this walkie-talkie, then said to Sally, "How did you know? We'd never have gone that far down without you pushing."

"It was an educated guess."

"This car was deliberately hidden. It would have been difficult to drive it down there with all the obstructions in the way, but not impossible."

"It would have been hidden nearly a year ago. Before the hurricane. I wonder why no one called it in. The homeless go into these tunnels in bad weather. Kids party."

"It's way down there," Frank repeated. "There was a cave-in years ago, way before your time. The city sealed off many of these underground tunnels because they'd become a hazard. Sealing off usually means fences, easy enough to get through if someone is determined. Someone cut through this fence, drove in the car, and then used wire ties to reconnect the fencing. At first glance, you can't see that it was tampered with, which is why we missed it the first time around."

"He didn't want it found."

"It's going to take an hour or more to get the equipment here."

"Frank, I have a favor to ask. I want to bring in a civilian."

Frank looked her straight in the eye. "It's your call. I won't say anything to O'Malley, but I'm not going to lie if asked."

Sally hoped that O'Malley didn't ask.

Max and David found Sally standing apart from the rest of her team on the broken sidewalk next to the abandoned rail yard. There were at least a dozen people on scene, and they were busy unpacking a supply truck. Everyone was donning gear. Their helmets had lights. It was late in the afternoon, the heat of the day still radiating from the cement.

"Thank you, Sally," Max said.

"I shouldn't let you be here."

"I didn't ask."

"If it weren't for you nagging me, and David helping yesterday, we wouldn't have found them."

"You okay?" Max asked. Sally had always been sensitive. It's what made her good with victims and survivors, but it also made these type of scenes more difficult.

"I'll be fine."

Frank Morelli, one of the two most senior members of the Queens crime investigative unit, approached. "Maxine."

"Frank."

Frank gave Sally a look. "You didn't tell me you were bringing a reporter. If O'Malley hears"—he shook his head, then turned to David "Frank Morelli."

David took the offered hand. "David Kane."

"Okay, this is how it's going to go." Frank handed each of them hazmat coveralls. "This is for precaution only, but you're not to touch the vehicle or go beyond our tape. I'm sending in a small team to assess the stability of the car and verify there are human remains, but we don't know exactly what we're dealing with."

"Understood."

"Just put these over your clothes." He glanced down at Max's feet, clad in three-inch heels. "You can't wear those."

"I have boots," she said.

"Get them on, we're heading into the tunnel in five minutes."

Max climbed into the backseat of David's car and shut the door. The windows were tinted, so she pulled off her dress and slipped on a pair of jeans that she always kept in her gym bag. She grabbed a white tank top and pulled a lined Windbreaker over it. It was a warm June day, but it would be cold underground.

She slipped on socks and boots and was out of the car in less than three minutes.

David handed her the hazmat coveralls, and she pulled them on over her clothes. He and Sally already had theirs on.

"Yellow is not your color, David."

"I could say the same to you," he said.

"Which is why I own no yellow clothes."

Max looked pointedly at Sally. She'd pulled her mass of curls back into a sloppy bun and her skin was drawn and pale. "Sally, what are you afraid of?"

"Nothing. Don't start with me, Max."

David raised an eyebrow. Max didn't answer his unspoken question. Instead she said, "We know they're dead, Sally. This isn't the same as going into the compound where Jane was held. They've been dead a long time."

"I hate this part."

"It sucks," she concurred.

Sally smiled and almost laughed. "I don't think I've ever heard you say that word before."

"I have a new assistant. Her mouth isn't as clean as mine."

Now Sally laughed.

There were four cops and twelve people from the investigative and recovery unit. Sally rushed to catch up with Frank, so Max and David followed on her heels. Frank walked behind the two CSIs leading the group. "We set up two lanterns near where we found the vehicle, but it's going to be dark for about two hundred yards in. That's why my people have lights on their helmets. Stick with us. There're nooks and crannies all through here, maintenance tunnels, and much of it is unstable. The storm last October did serious damage to much of the city's drainage system, and years ago, before you were a cop, O'Hara, an underground rave was partly responsible for a collapse. The area was gated off, but someone got through. That's where we found the car."

The train tunnels were part of an old system that had stopped functioning decades ago. New York was filled with abandoned buildings and underground spaces. When Max first moved to New York, she and Karen, her college roommate, met two urban explorers. Karen started dating one of them and they took the girls on a few tours of the bowels of Manhattan. Homeless, gangs, runaways, urban explorers, criminals, the mentally ill—there was an entire culture that lived beneath the city.

Max had been fascinated by the buried history of New York, but the dark underbelly was unsettling. It was never quiet. Noises above, around you, below. Things moving that you couldn't see. The constant sound of water. If *damp* had a smell, it was under the city. She wasn't squeamish about the dark or even being underground, but the rodents and bugs . . . they got to her.

She walked between Sally and David. It helped.

The ground was wet, and shallow pools of standing water gave the entire cavern a moldy stench. The lights from the powerful flashlights, both the ones that the investigative team held and those on their hats, bounced off the curved walls.

"Another hundred yards," Frank said. "There's a curve up ahead, and then a fence."

Frank led the way through a chain-link fence that had been attached to poles on the sides and bolted to the brick ceiling. "Here," he said, using his bright flashlight to illuminate the fencing. "Can you see where it was cut?"

David responded. "Someone cut it away at both poles and lifted it up from the bottom."

"Bingo," Frank said. "When we got down here earlier,

we saw the fence had been resecured with zip ties. They're all bagged and tagged, but they're common supplies. We'll process the entire area but if the Palazzolos are in the car, this is a year-old crime scene. We're not going to get much that isn't contaminated. I don't know that we'll be able to get the car out without taking it apart down here. We'll talk to a towing company, figure out our options."

Frank motioned for them to stop, then said to his team, "Set up the lights along the perimeter. We're going to photograph and assess the status of the vehicle before we attempt to search it. Everyone who approaches the car will wear full gear."

"Is sodium hydroxide still dangerous after a year?" Max asked.

"Not usually—it dissipates, the chemical reactions will have long been over. But if there are pockets of undissolved crystals, if they're introduced to liquid it can create a noxious gas, destroy evidence, or burn the skin. If there are human remains in the car, they present their own biohazard issues, depending on the condition of the bodies."

Max stood with David out of the way, but she had a clear view of everything the investigative team was doing. The lights were set up in six different spots, minimizing shadows as they overlapped. It was nearly blinding and some of the crew wore sunglasses.

After photographing the area, Frank and two of his people put on headgear and oxygen tanks and approached the sedan. Frank cleared dirt and gunk off the license plate.

Ohio.

The car was wedged into the far left side of the tunnel, in an area where the roof hadn't completely collapsed. Two members of Frank's team were inspecting the supports, making notes, and checking the stability of the immediate area.

The car itself was intact. The windows were rolled up, so dirty that Max couldn't see anything inside. The front end of the vehicle was inaccessible, but the back doors were clear.

Frank and his team inspected the vehicle's interior with a flashlight, then he approached them, speaking directly to Sally. "There are no bodies in the car, but three suitcases are visible. We're going to pop the trunk."

He stayed back with them as a man and woman in full hazmat suits broke the lock on the trunk and it popped open. They looked inside, then both turned away. One walked over to them and took off his headgear. "We can't confirm the identities, but there are definitely two bodies."

"Decomp?" Sally said.

He shook his head. "They were dissolved, most likely by chemicals."

"Sodium hydroxide?"

"Very possible. It's a mess in there, the bodies were essentially turned to sludge. But the process didn't finish. There are some bones still intact, including the skulls. We should be able to get DNA to confirm, but that'll take some time."

"It's their car," Sally said. "It has to be them."

"We still need to run DNA or dental to confirm," Frank said.

Max slowly let out her breath. She hadn't realized that she'd been holding it.

"We found them," she whispered.

"Max, let me call the family first," Sally said. "I'll let you know when I'm done. I'm sure you'll want to talk to them."

Max asked Frank, "Do you think prints would have survived? Could there be evidence pointing to their killer?"

"I don't know," he replied. "Doubtful. It's wet down

here, a lot of time has passed. But I promise, we'll process this scene as best we can. I need to bring in a specialist to figure out the best way to get the bodies and car out. I'll walk you back out. We'll be here all night. Maybe even longer."

Chapter Fifteen

It took Max fifteen minutes to convince David to stay with Sally at the crime scene and pick up any information he could. Sally seemed agreeable to it, maybe because she was as upset and relieved as Max. Max was a bit worried about Sally's state of mind, and knew the call to the Palazzolo family would be difficult. She was a cop, she would hold her own, but the scene was gruesome. It would give Max nightmares, but she'd be seeing Nick tomorrow. That would help.

David didn't want to leave her side because of Bachman's unidentified partner.

"He's still out there, Max," David said.

"I need to talk to Richard," she said.

"Sally is a big girl, she'll handle this."

"She needs someone, David. I promise—I'll take a taxi straight to the studio. I'll take Ben with me to meet Richard."

"If he'll meet with you."

"I'm not giving him a choice," she said with a half grin. "And I'll have the car service take me home. Fair?"

"Don't deviate from the plan," he said.

"I promise."

He grunted. "I'll call the car service."

"Eleven," she said. "I should be done by then."

"Eleven thirty. I know you."

"Fair enough."

She went back to the office in a taxi, calling Ben on the way.

"I need to see Richard now."

"The night of closing arguments?"

"Queens PD found the bodies. They're contacting next of kin, so you can't report anything until Sally gives me the go-ahead."

"They found the Palazzolos?" Ben repeated.

She gave him the minimum details. "Get me in to see Richard. I've given both him and Charlene good press this week, he should be agreeable."

"Don't you think that he would know by now?" She heard Ben clicking away on his keyboard.

"Sally is coming around to my theory, but no one else in law enforcement thinks that Bachman had anything to do with their murders. I want to push Richard to jump on this now."

He said, "Milligan's having a fund-raising reception from six to eight at the Sky Room."

It was already six. "Get me in."

"You? You don't donate to political campaigns."

"This is Richard. I'll make an exception."

"Fortunately, I do donate, and I've supported him from the beginning. I'm going with you."

"No." Then she remembered what she promised David. "Fine."

"Wow. That was easy."

"Not my decision."

"Thanks, David," Ben said sarcastically.

"Give me room to do my job."

"Hardly. Everyone who's anyone is going to be there, and I know you, Max—if you see someone you don't like, you can't keep your mouth shut."

"I can."

"Yes, especially if I'm close by holding your leash."

"Asshole."

"Bitch."

Max laughed, then said in her best trust baby impression, "Be a doll and find me a dress in wardrobe? I'll be at the studio in five minutes."

District Attorney Richard Milligan's fund-raiser was at the Sky Room on the thirty-fourth floor with rooftop views of the Hudson River and the Empire State Building. It was probably a good thing Ben came with her—in the first five minutes after they arrived, she found three people she disliked. They were liars and cheats. It was one of the reasons she detested politics—Richard was a good guy, yet he took money from people who had no scruples. It was all a game, and she detested political games most of all.

Ben Lawson was well known in many circles, including among the movers and shakers in the great city of New York. He glad-handed and schmoozed his way to where Richard was standing in the corner greeting his donors and other dignitaries. They had almost reached him before Charlene Golden stepped in their path.

"What are you doing here?" She almost couldn't get out the words.

"You look nice tonight," Max said. "Love those earrings."

"I cannot believe you're crashing this party."

"I'm a plus-one tonight." Max linked arms with Ben. Ben smiled and held out his hand. "Ben Lawson." Charlene recognized the name, but apparently hadn't put two and two together. "Ben's my producer," Max said. "And longtime friend. I need to talk to Richard."

"No."

"Now."

"*Hell* no."

"What are you, his campaign manager?"

"I'm a supporter. And a friend. And you're neither."

Max raised an eyebrow and stared. Charlene looked away first. Not very prosecutorial of her.

Max leaned over. "Queens PD found the Palazzolos. Dead, in the trunk of their car. I *really* need to talk to Richard."

Charlene couldn't hide the shock. "Are you lying to me?"

Max refused to answer the insult.

"This can wait until tomorrow," Charlene said. "There's nothing the D.A.'s office can do until there's a suspect and an arrest."

Max raised her eyebrows. "There is a suspect."

Now Charlene understood Max's meaning immediately. "No. That's *your* theory, no one else's. Do not do this. The jury is in deliberations." She sounded desperate.

"Do you really think I can sway the jury *now*?" Max stepped forward and had a modicum of satisfaction that Charlene stepped back. Ben had his hand on her arm. He tightened his grip. "Dammit, Charlene," Max said, "I'm not going to screw with your case. Did I say or write anything that hurt you? *No.* Get me time with Richard in the bar downstairs, or I *will* print something you won't like."

"Are you threatening a prosecutor?"

"I only print the truth," she said in a low voice. "I know a lot of truths."

"You are such a bitch."

"So I've been told." And getting sick and tired of it.

She'd done nothing to jeopardize Richard's career and, in fact, had helped when she could. She was a bitch for asking questions? For seeking answers? For wanting to know who killed two innocent people?

Ben pulled Max back a step. She shrugged off his arm. He was going to leave bruises on her if he held on any tighter.

"Max," he began, his voice low. He put his hand on her again.

Richard had seen them. He stared at her, but didn't make a move to approach.

"Well?" Max said. She put her hand over Ben's and squeezed his fingers until he let go of her.

Charlene was clearly agitated, but said, "Let me talk to him first. Stay put."

Max smiled, but felt no pleasure at the small victory. She grabbed a glass of champagne from a waiter who walked over with a tray. Through clenched teeth she said, "Of course."

She moved over to the edge of the roof and looked at the Empire State Building, trying to calm herself down. She usually had better control over her emotions. But she was so tired of being told she was wrong when she knew she was right. Would it hurt anyone to follow through on her theory?

She took a deep breath. Ben said, "Max, I know you're emotionally wrapped up in this case, but you need to see the bigger picture."

"I do," she snapped.

"Do you? Really?"

Maybe. Maybe not. She had been so invested in finding the Palazzolos that now that she had, she didn't quite know what to do. She couldn't even enjoy the view of the sinking sun reflecting off the buildings throughout midtown. New York was most beautiful at dusk.

"You normally don't let comments like that bother you," Ben said.

"It doesn't."

"Max, I've known you a long time. You're loyal. You're frustrating. You're smart. You're arrogant. I don't know anyone else like you, and that's a good thing because I couldn't handle two of you. You intimidate people because you're confident and usually right. I don't know why you let Charlene get to you."

Max didn't know, either. "It's not her. It's just . . . today. Two hours ago I was underground, in an abandoned train tunnel, watching the crime scene investigators open the trunk on a car with Ohio plates and tell us that two unidentifiable bodies were inside. And now I'm on top of a skyscraper drinking champagne surrounded by people who should have cared more that the Palazzolos disappeared in their city."

"They do care. I know Richard does, otherwise I wouldn't be giving him my hard-earned trust fund money." Ben smiled, trying to lighten the mood, and Max gave him a half smile in appreciation of the effort. "I can't tell you to let these things go, because I know you won't. I understand, Max."

In college, Ben and Karen had been best friends. Ben and Max, however, were oil and water. Because they both loved Karen, they made it work, but they didn't particularly like each other. But when Karen was gone? Something changed. Ben was the only person who cared for Karen like Max did. Ben was loyal. He was sharp. He and Max sparred constantly, but she respected him, which she couldn't say about many people.

Charlene approached them. "Richard said you can come to his office in the morning."

Max brushed past Charlene without comment and

walked up to Richard. She smiled and said, "Excuse me," to the couple who had claimed his attention. "I only need him for one minute."

Richard forced a smile at the couple, but he glared at Max as she took his arm and steered him ten feet away. His assistant—probably a bodyguard—approached, speaking into his cuff.

"It's okay, Stuart," Richard said. "Give me a minute."

She smiled. "Thank you, Richie."

"You are unbelievable," he said. He had a bland half smile on his face because people were watching them.

She held up her phone. On it she'd brought up the picture of the Palazzolos' missing sedan. The Ohio license plate was clearly visible. The trunk was open. The contents were unclear, but the expression on the face of the crime scene tech who stood nearby clearly showed this was a bad situation.

"A picture says a thousand words, Richard. We need to talk tonight. Or I'm going back to the studio, cutting into programming, and running this story along with my theory as to what happened."

"You wouldn't. The jury is still out. And there's no proof—*none*—that Bachman had anything to do with it."

"It's not illegal for me to report on the truth."

"Maybe it should be. Don't you care about the families of the victims?"

As he said it, he knew he'd way overstepped. Max buried her anger and said through a false smile, "If you're not in the bar downstairs at eight thirty, I'm leaving for the studio at eight thirty-one. I'm not bluffing."

She left, Ben right on her heels.

They went down to the bar. She switched to a vodka martini because she wanted something stronger than champagne, and she honestly didn't feel like celebrating anything. Ben got on his phone immediately, which was fine with Max because she wasn't in the mood for conversation.

She definitely needed the weekend in San Francisco with Nick. She made the reservations on her phone right then, a first-class ticket that left at eleven in the morning. That would give her time to wrap up everything in the office tonight and pack. She sent the itinerary to David.

Richard Milligan exited the elevator at eight twenty, spotted her, and crossed the bar. He sat down, alone.

"Five minutes," he said.

Max motioned for the waitress. "Another round, and add a Tanqueray on the rocks for Mr. Milligan."

"I'm not drinking."

"Make it a double," Max said.

The waitress left.

"You're impossible, Maxine."

She wanted to yell at him, to threaten him not to ever doubt that she cared, but she didn't. She ate the last olive on her toothpick and spun the small stick in her manicured fingers. "Adam Bachman had a partner," she said. "His partner killed the Palazzolos and Bachman helped. In turn, his partner helped Bachman clean up his five murders. There's a killer still out there, and Bachman knows who it is."

"I'm the district attorney, Maxine. I'm not a cop. There's no evidence that—"

"Stop saying that! There's circumstantial evidence. Bachman is in *your* custody. He's on trial. You're the one with access."

"If I go to him, he'll ask for a deal. I'm not cutting him a deal."

"You won't have to. You get the right person in there and he'll talk. I can't access the records, but you can."

"What records?"

Hook.

"Greenhaven, outside of Hartford. It's a private mental health facility. Bachman was there for ninety days when he was twenty. I have a source who said Bachman had a friend—a friend from New Haven—with tattoos. A few years older than Bachman. My theory is that they met there. I don't have that person's name, but Melinda Sanchez at Fringe can give us a description. She's good—she might be able to work with a sketch artist. But your office can contact Greenhaven, find out what doctor was responsible for Bachman, and get a copy of his records. Find out if he had a friend there, narrow it down."

"That is so vague I don't know where to begin to refute you."

"Get a patient list from the same time Bachman was there. Cross-reference it to this man—I have a good description, particularly of his tattoos. He likely has a record, based on what my source said."

"Maxine, you're insane if you think I can get private, privileged medical records."

"Nanette Jackson, the CAO, may help, if given the right incentive. She's very concerned about Greenhaven's reputation. She might know who this unsub is, could give you a name simply because it's the right thing to do."

"Getting doctors to talk without a court order is next to impossible."

The waitress came back with the drinks. Max sipped. She waited. Richard had said he didn't want to drink with her, but he picked up his glass and sipped, too. He leaned forward. "Look, Max, I'm sorry about what I said upstairs. Truly." He glanced at Ben, as if wondering how much he should say.

Max said, "I don't have secrets from Ben."

"Don't drag me into this," Ben said.

Max leaned forward. "Richard, there's another killer

out there. And Adam Bachman knows who it is." She slid forward a flash drive. "I don't share, you know that, but I'm breaking my own rule. These are my notes, including interviews with witnesses. I know you have a task force of investigators in the D.A.'s office who work these kind of cases. Multijurisdictional, complicated cases. I also added the contact information of an FBI-trained forensic psychiatrist who will consult if you ask."

Richard stared at the flash drive, but didn't pick it up. "I can't take that, Max. It's fruit from the poisoned tree."

Her heart sank. She thought for sure he'd grab it. He'd always wanted to see her notes before. "I don't understand."

"If you obtained any information illegally, I can't use it."

"That's not true."

"It's a gray area, and I'm not willing to jeopardize a case because I was overeager and cut corners. I have rules—rules I believe in. Rules I stand for." He drained his gin and stood. "But I will talk to Queens PD and get an expedited report about the car they found, and I will find some excuse to talk to Adam Bachman. I can bluff with the best of them. You think if I say to him that we have evidence he had a partner that he'll talk?"

"With the right questions."

"What cop?"

"Excuse me?"

"Who's been helping you? You couldn't have been at that crime scene if you didn't have someone on the inside."

"I'm not revealing my source, Richard."

"You think I can't find out? There had to be at least a half-dozen cops and investigators out there. All I have to do is ask one, and they'll tell me. I'm not going to get him in trouble—I need a cop with knowledge of the case to be in the interrogation room with Bachman."

He was right, on both counts.

"It's a her. Sally O'Hara. Detective out of Queens."

"O'Hara," he mumbled. Recognition lit his eyes. He stared at her, surprised. "That O'Hara."

"She's a good cop, Rich. Don't burn her."

"That's not me, Max. You should know that."

Chapter Sixteen

"No, no, no," Ben said as they drove back to the studio. He was beginning to sound like a broken record.

"The jury isn't going to come back until Monday, Richard is pursuing the lead on the partner, and I need a break. I'm going to San Francisco."

"I need you here!"

"Riley's here. David's here. You have a dozen staff members who'll come in at a moment's notice."

"You just came back from San Francisco."

"Six weeks ago. And I've been working twenty-four-seven ever since." She hadn't told him she'd snuck away for an overnight two weeks ago, and it was probably best not to mention it now.

"You never complained about the hours before."

"And I'm not complaining about it now. Maybe I just want a weekend of sex."

"It's that detective, isn't it."

"So?"

"You have boyfriends all over the country. You don't have to fly three thousand miles away just to get laid."

Ben was making her angry. She didn't appreciate her love life being used against her. "That's low."

"I need you here."

"I need to get my head clear. I'll be back Sunday night."

"You're driving me to a heart attack."

"Stop being so damn melodramatic. I'll be working. I'll write on the plane. I'll write from Nick's bed. I'll write from the pool if I have to."

"But you won't be *here*. And what about the Oregon trip? You made a commitment to cover those kidnappings, and you don't have as much time because of this trial, plus—"

"Don't tell me everything I have to do. I'll do it, do it right, and do it on time. I want to see Nick, and I'm going." Maybe she was being stubborn. Maybe she was being selfish. But it was only for a weekend. There was something niggling at her brain, an itch she couldn't scratch, and her insomnia was worse than usual. If she could just clear her head maybe she could figure out what was bothering her.

"You'd better answer your phone if I call."

"Anytime, day or night." She leaned over and kissed his cheek. "It's going to be fine."

Ben grunted and refused to look her in the eye.

Their driver stopped outside the studio. "You coming up?" Max said.

"No. I'm going to get drunk and be miserable because you're leaving in the middle of a trial."

"You're such a baby."

"Sunday night. I'm holding you to that."

She blew him a kiss and went into the building. The night guard nodded a greeting. "Good evening, Ms. Revere."

"Hi, Toby." She used her card key to get through the security gate and into the elevator, which was locked at night.

It was late, and she was tired, but she finished up the series of articles that would run on the Web site about the trial. Then she called Riley, filled her in on everything that had happened, and instructed her to handle any editing issues that came up on Friday.

"You're letting me touch your articles?"

"Lightly. You have a good eye, so when the copy editor sends them back and the fact-checker is done, you give them the final once-over."

"Thanks for trusting me."

"You did a good job this week. Even David is less grumpy."

"Why doesn't he like me, Max? I'm really trying— God, I sound like a whiny brat."

Max laughed. "Maybe you're trying too hard. Part of it's my fault. My previous assistants didn't do any legwork. They stayed in the office and handled correspondence and technical issues. Answered my e-mail. Talked to people if necessary. But you have a different skill set, and Ben agreed to move things around so you could be in the field more. So far you haven't disappointed me, though you could respond to my public e-mails faster."

"Where are you going?"

"To see a guy in California."

"Work?"

"Play. Be good, Riley. We did well. If the D.A. handles this right, Bachman will flip on his partner."

"You should be here for that."

"I will be. It's only a three-day weekend. Besides, I'm not a cop." As her ex-boyfriend Marco told her repeatedly. "I find the evidence when the police don't have the time or resources; get the scoop; expose injustice; and they get to arrest a bad guy. It works. But tomorrow, stick close to the studio. We ruffled a few feathers up at Greenhaven, and I don't want you getting the heat."

"Did C. J. find Anna Hudson?"

C. J. had sent her an e-mail before he'd left the studio with a status report. It wasn't promising. "Not yet. It seems she doesn't want to be found."

"Odd?"

Max didn't respond. She wasn't sure. C. J. was good at his job, and if he couldn't find her it made Max think she was hiding. But it might not have anything to do with Adam Bachman.

Or it might have everything to do with him.

Max said good-bye, hung up, and checked the time. It was only seven in California so she called Nick.

"Santini."

"It's Max."

"Did the verdict come in?"

"No, but it won't happen until Monday. I booked a flight for tomorrow."

"In the middle of the trial?"

She rolled her eyes. "You sound like Ben."

"What's wrong?"

"Nothing's wrong." She paused. "The D.A. is considering my theory of a partner in crime, but there's a whole bunch of little things nagging me and I need a break."

"What partner theory?" Nick asked sharply.

Max bit the inside of her cheek. She hadn't meant to let that slip to Nick, at least not until they were face-to-face.

"It's a theory I've been developing for a while."

"You didn't tell me."

"David has been keeping a watchful eye on me, don't worry."

"With you, I can't help it."

She was getting uncomfortable with his tone. It wasn't the angry overprotective rant that she often received from Marco. Nick's genuine concern was far more subtle, but hit her harder with its tinge of emotion. Unlike Marco, she couldn't tell Nick he was an egotistical prick and slam down the phone.

"I'm being careful, sweetheart," she said lightly. "I promise."

"Maybe it's a good thing you're coming out here for the weekend."

"Maybe it is," she said with a smile. "I thought if I bring all my notes and theories, your gorgeous eyes and brilliant brain might see something I missed."

"It sounds like we'll be having breakfast *and* dinner in bed."

"Even if I didn't bring work with me, I'd expect that."

He laughed, genuine and full of good humor. Nick wasn't a demonstrative person, and she enjoyed getting the piece of him that was. She didn't know where this relationship was headed—they lived three thousand miles apart—but for now, it worked. In fact, it probably worked *because* they were three thousand miles apart.

"I'll be at SFO at two twenty tomorrow afternoon. I'm forwarding you the confirmation."

"I'll pick you up."

"You don't have to."

"I want to. Besides don't they charge you ten times the going rate for car rentals?"

"That hurts."

"It sounds like we don't have a lot of time. Let me spend all of it with you."

"I'm not going to argue."

"That's a first."

She smiled and hung up. Nick was . . . special. She wasn't going to think too much about their new relationship because as far as relationships went, they'd always taken a backseat to her career.

Career. It wasn't a career, it was a vocation. She couldn't *not* do what she did. She couldn't stay home and raise a family; she couldn't take a nine-to-five job. She didn't want to. She had two nephews she adored, she considered David's daughter Emma the little sister she'd never had, and she loved her career. She needed it. She could write, she could investigate, and she had instincts that were as good—or better—than any cop out there.

That's why Nick was good for her. He was divorced, had a son with his ex-wife, so there was no pressure for commitment or family. He'd been there, done that, and she was content with living three thousand miles away as they explored what it meant to be . . . whatever it was that they were.

She called David. "I'm confirmed for San Francisco."

"Is Nick picking you up?"

"Yes, why?"

"Just making sure you don't need me with you."

"You're not my chauffeur," she grumbled.

He grunted a laugh. "I'll get you to the airport, then you're Nick's responsibility."

"That sounds insulting. Are you still in Queens?"

"Yes—but I can leave and pick you up. Otherwise, your car service will be out front at eleven thirty."

"Stay with Sally. She needs a friend."

"She told me about Jane. You've been a good friend to her."

She shifted uncomfortably. The O'Hara family had been through so much, she wished she could have done more. But some things couldn't be fixed with money or love. "It's just part of the job."

"No, it's not. She's been drinking, I'm going to make sure she gets home safely. What time do you want to be picked up?"

"Nine? Flight leaves at eleven out of LaGuardia. I'm not checking luggage."

"I'll be there at quarter to. You cut things too close."

"Thanks, David." She hung up and started organizing assignments so she could feel better about leaving.

Shortly after eleven, Sally sent her a message that she'd talked to the Palazzolo family. Max called J. J. on his home phone. He answered on the first ring.

"Detective O'Hara said she called you about your parents' car," she said.

"Yes." His voice was raw. "She also said if it weren't for you, they may never have found it. I don't know how to thank you."

"I wish there had been a happier ending."

"You never said they were alive, Maxine. But now, they can come home. We can lay them to rest." His voice cracked.

"It's late," she said, the emotions of the evening catching up to her. "I'll talk to you in a few days, see if there's anything else I can do."

"And, Maxine, if there is anything my family can ever do for you, call."

It was nearly thirty minutes later when she made it down to the lobby. She saw the black Town Car idling outside. "'Night, Toby."

"Take it easy, Ms. Revere." He buzzed her out of the main doors. The night was beautiful, neither warm nor cold. It was a night like this she would have enjoyed walking the three miles to her Greenwich Street apartment. But it was after eleven thirty and having David in her life had made her more security conscious.

The driver got out. Like all the drivers for her preferred car service, he wore a suit and cap. This guy was new. "Hi, I'm Maxine Revere. Do you need my address?"

"No, ma'am, it's in the log." He opened the door for her. She slid in and leaned back. She was definitely too tired to walk home.

He closed the door and walked around to the driver's side.

Normally, she'd make small talk—she liked talking to the drivers. They knew so much about the city that she found their insight and observations interesting. But all she could think about was sliding open the doors on her deck and slipping into her hot tub with a glass of wine and some cheese and crackers. Or maybe another martini—the two she had earlier had been tasty.

She leaned back and closed her eyes.

Chapter Seventeen

Friday morning, David parked in the loading zone in front of Max's apartment building because it was faster than circling the block and parking in the underground garage. He'd tried calling her ten minutes ago when he picked up the car. That she didn't answer wasn't unusual—especially since this trip to California was last minute—but she hadn't sent him a message that she was coming down. He got out of the car and approached the doorman, Jorge.

"Do you need something from Ms. Revere's apartment?"

"Ms. Revere," David replied.

Jorge frowned. "She's not in."

David clicked his car to lock and went inside. Jorge was an old-time doorman. Max had lived in this building for nine years; Jorge had been here for thirty. He knew everything about everyone. If he said Max wasn't home, she wasn't home.

"Is everything okay, Mr. Kane?"

"I'm checking her apartment," he said and punched the button for the elevator.

"Can I call anyone?"

"Call Henry and see when she came in last night."

"She didn't, and she didn't pick up her mail. But I'll double-check," he added quickly when he caught David's eye.

David didn't like elevators. He wasn't a fan of small, enclosed spaces, but Max lived on the top floor of a ten-story co-op on Greenwich Street in TriBeCa. Sometimes, he would walk it. Not today.

Jorge worked from six in the morning until three thirty in the afternoon; Henry worked three thirty until one in the morning. Weekends were covered by a service from seven until seven at night. The lobby was locked and unattended for the remaining hours, but the security system was state of the art. David made sure the co-op board upgraded it when he started working for Max nearly two years ago. Max wasn't the only at-risk resident.

David immediately checked her door for signs of a break-in. Clean. He unlocked the door with his key and it opened, meaning she wasn't home or had forgotten to engage the secondary security dead bolt—which was, unfortunately, her MO. No luggage by the door, no sound of running water from her shower, no sign that she'd been home at all.

He checked the apartment, including closets and under beds. There was no sign of Max. Her favorite overnight bag was in her closet.

David knew Max almost better than she knew herself. He didn't need to make calls to know that something had happened to her. If she had a change in plans or went off on an investigative tangent—which she often did—she would have called him or sent him a message. They'd had too many bumps in the road when he first started working for her, and he required her to inform him of her

whereabouts. Always. It had been hard for her initially—
Max didn't like answering to anyone. But she had a strong
self-preservation instinct, and trusted David.

He went through the motions because when he talked
to the police, he needed to give them good information.
He didn't want them chasing their asses for facts David
could easily, and quickly, verify.

He logged on to her computer to check her flight status
while he called Ben Lawson. There was a slim chance she
had changed flights.

But she would have told him.

If she had changed her plans and not told him, he'd quit.

"It's Kane. When was the last time you spoke to Max?"

"What?"

"Max. Time."

"What's wrong?"

"Answer my question."

"Last night when I dropped her off at the studio." Ben
sounded confused. "She's going on a trip, the most important case she's worked on this year, and she just left for
the weekend. Didn't you drive her to the airport? Staff is
going to be working all weekend in preparation for the presumed verdict on Monday, and—"

"What time did she leave the studio?" David repeated.

Ben hesitated. "Should I be worried?"

"I don't know." He wanted to say yes. But sometimes
Max was so focused on her job that she neglected to keep
in touch.

He didn't feel this was one of those times. Especially
since she had a flight. Especially when they had the conversation about what she would need to do to make him
quit. She might forget to call in, but she always answered
her phone.

"Hold on. I'll check the log."

David scanned her e-mails. She hadn't been online since last night.

Ben got back on the phone a minute later. "She left at eleven thirty-five. A car from her service picked her up."

"I scheduled it," David said. "Ben, have someone check ERs. I'll call you back when I know more."

Max's flight schedule popped up on her computer. She was still booked on the 11:00 A.M. direct flight to SFO.

It was possible, however unlikely, that she'd left on an earlier flight. Maybe forgot to tell him.

David opened her e-mail and scanned the inbox for any alternate flight confirmations. Nothing except for the 11:00 A.M. United flight. No messages had been marked as read after she left the office last night. The last message was at 11:32 P.M., it was from Nick in response to her itinerary and it read that he'd pick her up at the airport as they'd discussed. She hadn't responded. Not only had she not replied to Nick, she hadn't read the message.

He had several hours before Nick would be leaving for the airport. There was nothing the cop could do three thousand miles away, so David wasn't going to call him yet.

David turned on his phone's GPS tracker. He'd insisted on Max running a security GPS program on her phone. Only he had the password to access her unique signal. The software was state of the art, developed by one of David's close friends from the army who now worked research and development for a military tech company. Max—or, at least, her cell phone—was nowhere.

The program also maintained an archive, and if her phone was dead or the battery removed, her last location would be tagged. He pulled up the data.

The last ping from her cell phone was in the middle of the Brooklyn Bridge at 11:50 P.M.

What the hell was she doing going to Brooklyn in the middle of the night?

Though David didn't believe Max had made it home last night, he reviewed the security data from the building's system while he called the car service company. Because they were the preferred car service for NET, David knew most of the drivers as well as the owner.

"Mr. Vance, it's David Kane. Ms. Revere was picked up last night at eleven thirty-five outside her office building, but she didn't make it home. I had a ping on her cell phone that she was on the Brooklyn Bridge. Where did the driver take her?"

"Mr. Kane, I don't know what happened. I just got off the phone with the police because Omar didn't return the car last night. His personal car is still here. Sometimes, if they're scheduled to work the next day, they take the company car home. But his wife said he didn't come home last night. She's been calling and he hasn't answered his cell phone. I've called him repeatedly and—"

David cut off the man. "Horace," he said, "GPS."

"I contacted our tracking company. The car is nowhere. They tell me the GPS has been turned off."

The last ping on Max's cell phone was from the Brooklyn Bridge.

"When was the last time you spoke to Omar?"

"He called in at eleven twenty-five that he'd arrived at the NET building."

"Did you speak to him personally?"

"No, he called into dispatch."

"I want to listen to that recording. Have your dispatcher splice it off and e-mail it to me. I also want a copy of the GPS log for that car from the minute Omar picked it up until it stopped transmitting. Have you filed a police report?"

"I was trying to reach Ms. Revere first, because the police will ask, what was the last pickup, and—"

"Ms. Revere did not make it home last night. Call the police. File the report. Send me the officer's name and report number."

"What happened, Mr. Kane?"

"I will find out."

He hung up. He knew Omar. He'd been with the company since before David started working for Max. He'd run background checks on all Horace Vance's drivers, and they were clean. Vance ran his own background checks before he hired them. Omar preferred working nights because he had a son and coached his Little League team. Omar had ties to the community. He had a wife. He had family who lived nearby. David was good at picking out people who could be for sale, and Omar wasn't high on the list.

But there were other ways to force people to do what you wanted, and Omar had the baggage of a family.

He called Ben again. "Where is she?" Ben answered.

"Get whoever was on security duty last night into the building now. I want Riley there and anyone who was working with Max on *anything* related to the trial, the Palazzolos, or that excursion on Wednesday to Connecticut. You know damn well Max has people working on her pet projects; I want everyone to come clean. I'll be there in ten minutes."

"Why haven't her kidnappers called us?" Ben said.

"It's not about money," David said.

"Of *course* it's about money! Max is rich, richer than even my family. So why *isn't* it about money?"

"Because Max is nosy. She found something, did something, said something—we know where she was and who she talked to, but we need to retrace her steps, talk to them *again,* because the police aren't going to do it for at least another twelve hours. Even then—"

"You have to call Marco Lopez."

David didn't want to call Max's ex-boyfriend. He was in Miami for one, and for two, David didn't like him.

But this was Max's life. Marco Lopez was a fed. He could make things happen.

"I'm going to talk to the police first," he said. "If I can't make them move mountains, I'll call Marco."

He left the apartment. Nick called while he drove to the NET building.

"Max hasn't returned my calls. Did you take her to the airport early?"

Shit. David hadn't wanted to do this until he had more information.

"Max is missing."

"Define missing."

"A car service picked her up at eleven thirty-five at the studio and she didn't make it home."

"Hospitals? Police?"

"The car and driver are missing. Ben has staff calling the hospitals. I'll call the police when I have more information, but she hasn't been missing for even twelve hours."

Nick was silent on the other end, but David knew he was there. Processing.

Nick said in a low, rage-tinged voice, "Why did it take you so long to figure it out?"

David bristled, but responded calmly. "She wasn't at her apartment when I went to pick her up for the airport. That was less than an hour ago. It took me some time to piece together what happened last night, talk to people. I'll send you what I have, but right now I have two theories. The first is that Max followed a hunch and instructed the driver to go to Brooklyn last night, where they both disappeared. Or someone hijacked the car and dumped her phone over the Brooklyn Bridge."

"Ransom?" He sounded like a cop now. Good. David could deal better with someone who was professional, not emotional. Especially since David was having a difficult time with his own emotions.

"It's crossed my mind," he said. "We haven't received a demand, but she has kidnapping insurance. I wish it were a simple kidnapping for ransom." Then he would know exactly what to do and how to get her back.

"Is this about the investigation? Her theory that Bachman had a partner?"

"She's filled you in?"

"Basics. You have to bring in the police, David." It sounded like an order.

"If I thought the police would lift a finger, I'd have called them first. They're going to do shit, and you know it." David was agitated. He prided himself on remaining calm in any situation, but he was rattled. Max was his responsibility; she was missing. "Twelve hours, and it doesn't matter that she's a public figure. I'll work it, but—"

"I'm coming out," Nick said, cutting him off. "I'll let you know when I arrive."

He hung up before David could tell him to stay put.

David called Sally O'Hara. There were cops higher up the ladder he could call, or Richard Milligan himself, but Sally worked missing persons, and she could get the notice out faster on the car, driver, and Max.

"Sally, it's David."

"I'm hungover," she groaned. "Thank God today is my day off."

"Max is missing." David told her everything he knew.

Sally didn't say anything when he was done.

David said, "Do not tell me you can't do anything until twenty-four hours has passed."

"It's seventy-two," she said. "Unless you have proof of foul play."

"Sally, you know damn well something's wrong."

"You think it has to do with the Bachman case."

"Yes."

"I can meet you at the station—"

"Max's office. I've called in staff, we're going to retrace her steps, find out what she was working on related to Bachman's partner. She and her new assistant spent all day in Connecticut on Wednesday. I didn't think they'd found much, but maybe I'm wrong. I need the police to be looking for her and the car. Horace Vance, the company owner, is filing a police report about his missing car and driver."

"Okay. I can run with that. Send me his information and I'll follow up with his precinct and get a BOLO out. But you must have an idea as to what happened."

"Someone took her. Of that, I'm certain"

Pain brought Max to consciousness.

Through the fog in her head—a fog that Max was certain was drug-induced—several things became apparent all at once.

First, and foremost, the pain.

It was everywhere and nowhere, as if her entire body was being pricked simultaneously. As she came aware, it was her head that ached the most, a heavy, throbbing beat that kept her from lifting her neck or opening her eyes. Her mouth was impossibly dry, so dry and heavy she couldn't move her lips.

She was extremely thirsty. She'd been this dehydrated before. She knew exactly how it felt. Memories of a time she wanted to forget clawed to be heard.

She tried to move and failed. Restrained? Drugged so heavily that her limbs seemed to be weighed down by sandbags? She tried to open her eyes, but they were heavy, as if they were glued shut. Her head moved just a bit and something made her itch. The realization broke through that a bag covered her head, canvas or mesh. Something breathable and scratchy. Her arms were pulled above her head. She tried to pull off the mask, but binds cut into her bruised wrists, forcing a moan from her throat. Her hands were numb, tied together. Tied to something rigid.

She was lying on her back, on a flat, cold, hard surface. A metal table? A cement floor? The stench of oily dirt filled her nose, making her cough.

Don't cough. Don't let them know you're awake.

She had no gag in her mouth. Because no one could hear her if she screamed?

Them.

Why did she think two people had taken her?

The car.

She'd left the office and gotten into the Town Car. Almost immediately she knew something was wrong. She'd closed her eyes because she was tired—when she realized they were heading to Brooklyn she leaned forward to tell the driver. He sprayed something in her face and she couldn't speak.

That was the last thing she remembered.

She squirmed and instantly a sharp pain hit her feet. A thousand pinpricks and she froze. Where was she and what was under her feet?

Humid. Cloying. Oil, dirt, mold. A warehouse, maybe. There were no sounds except the ringing in her ears.

No sounds? Impossible. This was New York City.

Or was it? They could have driven her anywhere.

Ten minutes after he pulled away from the curb he stopped. Someone got in the passenger seat.

Maybe she remembered more than she realized. The mist in her face. Did she try the door handle? She thought she might have, but her hands hadn't been cooperative. She couldn't force them to grasp the handle.

She thought she was dying.

She'd seen a gun. But it wasn't a gun like David carried or Nick. It was smaller.

The sharp pain of a thick needle pierced her neck and she slumped over in the seat, her hand reaching for the protrusion. Tranquilizer.

Who was he? She hadn't seen his face. Her vision had been blurred. All she knew was that it was a man.

And then she slept.

Her neck still ached where the tranquilizer dart had pierced her skin. Her entire body felt sticky with sweat and blood.

But she was alive. She had to find a way to escape.

Did they want a ransom? Her trust had insurance on all members of her family in the event of abduction. They would pay the ransom. But no one in the Revere or Sterling families had ever been abducted.

How do you know? You haven't seen your mother since you were ten.

She pushed that thought from her mind because it was wholly unproductive. She focused on now. They weren't celebrities, they weren't in the public eye. Except for her, but she'd hardly consider herself in the public eye. Maybe on the fringe of the public's peripheral vision.

Max shifted, almost reflexively, as her arm began to tingle. More sharp pinpricks of pain hit her, this time in her back, through her clothes, as if a million needles punctured her simultaneously.

"Hello, Maxine. I see that you're awake. That was fast. We can now get started."

She involuntarily jumped. She'd had no idea someone was in the room. Had he just walked in? Had he been watching her the entire time? Seeing her squirm? Panic?

Don't panic. You can't panic. Keep your head, Maxine.

She opened her mouth. Her voice was rough, dry, but she managed to croak out, "What do you want?"

It had to be money. Wasn't it always about money? It was no secret that she was wealthy.

"To break you. Then my friend will kill you." There was a lilt to his quiet voice, as if he were having fun. As if this was a game for his amusement.

A sick predator pulling the wings off butterflies.

She was the butterfly.

"You won't." Her voice sounded stronger, but deep inside she wondered—feared—what it would take to break her. She'd suffered those eight days of hell in a Mexican jail. She'd been on the verge of losing her mind when Marco had finally found her. She'd told Riley that the reason she didn't write much about her imprisonment was because the story wasn't about her, it was about the victims of human trafficking. But the truth was, she didn't want to remember. She didn't want to expose that rawness to anyone, even herself.

But she hadn't broken, even after eight days. Marco had helped her escape and they traveled across Mexico and Max ended up writing an exposé on how Mexican gangs kidnapped tourists and businesspeople for ransom. She wrote about human trafficking and the cost in human life. She'd won several awards for that series of articles, a series she was particularly proud of because it shined a light on corruption and evil.

But she'd always wondered how much longer she could have taken confinement. Not just being in prison, but being in that pit with little to eat and drink, the heat of the day and the cold of the night. Freedom was one thing she valued more than anything else. What kept her going each day was that others had survived worse. Prisoners of war. Abused children. Sex slaves. There was always someone who'd suffered more. If they survived, and she knew many who had, she would survive.

But each passing day had been harder than the last.

She'd survived eight days in hell. Certainly she could survive whatever this bastard had planned.

The voice said, "I know everything about you."

He was messing with her head. But she didn't say anything.

There was something familiar about his voice. Now that she was fully awake, she realized that she'd talked to this man before. She couldn't place it. Her head was thick and pained. But her life might depend on remembering.

"I've read everything you've written. *Everything.* I've watched and analyzed your television interviews. There is so much information to mine. You think you understand what motivates people like me, like Adam? You have experts and you analyze us, dissecting us like a body on the slab?" He laughed, but it was cruel, the kind of meanness she expected from bullies.

"*I* am the expert," he said. "What you've written is nothing compared to what's between the lines. What you say when you think no one is listening.

"I listen, Maxine. I read what you don't write. I know you better than anyone. Better than you know yourself."

There were footsteps. Soft, echoing, moving away.

"We'll explore that shortly," he said, his voice far off, almost down a tunnel. "And I will turn you inside out. Until then, think about it. About what you think I couldn't possibly know. And realize, I know. I know everything."

Then he left. And in doing so, tapped into one of her greatest fears.

The unknown.

Chapter Eighteen

The head of building security greeted David as soon as he stepped into the NET building. He led David to the security office.

"She left the office and used the elevator to the lobby," the security chief said. "There's nothing important on those feeds, but I've made a copy. Here's what you want to see."

The chief pressed play. It showed Max walking across the large lobby and waving at the night guard. When she got to the door, he buzzed her out. The door closed behind her. The chief switched to the external camera feed.

"I backtracked this camera feed so you can see the car arrive."

A black Town Car drove up identical to nearly every other black Town Car that New Yorkers used. The driver didn't get out. Three minutes later, Max exited the building, visible only from the back at first. But there was no mistaking her long hair and confident stride. The driver got out and walked around the front of the car. He wore a dark suit and cap like all of Vance's drivers. His face wasn't clear on the black-and-white feed, but technology might be able to clean it up even with the cap partially obscuring his image. The driver opened the rear passenger door for Max. She looked up at him and they exchanged words. She didn't appear to be in distress. He closed the door, walked back around, and drove off.

David didn't recognize the driver—the image wasn't clear enough—but it certainly wasn't Omar. Omar was Pakistani and barely five and a half feet tall. This driver was Caucasian and at least three inches taller than Max.

David watched the entire video one more time. When the driver got out of the car initially, he looked both ways on the street.

"That pharmacy." He tapped the corner of the screen. "It's open twenty-four hours and they have security cameras on the outside of the building," David said. "Call them, get their feed from last night. Original, if possible. And get me the original of this. We need to enhance that guy."

"Of course, Mr. Kane. I'll personally deliver them to your office."

"Thank you."

David went up to the eighteenth floor and strode toward the main conference room where Ben told him everyone was assembling. Catherine Crossman made a beeline toward him. The petite brunette was dressed impeccably as always, but her brows were creased in worry. Catherine owned NET with her husband, Rob. They'd been instrumental in launching *Maximum Exposure* two years ago.

"What can I do?" she asked, putting her manicured hand on David's arm. "Break through programming?"

David hadn't thought of that. "Maybe—but right now we need more information before I make that decision."

It wasn't lost on him that he was now de facto in charge. It was a role he didn't enjoy, though he was capable of it. He much preferred staying in the background.

"Anything," she said. "I mean it. Was this related to one of her investigations?"

"I don't know yet," he said. He stepped into the conference room. Everyone stopped talking at once. A dozen people were there, all *Maximum Exposure* staff, including Riley and Ben. Sally hadn't arrived yet.

David walked to the head of the table but didn't sit down. "Maxine hasn't been seen or heard from since eleven thirty-five last night when a car picked her up outside this building. I've viewed the security footage and she left with her car service in no apparent distress. The car and driver are both missing, but I've confirmed that the driver who picked her up was not the driver dispatched by Vance's service.

"I want reports from everyone on what Max has you working on. Even if you don't think it's important, write everything down and send it to both Ben and me. But if there's something you think stands out, tell me now."

He looked at the faces of the staff, then his eyes rested on Riley Butler. She looked shell-shocked.

"Nothing? Anyone?"

Then everyone spoke at once, and Ben whistled and the voices stopped. Ben went around the room, and each person relayed what they'd been working on for the past week. Most projects related to future *Maximum Exposure* spots, primarily research. David was familiar with all the cases they were considering for upcoming shows, and dismissed anything not related to Bachman or the Palazzolos.

"C. J., you were working on something in Connecticut?" Ben asked the head of the research department. C. J. was Max's favorite staffer. He was older than nearly everyone else who worked for the show, and nothing seemed to faze him from the workload to Max's odd requests, though he could be tempermental.

This morning, however, C. J. looked troubled. He ran a hand over his shaved head and said, "I'm trying to locate a woman, Anna Hudson, who was a counselor at the same time that Adam Bachman was a patient at Green-haven."

"And?"

"I haven't found her. I know she exists, and I've been able to confirm the information Max learned. I then tracked her to a graduate program in Chicago, but lost her trail after that."

David said, "Send me everything you have. Why was Max looking for Hudson?"

Riley cleared her throat. "Anna quit Greenhaven while Bachman was there. Her friend believes Anna's leaving was directly related to an incident with Adam Bachman, and Max thinks Anna can lead her to Bachman's partner."

Debbie Starr timidly raised her hand. C. J. was the oldest, most senior member on staff; Debbie was one of the youngest, but she had a knack for being extremely thorough with fact-checking. "Um, Mr. Lawson? Max asked me to run deeper background checks on staff at Greenhaven, particularly the administrator, counselors, and doctors."

"Shit," Ben mumbled. "I told her to use C. J. only."

"I'm sorry," Debbie whispered and glanced down.

"Did you find anything?" David snapped. Debbie, though competent, was also shy and nervous, and David didn't have the patience to coddle her. "Debbie, anything important?"

"She was vague. She said she'd know it when she saw it, and to verify all public facts. There are no criminal records for any of the individuals she gave me, and so far I've verified each curriculum vitae, though I'm still going back to previous employers."

"Send me everything you've already completed," Ben said. "You might have raised a flag with someone. Then finish the research and send reports to both David and me."

David said to the group, "If you leave this building, let security know where you're going and when you will return. Stick in pairs or groups, and we'll arrange for a car service to take each of you home tonight. Until we know what's going on, I'm keeping close tabs on everyone."

The staff filed from the room, but David squeezed Riley's shoulder. "Stay," he said.

She sat back down, worried and scared. Good. She should be. David didn't know what Riley had been up to with Max, or on her own, but she'd better not be holding anything back.

Before David could question Riley, Sally O'Hara came in. She wore jeans and a polo shirt and no makeup. She looked as hungover as she'd sounded on the phone. Ben called his secretary to bring in coffee for four.

Sally collapsed into a chair. "This is so fucked. What do you have?"

"Not much, except a security video that I need enhanced," David said. "Can you do that?"

"We have people."

Ben said, "It'll be faster if our tech guys do it."

"Good." David much prefered to maintain control over the evidence until they had something solid to give to the police. "Security is bringing up the original feed."

Ben's administrative assistant, Lara, came in with a tray of coffee. Ben said, "Lara, when security arrives, let me know."

"Of course." Lara put her hand on David's arm. The woman had a motherly demeanor while also being one of the best gatekeepers David knew. "David, anything," she said softly. She and Ben exchanged a look as she walked out. David didn't ponder what it might mean.

David turned to Riley.

"Tell me what you've been doing for Max. Everything."

"I—you know everything."

"If I knew everything, I would know why somebody grabbed her last night," he said, enunciating his words clearly. His temper was coming frayed because he didn't have answers. Each passing minute increased the tension. "Start with Greenhaven. Why did Max ask Debbie to run deep backgrounds?"

"We toured the facility on Wednesday and Max thought that the chief administrator didn't dress as well as she should have."

"Excuse me?" Sally said. "What does that mean?"

"I don't know," Riley said. "Max determined what her salary should be based on like positions and because she had no family or elderly parents, Max said she probably spent her money on something she shouldn't."

"I've warned her about those gut impressions," Ben said.

David ignored him. "Why was she looking at Jackson? Does she think she's involved with Bachman?"

"God, no, she's in her fifties."

"That wasn't what I meant."

"Oh. No, I don't know, she just said that someone who lied in their appearance would lie about other things. It was cryptic."

"Were you with her the entire time?"

"Yes—I mean no. She arranged to talk to Jackson without me, and I think she might have looked at confidential files."

"Might?"

Riley bit her lip and glanced at Sally.

"Forget I'm a cop for five minutes," Sally said.

David slammed his palm on the table. "Riley! Everything!"

"I don't know quite what she did, but she came out with the names and addresses of employees who'd been fired, and determined which one was most likely to have worked there when Adam Bachman was there."

Sally slowly lowered her head to the table and put her hands over her ears.

Ben said, "And?"

"We tracked down a woman named Janice Brody. She's the one who clued Max to Anna Hudson, and Max asked C. J. to find her."

"Then why was Max pushing Milligan?" Ben interjected. "She had no hard facts."

David said, "Our witness from Fringe described Bachman's friend from New Haven. Did she ask this Janice about the guy?"

"I don't know—she asked me to leave."

Ben snapped his fingers. "That's why Max was pushing Milligan last night. She was stuck, couldn't get the information on her own."

"Or couldn't get it fast enough," David said. "If Bachman is sentenced on Monday, wouldn't it be more difficult for her to gain access to him?" He answered his own question. "Of course, Milligan can get Max in now. For her to get inside a prison will take weeks, sometimes months."

"Then why was she planning to run off to San Francisco?" Ben said.

"Because it wouldn't have happened today," David said. "She was stuck and frustrated." And, he suspected, she was still enamored with Detective Santini. It hadn't taken David long to figure out how Max handled her relationships, and with Santini it was still new and fun for her. As soon as it became too serious on either side, she'd pull back. He'd seen it more than once.

He turned to Riley. "Anything else? You spent nine hours with Max on Wednesday. Did she have any plans to go to Brooklyn?"

"Not that she told me."

"I want the contact information of everyone she spoke

to, including the former Greenhaven employee," David said. "Five minutes ago."

Riley ran from the room, passing Lara on her way in. "The tapes are here from security."

"Take them straight to tech, priority enhancement," Ben said.

"Of course." Lara left.

"I need to talk to Milligan," David said. "As soon as we have an image from the tapes."

"I'll go with you," Ben said. Before David could object— and he wanted to—Ben said, "I know Richard. Trust me."

"I'll work the image on my end," Sally said.

"Can you get footage from the bridge? Maybe we can figure out which way they went, follow the cameras," Ben said.

"Not as easy as it sounds," she said. "But I'll try." She stepped from the room to make a call.

David turned to Ben. "I'm going to call Lopez."

Ben nodded, but he wasn't smiling.

David had FBI Agent Marco Lopez on speed dial.

"Lopez. Is this Kane?"

"Yes."

"Maxine needs something but isn't willing to apologize, so she has you call me? The answer is *hell* no."

"She's missing."

Lopez didn't say anything for a beat. Then gruffly, "Explain."

"She left the studio last night at approximately eleven thirty-five and didn't make it home."

Lopez snorted. "Hell, Kane, thirteen hours? That's nothing, especially for Max."

"I viewed the security footage. The driver who picked her up isn't the individual dispatched by the car company. That person is also missing, and so is the vehicle. She missed a scheduled trip this morning. Didn't call me. Didn't check in."

"She doesn't check in."

His fist tightened around his cell phone. Why did Lopez sound like such a prick? If that fed was in the room right now, David would deck him.

"With me she does. Do you think I would call you if I didn't *know* that Max was in trouble? A detective is helping, but the police aren't going to do anything at least until tomorrow."

"And that surprises you?"

"Dammit, Lopez, this is fucking serious and I don't need your wounded ego in my way. She's completely off the grid and yes, she still does that, but not without telling *me* first. Believe me, you're the last person I wanted to call for help."

"Send me everything you know. I'll be there first thing in the morning." He hung up.

Prick.

David took a deep breath. Marco was a prick, but he was coming to New York, and having a fed working the case would help.

He just hoped that tomorrow wasn't too late for Max.

"Ben, we're going to make a stop before we go to the D.A. I want to show the photo of the driver to a potential witness, someone who worked with Bachman at Fringe. If she recognizes him, we'll be one step closer to finding him."

The blindfold distracted Max. How much time had passed? One hour? Ten? A day? In the darkness, she couldn't tell the passage of time. The initial panic she'd felt had given away to a dull throb in her head, partly from the drugs they'd injected her with, and partly from her fears.

Her mouth was parched. So dry she knew she hadn't

had water in hours. Possibly a day. If it were longer than a day, she would show more signs of dehydration. Her stomach churned, empty. But she wasn't hungry. The thought of food made her ill, possibly a side effect of the drugs. She tried to clear her mind, get her thoughts together, because she needed to focus on figuring out where she was, who had grabbed her, what they wanted.

Her thoughts were fuzzy.

Focus, Max.

She had to escape.

What if she couldn't escape? She was restrained. What if no one found her?

What if I end up like Karen?

Her heart skipped a beat. She didn't want to disappear without a trace. She didn't want her friends and family to never know what happened to her. Was that his plan? But that wouldn't hurt her . . . it would hurt the people in her life. What would be the purpose in that?

Unless they kept her alive and forced her to watch the news, read the articles as her case turned from hot to warm to cold. Watch her friends go on with their lives, haunted—or not—by her disappearance.

You're being ridiculous.

This wasn't like her, to be waylaid by fear. She wasn't naturally a fearful person. She'd risked a lot for the stories she wrote. Going after Karen's suspected killer. The time she'd spent in a Mexican prison. Being tortured. She didn't talk about that, and only touched upon it briefly in the book she wrote after her captivity.

She'd survived. She would survive this—whatever it was.

It took all her mental courage to take her eyesight out of the equation. She relied too much on what she saw and less on what she heard. The captivity troubled her, but she'd been in worse. She'd been naked in the Mexican prison. Humiliated. Whipped. And they still hadn't broken her.

She breathed deeply.

Focus on your other senses. Hearing. Smell.

The sound of water was the first. She'd heard it when she'd first woken up, but she'd been half-conscious, not really paying attention. Not running water, but steady drips. It hadn't rained in the city in weeks, this was like the sound of water moving through pipes. She breathed deeply, ignoring the pain in her chest. A musty, damp smell invaded her nose, her mouth. Moldy. Underground? They hadn't gagged her, which meant no matter how loud she cried for help, no one could hear her. If she wasn't underground, she was definitely somewhere secluded.

Was this where Adam Bachman had taken his victims? Is this where he suffocated them?

Why did she think her imprisonment had to do with Bachman?

Because he mentioned Adam before.

She shook her head to clear it and as she shifted pain hit her. What did they restrain her on? Some sort of table? A chair? She couldn't move without getting jabbed by a million pinpricks. She had to be calm. Focus. Get her head together so she could take advantage of any opportunity to escape.

She wasn't in her own clothes, but she wasn't naked, either. Though her body was partly numb from the drugs, she didn't think she'd been raped. The material on her skin felt rough and bulky, like cheap cotton. A hospital gown? Scrubs? Why would they remove her clothes?

He wants to break you.

Her clothes personalized her. But she didn't care if anyone saw her in something impersonal. She was vain, but not like that. Why would changing her clothes break her?

Solitude didn't bother her. She could think better now

that her captors were gone. She liked being alone. Living alone. Writing alone.

She breathed in again, tasted the air on her dry tongue. Definitely mold, almost a mushroom taste. Moist. Humid, but not hot. A basement, perhaps. Or in one of the underground mazes that held up New York City. She'd done an article about the hidden underground. Those two urban explorers she'd befriended had taken her to places most people who lived here didn't even know existed.

Underground. This place didn't have the same smell as the tunnel where they'd found the Palazzolos' bodies. That was wetter, louder. There was no free-running water here, it was underground pipes. A subbasement in an apartment building? A warehouse? Abandoned most likely, because that was Bachman's MO.

But what was his partner's MO?

Where had Max heard that voice before?

Why had they taken her?

Because they're going to kill you.

For the first time since she'd woken up, the fear took over.

She didn't want to die.

"Hello again, Maxine," the voice said.

Her body involuntarily jerked at the sudden sound. Pain shot up through her feet. She hadn't heard him approach. Had she been panicking? Had she passed out? How could she not have heard him walk in?

Had he been there the entire time, watching her?

"I brought a friend." A familiar voice. She knew who this bastard was, she just had to *think!*

But her mind was cloudy, unfocused. She suspected that she'd been in and out of consciousness for quite some time, that all her thoughts had been fragmented.

"You were close. I was surprised that you got so close. But not close enough."

She wasn't going to give him the satisfaction of asking questions, though a dozen burned on her tongue.

A pinprick in her arm made her involuntarily cry out.

"Just a little something to make sure you stay awake. Because we have a lot to talk about."

Her arm burned, as if a million fire ants crawled up her skin.

A chair rolled up next to her. Her body jerked again as he touched her hand, and he laughed softly.

"Oh, Maxine, if you keep fighting you'll only prolong the inevitable."

Her body tingled, the ants spreading from her arm up her throat, as whatever drug he'd given her flowed hot through her veins. The blood rushed through her ears like running water.

She tried to swallow, but had no moisture in her mouth.

Her heart pounded, faster and faster until the pain made her gasp.

She was going to overdose. Whatever they were feeding her was too much. Her body shook uncontrollably.

"Shh," the voice said. "Just breathe normally. This feeling will pass."

Thud. Thud. Thud thud thud thud.

Faster and faster.

Calm down, Max.

She forced her breathing to slow as best as she could.

"Good girl."

Asshole.

The sound of metal against metal as something moved away.

"We don't need those right now."

She stretched, just a bit, and realized that he'd removed whatever sharp instruments had been under her feet. She refused to say thank you, though she was relieved.

Her heart was still beating too fast and loud, but she focused on regulating her breathing.

"Where to start," he said lightly. "Let's start at the beginning? Because that's where your real fear comes from, doesn't it? Being abandoned."

"You don't know me." Her words were thick off her tongue. Weak.

"You think I'm talking about your mother leaving you with your grandparents. No. It started before then, didn't it? When your mother would leave you for days. With friends, strangers, alone. You never knew if she would come back."

He could not know any of that. It was a guess.

It's the truth.

"It's classic, Maxine. You're common. Fear of abandonment so you don't make strong attachments. Keep everyone at arm's length. Everything you write seeps in the emotion. But it goes even deeper, doesn't it? It goes all the way back to the womb. To your conception. To the fact that you would do anything to find out who your father is. That everything you believed as a child has been proven a lie."

That voice.

Everything you write.

Not the words, but the tone. The familiarity.

"You don't care who you hurt, as long as you get the truth The all-mighty, all-powerful *truth*. You wouldn't know the truth if it bit you in the ass. You waltz into people's lives, destroy them, and walk away as if you haven't a care in the world."

She'd heard this voice recently. But where? If only she could think clearly! If only she could concentrate. But every time she tried to focus, her mind slipped. She had no other explanation. She'd be on the verge of remembering and then she'd feel dizzy and everything would disappear.

It was like every few minutes she had to reteach herself how to think.

He was talking to her about something she felt she should know, an event he kept talking around, and she couldn't focus, couldn't figure out what he was talking about.

Betrayed. Destroyed. Stole. Ruined.

You took from me. You destroyed my life.

Every other word dropped off. Was that because of whatever they'd injected her with? Did she have a concussion? She strained to hear, but it was a mishmash of vitriol. Was he deliberately trying to drive her crazy?

She didn't know him . . . but she recognized the voice. He thought she'd destroyed his life and she had no idea why.

That's when she really started to be afraid.

Chapter Nineteen

It didn't take NET's tech team long to enhance the image of Max's suspected kidnapper. Once David and Sally approved, they printed off several copies and e-mailed the digital image. Sally sent hers to the NYPD Missing Persons Unit; David sent his to Marco.

He didn't want Ben to join him when he talked to Melinda at Fringe, but he couldn't rid himself of the producer. He couldn't articulate why he wanted to do this alone. Mostly, he didn't want to make small talk. He didn't want Ben—or anyone—to tell him that Max was fine, that she was probably following a lead. That there was a logical explanation.

There *was* no logical explanation for what had happened. Max was in danger and David knew it. He was supposed to protect her, and he hadn't done his job.

Ultimately, he let Ben stick with him because Ben knew more people—and more important people—in New York than David did.

Ben was the one who had hired David originally. David was paid by *Maximum Exposure* and had revamped the security for NET, the parent company owned by the

Crossmans. His official title was chief of security, though he had a trusted person in charge of the day-to-day operations in the studio. In reality, David worked for Max and that was the way he liked it. He understood Max. He respected her. And she gave him space when he needed it.

Ben had already started taking over, and he was out of his realm. Ben was a talker, a schmoozer, a mover and shaker; David was muscle with brains. And while Ben's maneuvers were subtle, David had felt it in the conference room. He understood that Ben was worried about Max, but David couldn't be concerned with Ben's feelings.

He didn't want to talk. He just wanted answers.

And Ben talked the entire drive to Fringe, working himself up into a near hysteria. David shut him out so he wouldn't have to toss him from the car.

"David! You're not listening to me. This is important."

David pulled the car into a space a block from Fringe that only the best parallel parkers could access. He shut off the car, his left hand gripping the steering wheel tightly. "Lawson, you're not helping. You're panicking. I called Marco. Sally will take care of the local police alerts, but you know damn well that if the kidnapper turned off the GPS on the car and dumped Max's phone that they aren't going to be easy to find. The good news? She's probably still alive. The bad news? We have no fucking idea where to start looking. The police will do their thing, and I will do mine, and you can either shut up and follow or walk back to the studio."

David got out of the car and slammed the door. He took a moment to breathe.

Ultimately, his rage came from the fact that it was his job to protect Max and he hadn't been able to. He might not be a traditional bodyguard, but he knew watching her ass came with the territory. He'd failed.

It wasn't the first time.

He walked down the street. People got out of his way, though he barely noticed. Ben followed at a distance. David crossed the street and turned into Fringe. The restaurant was at the tail end of the lunch rush. He recognized the hostess from the other day when he'd been here with Max. "Is Melinda upstairs?"

The hostess looked scared. He sometimes had that effect on people, the long, narrow scar on his cheek making him look more violent than he was. He tried to soften his expression, but the girl didn't notice.

"Melinda Sanchez has been helping with an investigation," he said. He could pass for a cop, he figured he could play the role when needed.

"Oh. Um. She doesn't get on until four. But, um, she might be with her boyfriend at the theater."

David pulled out his cell phone, accessed Max's contact list, and called Melinda. It went to voice mail. He sent her a text message.

This is David Kane, Maxine Revere's assistant. I have a photo of the guy we discussed the other night. I need you to look at it ASAP.

The manager approached. "Is everything okay? Sir?" He looked from David to Ben who stood behind him.

David showed him the picture. "Do you recognize this man?"

"I don't know. Are you with the police? We should go into the back room. This situation has been difficult for the club."

"Hasn't seemed to affect your business," David said, looking around at the packed dining room.

"It does, but not in ways you might notice." He led the way into the back where he had a small office. "Come in. It's crowded. Sorry." He started to clear off a chair.

"I'm not sitting," David said. He gave the manager his card. "Melinda Sanchez gave us information that Adam Bachman had a regular visitor. I need to find out if this is the man. Look at the picture."

The manager did. "I don't know. Really. I see a lot of people, and Adam has been gone for nearly a year. But I'll call the bar manager." He stepped out of his own office.

Ben said, "Dammit, David, you know the expression you get more flies with honey?"

He didn't respond. Ben muttered something, but David tuned him out.

Melinda responded to his text message.

I'm at the Fifth Street Studio. A rehearsal hall near 47th.

It was only a few blocks away. David replied.

I'll be there in five minutes.

"You deal with these people." David shoved an extra photo in Ben's hand. "I'll be back at the car in twenty minutes."

Ben started talking at his back, but David was already out of the room.

The Fifth Street Studio was a small venue used primarily for children's dance classes, David realized when he entered the building. Melinda was in the lobby. "Thanks for meeting here," she said. "My boyfriend is fixing their sound system. I came to keep him company."

"We have a photo I'd like you to look at, see if you recognize the guy."

"The friend of Adam's?"

David nodded. He showed her the photo.

She stared for two seconds. "That's him."

"You're certain."

"Absolutely."

"Even without seeing his tats up close?"

"I said yes. I'm positive."

"Thank you."

"Why?"

He hesitated. "We think he's involved in a kidnapping. I can't tell you more, but if you see him call me or the police immediately." He handed her a card.

"Oh, God," she whispered.

"You remember something else?"

"No, but if he's kidnapping people like Adam did, it's still going on, isn't it?"

"We don't know yet."

"It wasn't someone from Fringe? A tourist?"

"No." But Max had been in there with David the other night. Max had been to a lot of places. She must have gotten on his radar somewhere. At Fringe? Greenhaven? Queens?

Adam Bachman agreed to the interview the day after the sodium hydroxide was found. Someone knew the police had found the tunnel. They knew that it was only a matter of time before the Palazzolos were discovered.

Someone had been watching Max.

Sally called David to tell him she was canvassing the neighborhoods bordering the tunnel where they'd found the Palazzolos and their car. She had armed several cops with copies of the picture of the guy who'd kidnapped Max. David would have joined her, but he wanted to talk to D.A. Richard Milligan face-to-face. Fortunately, Ben remained silent during the drive to One Hogan Place, the criminal courthouse where Milligan had his offices. David nabbed the first parking space he saw even though it was three blocks away and got out immediately.

"David, hold up," Ben said, following him.

"We need Milligan to confront Bachman."

"David, please."

David stopped walking and turned around. "We don't have time to play nice. Milligan owes Max."

"You need to calm down. You look like you're ready to kill someone."

David ignored the comment and continued toward the courthouse. But he took several deep breaths. He'd been a soldier for ten years. He needed to be more objective, and forget that it was his closest friend who was missing.

His friendship with Max was odd—to him and to Max. David didn't have many close friends, and that was fine with him. He wasn't a friendly sort. He'd worked corporate security for a year after he left the military, then took the job with *Maximum Exposure* on a temporary assignment. But the temporary gig turned into full time, and now he couldn't imagine going back to Wall Street to work for the suits. Working for Max gave him a purpose not unlike when he was an army Ranger. Max was dedicated and driven. She didn't have to risk her life or spend eighty hours a week investigating cold cases. She was wealthy enough that she could travel the world, do nothing, live a life of leisure. But it wasn't in her nature. David respected that.

Maybe he did understand why he cared for her, more than just as a job. It was respect and an admiration that was born from watching her for so long. When they first met, he'd strongly disliked her. Hate might have been an accurate word. She was abrasive and far too independent. She didn't like taking orders, even from him, the person hired to protect her from very real threats.

But then he'd watched her with the parents of a murdered teenager, a cold case she'd solved because she risked her life and her reputation to uncover the truth about a corrupt sheriff in a small town. She'd sat with them, listened—really listened—and gave them the closure they so desperately needed in order to be parents to their surviving two children. She didn't exploit their grief, but instead turned the story around to praise their dead son and highlight flaws in the system that prevented for years his killer coming to justice.

She was demanding, arrogant, and judgmental. She was also compassionate, intelligent, and worked harder than anyone David knew.

Her job had risks, and it was his job to minimize the risks while still giving her the freedom she required. And he'd failed. He'd bought into her partner theory, why hadn't he recognized that her snooping put her on the killer's radar? Had he subconsciously doubted her? He honestly hadn't believed that she was a target.

He blamed himself. And he blamed Riley Butler. If he'd gone with Max to Greenhaven, he would have picked up on potential threats because that's what he did. Except he hadn't gone because he thought it would end up being irrelevant.

"We have an appointment with Richard," Ben said, keeping up with David's purposeful stride. "He's expecting us, so you don't have to bully your way in."

David didn't respond. Ben was high-strung, a gladhander, and often got under David's skin. David would never mistake the positive aspects of *Maximum Exposure* as the driving force for Ben's involvement. Ben used Max solely to gain ratings and more advertising revenue. He pushed her to work high-profile cases like the Bachman trial. This hadn't been Max's choice—not initially. It was the disappearance of the Palazzolos that spurred her involvement. Because when their three grown children had contacted her, Max was their last option. When she researched the disappearance of Jim and Sandy Palazzolo and developed the theory that they were connected to Adam Bachman, she agreed to cover the trial.

If Ben had his way, Max would be hosting a weekly show instead of doing a monthly newsmagazine format. He'd push her to do more "sexy" cases—brutal, violent, controversial—instead of the cold cases Max preferred. Max had held firm, for the most part. But lately she'd been unsatisfied, contemplative, and questioning. David didn't know if it had to do with what happened with her family in California six weeks ago, her breakup with Marco, or her new boyfriend Nick Santini. But she hadn't been herself, and David wondered if he should have been more worried.

Or maybe she'd been keeping something from him.

They had to wait twenty minutes in Milligan's exterior office. David stood with his back to the wall, his eyes surveying each person in the office, everyone who came in and went out, until finally Milligan's secretary said the D.A. was ready for them. David was used to waiting. There was plenty of high tension waiting in the military.

But he didn't like waiting for a suit.

Milligan was sitting at his desk, signing a stack of papers. An assistant stood next to him, taking the signed papers and putting them in the appropriate folder.

"Ben," Milligan said, "I told you and Maxine last night that I would help, but demanding a meeting now is not helping your case."

"Richard," Ben said, "we need to talk to you alone."

He finally looked up at Ben and David. "Do you understand how busy I am? Maxine acts like she's the puppet master and I'm on her string. And now she sends you and her pit bull?"

Neither Ben nor David said a word. A moment later, Milligan told his assistant to leave. She closed the door behind her.

"Maxine is missing," Ben said. "She was taken last night from the studio." He put a folder on Milligan's desk. "That's a security photo of the man who took her. The driver assigned to her is also missing, the car they were driving is missing. No one has seen Max since eleven thirty-five last night."

Milligan looked at his watch. "Fifteen hours. Are you sure she isn't—"

David stepped forward and put his hands on Milligan's desk. "This isn't a game, Richard. This isn't a joke or Max going off and doing her own thing. The car was supposed to take her home. It didn't. Now Max, car, and driver are gone." He opened the folder and pointed to the suspect. "This man took her. He has been seen at Fringe on several occasions talking to Adam Bachman, but hasn't been seen there since Bachman was arrested last year. Max was looking into Bachman's stay at a mental health facility near Hartford called Greenhaven, where she suspects he met this man, and now she's missing. We need to talk to Bachman *now*."

Milligan stared at the photo, then at Horace Vance's police report about his missing driver, the BOLO Sally issued on Max, and a brief statement by Melinda Sanchez.

Quietly he said, "If this is what you think, I can't deal for Max's life."

"Talk to him. Talk to the detectives who worked his case. Find out what they might have overlooked," Ben suggested. "They weren't looking for a partner; now that we know Adam Bachman had one, maybe the evidence will look different."

"We don't know that he had—"

David slammed his fist on the desk so hard that everything on the surface jumped. He walked away before he hit something softer.

Like Milligan's jaw.

Silence descended.

Milligan said, "I'll make some calls."

Calls. Calls weren't going to save Max.

David turned around. "Let me talk to Bachman."

"I can't."

"Yes, you can."

Ben said, "Send David in with Charlene. Plausible deniability."

"I don't operate that way."

"It's better than finding Max's dead body."

"Give me an hour, Ben. Stay by your phone. I will call you. I promise."

Ben nodded when all David wanted to do was pound heads. "Thank you," Ben said.

David walked out. They might not have an hour.

Max couldn't stop shaking. Her heart raced, the pounding vibrated in her ears. She'd tried to control her body, but nothing she told herself worked.

"You gave her too much," a male voice said.

"I know what I am doing, Cole," the familiar voice said, angry.

Max tried to concentrate on where she knew the man. She'd heard his voice, she just had to place it. The knowledge might save her life.

Or, it might kill you. You're blindfolded. Maybe they mean to let you go.

Hardly.

"Water," she said before she could stop herself.

"See?" the familiar voice said. "Exactly what we want. Maxine, I'll give you water when you give me something. Answer a question."

She shouldn't agree. Her head told her that. Her head, aching though it was, told her to resist giving this bastard *anything* that he wanted.

But she was so thirsty escape wasn't an option unless she could build up her strength. She needed something to keep going. At least, that's what she told herself.

She managed to nod.

"Thank you. Your cooperation will make this all much easier for both of us.

"I've researched you," he continued, "simply by reading your words. I wondered why you picked the cases that you worked, and then I saw the pattern. Do you realize that every cold case you've worked takes place in a town your mother took you to?"

What the hell was he talking about? Research? Her mother? Her head spun and she tried to focus on his words. To listen to his voice. To *remember*.

"I see the confusion on your face, Maxine. All the clues are there. In the book you wrote about your poor friend Karen's disappearance, you mentioned that you were in Miami when you were seven staying with family friends. We know that's not true—your mother's friends were not family friends—but it's an honest lie. You might not have comprehended that your mother was a pathological liar."

What the *hell* was he talking about? Her mother? What did her mother have to do with any of this?

"You mentioned in an article you wrote two years ago about the college student who was found dead in the Rocky Mountains that you'd stayed at the Broadmoor for a month when you were eight. I learned that your mother had a lover then by the name of Martin Flores. He was married, but kept your mother in a town house at the Broadmoor, most likely for sexual purposes. You didn't mention that, but I can read between the lines."

She was shaking her head. He was wrong.

Except he wasn't. She remembered Martin Flores. She remembered the town house she'd lived in, and the sounds that came from her mother's bedroom. She knew now that they were sounds of sex; then, she thought they were playing games. That's what her mother had called it.

"It's all just fun and games, Maxie. Just ignore it."

"Your mother was a whore. You knew it then, you know it now. How many men had she been with? So many she didn't know who your father was. But that's not what she told you, is it? Because you're a curious little bitch, and you just had to know. So she made something up, something that satisfied you until you found out she was a liar."

"How?" How did he know? She'd never hidden the fact that she didn't know who her father was, but she'd never publicly discussed how her mother lied to her. How did this man know? Was she really that open in her writing? She would have known . . .

"You investigated a disappearance five years ago in Jackson, Wyoming," the man continued. "You mentioned that you'd been there once, in winter, snowed in when you were only six. You couldn't remember much about the trip, but there was fear between the lines."

He was crazy. Certifiably a lunatic. Wyoming? Had she really written about going there when she was six? She couldn't have. She didn't remember.

The drugs. You don't remember because of the damn drugs they're feeding you.

Yet, she vaguely remembered that cabin. It was a blur, something that came to her when she was deep in sleep. A cabin that scared her, gave her nightmares that, when she woke, she couldn't remember. Except for the quiet. The white. The cold.

She'd been left alone because her mother went shopping with friends. A snowstorm came in and stranded her there. Her mother couldn't get to her—at least that's what Martha had told Max when she finally arrived days later.

Max had never told anyone about that. Not Marco. Not

David. She certainly hadn't written about it. It was the nightmare that she didn't completely believe was real.

"I see you remember."

"No," she squeaked.

"You're lying. Do you want the water?"

Cold liquid brushed her lips. She involuntarily opened her mouth. A few drops moistened her tongue; then no more.

"What do you want to know?" Her voice was hoarse.

"Just tell me you remember."

She didn't speak for several minutes, but felt his presence, his eagerness to hear her answer.

He wanted to talk to her about her childhood? What the hell for? What was his game? She never voluntarily thought about the first ten years of her life. She'd never forgotten, but the memories now came only in dreams and nightmares.

But if this is what he wanted, then she had to play the game. She needed water. She needed to regain her strength.

She said, "I remember."

"I knew it!" He clapped his hands.

"Water."

"Oh, please, it's not going to be that easy."

Her body betrayed her. She was shaking again. The pain, the feeling of being so out of control of her own body, made her head spin. Fear crept in, no matter how much she told herself she couldn't give in to what he wanted. The fear was there. She hated herself for being scared.

"Was that time, that week you were left," he whispered, "was that your earliest feeling of abandonment?"

She needed to make something up. Anything to stay alive.

"Yes." She didn't know if that was a lie or not. She didn't remember. She didn't want to remember.

You live by the truth. How could you not want *to re-*

member something in your past? Have you been lying to yourself all this time? Are you a fraud, Maxine?

She barely remembered that week. It was Christmas, a week before she turned six. Her mother left her, told her she was buying Christmas presents and would be very late getting back, but not to worry. There was plenty of food and water in the kitchen, just in case.

"Stay inside, Maxie. I'll be back before you wake up in the morning."

She'd left two days before Christmas. Left her alone. Max was okay with playing alone because she was used to it. And she had learned to read early, because of her mother. Martha Revere had been very well educated, loved books, loved museums and culture and made sure that Max saw everything.

I'm giving you the world, Maxie. Every day, a new world.

Every month they moved. Martha would get her paycheck, as she called it, on the first. Max later learned that it was her trust allowance. Feast and famine. Martha didn't understand budgeting, and it didn't take Max long to figure out she needed to save dollars here and there for when the month's allowance ran out.

You're the luckiest girl on the planet, you know that?

Whether her mother believed it or wanted to believe it, Max didn't know. But Max didn't think she was lucky when she was left alone for nine days. Her mother said later it was a storm. That she couldn't get back. But it wasn't. It was Martha stuck because she had no money. She came back January 2, the day she got her paycheck because the banks were closed on the holiday. It was nine days, not a few days. Not a week.

Her mother had left her alone for nine days.

I'm so sorry, baby. I didn't think I would be gone so long. Look what I got you!

Max had cried. She wasn't an emotional child, but she'd hugged her mother tightly, her whole body shaking. She couldn't stop the tears. She'd never been so scared, so terrified, so worried that her mother wouldn't come home.

Don't leave me, Mommy. Don't leave me again.

And Martha cried. Maybe she realized what she'd done, maybe she regretted it. She must have because for nearly four years she rarely left Max alone for more than an hour. And it was better, even if Max knew their life wasn't normal.

Until Martha left her at her grandparents the month before her tenth birthday. Max hadn't seen her since.

"Maxine, you're not listening to me."

Had this bastard been talking to her while memories flooded her? Max didn't want to be six again where the one thought in her head was that she would be alone for the rest of her life, trapped in a house she didn't know. No one would find her. For nine days she came up with hundreds of scenarios about what had happened to her mother. And the fear—the deep, primal fear—that she would never know what happened to her. That she would die in this cabin because no one knew where she was. That her mother had left her because she never wanted her in the first place.

She'd been an accident. Her mother had said that once. Not to Max, but to a friend.

Max was supposed to be sleeping. But even as a child, she'd never slept well.

"Fucking bastard," she mumbled. She didn't want to think about her mother. She didn't want to think about any of this.

He laughed. "That's good! You're making progress, Maxine. You're remembering. Now you can recognize that everything you've done is because of that fateful week. Your life isn't about Karen Richardson or your poor dead high school friend Lindy Ames or even your pathetic mother. It's about *you*. Everything you've done is because of how *you* felt when you were six years old and alone."

It wasn't true. Max barely remembered that time. This man was a lunatic.

There was whispering. At least, Max thought it was whispering. Maybe it was ghosts in the air, calling to her. Telling her to close her eyes and give up. . . .

Keep your head together, Maxine.

"We need to go. I don't know when we'll return. Maybe never. But because I want to talk if I come back, I have a treat."

He poured water into her mouth. She coughed and gagged and then eagerly drank, hating herself for feeling grateful for the few ounces he fed her.

Then he left without a word and she was alone.

For the first time since she was six, Maxine cried.

Chapter Twenty

David checked with everyone at NET, touched bases with Sally O'Hara, spoke again to Vance at the car service, and skimmed all the files related to everything Max had been working on.

And still Milligan didn't call.

David couldn't think of anything else to do. He would've helped Sally canvass the areas in Brooklyn and Queens, but he didn't want to be far from the D.A.'s office when Milligan finally called. Nothing popped out from Max's notes. It was all stuff he knew—or he learned this morning—and he didn't see what she'd stumbled upon that landed her on a killer's radar.

Maybe it wasn't any one thing. Maybe it was a culmination of several things.

Or maybe this had been part of Bachman's sick plan from the beginning.

"Milligan called," Ben said, stopping by Max's office where David sat at her computer reading recent e-mails one more time. "We're to meet him at the Manhattan Detention Complex at four fifteen."

"It's about time," he grumbled. He shut down her computer and rose.

Ben handed him a sandwich as they walked to the elevator. "Lara ordered out. Told me to tell you to eat."

David wasn't hungry. But he ate half the sandwich in the elevator and tossed the other half in the trash before getting into the car.

David and Ben were processed through the Manhattan Detention Complex and brought into a small conference room where Milligan was on his phone. He quickly hung up. "I haven't been able to reach Bachman's lawyer," he said. "However, because Bachman signed a waiver to be interviewed by *Maximum Exposure,* I'm comfortable that I can let Mr. Kane speak with him."

"I don't care about your red tape," David said. "He has information that we need."

"The guard is bringing him in from holding. They'll be in the interrogation room down the hall in a few minutes. I have to say, for the record, that I'm not comfortable with this."

"Of course you do," David muttered.

Ben stepped forward. "Richard. David. This is a difficult situation for all of us. We truly appreciate the delicacy of your position, Richard, and I can assure you that we will not abuse your trust."

Milligan didn't look confident, and he said to David, "I look at you and see a man who would snap Bachman's neck if he could get away with it. Stay on your side of the table, Mr. Kane."

"I won't touch him," David said.

"And do not make him any promises relating to his sentencing or trial. I will not negotiate for a reduced sentence. I'm confident that the jury will come back Monday with a guilty verdict; Adam Bachman will spend the rest of his life in a jail cell for what he's done. But how you run your show and what you promise him in the media? That's up to you."

Ben said, "Thank you, Richard."

"I still don't know what you hope to accomplish here," Milligan said. "I don't believe he's going to say anything."

David said, "You could offer him immunity from prosecution for other crimes."

"Not without knowing what crimes, what evidence is out there, how many potential other victims there are. I have him on five murders."

"But I can."

The three men turned to face FBI Agent Marco Lopez.

"Excuse me," Milligan said, stepping forward. "Who are you?"

"Supervisory Special Agent Marco Lopez with the Federal Bureau of Investigation. Bring me up to speed."

"What?" Milligan looked blindsided and angry. No one in local government liked the feds coming in, especially without warning.

"You said you'd be here tomorrow," David said.

Marco shook his head. "I thought about it for about five minutes and hopped on the first flight I could get out. I've already checked in with the New York field office and given them a briefing on the situation. I reviewed the security footage you sent, and ran the guy through our facial recognition program."

"And?"

"Nothing yet, but it could take a few days."

"Agent Lopez," Milligan said with barely restrained anger, "I'm District Attorney Richard Milligan. Our case is closed. The jury is deliberating. Bachman will be convicted." Milligan seemed more concerned that a federal agent was stepping in to his case than with David talking to Bachman. "You can't walk in to the middle of my case—"

"I understand the complexities and I assure you I'm not going to touch your case. But if Adam Bachman had a partner, and that partner has Maxine, we need to find him now."

"If you talk to him, I have to get his attorney down here," Milligan said. "We'll be jeopardizing future charges if he says anything incriminating."

"You said you were confident the jury will return a guilty verdict," Marco said. "There's no going back on that."

"There's an appeals process, there's—"

"I'll take the heat," Marco interrupted. "I'm used to it whenever Maxine is involved."

Without waiting for an answer or argument, Marco turned to the guard. "Please take me to Bachman."

"I'm going to be in the observation room, Agent Lopez," Milligan said. "Don't screw this up."

David followed Marco. "I can't let you in there," Marco said. "I don't know what deal you had with Milligan, but I'm doing this on my own."

David stared silently at Marco. Marco swore under his breath. "Shit, David, I can't have you losing it."

David again said nothing. Marco thought he knew him, but he really didn't.

"I'm lead," Marco said, relenting. He nodded to the guard to let them both into the room.

Bachman was cuffed to the table. He had bags under his eyes. He looked like shit. Like a prisoner of war, David thought.

"Mr. Bachman," Marco said, "I'm Supervisory Special Agent Marco Lopez with the Federal Bureau of Investigation."

"Where's my lawyer?"

"I'm not here to discuss your case. Nothing you say to me will be used against you. This interview is not being recorded."

Bachman looked skeptical.

"Why are you here?" Bachman said to David. "You work for Maxine Revere. I want to talk to her. I only agreed to talk to her."

David stared at him so hard that Bachman turned away.

Marco cleared his throat, "Mr. Bachman, I need to know the name and location of this man."

He put a photo of their suspect in front of Bachman. David watched him closely. The killer couldn't hide his recognition.

"I don't know," he said, his voice cracking.

"We have a witness who saw you with this man on several occasions at Fringe," Marco said. "We know you know him. He's wanted for felony kidnapping."

Bachman blinked rapidly. "What?"

"If you were involved in a crime with this man, I can help you."

He laughed, but he sounded sick and weak. "I'm still going to prison for the rest of my life."

"Federal prisons are much nicer than state pens."

"It doesn't matter." He shrugged. "I'll be dead."

"Have you been threatened? I can offer you protection. A secure wing in a federal prison."

Bachman didn't say anything. David stepped forward and Marco put his hand up to stop him.

David ignored Marco. He sidestepped his hand and put his palms on the table. He waited until Bachman looked at him, then he said slowly and clearly, "Adam, we know you met this guy at Greenhaven. We know you've been in contact with him up until you were arrested. And we know that he's the one who killed the Palazzolos. You helped cover it up." As he said it, David saw in Bachman's wide eyes that he was guilty. Max had been right all along. Somehow, that didn't make him feel any better. "Give us his name."

"What did he do?" Bachman asked, blatantly curious.

"We have him on tape kidnapping a woman," Marco said.

"When?"

"Last night. Now talk."

Bachman's eyes rested on David. "He really did it? He kidnapped Maxine Revere?" His voice was filled with awe and pride, and David's fist clenched.

"How do you know that?" Marco snapped.

"It's obvious. Her pet is here, not her. And you think I don't know who you are? You think I haven't read all her books? They were practically required reading. Marco Lopez, the federal agent in charge of the Karen Richardson disappearance. And didn't you arrest her once for obstruction of justice?"

David froze. Why would Bachman have read Max's books? Why would he have remembered those details? He was in high school during that investigation, more than a thousand miles away from Miami.

What the *hell* did he mean by *required reading?*

"Were the two of you planning on kidnapping Ms. Revere from the beginning?" Marco asked.

Bachman opened his mouth, then closed it. He looked down at his hands. There was a shift in his body, a sag, as if he'd made a realization and now didn't know what to do.

"Give us his name," Marco said sharply.

"Guard," Bachman called out. "I'm ready to go back to my cell."

David lunged. His fist was inches from Bachman's face when Marco stopped him. David pushed Marco off him and left as the guard entered the room.

That bastard knew exactly what was going on. And it was orchestrated, and not by Bachman who'd been in jail for the last nine months. Why had they planned on grabbing

Max? Was that their endgame? Or one more crime in a long list of felonies?

David ignored Ben and Milligan as they stepped out of the observation room. He had to get out, get some space between him and the world, just to breathe.

He left the building and started the long walk back to the studio. He couldn't think with a crowd. It took two blocks before his heart rate slowed enough that he stopped hearing the pounding behind his ears.

Another block passed before he let himself think about the conversation with Bachman. He considered it clinically.

Once confronted with the truth that the police knew Bachman was associated with Max's kidnapper, Bachman had relaxed, almost as if he was relieved that the game was over. He was curious about what his friend had done and yet he didn't seem surprised that Max had been kidnapped. He knew about Max, her books, her background. Had he done the research from jail?

Practically required reading.

Had she been a target from the beginning? Why? She didn't fit the profile of any of the other victims. But this action didn't fit the other victims, either. This didn't fit anything, except for the niggling idea that Max knew something and was being silenced because of it.

Which meant that she was already dead.

If they planned to kill Max anyway, why kidnap her? Why not just shoot her and leave her to be found in the car? Why not make a big splash? Or set it up to be an accident? They had her alone in the car. They had time to do anything they wanted.

Except if Max had learned something recently then the kidnapping couldn't have been planned. It would have been spontaneous. Yet everything about it pointed to a plan. The kidnapper knew what car service she used, knew she was working late, knew she would be leaving alone. They must have staked out the car service or tapped into the company's dispatch to know that David wasn't picking her up.

That might be traceable.

By the time David reached the studio twenty minutes later, he came to the conclusion that Bachman's partner had kidnapped Max as part of a larger endgame and he had several directions to go. But he still couldn't see *why*.

He stood outside the NET building and called Dr. Arthur Ullman's private phone.

"Dr. Ullman, it's David Kane. I need your help."

Riley parked in front of Greenhaven and took a deep breath.

She had to do this.

The entire drive to Hartford, she'd debated with herself about her crazy idea. She didn't care (much) that Kyle thought she was way off base; she didn't care that it was a long shot. She needed to ID the guy who kidnapped Max. He had been here, in Greenhaven, and as David said, the police weren't going to be able to do anything for days.

Max might not have days. She might not even have tonight.

Finally Riley asked herself what Max would do. Max had risked her life picking through lies in order to learn the truth. She'd started when she was younger than Riley. Riley had read her book about Karen's disappearance, about how she hounded the police, the FBI, the resort, guests, everyone who might know what had happened to Max's friend. And Max had only been twenty-two.

Riley's plan was a much safer idea than what Max had done. She wasn't confronting a killer. She wasn't hounding the police or risking her life or freedom. And Riley had a car, she could leave whenever she got the information she needed.

She convinced herself that this was the only way. That this was exactly what Max Revere herself would do.

Riley hid the small, thin laptop that Kyle had loaned her under the front seat of the rental car. She also hid a second cell phone, just in case. And it wasn't like no one knew where she was—Kyle knew, and she'd left a message with Lara Smith, Ben's administrative assistant. Gave her Kyle's number in case there was an emergency. She hoped she'd find the answers tonight and be back early Saturday morning to tell David that she had found Max's kidnapper. She hoped to be back before anyone at *Maximum Exposure* even knew she had slipped out.

Maybe then, David would finally believe she added value to the team.

Riley took a deep breath, grabbed her overnight bag, and walked up the steps to the main entrance of Greenhaven. The receptionist who'd been there on Wednesday smiled kindly, and immediately Riley knew she'd done the right thing.

"Ms. Jackson told me you were coming in this afternoon," the receptionist said. "I'll show you your room, you can leave your bag, then I'll introduce you to your counselor. There's a lot of paperwork to fill out."

"I'm ready," Riley said.

"You've made the right decision, Ms. Butler."

Riley was confident she had.

Chapter Twenty-one

David debated ditching Marco so he could meet with Dr. Arthur Ullman one-on-one. David *wanted* Marco to move mountains to force the police to focus on Max's disappearance, and his take-charge attitude could benefit them on that end, but with Ullman, Marco's annoying habit of taking over could work against them.

In the end, David told him about the meeting he'd set up and Marco insisted on joining them at Max's apartment. It was seven in the evening, and David eyed Marco's overnight bag as they rode up the elevator, but didn't say anything. Max would be furious if Marco stayed in her apartment, but right now David yearned for her fury.

Max had been missing for twenty hours.

Marco went right up to Max's bedroom with his bag, dropped it on her bed, then went up the half flight of stairs into her office. David was about to follow when the house phone rang. He answered, expecting Dr. Ullman had arrived early.

"Mr. Kane, there's a Detective Nicholas Santini here requesting access to Ms. Revere's apartment."

Santini? What was he doing here? He must have jumped

on a cross-country flight not long after David talked to him that morning.

"Send him up," David said. "And when Dr. Ullman arrives, please send him directly up as well."

"Of course, Mr. Kane."

If the situation wasn't so dire, David would have enjoyed introducing Marco to Nick and watching the fed size up Max's new boyfriend.

David liked Nick. He'd been a Marine, honorably discharged with honors, and now was a cop in California. He and Max had met six weeks ago, and David wasn't surprised that Max was attracted to him. Nick was level-headed and smart and could meet Max on her own field yet stand his own ground. David admired that. But David didn't form close friendships with Max's boyfriends. The relationships never lasted long. David wanted to believe Nick was different, but only time would tell.

When Nick knocked, David let him in.

"Any word?" Nick asked.

David shook his head. "We have a photo of the kidnapper and the FBI is working with NYPD to ID the guy."

"So the police did get involved."

"Contrary to rumors, Max has some friends there."

"Let me see it."

David handed him a copy of the image.

"You said the FBI is running him?"

"So far, nothing."

"What did she get herself into?" Nick asked, almost to himself.

"I should have seen it coming, Nick," David said quietly.

Nick clamped his hand on David's shoulder. "We will find her. You're not alone here."

The phone rang again, and it was Jorge telling David that Dr. Ullman was on his way up.

"Who's Ullman?" Nick asked.

"Retired FBI profiler. A friend of Max's. I hope he can give us a direction to go in. I feel like I'm running in circles, not knowing what the hell this is about."

David opened the door for Arthur. "Thank you for coming," he said.

Arthur waved off his comment. "Anything I can do." He walked in with his well-worn leather briefcase. "Did she put anything new on her wall?"

"A few things. This is Nick Santini, a detective from California."

"Yes, yes, Max told me she was taking some personal time in California. I see why now." He smiled, but his eyes were worried. "And you said Marco was here?"

"Upstairs."

"Time, David. We don't have a lot of time."

Arthur crossed the great room and walked up the curving staircase. David followed with Nick, feeling like he'd been kicked in the gut. What did Arthur mean by that? Why didn't they have time? What did he know?

"Arthur," Marco said and shook his hand. Marco had already made himself at home at Max's desk.

"Marco. I'm glad you're here. We all need to work together on this."

Marco frowned at Nick, then glanced at David. David made quick introductions, but didn't feel inclined to explain Nick's presence to Marco.

Arthur went right over to the wall. "There's nothing new here except this—what is this about Greenhaven on Wednesday? Who are these people?"

On the wall Max had put up the names of the director, the doctors, the staff member who was fired, and Anna Hudson, Bachman's counselor.

"Max determined that Bachman spent at least three months at Greenhaven, a mental health facility outside Hartford," David said. "Jackson is the director, the three names under her are psychiatrists, Janice was a former staffer who told Max that Anna Hudson spontaneously quit after something happened with Adam Bachman. We haven't been able to find her."

"Max talked to all these people, except for Anna?"

"Yes." David clipped a photo of the unsub to the wall under the word *partner*. "This is the man who kidnapped Max. He was identified by one of Bachman's former colleagues as someone who visited Bachman at Fringe several times prior to his arrest. He's approximately six foot one and close to two hundred pounds. Large guy, sleeve tats on his arms, older than Bachman by a few years."

Arthur didn't say anything for a minute. He looked at the new information, then opened his briefcase and removed a file. "I contacted a friend of mine in the crime lab. This came out in the trial, according to Max's notes, but the prosecution didn't understand the dual purpose of the drug. Trifluoperazine is a sedative that can incapacitate an individual immediately if injected, make them weak and compliant and in higher doses render them unconscious. All victims had traces of this drug in their system. It's a Class-C regulated drug used by some psychiatrists treating anxiety and depression. There are some nasty side effects, so it's rarely used anymore in treatment except as a last resort.

"The other point that the prosecution missed is that there were trace elements of another drug in the victims. Ritalin."

"Isn't that used for treating ADHD in kids?" Marco asked.

"Yes, among other things. But in many adults it's a stimulant. I checked the medical records of the victims, and none of them had a current prescription for Ritalin, and only one had been prescribed the drug as a child. I suspect it was used to either wake the victims up after they were secured or to keep them awake."

"I'm familiar with the case," Marco said. "Bachman suffocated his victims."

"There was a third, unidentified drug in three of the victims. I've flagged the information and want the FBI to run additional tests on the blood work, but I think this particular drug dissipates after time, even after death. They may not have a clean enough sample."

"How does that help?" Marco asked.

"I don't know yet." Arthur frowned, regained his focus, and said, "The prosecution didn't press the fact that they suspected Mr. Bachman kept his victims alive and in a state of extreme agitation for twenty-four hours. They gave basic information about empty stomach contents, dehydration. It was probably too scientific for the jury, and because it would equate to torture, they might have felt it was harder to prove because none of the bodies had signs of external torture. Psychological torture is a completely different matter, and that's what I believe Mr. Bachman was doing. Tormenting his victims until they died on their own, or he decided he was bored."

David kept his face impassive, but inside he was agitated, picturing Max suffering as Bachman's other victims suffered.

"How? Why?" Marco asked.

"I believe that Bachman and his partner wanted to terrify their victims. With the drugs their fear would be exponential. At this point, I can only guess to why. The pathology seems too . . . sophisticated for a hands-off killer like Bachman."

"Hands-off?" Nick asked.

Arthur nodded. "Maxine was right about that, Bachman had a lifelong phobia about germs and dirt. He would touch the victims only as necessary. But your unsub is far more brutal." Arthur gestured toward the photo of Max's kidnapper. "And I don't see him being so restrained."

"Why do you think the unsub is more brutal than Bachman?" Marco asked.

"I'm sorry, I'm still formulating my theory." He looked down at his notes. "O'Hara, right, David? The detective?"

"Yes," David said. "I asked her to send you everything she had."

"Thank you, she did. I reviewed the preliminary report on the Palazzolos' murders. The autopsy hasn't been completed, but the killer didn't understand the properties of sodium hydroxide, or the necessity to keep the reaction going by adding water over time. The bodies were well dissolved, all the flesh gone, but the skulls and many of the bones were still intact. These showed, particularly on the male victim, extensive blunt force trauma. He may have been beaten to death, or close to it. Based on Bachman's pathology, he would not and could not do this. Bachman's MO is clear, and based on what I've read about his case, he likes to watch. He may have watched his partner kill the Palazzolos. He would have been disgusted by it. It's dirty and messy. He may have refined his own killing process because of it. He suffocated his victims by tying a clear plastic bag over their heads and watching them die. Hands-off. Your other killer is not hands-off. He has impulse control issues, though he's able to keep them under control for long periods of time. However, he'll become increasingly violent and unpredictable."

"We haven't found him in any criminal database."

"He may not have been caught, or not since he was a minor. He picked the Palazzolos for a specific reason. They may have reminded him of his parents or grandparents or someone else close to him. If he was in Greenhaven as

Max suspected, he was likely there for anger management or substance abuse."

Nick said, "Doctor, go back to what you said about psychologically torturing your victims. You said that the pathology was too sophisticated for either Bachman or the unsub. Are you saying that there is a third individual?"

"Yes, Detective, I'm saying that there is another person involved. A third killer."

David stared at Arthur. A third killer? It seemed too unbelievable. He glanced at Nick and Marco. Nick had a dark expression. He'd been the first to pick up on what Arthur was suggesting, and it was clear he believed it. Marco dismissed the idea.

"Do you realize how unlikely a third killer would be?" Marco said. "The partner—I can buy into that. It makes sense. Killing pairs aren't uncommon. But three? I don't see it."

David was skeptical, but he had great respect for Arthur. "How certain are you, Arthur?"

"As much as I can be." Arthur glanced at Nick. "You see it, Detective, right?"

Nick gave a brief nod. "If you're accurate in your profile of Bachman and the unsub, it makes sense that there is a third more organized thinker involved."

Marco opened his mouth to argue but David caught his eye, and said, "If there's a third, where does he fit in? I'm assuming it's a man."

"Most likely," Arthur said. "I would be looking for an individual who is older, above-average intelligence, and has training in medicine and psychology—possibly a medical school dropout, possibly a doctor or nurse or psychologist."

"A counselor? A psychiatrist?" Nick suggested, gesturing toward Max's board and her list of names.

"Possible. Someone who had been working closely with doctors for years, especially someone who was smart and driven, could learn about these drugs and how they interact through watching and reading, asking the right questions."

"Assuming you're right," Marco said in a tone that told David he was still skeptical, "did Max tip someone off? Maybe her trip to Greenhaven?"

"I couldn't say, but the timing would suggest that."

Practically required reading.

"No," David said. "That wasn't it."

The three men turned to him. David needed to think his analysis through. He wasn't driven by instincts like Max. He liked evidence he could see and touch and smell. But he never discounted the "gut feeling" some of the guys in his Ranger squad had. There were times when his acute senses had picked up on danger for no tangible reason. So David tried to articulate this gut feeling he had about why Max had been kidnapped.

He said, "I think Max was a target from the beginning."

Marco said, "The beginning of what?"

"I don't know how far back, but Bachman said something that I haven't been able to shake. He said that Max's books were 'practically required reading.' Why would he say that?"

"It could mean anything," Marco said.

"The day before Bachman agreed to the interview with Max, Detective O'Hara found the empty container of sodium hydroxide."

"That's a thin connection."

"Yes, it is," David said, irritable. "Nothing that could stand up in court, but I don't care about court. It proves to me that Bachman lured Max in. He implied that she would never find the Palazzolos, and then three days later, Sally O'Hara found the bodies. *Because* Max pushed her."

"Maxine pushes a lot of people," Marco said. "She gets obsessed with these cold cases, to the point where she makes mistakes. I've known her a lot longer than any of you, and a lot better."

"Knock it off, Lopez." David narrowed his gaze. "You're hardly unbiased when it comes to Max. You didn't even want to come here because she refused to apologize for embarrassing you on the Garbena farce."

"You have *no* idea, Kane, what I had to clean up there."

"Then go, Marco. I don't need your shit right now."

Arthur Ullman cleared his throat. "I think we can all agree that Maxine obsesses about missing persons cases. That doesn't mean she's blind. I need to speak with Mr. Bachman. I listened to his interview, and as David said, Bachman knows more about Max than a cursory interest. It's hard for me to make a psychological judgment based on limited information and third party analysis."

Nick said, "David, are you suggesting that Max was abducted because Detective O'Hara found the dead couple?"

"I don't know," David admitted. He rubbed his temples with the tips of his fingers. Now was the time he wished he could think more like Max and less like a soldier. He sometimes didn't know how she made the connections she made, pulling seemingly unrelated facts into a truth no one else could see until she laid it out.

Arthur turned to Marco. "Can you get me in to talk to Bachman? The sooner the better."

"First thing in the morning," Marco said without hesitation. David didn't know if Arthur had convinced him or if Marco came to the conclusion himself or if Marco was simply placating the rest of them. David didn't feel at all confident in their investigation if Max was ultimately the target. Maybe she *was* their endgame.

"I also suggest you find a way to subpoena Greenhaven records. Start with Adam Bachman's file."

"You know that's going to be next to impossible."

"There's precedence. I can help you with that."

Nick said, "Doctor, go back to the third individual involved. How are they working together? Like a killing team? Or that Bachman and the unsub were a pair, with a . . . a *master* for lack of a better word, directing them?"

Arthur didn't say anything for a moment. He looked at Max's wall, at the time line, and the facts.

"I don't know if they worked together, but I believe based on what we know, that three people were certainly privy to the details either before or after each of the murders. It's clear from the evidence I've seen that Bachman killed those five people, but I concur with Max that he didn't move the bodies. He had a partner to help him dispose of the bodies, like he helped his partner dispose of the Palazzolos. And there may have been more before them. There are too many unknowns at this point.

"But I think it's clear from Bachman's interview with Max and from your conversation with him today that she has been on his radar for far longer than she's been involved in this investigation. And without the *why* it doesn't make sense." Arthur waved his hand to Max's wall. "There is nothing here that suggests that Bachman has a personal connection with Maxine. She would have picked up on that. But the interview she had with him tells me he knows a secret about her. I can't explain exactly why, but she's at the center of this somehow."

David didn't want to believe it, because that meant not only was Max being stalked—either physically or through digital media—but he hadn't known. He hadn't even picked up on the threat.

Arthur continued. "Bachman's comment to you was odd, David, truly unusual. Have you looked into her old investigations? People she may have butted up against?"

"Ben has the research unit reviewing her files, but it's a vast landscape."

"Excuse me," Nick said, "but if her kidnapping is related to a past case, how does Bachman fit in? She would have known him from the start, or she would have figured it out along the way. His life was turned inside out by the police and by Max herself."

"That's an excellent point," Arthur said. "Which is why identifying the two partners needs to be a priority. There's a personal component here."

"Why do you say that?" David asked. "Personal how?"

"I keep going back to, why Max? If Bachman deliberately pulled her into the investigation, baited her with the interview, it isn't a simple game."

Marco leaned forward. "Wait—so you're thinking that one of these two unidentified individuals has a *personal* beef with Max? Do you realize how many people she's pissed off in her life?"

"Stop," David said. He was beginning to hate the fed. "Marco, you need to either be on board with Arthur or leave. We don't have the time to debate every single point. If Arthur says this is personal, it's personal."

He stood in the doorway and looked across Max's open bedroom, through the windows to the dark Hudson River beyond. *Personal.* Of course it was personal. They hadn't received a ransom letter, they hadn't received any demands at all. And they hadn't found her body.

"I'm having a hard time buying into the theory that Bachman and the unsub killed five or seven people in order to lure Max into their case," Marco said.

"Gentlemen," Arthur said, "it's probably not that. Meaning, these people would have been dead no matter what. But at some point, they wanted Max involved and knew how to draw her in. Like I said, there're too many unknown variables."

"I'm going to call Ben," David said. "He's known Max longer than any of us. He might have an idea of where we can start."

"Start with her four books," Arthur said. "Bachman specifically mentioned books to Max, and she's better known for those than she is for her journalism. The 'required reading' comment makes me think of books as well."

David left Max's office to get some distance from the others. Arthur gave them a direction, and while the information made the task ahead of them seem daunting and the situation in some ways shocking, David had something to do, and that made him think they'd find her.

Because if he didn't have something to focus on, all he'd be able to do is picture his best friend dead.

Riley waited until it was quiet and close to midnight before she snuck out of her room and walked along the perimeter of the Greenhaven property to where she'd parked her car. There was a private security patrol that drove through the property several times a day, but she'd quickly realized they weren't there to keep patients in so much as to make sure the property itself was secure.

She retrieved the small laptop and her cell phone, then went back to her room. She saw no one.

Her stomach flipped as her nerves hit her. Her dad would have her head. He didn't like that she was working for Max. Not specifically *Max*, but any reporter. He didn't like reporters, on general principles. But this was what she'd always wanted to do, from the day she wrote an article in third grade for the classroom newsletter arguing in favor of longer recesses. The administration had come back with an article about how students needed to be in school a certain number of minutes a day, and Riley had countered with an article she'd clipped from one of her mom's early childhood education magazines, citing that kids needed playtime in order to be more productive in school. In the end, the administration extended lunch by five minutes. A small victory, but one Riley had cherished.

She wanted to make a difference. She wanted her words, her ideas, to change people's minds, no matter how small.

What she was doing now wasn't small. It was huge. It would save lives. It would save Max. She was certain the answers were here, she just had to find them. She had to put herself in Max's head and figure out what her boss—her mentor—would do in this situation.

By the time she left the city earlier that afternoon, they still hadn't been able to ID the guy who'd kidnapped Max. Max had been positive Adam had met him while here at Greenhaven. That meant she needed to get a list of all the patients who were here at the time Adam was here. Logical. Yes, it was a felony. Yes, she would get in big trouble if she were caught. So she had to be careful and not get caught.

But hadn't Max done similar things? When she investigated the elder care facility in Miami, she'd worked with someone on the inside to gather information. Riley didn't know all the details about the case, but she'd read the articles and the subsequent book. Max had won awards. She'd also once gone undercover in a women's prison to expose systemic abuse when she wasn't much older than Riley.

Now or never.

Grow up, Riley. You can do this.

Kyle had created a program on the minilaptop that could help her break into any computer. She'd lifted a card key from one of the staff, and planned to leave it somewhere when she was finished so that the individual would think they'd dropped it.

She took a deep breath. Max had always told her to have a clear objective when researching, but to be open to new ideas if they presented themselves. Her objective was to

ID Max's kidnapper. If they could find him, that would bring them one step closer to finding Max. And, if Riley was going to be perfectly honest with herself, prove that she was indispensable to the team. That she could gather information just like Max, that she could crack a case wide open. Maybe even solve the Palazzolos' murders at the same time. Prove that she belonged.

Riley exited her room. The hall was quiet, except for a light snore coming from the room next to hers. She left through the side door, wincing as it clicked shut behind her.

Though it was the first week of June, it was cold here at night. She had a sweatshirt on, the small computer hidden in the front pocket. She had an excuse if caught. Going for a walk. Needing fresh air. Unable to sleep.

But no one was around. No security guard, no patients, no staff. She could see why addicts would come to a place like this. Away from the city. Away from stress and family and people with expectations. Riley had recognized when she was fifteen that her addiction came from her own brutal expectations, to be the best at everything. To go, go, go, do, do, do, never slowing down because she didn't want anyone to think she was lazy or dumb.

She still had the overachiever gene, but she'd hoped she'd tempered it with age. She didn't crave drugs like she used to. She still worked hard. She still demanded a lot from herself. But that was okay, because she was doing it without artificial help.

Her heart raced. The first hurdle was getting into the administration building; her purloined card key worked. She breathed easier. If the individual had reported it missing, it might have been deactivated; fortunately, she was in the clear.

A low hum of computers and printers in sleep mode. A settling of the building. The faint buzz of lighting. It wasn't pitch-black; a low glow from intermittent lights illuminated the halls.

She took the carpeted stairs to the second floor.

She found the main records room. She feared the key she had wouldn't access it. She held her breath as she pressed the key against the access panel.

Click.

The door unlocked, and she slipped inside. Now she felt more confident, secluded in this room.

There were file cabinets, two desks, and a computer. She carefully closed the venetian blinds hoping they would block the light from the computer.

She turned on the computer and plugged Kyle's decoder into the USB port. As the computer booted up, Kyle's minicomputer flashed a couple of lights and the small disk drive inside spun.

Please work, please work.

She bit her thumbnail as she waited. And waited. It seemed to take forever, but only ninety seconds passed before a bunch of stuff flashed on the screen. She feared she'd crashed the system, then suddenly the desktop appeared.

It worked!

She sat down and quickly looked through the root directory.

And quickly discovered all files were saved by number.

No, no, no!

There were far too many records in the database to download. She opened up a couple and skimmed them. They had everything she needed, but how could she weed through and find the people who were here at the same time as Bachman?

Riley rubbed the back of her neck and considered her options. She knew the year Bachman had been here, so she sorted the files based on *when* they were created, then copied more than nine months' worth of files—those created three months before, during, and after Bachman was here. She hoped that would be enough.

She hoped this worked.

When the files were copied to Kyle's computer, she shut everything down and waited. Listened. Except for the low hum of equipment, it was quiet. Riley left the office and walked back the way she'd come. Down the stairs, out the side door, back to the dormitory-style rooms. She saw no one and heard nothing, and was grinning when she opened the door to her room. She'd send the files to Kyle and he could help her quickly sort through them. Once she knew she had what she needed, she'd leave.

She shut her door and flipped on her light.

A man was standing in her room. He was familiar . . .

The courthouse. You bumped into him at the courthouse when you were texting on your cell phone.

She turned to run out, but he grabbed her arm and held on so tight she lost her breath.

"You think you're smart, Ms. Butler. But you just signed your death certificate."

Chapter Twenty-two

Max had been hungry before.

In her early years, when her mother roamed the country in search of something intangible, Max had always been fed. There were lean times—which meant hamburgers and fries instead of steak and potatoes; fish and chips instead of sushi. And there were times that Martha had forgotten to make dinner or neglected to shop, but Max learned early on to keep a box of granola bars and a bag of dried fruit in her suitcase.

When she was working, she sometimes skipped a meal and found herself starving at ten at night, searching for a decent restaurant because she hadn't had time to go to the market, or didn't feel like cooking. She spoiled herself, and she knew why: for years, her mother flitted about, meals a second thought, as content to dine in a five-star hundred-dollar-a-plate restaurant as McDonald's. She had never cooked for Max.

Max liked—she *appreciated*—good food well prepared. It's why she'd learned to cook for herself.

She didn't know how much time had passed, but if her stomach was to judge, it was at least twenty-four hours.

Longer. Forty-eight? The water her captor had trickled down her throat had long lost its freshness.

She was going to die of starvation.

No, she corrected herself, she'd die of dehydration. A human could survive a lot longer without food than without water.

Something crawled up her leg.

She let out an involuntary cry. Her voice was foreign to her. Weak and empty.

But she'd been weak before. She'd faced death before.

She sat on the dirt floor of the prison cell, if that's what her cage could be called. The bars looked out into a square full of light. It was hot, so hot, but she wasn't sweating because she was so dehydrated. She'd be dead before the American embassy found her.

If they even knew she was missing.

If they'd even been told she was arrested.

If they even cared.

One bottle of warm water for each of three days. It could be worse. It could be the disease-infested water that ran through Mexico. For all she knew, they refilled her bottle from the river, and she'd die of diphtheria or worse.

The smell of rot filled her. Her own filth, the smell of blood. Her blood. The dried blood of her informant. She didn't know if he was dead or alive, but he wouldn't live long with the gut shot she'd witnessed. She didn't know where the rebels had taken him.

There was no free speech in this hellhole deep in Mexico. Being a reporter meant nothing to the people who had arrested her. Arrested? Were they even the real police? More likely a private squad working for the bastard she'd been investigating. She'd be dead and no one would know. No one would find her.

A rat ran in through one of the openings in the bars. She

hated rats. They were filthy and carried disease. It scurried over to her, skinny and dirty, with feral eyes. It sniffed her bare foot; its whiskers brushed against her skin. She kicked at it. The thing bared its teeth at her, and she thought for a brief, terrifying moment it was going to bite her.

Then it ran out.

She would never be able to sleep again.

But a minute later, she wished the rat was back, because there was something worse than rats.

Scorpions.

She wasn't in a Mexican prison; she was somewhere in New York City. She could hear distant traffic. There were no scorpions in the city. The worst of the bugs were cockroaches.

But there were rats. She could hear them scurrying about in the walls, their purpose to survive.

She had the same purpose.

She didn't know what this bastard really wanted, but he hadn't removed the blindfold. Maybe that was good news—maybe he didn't plan to kill her. She could survive anything—she *had* survived a Mexican prison, the disappearance of her mother, the murder of her best friend. She could survive some psycho who wanted to talk to her about her childhood, about her feelings of abandonment or whatever it was he wanted to know. She didn't hide behind lies or sugarcoat who or what she was. And *damn* if she was going to let him win.

He wanted to break her? She couldn't be broken. She wouldn't *allow* herself to be broken.

He'd been gone long enough that the drugs had worn off, or at least they weren't messing with her head as much. She was uncomfortable, her head ached worse than the worst hangover she'd ever had. Her mouth was thick and her body numb and bruised. But she was *alive* and her mind was finally beginning to work again. She needed a plan, or a way to stay sharp enough to take advantage of an opportunity.

He'd forced her to remember her past, whether because it was always in the back of her mind or because the drugs he fed her forced the memory to the surface. Those dark days when she thought her mother was gone for good and she would die in that cabin.

Except . . . she hadn't thought she would die. As the buried memory returned, she remembered being afraid—very, very afraid. She remembered being cold because she didn't know how to restart the fire. But she'd found blankets and then the instructions for the woodstove. The fire was still there, smoldering, and she fed it more wood. She'd burned her hand; that she remembered. She'd been angry with herself, because she *knew* stoves were hot and she *knew* she should have found a pot holder to open the handle, but she hadn't thought it through.

She'd been scared, but not about dying.

She was scared her mother would die and no one would know where she was. That the people who owned the cabin would find her and be angry that she ate their food and slept in their bed like Goldilocks.

But she hadn't thought *she* would die.

Maybe he *would* break her, but he'd need more drugs to do it. Of that she was certain. So what if he'd uncovered that she'd revisited towns her mother had taken her to? Her mother had brought her everywhere. Maybe she hadn't consciously realized it, but if he thought the knowledge would somehow make her cry and beg for mercy, he was wrong.

He'd already gotten tears from her once.

She wasn't giving him anything else that he wanted.

She just had to wait. Think. Plan. Figure out who he was

and why he was doing this. There was something she was missing, something familiar about him. She'd recognized his voice—she had to focus on that. If she knew who he was, she might be able to turn the tables.

She might have drifted off, remembering his words, that tone, a word . . . a specific word . . .

Try to remember everyone you've met. The voice came with a smile. A secretive smile like he knew something no one else knew. Like he knew her. . . .

"*I'm glad we caught you, Doctors. This is Ms. Revere. One of her employees is looking at our facilities. Ms. Revere, Doctors Abrams, Schakowsky, Duvall.*"

Courteous hellos. And a surprise in his voice.

Duvall.

"*I read one of your books a while back.*"

"*In the book you wrote about your poor friend Karen's disappearance . . .*" *he'd said later. A second conversation.*

He'd read her books.

The way he said "book." The secret smile in his voice.

Dr. Carter Duvall.

Max moaned involuntarily. Her head was so heavy. She'd fallen asleep, but it certainly wasn't restful.

Duvall.

Why had he kidnapped her? What the hell was going on? Why had he said he wanted to break her? None of this made any sense!

Had she learned something about Adam Bachman that Duvall didn't want her to reveal? What could it have been? She didn't know squat, which was one of her frustrations. And if this kidnapping had to do with the Palazzolos— well, their murders weren't being investigated by *her*, they were being investigated by the NYPD.

The time line works. Duvall was at Greenhaven when Bachman was there.

It still made no sense to her. Why would a psychiatrist work with a psychopath to kidnap her? To kill people? What was she missing?

Was Carter Duvall his partner?

Max shook her head to clear it, but that only made her head ache more. Duvall wasn't the person Bachman met at Fringe. Melinda's description couldn't have been more different. The partner was large, tattooed, only a little older than Bachman. Carter Duvall was in his late forties, Max's height, and skinny.

Maybe the guy at the bar wasn't his partner, just a friend. Maybe Max got it all wrong, and now she was going to die for being wrong.

There's two of them.

Cole. Duvall called the other guy in the room Cole. Did that mean there were three of them working together? Duvall, Cole, and Bachman? Could that even be possible?

Of course it's possible! You knew he had a partner, why not two?

Something crawled over her skin and she cried out. Was something on top of her? Or was this a reaction to the drugs? She thought they'd worked their way through her system, but what if she was hallucinating? What if her mind was making things up? Why would one of the doctors at Greenhaven be party to murder?

It makes sense, Maxine. Focus. Calm down.

She had to be alert enough to pay attention when her captor spoke again. Now she had a reference. If she was right, she'd know it as soon as he returned.

She prayed she survived long enough to tell the bastard to go to hell.

* * *

David sat up early Saturday morning and got his bearings. He'd fallen asleep on Max's living-room couch. He hadn't closed his eyes until nearly dawn. It was now 6:30 A.M.

David had shown Nick to a guest room, because Marco had taken over Max's bedroom. David wanted to tell Marco to use the other guest room, but he didn't want another argument. Marco always came into Max's life like a bull in a china shop. David had been around long enough to watch her work through several different men, but he didn't usually like—or dislike—any of them. Max once said he was the overprotective brother she never had, but that was far from the truth. Sometimes, David felt sorry for the guys who had fallen for Max. She didn't let people get close. That he understood. He had few friends and even fewer people he trusted. He hadn't left the Rangers on good terms, though he'd been honorably discharged. He'd thought he'd known people . . . but he hadn't. Not really.

Which is why he cared for Max. They had rough spots, but she was honest with him and with herself. But mostly, she gave him something he'd never had before.

Purpose.

Everything he'd done in his life was because of someone else. He'd slept with Brittany in high school because he wanted to prove to his football team buddies that he wasn't gay and could screw the hottest girl in the school. The only good that had come out of that volatile relationship was his daughter. He'd joined the army for his father, a patriotic veteran whom David admired and respected above all other men. He'd become a Ranger because his best friend joined the Rangers. He'd left the military to save his one long-term relationship, but it hadn't ended well— and then Chris had committed suicide and in his suicide note blamed David. He'd even started working for *Maximum Exposure* as a favor to a friend.

He'd been lost. Angry. Borderline depressed. He hated Chris for killing himself, for leaving David to clean up the mess. He hated himself that he hadn't seen the signs, hadn't been able to stop it from happening. And he hated himself for being less than he should have been, questioning everything he'd said and done, thinking he could have said and done something different. Until Max, he only saw the negative in humanity, rarely the good. The only good was his daughter, and Brittany didn't give him a minute of time with her over the court mandate. All the rage made him bitter.

David was still angry at times, but over the last two years he'd developed a peace that he hadn't had before. A focus and purpose that saved him. He'd made it his secret mission to give Max the one thing she didn't know she needed. Unconditional love.

He would find her. He would tell her.

Nick stepped into the room. He'd showered and changed, and wore his gun belt and badge, though he was far out of his jurisdiction. He didn't look like he'd slept any more than David. The shower upstairs went on and Nick glanced up, a hint of anger in his expression.

Nick was similar to Marco in career choice, but in most every other way different. Which was a good thing, as far as David was concerned.

"What's the plan?" Nick asked.

"Coffee," David said and got up. He walked into the kitchen and started a pot. "Sally O'Hara—the detective from Queens—is canvassing the area where we think our unsub might have been recently, and so far nothing. She's going back out today."

"Do you think that Dr. Ullman can get information from Bachman?"

"I don't know. Arthur is close to Max, I've only met him

a couple times. But whenever she's stuck on something, she calls him and he comes."

"And Lopez?"

David knew what Nick was getting at, but he didn't want to go down that path. He said, "Ignore him or he'll get under your skin. But he has clout in the bureau, he'll move mountains to find her."

"He's sleeping in her bed," Nick mumbled, but walked away before David could comment.

Marco came downstairs shortly, his black hair wet and curling at his collar. He was in a suit, sans jacket, and also had his gun. He was talking on the phone. He poured coffee as he spoke, then hung up. "Arthur," he said. "He worked with the assistant director in New York on the warrant to put Bachman into federal custody so we can take a crack at him. It's Saturday, but we have a federal judge on call who Arthur thinks will be amenable. All we can do is wait."

"I'm not waiting," David said.

"You have to leave this to me. It's been nearly thirty six hours. There've been no ransom demands. The driver is still missing. The car hasn't shown up. They're down a rabbit hole somewhere. This isn't about money."

"We knew that yesterday."

"We have to cross the t's and dot the i's, Kane. You've worked kidnappings before, haven't you? Right—you're not a cop."

Marco could get under his skin like no one else. But David refrained from comment. "We need an ID, Marco."

"You think I don't know that? I'm pushing everyone I can push."

"Have you found Anna Hudson?"

"No, but considering the FBI has been working on this for less than a full day, cut me some slack, Kane."

"I may not be a cop," David said slowly, carefully, "but

I know when something is personal. This is personal." Arthur had said it the night before; David had been turning it over in his head throughout the sleepless night.

"We don't know that." But Marco didn't look at him.

"You think so too."

"It can't be that personal if Max didn't recognize the guy who grabbed her."

"He could have been hired, but it is still personal."

"Personal how? I need evidence, Kane. Not speculation."

"Arthur agrees."

"Psychology is educated guesses, and even educated guesses can be wrong."

David's phone rang. He grabbed it. It was Ben. "What?"

"We found Anna Hudson. C. J. traced her. She's an elementary schoolteacher in Levittown, a suburb of Philadelphia. She changed her name to Anna Bristol, her mother's maiden name."

An hour and a half drive. "Tell C. J. good work."

"What are you doing?"

"I'm going to talk to her."

"Shouldn't you leave that to Marco?"

David glanced at Marco. Without breaking eye contact, he said to Ben, "He can join me if he wants. E-mail me the information, including a photo if you have it. I'm leaving in ten minutes."

He hung up. Marco said, "You can't—"

"Don't say it. You and Arthur handle Bachman, I'll take Santini with me to interview Ms. Hudson. Maybe one of us will have put a name to Max's kidnapper before noon."

Nick stepped back into the kitchen. "I'm ready."

"You're out of your jurisdiction," Marco told him.

Nick didn't say a word. He turned to David. "I'll meet you in the lobby," he said as he left.

David was beginning to like Nick even more.

* * *

Riley woke up feeling sick to her stomach. She tried to open her eyes, but couldn't.

She knew this feeling. She'd had these sensations before, when she popped too many pills.

But she'd been clean for eight years.

She tried to sit up, but her stomach rolled, and she almost puked. She was desperately thirsty and for the first time in a long time she wanted *something* to pick her up. Just one pill, to take off this edge.

No. No. No! What happened last night?

The last thing she remembered was leaving the records room. No . . . that wasn't right. She had left the room and went outside. She'd opened the door to her room. It was fuzzy. But she knew she'd returned to her room . . . and there was a man.

They were standing in the courthouse.

That's not right! You were in your room at Greenhaven. You admitted yourself so you could ID Bachman's partner. You got the files, returned to your room, and . . .

The man from the courthouse, the one she'd bumped into, was there. In her room at Greenhaven.

"Ms. Butler," a voice said. "You're awake."

She didn't recognize the voice. Or did she? It wasn't the counselor she'd met yesterday. Or Ms. Jackson.

It's the man from the courthouse. Why is he here?

"You have a serious problem. You came to the right place for help, but we can't help you if you aren't honest with us."

"I—what?"

"You brought drugs into Greenhaven. You nearly overdosed last night."

"No." But she wasn't sure she'd spoken out loud. She hadn't taken anything. Not voluntarily.

He'd said something to her in her room, but the image

was blurry, like opening her eyes under water. She couldn't remember his words. What did he say?

Her body told her she had taken a lot of pills. Or something. It was different, not what she'd been used to. It was worse that the oxy she'd been addicted to.

A sharp prick in her arm.

"Ouch! What? Wh-wh-wh?" Her tongue was thick.

"To help you with the withdrawals."

"No. Please. No."

She felt someone lean over her. Touch her face. She was hot, so hot, but she was shaking.

She felt another prick in her arm, then she couldn't speak.

The door opened, then closed.

Riley forced her eyes open, but she saw nothing. She was blind. That couldn't be right! But everything was white and out of focus. She wanted to throw up, but she couldn't force herself to puke. Her head was spinning.

She tried to scream for help, but no sound came out. The pain was fading away, along with everything else.

The noises were far away.

"She's crashing—call 911."

A voice—it was panicked.

"Riley? Ms. Butler, what did you take?"

Nothing! He drugged me!

But no words escaped her. She gagged.

"Riley, help is on its way. Doctor! Doctor, please help—Ms. Butler is a new guest, I think she smuggled in drugs. She's nonresponsive."

That voice was Ms. Jackson, and she sounded very concerned.

Nonresponsive . . . because she'd been drugged. The sounds were fading.

"An ambulance is on its way," someone else said. How

many people were in her room? Where was the man who drugged her? How long had she been here?

"Where are the drugs?"

"Here," someone said. "Two syringes on the floor. I don't know what was in them, but they're empty."

"Keep them for the medics. They need to save her. This can't be happening!"

It was happening.

Help me.

She cried, but no sound came out.

I don't want to die! He did something, he did this to me, stop him, don't touch, help me help me help me . . .

Her body convulsed and she heard voices, panicked voices, felt hands on her, holding her down.

God, I'm dying . . . I'm going to die . . . please, no.

No.

Chapter Twenty-three

Levittown was more than just a suburb—it had been built in the 1950s and every house looked like nearly every other house. It was a perfect place for a person to disappear—its population was mostly white, mostly middle income, mostly commuters.

Anna Hudson—Anna *Bristol*—lived in one of the identical houses, updated only by a fresh coat of pale yellow paint, colorful flowers in pots along the front walk, and two new trees in the front, planted a year or two ago. She spent a lot of time on her yard and it showed. An old Honda Civic in the driveway was in dire need of new tires.

It was nine in the morning when they arrived and kids were playing ball on the quiet street. David knocked on Anna's door, Nick standing beside him.

A security chain allowed Anna to open the door a mere two inches. She looked only marginally like the photo C. J. had found—she'd dyed her blond hair dark, and she'd lost weight she didn't need to lose, leaving her face gaunt and strained.

"Yes?" she asked, looking nervously from David to Nick.

She was skittish, fearful. David wished he'd thought to bring Riley with him—a female might make her more comfortable.

"I'm David Kane. We need your help."

"I don't know you."

She was about to close the door.

Nick showed his badge. "Detective Nick Santini. We're not here on official business, but this is a serious situation related to Adam Bachman."

Her voice was a mere squeak. "I don't know who you're talking about."

Nick said, "Your friend Janice Brody said you quit Greenhaven and disappeared because of Adam Bachman, and now we believe he's responsible for kidnapping a woman."

"He's in jail. Oh, God, did they let him out?"

"No. He's still behind bars, but we are desperate for information and need your help. Please."

Nick had a calm, soothing, commanding voice. His "please" wasn't a request, it was a polite demand. Anna's lip trembled.

"I don't want to move again."

"No one will know you talked to us. This isn't official."

She closed the door and they heard the chain slide, then she opened it again and let them in. Her living room was sparse and clean, but her dining-room table was covered with paper. "I teach second grade," she said with the first smile David had seen. "I'm cleaning out my files from last year, to start the new school year fresh."

Her smile wavered. "How did you find me?"

"I'm head of security for NET programming," David said. "We have a good research staff. Bristol is your mother's maiden name."

"I probably overreacted, but—it's—I was so scared back then."

Nick leaned forward and said, "It's good to trust your instincts, Ms. Bristol. We have a picture for you to look at. We're hoping you can identify this person."

"I thought this was about Adam?"

"It is," Nick said.

"Did he really kill all those people?" Her voice was growing smaller, more fearful.

"Yes," Nick said.

"I—I knew."

"You suspected him of murder? When he was at Greenhaven?"

"No—but—there was something off about him, and it just got worse the longer he was there. I can't really explain it, just . . . he came in for one thing, but his treatment was completely different from the others. I asked questions and no one would tell me why. I was a counselor, trying to help, just doing my job. And he wasn't one of my patients, so I forgot until one of the counselors quit and then he was assigned to me. That first session . . . he looked at me . . . and something was wrong. He'd always been quiet, clean, obsessively neat, and polite. But he'd been watching me, he told me he saw that I loved flowers, that I cared for them in the garden. I thought maybe this was a breakthrough for him, because he'd never have put his hands in the dirt when he first came. I asked if he wanted to help prune the roses. He shook his head, said he didn't want to touch them. And he said, and I'll never forget it, " 'What do you feel when your flowers die?' "

She visibly shuddered.

"It wasn't what he said as much as how he said it. And it freaked me out."

"And you quit?" Nick prompted.

"Not then—I told Janice I was upset about a patient, but that was all. We're not supposed to talk about the patients, and Janice wasn't a counselor. But the next day . . ." Her voice trailed off and she looked at her tightly clasped fingers.

"Janice said you left in the middle of the day," David prompted.

"Adam was watching me and I was so upset that I ran to my office. Not an office, really, we all had semiprivate cubicles. I was writing up a report and Adam walked in and handed me a bouquet of roses."

"And that made you feel uncomfortable," David said.

"Yes. Because they were my roses, from my bushes, and they were all dead."

David took the picture of Max's kidnapper from a folder. "We believe that this person was at Greenhaven and may have known Adam. Do you recognize him?"

He turned the picture so she could see it.

"Cole Baker," she said immediately. "He was at Greenhaven for anger management issues. He should have been in prison. He was seventeen when he hit his mother. His mother didn't want to press charges, but his dad insisted he get help, and Nanette Jackson, our director, agreed. Cole was the type of guy you avoided. If he looked at you, you looked away."

"Was he there the same time as Adam?"

She nodded. "He might still be there. He began working at Greenhaven after his treatment. Maintenance. I saw him all the time because I used to care for the roses. He trimmed hedges and mowed the lawn and fixed things. He was actually very handy. But everyone was a little scared of him."

"Who was his doctor?"

"Same as Adam Bachman. Dr. Duvall."

Marco Lopez had to admit that Dr. Ullman, even retired, had more power than most of the active FBI agents he knew. Dr. Ullman had put in thirty years, helped grow the

Behavioral Sciences Unit, and even though he'd retired ten years ago, he was still called to consult several times a year. Marco had helped secure the warrant to allow Dr. Ullman to conduct a psychiatric assessment of Adam Bachman. But before calling Milligan, Marco called Bachman's lawyer as a courtesy. The counselor didn't answer and Marco left a message.

"His client is waiting for a verdict and he's unavailable?" Marco muttered.

"The calm before the storm," Ullman said. "Max believes he took the case for the ancillary benefits."

"What defense lawyer doesn't?" Marco said.

"There are a few who are reputable."

"You're being sarcastic."

"You're being judgmental, Marco. The system works more than it fails."

Marco had his faults, but he was a decorated FBI agent who closed cases and put bad guys away. That satisfied him completely.

He frowned. Not *completely*. He missed Max. He loved her with a passion that she'd never understood. And he knew she loved him back, though she'd never said it. He'd often wondered if she would even recognize the emotion, because they were combustible together.

Thinking of her hurt—or worse—made him see red. When they'd been together, he'd done everything he could to protect her, but she always crossed the line. She always risked herself. He wanted her safe, and that damn bodyguard was supposed to protect her. How had she slipped away? How had someone gotten close enough to take her?

Was she even alive?

"Marco?" Arthur said quietly. "Are you going to call the D.A.?"

"Yeah. Sorry." He punched in the numbers to Milligan's private cell phone.

"We're all worried."

"I know," he said brusquely. Milligan answered and Marco said, "Counselor, this is Marco Lopez. I have a federal warrant requiring you to grant Dr. Arthur Ullman access to Adam Bachman immediately. We're on our way to Manhattan Detention now, but I can hold off if you'd like to observe. As a courtesy," he added.

"I'm sorry, Agent Lopez, but that won't be possible."

Marco mentally swore. "I have a warrant. You can't stop this interview."

"You'll need more than a warrant, Lopez. You'll need a psychic. Adam Bachman killed himself last night. He's at the morgue."

"Answer it," David said. "Put him on speaker."

Nick glanced down at David's phone. Marco Lopez. He answered the call and pressed speaker. "Santini."

"Where's Kane?"

"Driving. You're on speaker."

"Bachman is dead. He killed himself. Where are you?"

"On our way to Greenhaven."

"Turn around—"

David interrupted. "Like hell I will."

"Dammit, David! I told you to let me handle it!"

"I told you what Ms. Hudson said to keep you in the loop."

"This is a federal investigation—"

"Hang up, Santini," David said.

Nick's finger hovered above the off button.

"Don't!" Marco screamed. "Shit, David."

"Are you certain Bachman committed suicide?"

"They haven't done the autopsy, but initial findings are fairly conclusive. Dr. Ullman and I are on our way to see his attorney. David, please turn around and come back to New York."

Nick asked, "Have you located Maxine?"

"No, but—"

"Then no," Nick said, catching David's eye. He nodded. "We sent you the name and last known address of the individual who kidnapped her, and we're following up on this end. We're nearly there. Time is against us here. I've been a cop for a long time, Agent Lopez."

Marco didn't say anything for a minute, and Nick thought he'd hung up on him. Then he said, "Just keep me in the loop, Santini."

"Scout's honor." He hung up.

"Marco's competent, but he likes being in control," David said.

"It's amazing he and Maxine didn't kill each other."

David smirked. "Luck. But that's in the past."

"Is it?"

David glanced at him. "Yes."

Nick wasn't so sure. At least on Marco's end. Nick was good at reading people—most cops were.

He'd had his share of failed relationships, including a bad marriage. He didn't always know why they failed, whether it was him or the woman or a combination of both. He hadn't planned on getting involved with Max, the weekend they spent in bed together notwithstanding. But he couldn't get her out of his head. He enjoyed their Skype calls. When she had flown out to California spontaneously two weeks ago, he thought she was insane. A cross-country flight for one night with him?

He'd also felt pampered and happy. And happiness had been eluding him lately.

David said, "Max met Marco when she was twenty-two and her college roommate disappeared."

"I read her book. After I met her, I was curious."

"So you know what she went through down in Miami. If you think that Marco is a threat to you, he's not."

"I know."

"Sounds like you're worried."

"I'm not worried about anything except Max's life right now." He paused. "And I know Max well enough to know that she's the only threat to any relationship she has."

After a long pause David said, "You already know Max well."

David's phone rang again. Nick said, "Caller ID reads Sally O'Hara."

"Speaker."

David turned off the highway and headed toward Greenhaven. He said, "Sally, you're on speaker with me and Nick Santini. Find something?"

"No one has recognized Baker from the photo, but now that we have an ID, I put out an APB."

"What?" David exclaimed. "I thought we agreed to keep this as quiet as possible."

Sally paused. "The FBI wanted it."

"Marco. Damn him."

"David, I understand what you're thinking, but the feds handle cases like this all the time."

"And if this bastard knows we're on to him, he could easily kill Max and disappear."

Nick agreed with Marco on this one—the more people looking for Max and her kidnapper, the better. But he didn't comment.

"Marco didn't release the information that Max is missing," Sally said. "The APB is for a material witness, he's keeping the rest close to the vest."

"Anything else?"

"I have a preliminary report on the Palazzolos' murders. I told Marco, because I thought it might help Dr. Ullman with Bachman, but I guess you heard that he killed himself."

"We did."

"We don't have much because of the condition of the bodies, but cause of death for the female was strangulation. Her hyoid bone was broken, and the M.E. is certain of the cause of death."

"I thought the bones were melted or destroyed."

"Only below the shoulders. The male victim is preliminary—he had a severe blow to the head, but the M.E. said it wouldn't have killed him. They don't believe he was strangled, but that's all I know now."

"Thanks, Sally."

They hung up and David pointed to a vast expanse of lawn on his left. "Greenhaven. We made good time."

Nick said, "You going to be okay in there?"

He glanced at him. "I'm good. Let's do this. You play the cop."

Nick raised an eyebrow. "Play?"

"Figure of speech."

They parked in the visitor lot and walked up the grand stairs to the main doors. Inside, it was cool and quiet. Nick showed his badge to the receptionist and said, "We need to speak with Dr. Duvall."

"I'm sorry, he's not in this afternoon. I'll get our director for you." She practically ran, doe-eyed, from her desk.

Nick said to David, "I'm going to push on the employment records. Those will be easier to obtain than medical."

"We still need to talk to Duvall."

"Agreed."

Nanette Jackson was an attractive, nervous woman. She seemed surprised that a cop was standing in the lobby. "What may I help you with?"

Nick showed her the photo of Cole Baker. "We're looking for this man, Cole Baker. We have information that he's an employee of yours."

She looked momentarily confused. "No, no—I mean,

he was, but he hasn't been working here for over a year. He worked in maintenance."

"I need your last known address for him."

She hesitated. "I don't know if I can give that information out."

"He's wanted for felony kidnapping and is a suspect in a murder investigation," Nick said, his voice low and steady. "I can and will get a warrant, but if the delay causes the death of another person, I will make sure the media knows exactly who caused the delay."

She caved. Nick saw what Max must have seen—an inner weakness that Max had exploited to gain information.

Employment records were not sacrosanct. Businesses could hide behind privacy laws, but in a criminal investigation those laws were much grayer. And she knew that a warrant was inevitable.

"I didn't know him well," she said quickly as she led the way to her office. "He worked directly under our building and maintenance supervisor."

"We'll want to talk to him as well," Nick said.

"He doesn't work weekends. I'll give you his name and number."

She was flustered, but had begun to recover. She unlocked a file cabinet and pulled out a folder. Checked it, then handed it to Nick. "Is that what you need?"

Nick looked at the information. Baker had been hired nine years ago, and left employment nearly two years ago, in July. "Was he fired?"

"No. He gave notice and left."

"Forwarding address?"

"If he left one, it would be in the file."

It wasn't. But there was other information—parents, emergency contacts, social security number, previous addresses.

He handed it back to her. "Please make me a copy."

"Of course." She left the room.

"What do you think?" Nick asked David.

"She's worried about what he did and whether it'll bite Greenhaven in the ass."

"Now we're going to push."

"I thought you did pretty good getting that info without much effort."

"We don't have what we need yet."

Jackson came back and handed Nick a copy of the file. "Thank you," he said. "One other thing, we'll be getting a warrant for Mr. Baker's medical file as well."

"What? I—what do you mean?"

"He was a patient here prior to his employment."

"I can't discuss our patients."

"You don't have to. We know he was."

"How do you know? We have a strict privacy policy. Our guests insist that—"

Nick didn't answer her question. "We also know that Adam Bachman was a patient here, and that he and Mr. Baker associated together."

"I can't—" She stopped, mouth open. She wasn't a dumb woman, she made the connection immediately. He *had* said that Baker was a suspect in a murder investigation, and she must know about the Bachman trial. "I—you're not suggesting that Cole knew something about those murders?"

Nick didn't comment. "Please get his file ready, the FBI is in the process of getting a warrant, and the faster you comply, the faster we resolve this issue."

David said, "We need to speak with Doctor Carter Duvall. He was the psychiatrist for both Mr. Bachman and Mr. Baker."

"I—" She was going to stall, then she said, "I can give you his cell phone number. I can't discuss who might have been a patient of his. But he won't talk about his patients. He could be sued, lose his license—you understand."

"Yes, we do." David handed her his business card. "Send me all his contact information."

Jackson stared at the card. Confusion twisted her face. "You work for *Maximum Exposure*?"

"Yes."

"And you're here about Mr. Baker? I don't understand . . ." Her voice trailed off, then she shook her head and said, "I've been trying to reach Ms. Revere all morning, but she hasn't returned my calls."

"Why?" David asked.

"Her assistant. Riley Butler. She's in the hospital."

David didn't say anything, so Nick picked up the silence. "How do you know this?"

"It's, oh goodness, I don't think I should say—we take privacy issues very seriously."

"Privacy?" David snapped.

"Well—Riley did sign a waiver agreeing to keep Ms. Revere informed of her progress. For employment purposes."

"Start at the beginning," David said through clenched teeth.

"Were you aware that Ms. Revere and Ms. Butler were here Wednesday to tour the facility?"

"Yes," David said, but Nick was pretty certain this was the first David had heard about Max's excuse for visiting.

"Ms. Butler checked in yesterday. She has a history of addiction, and the stress of her job was creating problems. And though we search our clients, she managed to sneak in drugs. She overdosed last night and her counselor found her this morning in her room. We immediately called 911. I can give you the hospital she's at."

"Please," Nick said.

They followed Jackson back to the foyer. David left the building without comment while Nick waited for Jackson to retrieve the information. He wondered what he was getting himself into. Had Max sent a young intern into a dangerous situation without backup? What had she been thinking? He knew she was reckless with her own life, but reckless with the lives of others?

Ms. Jackson returned and handed Nick the information. "Here's the hospital, and Doctor Duvall's cell phone. I'll make sure he knows that you're looking for him."

"Thank you."

Nick walked out, expecting to see David on the porch. He wasn't. He'd brought around the car to the main doors and barely waited for Nick to get in before he sped off.

Nick said, "Did Max send that kid here? Does Riley really have an addiction or was that a lie to get her inside?"

"Max wouldn't have done it. Not like this."

"She takes risks, David. We both know that."

"I called Ben. He said Riley went completely off the grid yesterday afternoon, and he tracked down a friend of hers who isn't talking. I have his name. He'll damn well talk to me."

"Let's go to the hospital first," Nick said. "We need to talk to this girl, find out why she was here. Did she really have a drug problem? Or was that a cover?"

"I don't know. I did the background on her. She's had a clean record at least since she turned eighteen. Her dad's a cop. Her mom's a doctor. I'm going to have to call them."

"First, let's see what she knows." Nick had given parents bad news before. He preferred to have all the facts before they called the Butlers.

Chapter Twenty-four

"I can take you back to FBI headquarters," Marco said to Arthur Ullman as they left the morgue. They'd confirmed that it was indeed Adam Bachman who'd killed himself. He'd made a shiv out of a toothbrush and slit his wrists. He was found unconscious and died en route to the hospital. The M.E. said it was clear that the wounds were self-inflicted.

"I'd like to talk to Bachman's attorney as well," Arthur said. "Did the D.A. give you the visitor logs?"

"No one has been to see him since I talked to him yesterday," Marco said. "The last time he saw his lawyer was Thursday after court recessed."

"And the only time Maxine spoke to him was on Monday?"

"Yes. There have been no other visitors. Max, his lawyer, David, and myself."

"From my limited view of the information, he doesn't seem to be suicidal. I listened to Max's recording of the interview."

"She recorded the interview? Why didn't I know?"

"When we're done with the lawyer, you can listen, but she wrote the key points on her wall."

Marco frowned. "He said something odd yesterday, but I thought he'd been threatened."

"What did he say?"

"I suggested that if he cooperated and helped us identify and locate his partner, that I could get him into a federal prison. He said he'd be dead. I offered protection, asked who'd threatened him. He didn't answer."

Arthur didn't say anything and Marco squirmed. "Did I miss it? Was it that obvious?"

"I honestly don't know. I wasn't there."

"He looked like death warmed over."

"Was your interview with Bachman recorded?"

"By the D.A."

"We should listen, see if there's something he said that could have a dual meaning. Another set of ears."

Arthur was the expert. Marco was certain he'd missed something, and that comment about how nothing he could offer would matter because he'd be dead? That definitely took on a whole new meaning now that Bachman *was* dead.

"Let's hope his lawyer will be forthcoming."

They'd already checked out the lawyer's small office near the courthouse and he wasn't there, so they drove to his apartment on the Upper East Side where Gregory Warren had lived in the same small, ground-floor apartment for ten years.

Marco parked illegally and placed an OFFICIAL FBI BUSINESS placard on his dashboard. They got out and Marco surveyed the building. The apartment was below street level, down six stairs to a small patio in a five-story building. Every house on the street looked the same. All apartments, all brick and stone, trees growing out of holes in the sidewalk. Marco had never understood what ap-

pealed to Max about New York. Miami was a big city, but
it had beaches and sun and space. He needed the space.
New York made him claustrophobic.

Marco knocked on the door. "Mr. Warren, it's Marco
Lopez with the Federal Bureau of Investigation. We need
to talk." A little dog barked at them from inside.

Marco had misstepped with Max. Misstep was an understatement. He'd fucked up their relationship, but she had a
big part in that, too. She'd never admit when she was wrong
because she never *believed* she was wrong. She justified
everything she did as if exposing the truth was a noble goal
and could wash away any sin she committed. She never
thought about the repercussions, to herself or to others.
While he admired her determination and tenacity, he
wished she would just *listen* to him. Sometimes, the truth
should be shelved for the greater good. She never understood that, and he didn't know how to explain it to her.

But dammit, he loved her. She made him crazy, but
whenever they left things unsettled or—like last month—
over, he felt the void. She didn't just have a passion for the
truth. She had passion for everything in life. Good food.
Good fun. Sex—dear God, he missed having her in his
bed. For all the craziness she'd brought into his life, that
was the one area where they always did exceptionally well.

The new guy, Nick Santini, didn't know Max, and he
couldn't possibly understand her. He'd known Max for a
few weeks; Marco had known her for ten years. And when
he found Max—and he would—Marco would make sure
she understood that they were not over, that the Garbena
fiasco six weeks ago was just one more road bump, but
they would fix it, like they'd fixed all their other problems
over the last decade.

"He's not here," Arthur said. The dog still yapped fran-
tically.

"Where the hell is he?" Marco asked. "He wasn't at his

office, he's not answering his phone." He flipped through his notes and found the phone number of Warren's office manager. A moment later, Ms. Walsh came on the line.

"This is Special Agent Marco Lopez. We spoke yesterday when I left a message for Mr. Warren."

"Yes, Agent Lopez, how may I help you?"

"I still need to speak to him."

"I gave you his cell phone number. He always answers."

"He's not answering, he's not at the office, and he's not at his apartment."

"He must be there."

"Could he have left town? Who watches his dog?"

"Biscuit? No one—he doesn't leave town except to visit his brother in Virginia, and he'd take Biscuit with him."

"Biscuit is barking up a storm."

"Oh, dear. I haven't spoken with him. He left Thursday and said he was going to work from home while waiting for the verdict."

"Do you have a key to his apartment?"

"Yes."

"Can you get over here?"

"Twenty minutes." She hung up.

The woman sounded worried.

The dog continued to bark.

Arthur said, "Something is definitely wrong."

Marco put on gloves and tried the door. It was locked. "Does this place have an alley? A back way in?"

"Likely."

"You good to wait here while I check the back?"

Arthur nodded. While he had been an FBI agent for thirty years, Arthur was retired and Marco didn't want to put him in harm's way.

Marco had to walk half a block, then down another half block, until he found an alley lined with Dumpsters that was barely wide enough for a car. He counted the buildings and stood behind Warren's. No parking. Balconies off the upper three floors. Downstairs there was a tiny dirt yard—two doors led to it, one from below and one a few steps up. Both had screen doors with bars.

Again, how could people live like this?

He knocked on the lower door, the one that was Warren's. Tried the doorknob. It was unlocked.

He had probable cause. Unlocked door, frantic dog, no one had spoken to Warren since Thursday afternoon.

He unholstered his gun and opened the door.

The smell of death hit him. The little dog, Biscuit, ran out into the small yard and immediately started peeing. It was a Maltese or some other kind of small white fluffy dog, only this one had dark tipped hair.

It's blood.

Marco called out, "FBI! I'm coming in!"

But there was no one alive inside.

In the kitchen, Gregory Warren was sprawled facedown on the linoleum, the handle of a butcher knife protruding from his back. He wore sweatpants and a T-shirt that was now drenched in his blood. The blood beneath him was dry, but at some point the dog had walked through it, tracking little bloody paw prints through the house.

By the look and smell, he'd been dead for at least twenty-four hours.

Marco quickly checked the entire apartment—kitchen, living room, bedroom, bath, and a den smaller than Marco's closet. Clear. He opened the front door and told Arthur, "He's been dead for a while. Stabbed in the back. He didn't see it coming."

Max was alone.

She couldn't possibly still be in New York—it was too quiet.

She loved the sounds of the city. Her penthouse was ten

floors up in TriBeCa, and even that high up she could hear the steady hum of traffic, the low noise of people, machines, planes, and *life*.

But now she was underground, she could hear water or sewage flowing through pipes. Civilization was somewhere nearby, just not close enough to hear her if she screamed.

She wanted to go home. She wanted to see David. To shower for an hour under blistering hot water. To sleep in her bed with her mound of pillows. To eat at her favorite restaurant. To drink a gallon of water.

The smells in this room had grown worse, and she knew the stench came from her. How long had she been here? It seemed so important, but she didn't know. Time now had no meaning. Had it been a day, or a week? She was in and out, in and out. Humiliated and angry; what must she say for them to let her go?

Nothing, Max. They're going to play their games and then kill you.

She'd been soundly humiliated. If that's what they wanted, they'd achieved it.

She'd been humiliated before.

Max had been sixteen when she decided to confront her father.

Three events led up to her decision.

First, her mother didn't send her a birthday card on her sixteenth birthday. She'd forgotten, obviously. Martha had left her on her grandparents' doorstep one Thanksgiving. Stayed for dinner, was gone the next morning. But she'd always sent a birthday card in time for Max's New Year's Eve birthday.

Not this time.

Second, she'd had a major battle with her uncle, Brooks, who was having an affair. Max found out about it and made sure everyone knew. He was a liar and a cheat. Max learned the hard way that sometimes people wanted to believe lies—Aunt Joanne had known Uncle Brooks was a cad, but preferred blind ignorance than walking away. Max's announcement had started a chain of events that had hurt people she never intended to hurt. Everyone blamed her, and maybe she was partly to blame. But she wasn't the one having an affair and she didn't regret exposing her uncle.

And third, curiosity. Max had read an article about Victor Tracy in The Wall Street Journal *and was intrigued. He'd been under investigation by the FBI for insider trading . . . but had been cleared. The article was fascinating because it was clear that the government believed they had a case, but they couldn't prove it. It had been considered an embarrassment for the government and a victory for Tracy.*

She'd been following Victor Tracy and his career for eight years, ever since her mother told her he was her father.

Her best friend Lindy drove her to the airport. Max and Lindy had ups and downs in their friendship, but Lindy was the only person Max trusted with her plans. Lindy liked keeping secrets.

Lindy wanted to come with her to New York, but Max insisted she do this alone. Besides, she needed Lindy to cover for her with her grandmother if necessary.

"What if he doesn't know?" Lindy said. "You should call him first."

Max thought about that, but said, "Something like this, I need to do it in person."

Max didn't think Victor Tracy knew about her. Typical Martha Revere, always withholding information. She didn't even tell Max about her father until Max was eight and had asked—repeatedly.

"Victor is charming and handsome and fun. That's

*where you get your red hair, from his family. But Victor
is a black sheep, Maxie. He's always being investigated
for something, getting in trouble with the police. You can't
trust him. I don't want you associating with him."*

At eight, Max was scared of her father. But she was also
curious, and as time passed, she realized that Martha
exaggerated about everything. When Max was little, she
never called them lies, but now, at sixteen, she didn't know
what to believe about Victor Tracy because she'd finally
realized that her mother was a pathological liar.

She flew first class, because that was what she was used
to. She was already five feet ten inches and most people
who met her when she was sixteen assumed she was in college. She had the maturity, height, and poise to pass for
older. Partly because her grandmother insisted on the maturity and poise; partly because Max had grown up fast
with a wild mother.

She read all the articles she'd printed about her father
multiple times, but a few facts stood out.

The first was that he'd been married to the same woman
for twenty-two years. That meant that he'd been married
when he slept with her mom. It saddened Max, because it
wasn't fair to his wife, but it didn't surprise her. After all,
Uncle Brooks had done the same thing.

He was successful, having founded multiple businesses
and selling them for a profit. Max wasn't as interested in
business as her family, but she understood what a venture
capitalist was and how it could yield huge windfalls.

She didn't understand the nuances of alleged insider
trading, or how her father kept getting off. But she decided that she didn't care. She wanted to know more
about the man who'd made her than she cared if he was
a criminal.

She took a taxi to his Murray Hill town house in Manhattan. It was a beautiful four-story midtown brownstone with tree-lined streets and flower boxes in all the windows. April was beautiful this year, and all the trees were in bloom.

Max had always prided herself for being courageous, but she'd found it easier to stand up for others than to stand up for herself. Finding Victor Tracy's home address, flying cross-country without telling her grandmother, telling him she was his daughter . . . these had all been difficult.

But she did it. And she wasn't going to back down now.

She had the taxi leave her at the end of the block and she walked slowly up the street to build courage. Every step was both excruciating but exciting. She'd been looking forward to meeting her father even before she knew his name. She'd even kept a small picture, cut from a financial magazine, in her jewelry box. She planned on making it clear that she didn't want anything from him— not money, not even a place to live. She just wanted to know him.

It was Saturday, and she knew he came home from golf between three and four. She knew this because she'd called his secretary the day before to check his schedule, pretending to be a temporary secretary of one of his golf mates. It had been surprisingly easy to obtain the information. They played from nine until noon, ate at the club, and he had no other plans for the afternoon. So she'd arranged for the niece of one of his partners to meet Victor Tracy for an internship interview as a favor.

It was four thirty. She rang the bell before she ran away.

Victor answered the door.

"Maxine? John's niece?"

"Actually, I lied. I'm Maxine Revere. Martha Revere's daughter. Your daughter."

He stared at her for a long minute. "What does Martha want now?"

Max hadn't been expecting that response. She didn't know what she'd been expecting. Her knees buckled, but she held on to the railing. "I haven't seen her in six years. But before she left, she told me you were my father. I don't want anything, I just want to get to know you."

"I'm not your father."

How could he lie about something like this? "Yes, you are." Her voice cracked.

He stepped out and closed the door behind him. He was very tall, and he did have red hair—but it was more strawberry blond than the dark mahogany she had. She didn't see any resemblance, but that didn't mean anything. Lindy didn't look anything like her father.

"What do you want?" His voice was low and borderline mean. He was trying to intimidate her and he was succeeding.

"Nothing. I don't need anything from you. I just wanted to meet you." Her voice quivered and her eyes burned. She would not *cry.*

He softened, just a bit. "Look, kid, I feel sorry for you. I knew Martha, but I can promise you I'm not your father. She was already pregnant when we were together. But I'm married, and I was married then, and my wife is fragile. I'm not going to let you create a scandal when I just got out of one."

"I don't want to—" she began, but he cut her off.

"You should know one thing about your mother. You can't believe a word that comes out of her mouth. Now go. And honestly, if you come here again, I'll have you arrested."

That had been one of the worst days of her life. She'd flown back home that night, two cross-country trips in one day, feeling small and worthless. It had been later, when she was more angry than humiliated, that she'd pushed for the paternity test. He'd reluctantly agreed.

It had been negative.

He wasn't the one who had lied to her; it was her mother who had lied.

Chapter Twenty-five

David and Nick listened to the doctor explain that Riley had nearly died from her overdose, and to stabilize her they had to induce a coma. She'd listed on her Greenhaven forms to contact Maxine Revere in case of an emergency, but no one had been able to reach Ms. Revere.

"I can't tell you anything else, unless you're family," the doctor said.

"I'll call her father," David said. "Are you positive she OD'd?"

"Blood test came back positive. It's a designer drug, but we've seen it before. Extremely dangerous, especially when injected like Ms. Butler did. Greenhaven called the paramedics immediately upon finding her this morning. Probably saved her life. We'll know more in a day or two. Excuse me." He walked away.

David turned to Nick. "This isn't what it seems. There's something else going on. We need her things."

"Let me talk to the nurse," Nick said. "I may be out of my jurisdiction, but they're usually helpful with cops."

Nick walked away, and David stood outside Riley's room. He considered what he knew. Why would Riley admit herself into a rehab facility—obviously as some sort of farce to gain information—and then inject herself with drugs?

David dialed Riley's father, even though he dreaded the call. He spoke officially, hiding his anger. It was more than anger at Riley—he was upset. Max was missing and now Riley was in a coma. Had Max condoned this? Had she hinted to Riley that it was a good idea to go undercover?

Max went missing Thursday night. She didn't know what Riley had planned.

Riley was in the meeting Friday morning. She knew Max had been kidnapped, and she went off without telling anyone. Did she remember something important about Greenhaven? Why hadn't she told David?

She told someone. A friend—Ben knows who it is.

"My wife and I will be down there in a few hours," Lieutenant Butler said after David told him the facts as he knew them. "Mr. Kane, what the hell happened?"

"I don't know, sir, but I will find out."

"Riley had trouble with drugs when she was fifteen, but she hasn't used since. And I'm not blind to it just because she's my daughter. I can promise you she's not using again. And she popped pills. She's never used needles."

"I believe you, sir," David said, though he didn't know what to believe at this point. But he couldn't discount the information about Riley's preferred drug choice. Kids who popped pills or smoked pot didn't suddenly start shooting themselves up with heroin or whatever Riley had in her system. "I don't know what happened, but I suspect she was following through on a lead and got in over her head."

Silence. "That," Lieutenant Butler said quietly, "is something I do believe. My daughter has always been un-usually curious. Anything you need, Mr. Kane, let me know."

"You should know that Maxine Revere has been kidnapped. We haven't released the information to the press, but the FBI is working with us on recovering her."

"Is that what my daughter was doing? Looking for her?"

"I don't know what she was doing at Greenhaven. Not specifically, but I will move heaven and earth to find out who did this to her."

"You believe this wasn't a drug overdose." It was a statement, not a question.

"It was, but I don't believe that it was a voluntary overdose. She has a friend who she confided in, and I'm heading back to New York to interrogate him now. But until we know what's going on, I'm going to put a guard on her room."

"Thank you, Mr. Kane. I'll be down there as soon as possible."

David hung up and then called his former employer, a private security company, and hired a bodyguard for Riley. He informed the hospital that no one except hospital personnel was allowed in Riley Butler's room until her father arrived. David waited until the bodyguard showed up, instructed him, and called Nick to tell him he was leaving for New York. They met up at the car.

Nick said, "I have the name of Riley's friend, the one who covered for her with Ben Lawson. Kyle Callahan."

"Don't know him."

"He's a Columbia grad student and when he found out that Riley was in the hospital, he spilled everything to Ben and Marco. Marco has him in the NET offices."

"Let's go." David drove fast out of the parking lot.

"And one more thing. Bachman's lawyer was murdered in his apartment. Early forensics believe it happened late Thursday night or early Friday morning."

Around the same time that Max disappeared.

* * *

It was after five that afternoon by the time David and Nick arrived back at the NET offices and walked into the middle of what sounded like an interrogation. Marco was angry and Kyle, the young grad student, looked terrified.

"I want to help," Kyle said, "I really do. But I don't know what I can tell you. I told you everything I know."

Marco slapped his hand on the table. "You have to know what Riley was looking for! You gave her a computer, knew she was going to commit herself into rehab."

"I only knew that she wanted to look at records."

"So you aided and abetted in a felony?"

"No!" Wide-eyed, he looked from Marco to David, then back to the fed. "Do I need a lawyer?"

"I haven't read you your rights," Marco snapped. "But if you want to play it that way, I'm more than happy to."

David crossed the room and sat next to Marco. "I'm David Kane," he told Kyle.

"I know."

David raised an eyebrow.

Kyle shifted uneasily in his seat. "Riley mentioned you a few times. Is she okay?"

"She's in a medically induced coma because of a drug overdose."

"Drugs? No. No way. She doesn't use. I swear to God, she doesn't. She got in deep years ago, but she doesn't use anymore. Her best friend got wasted and nearly died. It woke her up, and, well, she just wouldn't."

"I believe you," David said. "Was Riley at Greenhaven because Max sent her to go in undercover? I promise you, nothing you say is going to get Riley in trouble, if that's what you're worried about."

Kyle glanced at Marco.

"Marco," David said sharply, getting his attention. "Give him what he needs."

Reluctantly, Marco said, "You have five minutes of

immunity if you spill everything now. But if you lie to us, all bets are off."

Kyle spoke rapidly, as if he believed Marco would hold him to the five-minute time limit. "Riley came to me Monday and I helped her find Greenhaven. She told her boss, Ms. Revere, about it and Riley wanted to follow up, you know, prove she was good. And Ms. Revere wanted to go with her. So they did. I don't know what they found, Riley wouldn't tell me anything, but she was upset that Ms. Revere didn't let her go undercover. There was another case, she said, down in Florida where someone went undercover at an old folks' place, and Riley had read that book a dozen times. I don't know the details, but Riley wanted to do the same thing. But Ms. Revere said no, they didn't have time to set it up. But when she disappeared Thursday night, Riley wanted to go in for the weekend and dig up all the information she could that might help find her. She kept saying that Max knew there was a connection to Greenhaven and couldn't prove it, but Riley would. She wanted so badly to prove herself. Please don't fire her—"

"Stop. We're beyond that. What did she plan to do?"

"I don't know! I swear! I gave her a decoder—"

"Decoder?" Marco interrupted.

"A small laptop that you plug into a USB port and it decodes any passwords. I, um, am still in my five minutes, right?"

"Yes," David said. He turned to Marco. "I checked with the hospital. Nothing was found in her personal effects. She had a cell phone, but it was a burner phone, not her work phone. No computer or decoder or anything."

Kyle piped up. "She did. I swear."

Marco asked, "Do you have a way to track it?"

"If it's on."

"Anything else? Anything at all?" David said.

"That's it. That's all I know."

"Mr. Callahan," Marco said, "you're very lucky this time. Next time—you won't be."

"I'm so sorry. Can I—can I go and see Riley? Please?"

"First, give us everything we need to track that laptop. And I want all your contact numbers. If Mr. Kane or I call, you pick up, got it?"

"Yes, sir. Absolutely, sir."

David sent Kyle off with Pete, the head of the IT department. Once he was alone in the room with Ben, Marco, and Nick, he said, "Who at Greenhaven knew what Riley was up to?"

Nick said, "Nanette Jackson seemed sincerely concerned about Riley. Could she have drugged her, called 911, and then faked her reaction?"

"Possible," David said. "She knew who Riley was and that Max had shown an interest in Greenhaven. Maybe she picked up on the game Max was playing."

"That would mean she thought Riley knew something or could learn something that would damage Greenhaven or Jackson personally," Marco said. "It seems a stretch."

"That's the thing," Nick said, "she's concerned about the reputation of Greenhaven and the privacy of its patients. She didn't confirm that Bachman or Baker had been patients there. But would she attempt to murder someone in order to keep that secret? Because it's not a big secret—staff knows, other residents, and we should have a warrant any minute for their records."

"It does seem far-fetched," Marco agreed.

Ben paced behind David. "I should have seen this coming," he said. "Riley has been going above and beyond since she got here. Trying to prove herself."

"Ben, it's not your fault. It's no one's fault," Marco said.

David didn't agree. It was Riley's decision to go off on her own. It didn't mean she deserved to be attacked, but it meant she wasn't ready for this kind of work. But he didn't say anything, because he also blamed himself. He'd seen it coming. He'd had Riley pegged from the beginning. She would do anything to prove her worth to Max. She was practically obsessed with her boss. David should have pushed harder with Max, harder with Riley, limited the girl and what she was allowed to do. Especially after the meeting yesterday, but David had been so focused on figuring out what happened to Max that he hadn't considered what Riley might do on her own.

Nick slid over to Marco the employment records on Baker that they'd received from Jackson. "Nothing in here jumps out at me, but his parents and previous home address are there. We need to talk to this Doctor Duvall. According to Ms. Hudson, Duvall was both Baker and Bachman's shrink. He should remember this guy, considering the patient turned into an employee."

"The New York office is working on getting a warrant for all Greenhaven records related to Cole Baker. Arthur has been helpful there."

David's cell rang: Sally O'Hara. He put her call on speaker.

"I have an address for Baker. Looks to be a good one. Plus I got a warrant to search his residence."

"That was fast," Marco said, impressed.

"Max saved my sister's life. I'll move heaven and earth to find her. Baker lives in Queens. Three blocks from where we found the Palazzolos. I'm sending you the address, but my boss is sending in a tactical unit, so be prepared."

"Thanks, Sally. I'll be there in twenty minutes."

Marco excused himself and left the room, putting his phone to his ear.

David said to Ben, "Stop pacing or I'll make you stop."

Ben stood in front of the windows and looked out. "Is she dead? Just tell me."

"No," David said. But he didn't know if he believed it anymore.

Marco came right back into the room. "We have the warrant for Greenhaven's records on Baker *and* Bachman. And the New York office contacted Duvall through Greenhaven's attorney. Duvall has agreed to talk with us."

"I'd like to join you," Nick said.

Surprisingly, Marco agreed.

Marco said to David, "Let me know what you find in Queens."

"Ditto with Duvall."

After the tactical team cleared Baker's apartment and determined he wasn't there, Sally and David methodically searched the small space.

The place was a clean dump. The building sagged with age, but the apartment was tidy. He wasn't as immaculate as Adam Bachman, but clean.

"Why is he living here when he works at Greenhaven?" Sally thought out loud.

"He left Greenhaven nearly two years ago," David told her. "At least that's what the records indicated."

Sally pulled out her notepad. "He moved in here September fifteenth of that year. It's three blocks from where we found the Palazzolos," she added.

"He could easily have known you found the sodium hydroxide," David said. "From the roof of this building there's a clear line of sight to the rail yard."

"Why pull Max into this now? It's like they were just waiting for us to find something, and then Bachman calls her?"

David had been thinking the same thing. He kept going back to Arthur Ullman's conclusion that something about this case was personal to Baker, something about

Max herself. And though they still had a lot to learn about Baker, there didn't appear to be any connection between him and Max.

"Are they smart enough to pull this off?" David asked as he opened Baker's kitchen cabinets. The contents were sparse and orderly. "To manipulate an investigation to such a degree?" Though based on Arthur's analysis last night, neither Bachman nor Baker were the brains. There was a third person with the vision, for lack of a better word. "Dr. Ullman thinks there's another person involved. Possibly the leader."

David opened the cabinet under the kitchen sink. Two twenty-five-pound sodium hydroxide containers had been pushed to the back. "Sally."

She squatted and swore under her breath. "Same size and brand as what we found in the tunnel. I'll alert the crime scene techs when we're done here."

They moved their search to the living room. Sally asked, "Why did Max start snooping around again three weeks ago?"

"I don't understand what you mean." A small television sat on a cabinet. Inside were DVDs of all kinds, but David knew they'd have to look at each disk in case he'd hidden something on them, using the cases as a disguise.

"It's because she pushed me then, started snooping around like she does, that I took another look at the files, found the chemicals, then found the victims. Why three weeks ago? Why not two months ago? Six months ago?"

"Time," David said. Suddenly, several things Max had been telling him over the last few months began to make sense. She'd been angry about being spread too thin. "Two months ago she was in Florida investigating an underage prostitution ring that ended up being tied to a drug cartel. Then she was in California for a funeral and ended up staying because of a cold case. Once she got back, she tarted prepping for the Bachman trial—and that put the Palazzolos front and center again."

"Someone who was that brutal to strangers isn't going to stop killing for a year," Sally said.

"That's a psych question, above my pay grade."

She shot him a glance. "Hardly. But it—oh, shit."

David crossed the small room to where Sally was standing in front of a small desk.

Inside the bottom drawer were all four of Max's books, in hardcover, lined up by publication date. Sally pulled out the most recent book, *Killer Nurse,* which had numerous sticky notes marking specific pages and passages.

Also in the desk was a day planner. David grabbed it and opened it up.

Baker had been tracking Max. He had blocks of time marked out when she'd been out of town. He had photos of her going in and out of a variety of places, including the NET building and her apartment. This planner was for this year; another planner was under the books. It was for last year. He'd started following her last March, fifteen months ago. Six months after he moved to New York City.

"He's been stalking her," David said. "And I didn't know." What good was he to Max—to anyone—if he couldn't identify a stalker?

"David, you couldn't have known. He didn't send her threats. He kept his distance. These pictures are zoomed in. He didn't need to get close."

That didn't appease David.

He grabbed the other three books. They, too, had been marked up. "We need to get this to Arthur Ullman. He might be able to make sense of why Baker marked these specific passages."

Chapter Twenty-six

Carter Duvall lived in a stately home in Stamford, Connecticut, less than an hour from the city and a little over an hour from Hartford in the opposite direction. Marco had been on the phone the entire time they were driving up, but Nick picked up on the important points. A team of federal agents had been dispatched to Greenhaven to pull the records covered by the warrant. David had also contacted Marco and said Baker wasn't at his apartment, but they'd found evidence that Baker had been stalking Max for more than a year.

Marco didn't attempt to lecture Nick or tell him he didn't have jurisdiction or authority, but his attitude was enough to keep Nick quiet. Sometimes, Nick could learn more simply by observing.

Marco knocked on the heavy door. A moment later, the doctor answered. He looked like his picture on the Greenhaven Web site. Late forties, distinguished, neither short nor tall, physically fit but a bit soft around the edges.

"Thank you for taking the time to meet with us," Marco said. "This is Detective Nick Santini. I'm Marco Lopez,

Federal Bureau of Investigation. My colleague spoke with
you on the phone."

"Yes, come in please." He closed the door behind them.
"Can I get you anything? Water? Coffee?"

"We're good, thanks," Marco said.

Nick looked around. Nice place, but a bit ostentatious.
Elegant, for a single man. A suitcase was sitting by the
staircase.

"Coming or going?" Nick asked.

"Coming," he said with a smile. "I spoke at a conference Thursday night in Boston. A group of psychiatrists
specializing in childhood fear. It's one of my areas of ex-
pertise. I came home yesterday afternoon, but had work
to catch up on. Today was supposed to be my day off."

Duvall led them into the living room. It was masculine
and elegant at the same time, if that were possible—dark
wood, light floors, leather furniture, and extensive artwork,
all landscapes. Nick had no idea if the art was worth anything, but each had individual lighting and small plaques
that he couldn't read from the distance.

Duvall sat in a chair and Marco took the couch. Nick
stood. Except for the brief exchange the night before,
Marco had kept everything with Nick all business. Nick
thought he had Marco's number, but he also thought the
fed was a bit more complex than at first impression, so
Nick was reserving judgment.

"Cole Baker," Marco said. "He was one of your patients
at Greenhaven."

"You know I can't discuss my patients with you."

Marco slid him a copy of the warrant. Duvall read it—
slowly, possibly for effect—then handed it back to Marco
without showing that it had affected him.

"You'll see when you read the files that I treated Cole
Baker for drug addiction, which manifested into some

serious anger management issues. That was nine or ten years ago, I'm not sure."

"But he continued to work at Greenhaven."

"On the maintenance staff. He'd shown an aptitude for manual labor, but because of his complex family issues felt it was beneath him. Only after accepting that he didn't have to live up to his father's expectations of him could he truly rid himself of the root cause of his addiction and the fear that was at the root of his anger."

"And Adam Bachman?"

"Yes, I'm well aware of his legal situation. He had never exhibited any signs of violence. He came to me because of social anxiety and an extreme fear of germs. Three months later, he was able to return to college and function normally."

"You gave Baker a letter of recommendation."

Nick saw what Marco was doing. He was going back and forth between the two patients in the hopes of rattling Duvall, keeping him on his toes. But the tactic didn't seem to work. The more formal Marco sounded, the more comfortable Duvall appeared.

"I'm sure I did. I don't remember specifics."

Marco pulled the letter from the file and quoted from it. "Cole Baker is a success story. He has shown aptitude for hands-on work, including repairs of all types. He's enrolling in a community college and a part-time maintenance job would achieve his goals, plus provide a much needed service to Greenhaven."

Marco put the letter down. "Baker never completed a semester at a community college, and ended up working full time at Greenhaven after three months. He was there for nine years, until he moved to Queens. However, we don't have any record of him working in the city."

Duvall didn't say anything. Just shrugged, as if he didn't know or care. He leaned back into the chair, fully relaxed.

COMPULSION   311

"Did you give him any other letters of recommendation?"

"No."

"Have you spoken to him since he quit his employment?"

"No."

"Do you remember his friendship with Adam Bachman while Mr. Bachman was a patient and Mr. Baker was an employee?"

"I wasn't aware of a friendship."

Marco's body shifted slightly. He was barely hiding his frustration. And Duvall seemed to be acutely aware of his impact on the fed. The psychiatrist seemed even more relaxed as Marco became more agitated. As if Duvall was in charge and had all the time in the world.

"Dr. Duvall, Cole Baker is wanted for questioning in a kidnapping and a separate murder investigation."

"Kidnapping and murder? I can't imagine." He shook his head, as if in disbelief, but his eyes lit up with interest.

"We know that he was at Greenhaven for anger management issues. He hit his mother and his father arranged for his treatment."

Duvall put up his hand. "Honestly, I only remember the basics of these cases because they were so long ago. I have seen literally hundreds of patients since Mr. Baker and Mr. Bachman. I need time to refresh myself with my notes, look over the case files, review any diagnosis. You'll have to give me a day or two to bring myself up to speed. And then, if you still need my input, I'll be happy to share. But I'm sure, after fifteen years as a federal agent, you're more than capable of deciphering the files yourself."

Nick almost said something, but Marco noticed the same thing he had. "How'd you know I was in the FBI for fifteen years?"

"I read it. You were prominently featured in two crime books."

"You read true crime."

"I read a lot of things."

Nick didn't like coincidences. And while Maxine's books were widely available, he found it suspicious that the psychiatrist who had treated Max's suspected kidnapper had read her books. Bachman had told David that her books were practically required reading. That made two patients of Duvall's who had read Max's books, along with Duvall himself.

"Refresh yourself," Marco said as he rose from the couch. "I'll be requesting your presence at FBI headquarters tomorrow to go over each file piece by piece."

Marco was highly agitated, and Duvall had a half smile on his face, as if he had enjoyed getting the agent riled up. He walked them to the door.

But when Duvall looked at Nick, the smile disappeared.

"Detective Santini, you're a long way from home, aren't you?"

Nick tensed. "Agent Lopez didn't tell you where I'm from."

"I recently read an article about a case you closed in California. Atherton?" Duvall nodded, as if answering his own question. "An architect had been killed, and you solved the case and you arrested his killer five months later."

The only article about that murder investigation that named Nick personally was the article that Max had posted on the *Maximum Exposure* Web site. Nick thought it highly suspicious that Duvall had not only read that article, but remembered the name of the arresting officer.

Nick didn't break eye contact, and for one brief second he saw Duvall squirm. Then Duvall turned back to Marco and said, "If that's all, Agent Lopez."

"The news is going to break soon, so I'll give you a heads-up," Marco said. "Adam Bachman killed himself last night. His lawyer was murdered. Cole Baker is in the middle of it."

Duvall didn't seem to be surprised or interested in the information. "Agent Lopez, I don't know how I can help. I barely remember those two young men. But if you have questions after you read their medical files, I will be more than happy to answer them."

"Prick," Marco mumbled when he pulled away from Duvall's house.

"He's read Max's books and he knows who I am."

"It proves nothing. Maybe he knew that Baker had some sort of obsession with her. Maybe Baker said something during whatever therapy he had. Obviously, his therapy didn't work."

"It seems odd that, not only did he know you've been in the FBI for fifteen years, but he knew it off the top of his head. How many years did you have in when Max wrote the book?"

"Six."

"I read the book a few weeks ago and I didn't remember that, nor had I extrapolated how many years that would be now. But he read it, he knew who you were by name, and your tenure. It seems . . . unusual."

"Maybe he has a photographic memory."

"Hmm."

"What are you thinking, Santini?"

"I'm not. He could just be a prick, like you said."

Marco picked up his phone and Santini heard him order a full background on Carter Duvall. He hung up and said to Nick, "Just in case."

Then he called David and put him on speaker.

"Duvall's a slick bastard and we need to keep an eye on him, but there's nothing he can help us with now, until I have more questions," Marco said. "Tell me about Baker."

"He has a collection of Max's books," David said over the speaker. "All read and marked up, particularly the book on the nurse in Miami."

"She was an elder care facility administrator. Also a nurse, but not practicing," Marco said. "It was the last book Max wrote. The woman was a coldhearted bitch."

Nick said, "Didn't Kyle mention that Riley had read that book many times?"

"I was there," Marco said. "I arrested the wicked witch, as Max called her. Lauren Smith. Max was pulled into the investigation by Lois, a great-grandmother who thought the death of one of her friends wasn't of natural causes. Max posed as Lois's granddaughter. This was before she had the television show, when she did a lot more under-cover work. Between Lois and Max they uncovered a whole host of fraud, theft, elder abuse, and more. Smith's lawyer worked out a plea deal, but she won't see the out-side of a federal pen for at least twenty years."

Nick said, "Duvall told us he's read her books."

Marco said, "We can't bring him in for being well-read. It may mean nothing."

"Or he could have known his patient was obsessed with her," David said. Exactly Nick's thought.

"Even with doctor-patient confidentiality, if he had cause to believe that Baker was a threat to another person he would have an obligation to report it."

Nick said, "It's suspicious. Marco ordered a background on Duvall. Is there someone on your staff who can look into him as well?"

"Consider it done."

Marco glanced at Nick, but he ignored the glare. He said, "If Baker quit his job at Greenhaven two years ago, and has no known employment, how was he paying for his apartment?"

David said, "The neighbors say he works cash jobs—

fixing this and that. Probably under the table. His apartment is cheap, he lives cheaply."

Marco asked, "Anything that connects him to the Palazzolos?"

"Two containers of sodium hydroxide under the sink in
his kitchen."

"Can you match them with the one the NYPD found?"

"Sally is already working on it, but they're the same
brand and size."

"Were the containers full?" Nick asked. He thought he'd
kept his voice steady, but it sounded weak.

"Yes," David said. "Both factory-sealed. O'Hara has a
forensics team taking this place apart. Cops are canvassing the neighbors. We have a lead on a car he may be using, one of the elderly neighbors he does odd jobs for. She
said he borrows her car all the time, and it's not in the lot."

"Send me the details," Marco said. "Any word on
Riley?"

"Our IT department has a trace running on the laptop.
It's not on, but if someone turns it on, we'll have GPS coor-
dinates. You never told me what you found at the lawyer's
apartment."

"An FBI team is processing the scene. I don't have a
report yet. They know we're on a time crunch here."

"Do they?"

"David, I'm doing everything I can. I love her, too."

Silence filled the car. David signed off and hung up.

Marco didn't say anything for a long minute, then said,
"She always comes back to me, Santini."

Nick didn't dignify the comment with a response.

But he couldn't help wonder if Marco was right.

The grating sound of metal on metal woke Maxine from
her uneasy sleep. Or had she passed out? She was disori-
ented, thirsty, beyond hunger.

They'd fed her one small meal a day and a quart of water in the Mexican jail. It was crap, but it was sustenance. Enough to keep her alive, but not enough to give her the strength to fight back.

She wouldn't be able to fight back now. She was weak and miserable.

But she had to find a way to escape.

Footsteps crossed the floor and then a hand slapped her face.

"I'm. Awake." It took all her humility to beg. "Water. Please."

"It'll help you talk. And we need to talk." Cool liquid caressed her lips. She opened them greedily.

It wasn't enough, but it was something.

"I don't know how you do it, Maxine," he said. His voice was quiet.

She wanted to ask questions, but she needed her strength to fight, not talk. She had to find a way and be smart about it.

"It's truly stunning how you elicit so much loyalty when you hold everyone at arm's length. And why? That's what I've been trying to figure out for the past two years. *Why* do people gravitate toward you? You're attractive, but there are more attractive women. You're smart, but there are smarter women. You're overly confident to the point of being narcissistic, and yet they all flock to you. You destroy people's lives without a thought. You cut them to the quick, without any consideration that there may be damn good reasons for what they do!" As he spoke, his voice rose.

"I thought you had me all figured out," she whispered.

"I do. I have *you* figured out, it's all the others. You're selfish and egotistical, a borderline sociopath because you don't care about anyone but yourself. You pretend to care because it gets you what you want. Good sociopaths can do that well. You're one of the best."

"You should know, Doctor Duvall."

He didn't say anything.

"Surprised that I know you? It took me a while, thanks to the drugs you fed me. But it came. What did I ever do to you?"

"What haven't you done? You wouldn't remember, you're too self-absorbed."

"You encouraged Adam Bachman to kill."

"So close, yet so far. It doesn't matter. You were never going to survive this. I just wanted you to suffer before I let my protégé do what he does best."

"Protégé? Your pet killer? The one who helped Adam Bachman kill all those people? The one who killed the Palazzolos?"

He laughed. "Smart, but not smart enough."

"Kill me, but the truth will come out."

"Not if they never find your body."

She involuntarily shivered.

He leaned over so close that she felt his breath on her cheek. "If you thought the Mexican prison was bad, wait until my *pet killer* does what he wants. You'll beg to die. But I want you to know that I will destroy your legacy. I will unravel every case you worked on. I will set killers free. I will sue your estate and get every dime from your trust, and your family will be happy to pay just to make me go away. Your reputation will be annihilated."

"I've never printed anything that wasn't true."

"Lies are more powerful than the truth, Maxine. And I will be more powerful. By the end of the year, everyone you know will pity you because they'll believe *my* truth. You took from me; I'll take from you.

"Good-bye, Maxine. I refuse to lose any more sleep over you."

And then he walked away. A distant metal door closed. Silence.

Max began to work on her binds, a numbing fear washing over her.

She'd never met Carter Duvall before this week. What did he think she'd done to him?

She was stuck. Nothing she could do was going to free herself. How could she die like this? Without knowing *why?* Was that what this was? Payback for something she didn't know she'd done?

She'd pissed off a lot of people—cops, killers, even some of the victims she tried to help. There was a time when Sally O'Hara hated her guts because Max had told her the truth and Sally hadn't wanted to hear it. But they'd gotten over that, they'd become friends.

Did she truly have friends?

David.

He'd been her best friend for nearly two years, but it hadn't started well. He'd hated her, too, at one time. Maybe hate was a strong word . . . but he'd intended for the one protection assignment in Chicago to be his last. Yet . . . somehow they'd made it work. More than made it work—Max needed him.

Ben . . . they battled constantly, but they respected each other. Or was that her imagination? Was he placating her because he wanted her show? Did it even matter that it was his idea to begin with? Maybe he just saw her as the next step on his ladder. She'd accused him of worse.

Marco had told her time and time again that curiosity killed the cat. She'd meow at him mostly to annoy him, but he'd been right more often than not. But did that mean she should just sit back and do *nothing* when she could do *something?* She didn't regret the choices she'd made. She didn't believe in living with regrets. So much of her life had been because of the past—what her mother had done, what her friends had done, the cold cases she was drawn to. The past ruled her. Drove her. But she still didn't regret her decisions. How could she? She'd helped people, hadn't she?

Or maybe she'd really only helped herself. Maybe solving these cold cases was to give her peace because she could never solve the mystery of her past. She didn't know who her father was, she didn't know where her mother had gone, and only because she was willing to risk the love of her family had she learned what happened to her best friend from high school.

Her family . . . would they even miss her? After she'd gone back home six weeks ago and turned their lives upside down, they would be happy to think the worst of her. Whatever the worst it was that Duvall could make up.

What would Nick think? He barely knew her. And somehow that hurt more than anything. If her friends and family believed lies that Carter Duvall spewed, that was on them. She'd proven herself over and over again, and they should know her. But Nick didn't. They were just feeling their way around, and he might buy into it. She hadn't exactly started off on the right foot. She didn't want him to think anything about her that wasn't true.

Men. She'd had so many come in and out of her life. Most of them good men, powerful, driven. Smart men. She liked them smart, because while sex was fun, conversation could be far more stimulating. Maybe she was reading more into this Nick Santini relationship than there was. After all, it's not like they had a history. She'd thought that was a good thing—a relationship without all the baggage. But now, she didn't know.

Really, Max, you're going to die and you're worried about what people think of you? You'll be dead!

No. She wasn't going to die. She *couldn't* die, not like this, not without knowing why!

The metal door again, clicking shut, down a long hall. Above her. She was underground, and he was coming. Duvall's pet killer. Bachman's partner.

She would take the first opportunity to escape. She would have to make the opportunity. That was the only way she would survive.

She listened as he walked into the room. A door shut. And the voice of the man who'd kidnapped her, the one she was certain murdered the Palazzolos and helped Adam Bachman dispose of his victims, said in a gleeful voice, "You're my prize, Ms. Revere. Doc gave me a present." She felt a prick in her arm. Almost immediately her heart thumped painfully. He pinched her and she screamed as the nerve endings in her skin felt raw, exposed. "Just so you get the most out of everything. When you're ready to die, beg for it. I'll be happy to oblige."

Then he took off her blindfold. She blinked in the dim, artificial light. Looked around everywhere for a weapon. To her right was a tray of knives and hammers and a vise that seemed even more fearsome. To her left was a table with syringes. The drugs they'd been injecting in her.

It didn't take Max long to figure out she had no strength to wield a hammer and do any damage, but if she could get to those needles . . . she might have a chance.

Chapter Twenty-seven

Sally O'Hara called David. "Found the car we think Baker's been driving," she said. "I'm sending you the address. It's near an abandoned fishery in Queens. I'm on my way."

David hung up. It was just after dawn and Max had been gone for more than forty-eight hours. He had a sick feeling all night that she was dead. It didn't help that Marco was being a prick and Nick was brooding and Ben was panicked. Sally was the only one who seemed to understand that David just wanted the facts and to be left alone. They'd done everything they could and it wasn't good enough.

Until now. One small lead.

"Lopez! Santini!" he called out. "Sally has a lead."

Nick came out of the kitchen. He was dressed and ready.

David continued, "Baker's car. They found it near an abandoned building in Queens."

Lopez ran down the stairs pulling on his shoulder holster. "She should have called me."

David's fists tightened. Nick caught his eye. "Let's go," he said. "It's a solid lead."

Marco dialed his phone as the three of them left in the elevator. "O'Hara? Agent Lopez. What did you find?"

David tried to ignore that Marco was being a jerk.

Marco said, "Got it. Call in backup, have them keep a perimeter. If he's there, we don't want to spook him." He hung up.

"She knows what she's doing," David said.

"I didn't say she didn't."

"You just like giving the orders," David mumbled.

"What's your problem, Kane? You've been giving me shit since I arrived."

He didn't respond. He couldn't explain it to himself or to Marco. He was acting like a damn lover and there was nothing further from the truth. He'd like to say Max was like his sister, but their relationship was deeper than a beloved sibling. He'd never had to justify his relationship or his feelings, never had to think about them until now.

But at this point, he didn't know if he'd make it through the day without decking Marco Lopez. It started during the interview with Bachman, but it definitely continued when he took Max's bedroom as his own.

David drove Nick, and Marco followed in an unmarked federal car. "He's not a bad cop," Nick said to David. "In fact, for a fed, he's pretty good."

David grunted.

"As a person? Well, let's just say I won't be inviting him over for beer and steaks anytime soon." It was light, and it took the edge off David's temper.

A minute later, David said, "We're on the third day, Nick."

"I know what it might mean, David."

For the second time since they got in the car, Nick looked at his phone.

"What?" David asked, hoping Nick had something to help get his mind off Max.

"My ex-wife. I can't deal with her shit right now."

"Sorry, buddy."

"She's a liar. Maybe that's why I like Max so much. Honest to a fault."

"That's a positive spin. What'd your ex do?" They had ten more minutes of driving. He could think about Nick's problems or he could keep picturing Max dead.

"Yesterday my son had a championship baseball game. They won."

"That's great."

"Yeah. I should have been there."

"I don't know what to say to that."

"It's not because I'm here—it's because she didn't tell me about it. She told Logan, our son, that I would come, but never told me about the game. So he thinks I just bailed. And I can't fix it."

"Tell him the truth."

"That his mother is a lying, manipulative bitch?"

"Works for me."

"We're supposed to keep a happy face for him. Get along. Everything I've read about divorced parents—"

"Hey, I've read those fucked articles, too. And I'll tell you one thing, kids are smart. They know damn well what's going on. They'll use it against you if you let them. I'm sure as hell not the poster dad of the year, but Emma knows one thing about me: I'll never lie to her. Brittany has made my life hell, and Emma knows it. Not because I've told her, but because she's seen it with her own eyes. Tell your son you would have been there if you'd known about it. He'll put two and two together."

"What would Max do?" Nick wondered out loud.

"She'd send you home right now," David said. "When we find her, don't tell her."

"Lie? To Max?"

"Omission. Max has a thing about fathers. If she thought

that you had in any way picked her over your son, she wouldn't forgive herself, or you." He paused. "You're good for her, Nick. And when we find her—because we have to—she's going to need someone around who's good for her."

He pulled over a block from where Sally had spotted the car. Sally stood next to two patrol cars and four cops. She motioned to David.

"Let's find her, Nick."

Max didn't know how long the bastard Duvall called Cole had tortured her, but he'd made two mistakes.

First, he'd untied her in order to flip her on to her stomach. She had no idea what he had planned, but he whistled while he sorted through his tools.

And that's when he made his second mistake. He thought she was unconscious. He thought she was defeated. And so he turned his back on her.

This was her only chance. The opportunity. She couldn't outrun him; she didn't even know if she could stand. But the drug he last injected her with had made her heart race and gave her renewed strength, even as it made every nerve in her body scream in pain. Adrenalin, maybe. Something that gave her a jolt.

Which she now used.

She slid off the table, toward the needles. Swung her arm out and the tray fell to the floor.

Cole turned and laughed. She tried to stand and failed. Dizziness overwhelmed her.

You will fight. You will not faint.

He was on the other side of the table she'd been restrained on. She groped around for something to pull herself up on. As she did, she gathered up several needles in each hand. Three in one, two in the other. She crawled away from him. More slithered than crawled really.

And he continued to laugh as if he were enjoying the show.

"Maxine Revere. You are a wonder. The doc said you were a fighter, and I love fighters. Like the old fart. He fought and that just made beating him to death much more satisfying."

Out of the corner of her eye, she saw Cole pick up a knife. He'd already cut her. Nothing too deep, but the drugs made each incision agony. He had enjoyed her pain, her screams, and she knew in the back of her mind that when she stopped screaming, he would get bored and finally kill her.

She would only get one chance. If she failed, she'd be dead.

She grabbed the table to stand. Her legs wobbled beneath her. She backed away from Cole, the needles in both fists, using her arms on the table to balance herself. If she fell she might kill herself.

Blood smeared the hospital gown they'd dressed her in. Cole had hurt her, but aside from the shallow cuts, most of the pain was his cruel use of pressure points.

Cole smiled at her. He was a large man. Taller than her. Probably close to two hundred pounds. The tattoos on his arms writhed as if they had a life of their own, and she realized she was seeing things. Hallucinating? Seeing double? She shook her head to clear it.

Then she saw what she had to do. What she had to risk to survive.

She lunged for him, her left arm raised, the syringes ready to jam into his neck. Cole easily caught her wrist and squeezed until she cried out in pain and dropped the needles.

She took her right arm, her dominant hand, and plunged three syringes simultaneously into his bare arm. He pushed her away and she fell hard on the rough cement floor. His face twisted in anger, horror, and an underlying fear.

"Fucking bitch!" He pulled the needles out, but their contents had already been injected into his system.

She crawled away as he thundered toward her, walking like Frankenstein's monster. He crashed into the metal table and fell to his knees.

"B-b-b," he slurred and collapsed.

Max stared at the motionless body of the man who had tortured her. Her breath was labored, as if she were on the verge of drowning. Pain crawled over her skin like scorpions.

Her body shook at the memory.

The only thing that kept her from passing out was adrenaline. And that wouldn't last.

For a split second she considered waiting for Duvall. She wanted to hurt him, too. She could see herself cutting his skin, like his bastard pet killer had cut hers. She could see herself hitting him, pounding him with her fists. Kicking him in the balls. Raging against him until he told her the truth. Until he told her *why*.

Cole moaned on the floor. He wasn't dead. She had to run before he recovered. She pulled herself up, using the wall as leverage, and slowly made her way to the door.

Max had no time to think or wait. She was weak and bleeding. Her will to live was stronger than her desire for revenge, it always had been. Did that make her selfish? That she hadn't sacrificed her life to prove who killed Karen nine years ago? She was arrogant and forceful and reckless in many ways, but she'd never truly risked herself for anyone else. Not like David, the soldier, who'd always put himself in front of anyone who'd harm her. Not Marco, her ex, whose temper often got him into hot water, who had risked his career and life to find out who killed Karen, who risked his life battling those who smuggled humans for personal gain or sick pleasures. Or Nick, who had done both, been soldier and cop, a quiet hero who hadn't told her half of what he'd done. She'd learned his story through research.

She was nothing. She was a mouthpiece.

She was no one.

You let him get into your head. Dammit, Maxine, get your ass out of here!

Max glanced around the room that had been her prison for God knew how long. At least a day. Two? Maybe it had only been hours and she was still hallucinating.

Her head began to spin and she leaned against the filthy wall to keep from falling. Everything stunk in the room, including her. There were stains on the floor she didn't want to think about. Dark. Red. Blood? Had others been killed down here? How many?

The bastard groaned again and tried to get up. Blood poured from his scalp from where he'd hit the corner of the table. She turned away from the room, stumbled toward the doorway, keeping her hands near the walls. The light from the underground room faded and she was submerged into darkness. She blinked and realized that it wasn't completely black. Streams of narrow light came from boarded-up windows high above. A warehouse? What kind of warehouse had two-story ceilings but a basement with no windows? Or maybe it wasn't a basement, but a wide windowless warehouse. An alliteration.

Snap out of it, Maxine!

She didn't remember half of what had happened, and maybe that was a good thing.

Remember, dammit! Remember it all. You have to remember.

Her head spun, her mind wasn't all there. The Adrenalin must have kicked the drugs into overdrive. Cliché. She was thinking in clichés now, but that was better than alliteration.

She laughed, then grabbed her mouth. What if Duvall

was here? What if he was waiting for her? What if he staged the whole thing, to see if she had the capacity to kill? He'd wanted to break her, he said, and he hadn't. She'd won. She'd won!

She almost laughed again, but instead coughed, unable to catch her breath. She had won nothing unless she survived and exposed him to the world.

She'd been an experiment to him, just like Bachman, just like Cole. Like how many other people through the years? How many impressionable, troubled teenagers had gone to Duvall for help, only to be turned into something darker than they should have been?

Or were their crimes inevitable?

She couldn't think about any of that. Her head wasn't on straight, she was sluggish, and she wouldn't get out at all if she couldn't focus.

Get out of the building. Get help.

Get out, Maxine!

Max continued forward. She tripped over garbage, something foul and old. But as she pushed forward, the light grew brighter. Not bright, but lighter, and she had the sensation that she was walking up a gradual incline. Get out, get help. The mantra pushed her forward.

At the top of the incline, she stopped to catch her breath and stumbled. She collapsed across the hood of a car. She blinked, and in the dim light she saw it was a black Lincoln Town Car, much like the one she'd thought had been sent for her. She opened the door, praying for keys. None were there. But a foul smell came from the back. She knew, without looking, that the driver—the one who was supposed to pick her up Thursday night—was in the trunk. She searched the glove compartment box. There was nothing. No cell phone. The radio had been torn out. They'd likely disabled the GPS, otherwise *someone* would have found her by now.

A sob escaped. She wanted David. She wanted to call for help.

Clanging metal from down in the basement made her scream. The bastard was alive and he was coming after her. She hadn't killed him, she'd only slowed him down. But she was also slow. Every movement ached, every step shooting pain up her nerve endings. Her skin was on fire.

Max climbed out of the car. Her legs gave out and she fell heavily to the cement. She screamed as her knees seemed to explode.

Dammit, get up!

She was not going to die like this, in this bloody, filthy hospital gown. What if no one knew what happened to her? What if Duvall and Cole made her disappear? David would know she was dead, but would never rest because he wouldn't know the who, the what, the why. And Nick . . . did he think she just changed her mind about the trip and didn't call him? She was selfish, after all. Selfish and self-centered and arrogant.

Maybe they didn't know. Maybe they thought she had just left because she was Max Revere and could do anything she wanted. She'd said it often enough. She meant it, too. But she wouldn't have left without a word. She wouldn't have hurt the people she cared about. David was more than a brother. She would never hurt him, never never never never . . .

She shook her head to clear her thoughts. She wasn't even making sense to herself.

"Max-ine," the bastard's voice called. He was closer, too close. She shuffled around the car to the trunk. Looked around. Where was the door? How could she get out?

"Max-ine," he called again, his voice a singsong. "Max-ine. There's no way out, Max-ine. Here, bitchy-bitchy bitch."

She cowered behind the car, the smell of the dead driver filling her nostrils so violently that had she any food in her stomach, she'd have puked. The drugs made her panicked and she had the overwhelming urge to let him find her. To get it over with, because there was no hope. She didn't know where the damn door was. No door, no escape.

Who are you? You're not a quitter, Maxine. How did the car get in here?

Of course there was a door. A door big enough that this car could drive through.

"I'm going to cut you into small pieces. Maybe I'll pour sodium hydroxide on you and let it burn you alive. That would be fun. No one can hear you scream in here, Max-*ine*."

She looked behind her and saw the door. It was a big roll-up door, huge and heavy. It was bolted from the inside, but it wasn't locked. No one outside could get in, but she could get out.

But could she make it to the door before he found her? Did she have the strength to open it?

If you keep debating with yourself, he's going to find you. Just do it!

She stumbled from her hiding place, sparing a glance down the ramp. She saw him, tall and broad, scowling. Blood covered half his face. He was fifty feet away and coming slowly, unsteady, not walking in a straight line. Did he have a gun in his hand? A knife? A hammer? She couldn't see, he wore dark clothing, but he held something.

She walked no faster than Cole. She turned back to the door and he laughed behind her. It sounded like he was right in her head and she turned, lashing out, but he was still down the ramp. She staggered and fell on her ass next to the door. She crawled the two feet to the bolt and slid it free.

She pushed the door up. Pushed *harder*. But it barely budged. She had no strength.

He laughed again, closer.

She pounded on the door, the metal echoing in the vastness of the empty space.

"Help me!" she tried to scream. Her voice was weak. She looked up. Praying? No. Where had that gotten her before? All those years praying for a home? Praying for her mother to come back? Praying for answers to all the questions that had plagued her for her entire life?

She saw the chain above her.

The chain would open the door.

She pulled herself up and reached, standing as tall as she could, but she still couldn't reach it.

No, no, no! So close, and still she would die.

A ladder was propped up against the wall. She climbed it, her knees aching, her bare feet slipping, but she still climbed. She reached out and grabbed the chain. Her foot slipped and she screamed as she fell from the ladder. But she held the chain tight, and her weight forced the door open several feet until her hands slipped and she fell hard on the ground.

Ignoring the pain, she rolled under the door into bright sunlight reflecting off water. *Water.* Fresh air burned her lungs.

The door didn't close, it was stuck open three feet. She crawled away, simultaneously trying to figure out where she was, but she'd been in the dark so long all she saw was white. She couldn't tell if Cole was following. She couldn't hear him, the ringing in her ears getting louder and louder until she wanted to scream.

She staggered away from the building, praying for her sight to return. She needed a person, a phone, a car—anyone to call the police. To get her out of here and take her home.

She heard the door roll up behind her. She glanced back and saw a silhouette. Something in his hand. He was closer. Twenty feet? Less?

Run, Maxine.

She ran. Or, rather, loped. She fell and got back up and fell again. Her eyes were regaining their function, but everything was in shadows with splotches of light and dark as she attempted to focus. She'd been hit on the head, maybe this was a concussion.

You've been hit on the head before. You know *this is a concussion.*

Just get out of here. Find help. Run faster than that bastard.

She got up one last time, walked two feet. Her next footstep came down hard on broken glass. She cried out and fell hard. She rolled over and pulled her foot up into her lap. Blood poured from a gash that cut from her big toe to her arch. A thick brown shard stuck out. She didn't think twice, she pulled it out and got up. But she couldn't put much weight on her foot, and her already slow speed got a whole lot slower.

She only had one option.

Hide.

He was still trying to spot her, the sun blinding him temporarily like it had her. It was either morning or evening, the sun low, but she didn't know if she faced west or east because she couldn't make out any familiar structures.

She crawled over to a row of rusting, overflowing Dumpsters that had been left by the side of the dock. It seemed no one had emptied them in months. They were filled with garbage, broken furniture surrounding it as if a tornado had picked up, shaken, and dumped the contents of a house right here. She crawled in the filth underneath, not caring about dirt or bugs or garbage or anything but hiding.

Her heart raced as she wondered if she'd just signed her death warrant. He'd get his vision back, he'd see that this was the only place she could hide. She just hoped he thought she'd ran. She hoped he hadn't seen her fall, didn't know her foot was cut, wouldn't realize how bad off she really was.

She wiggled around, her face on the filthy, broken concrete as she looked under the Dumpster to see where he was coming from. He was standing thirty yards away, a speck in the distance, his hand over his eyes. He'd hit his head hard when he fell. He'd been unconscious, whether from the drugs or the fall, she didn't know. Maybe his vision was blurred. She hoped he had a concussion, worse than hers. She hoped he felt pain, that he was hallucinating.

Her breathing was labored and she was queasy. Cole started moving away from the docks, not coming right at her, but if she moved, he might see her.

But she couldn't move. She had no more energy, not even to crawl away. She couldn't lift her arm. She collapsed into the garbage, resigned.

The traffic she heard in the distance sounded closer. Was someone driving through? Coming to work? Going home? But Cole could have a gun. She didn't want to be responsible for anyone dying, not while they were trying to help her. But she needed help.

I don't want to die. I really, really, really don't want to die.

The car was coming closer. She couldn't see it. But the bastard Cole stopped. Then he turned and ran back toward the warehouse.

This was her only chance. She needed all her strength. She willed herself to move, to crawl to the other side of the garbage heap. She did, painfully slow, the cement digging into her flesh.

Max saw three cars pull up on a narrow, unpaved street parallel to the water. There were several cars parked on the street—they all looked abandoned or broken down. They surrounded one vehicle.

The police.

She grabbed the broken handle on the side of the Dumpster and forced herself to stand. Her foot ached, but really it was no worse than the pain that pumped through her body with each beat of her heart. She called out to them, but they were so far away. Farther than the warehouse and in the opposite direction. She looked around and saw a chair leg. She reached down, grabbed it, and hit the Dumpster. The vibrations made her ache worse, but she hit it again as hard as she could.

Help. Me.

Two men were running toward her. Odd. They looked like Marco and Nick.

She must really be hallucinating.

Chapter Twenty-eight

David had never seen Max so vulnerable.

There was blood on the gown she wore—it looked like a hospital gown—and she was barefoot. Her hair was damp and matted to her head, her face bruised, her eyes far too bright blue to be normal. She was filthy from crawling through garbage. She looked feral and scared.

But she was alive. Marco and Nick had grabbed her as she limped away from her attacker, and the ambulance was en route.

Nick had fired at Baker, but he'd run back into the warehouse. They were waiting for SWAT before they breached the facility. But with all the underground tunnels and drainage systems, David feared they'd already lost him.

But they'd found Max.

Marco and Nick were both searching for bullet and knife wounds, but they found only shallow cuts. Max brushed their hands away. "It hurts," she said.

"What hurts? Where?" Marco asked.

"I'm fine," Max muttered, then laughed. Or tried to laugh. Her voice was rough and faint and her breathing was labored.

"Are you shot?" Marco asked again. "Maxine, why are you bleeding?"

"Cuts. Scorpions. Don't touch me."

"Scorpions?" Nick said.

"That was a long time ago," Max said and closed her eyes.

Nick pointed to marks on her arm. "Those are needle marks."

"She's hallucinating," Marco said.

David's fists clenched and unclenched. Max had been tortured. The cuts, none deep enough to kill, were designed to elicit pain. The drugs likely made the pain unbearable. She had been stripped of personal items, dressed in a generic gown, kept without food and minimal hydration. David understood psychological warfare, and he'd been trained in criminal and military interrogations. He'd seen the results of torture. These methods were crude, amateur, but no less effective.

"There's two," Max said.

"Two what?" Marco asked her.

"The doctor left," she said.

"What doctor?" Marco asked.

Her head lolled to the side. "Which doctor?"

David called over to where Sally stood commanding the four patrol officers who were keeping an eye on the building. "How long for the medics?"

"ETA two minutes. SWAT is six minutes out."

They heard the sirens in the distance.

"That's fast," Marco said.

"I had SWAT on standby as soon as we ID'd Baker's car," Sally said.

"Maxine," Nick said, "stay with us. Focus."

"Water," she said.

"Don't," David said. "She can't have anything, we don't

know what's in her system." He wasn't a medic, but had plenty of on-the-job training in the army.

"She's obviously dehydrated," Marco said.

"They'll put her on an IV." David squatted next to Max. "Maxine, it's David. Can you hear me?"

"David." She still didn't open her eyes. "I'm sorry."

"You have nothing to be sorry for," David said. "This wasn't your fault."

"That's a first," she whispered. There was a little smile on her face.

David began to breathe easier. "You're going to be okay," he said. "Stay awake, okay?"

Her eyes were still closed but she nodded.

Marco said, "Max, you said there were two inside."

"One."

"Only one?"

"No. Two."

She was confused, or they weren't asking the right questions.

"Who, Maxine? We know one is Cole Baker."

"Cole." She squeezed her eyes tight. "Doctor. My head."

Her voice was so faint David could barely hear her. The ambulance turned on to the street. Sally ordered two officers to stand guard over the medics.

"Get them off me!" Max's arms flapped, as if trying to shake off bugs. "Off!"

The paramedics ordered Marco and Nick to stand back. One checked Max's eyes. They were unfocused and dilated. The other checked her pulse and put on a blood pressure cuff. Max screamed as the cuff contracted.

"What's she on?" one medic asked.

"We don't know," Marco said.

"History of drug use?"

"No," Marco said. "Someone drugged her. She's been missing since Thursday night."

"Severe dehydration," a medic said. "Let's get a saline drip in her ASAP."

"Heart rate two-twenty over one-ten."

"Dear God," Sally said. Her radio beeped and she walked away.

"We need to know what's in her system," one medic said. "Ma'am, stop fighting."

"It hurts."

"What hurts? Ma'am—"

"Everywhere. My skin. Water."

The two medics lifted Max onto the gurney and she began to convulse.

"Strap her down."

"No!" Max screamed.

David put his hand on one of the medics. "Don't."

"It's for her safety."

David pointed to her wrists and ankles, which were raw from restraints.

Nick said, "Every time you touch her, she's in pain." He leaned over Max and said, "Maxine, it's Nick. Listen to me. You can't fight the medics. They're going to make you better. But if you fight them, they have to tie you to the gurney."

She reached out and touched his hand. She had no strength to squeeze. "Okay," she whispered. "Okay."

"I'm going with her," David said. "I'm her bodyguard."

"I'll follow," Nick said. Then he looked at Marco. "Unless you need me here."

Marco hesitated, then shook his head. "Go. Let me know."

Nick nodded. "Call when you get inside. The doctors will need to know what they drugged her with."

"I will."

The paramedics hoisted Max into the ambulance and David jumped in behind them, tossing Nick his car keys.

The driver closed the rear doors and David sat with Max as the paramedic put an IV into her arm. "Saline only, until we know what's in her system," he said.

The ambulance pulled away and David prayed for the first time since he was a boy.

The hardest thing Marco had to do was let that detective from California go with Max to the hospital. Marco wanted to go with her, to be there for her, make sure she was taken care of, remind her that he loved her.

The bastard had tortured her. No one had said it, but they all knew. She'd been cut, drugged, denied food, water, and more.

The important thing was that Maxine was alive, and she would stay that way. They'd found her. She'd fought, freed herself because she was a survivor. It was why he loved her, and why she infuriated him.

Sally O'Hara said, "We have the warehouse surrounded. The SWAT team is two minutes out. Did you recognize the guy?"

"It's Baker," Marco said.

"You know Max is the toughest woman on the planet," Sally said.

He knew. "Who was she talking about? A doctor." He pictured Doctor Carter Duvall, but Duvall had been in Boston Thursday night until Friday morning. He'd been in Connecticut last night. It was possible—this warehouse was about an hour or so from Stamford. But it would be difficult. And what was his motive?

The New York field office had verified Duvall's alibi in Boston, but Marco called his liaison nonetheless and asked her to check the time line down to the minute, from the time he left Stamford for Boston, when he checked in, when he spoke, who saw him, when they saw him, transportation, the works.

"Do you really think Dr. Duvall is a suspect?" Sally asked.

"No," Marco said. "But I can't rule him out. And he was the shrink for both Bachman and Baker. He could have known, or suspected, that Baker had an obsession with Max. If he did, and we can prove it, that'll make him an accessory."

But *why* was Baker obsessed with Max? The FBI was in the middle of a full background on him, and there was no doubt that Ben had the NET research team working on it as well. Maybe, when Max was coherent, she'd fill in the holes.

"What did she mean by scorpions?" Sally asked.

"It was a long time ago," Marco said, noncommittal.

She had to be hallucinating. Marco knew what she'd suffered in the Mexican jail. Things she'd never written about. Rarely talked about. He'd been there, he'd found her. He'd been so angry at the time, and relieved. Dammit, he should be with her now, not that new guy, Nick Santini. Nick didn't know Max like Marco did. Nine years. No one could dismiss that kind of history.

The SWAT tactical truck and two SUVs rounded the corner. At the same time, a rumbling sound came from the direction of the warehouse.

"Take cover!" Marco yelled as the large door rolled up.

A black Lincoln Town Car burst from the building. It was heading toward them—they had blocked the only way out of the area. Baker planned on ramming them in his attempt to escape.

Marco and Sally drew their guns because the SWAT team hadn't yet set up.

"Tires!" Marco said. He wanted Baker alive. There were too many questions that needed answers.

Between him and Sally and the two patrol cops, they hit the tires. The car veered off, out of control, and hit a row of parked cars—including the car that Baker had driven here. The Town Car flipped onto its roof, then the momentum turned it over on its blown-out tires. The airbags had deployed inside.

Marco ran over, gun out, holding it on the driver's side door. Baker was trapped and dazed, but alive.

"Keep your hands where I can see them!" Marco shouted.

Baker looked at him through the broken driver's side window. He lowered his right hand.

"I mean it, Baker! Do not move."

Baker raised his hand. He had a gun. Marco fired and hit him in the head. Baker slumped over, dead.

"Well, shit," Marco said.

Sally was right behind him. "You had no choice."

Maybe not, but finding the answers to what the hell was going on was now going to be much, much harder.

Chapter Twenty-nine

Max hated lying in the hospital bed. She just wanted to go home, but the doctors said no. They were testing her blood, pumping fluids and antibiotics into her body, and her foot was heavily bandaged and in a boot because of the glass she'd stepped on when she'd escaped.

But what she hated most of all was the three men she respected the most staring down at her as if she were some fragile little child. And a female FBI agent she'd never met before, S.S.A. Rose Pierce, who Marco introduced from the New York field office. This was Pierce's case apparently. She was at least ten years older than Marco, and he was closing in on forty. She had a no-nonsense appearance, though Max thought her dyed hair looked just a little too blond for her sallow complexion. She should have gone with the warm browns.

You're being judgmental again, Maxine.

"Ask your questions," she said. *Then go away.*

She'd been missing for nearly three days. She'd escaped Sunday morning; it was now late Sunday afternoon. She couldn't fathom how that much time had passed. Maybe she'd sensed it, but she had been so confused so much of the time between the drugs and the dark and Duvall's twisted mind games.

"Ms. Revere," Agent Pierce began, "we understand you've been through an ordeal, and I won't take up much of your time. But it's important that we know what happened. According to Mr. Kane, you were supposed to be picked up by a car service on Thursday evening to go home, but you never arrived home. Is that correct?"

"Obviously," Max snapped. God, her head hurt. They hadn't given her any painkillers, which was fine—she didn't want to be on any medication. Their reasons were medical. They hadn't been able to identify the drugs she'd been injected with and were testing her blood at an outside lab. Their fears were of a potential adverse reaction. She didn't want to take anything, not even aspirin. But dammit, every muscle and bone in her body hurt under an odd sensation of numbness.

"Sarcasm," Marco said. "Always a good sign."

She was not up for an argument with Marco. She wasn't up to anything. But she wanted Carter Duvall caught. She would do anything to see him behind bars.

She detailed leaving her office and meeting the driver in front of the NET building.

"I didn't suspect anything was wrong until I was in the car for about five minutes," she said. "It doesn't take long to get from the studio to my apartment. I looked up and noticed we were about to turn on to the Brooklyn Bridge. I was irritated—I was tired and needed to pack for my trip. He stopped at a light and I leaned forward to explain that he was going the wrong way, and he sprayed something in my face. I tried to get out of the car, but my arms and legs didn't cooperate."

She'd been confused. Then scared.

Scared is an understatement.

"I woke up in a warehouse. They'd blindfolded and

undressed me. I didn't know it was a hospital gown until later. No one was there when I woke up. I tried to get free, but I was restrained and whatever drug they'd given me made me queasy."

"They? There were two?"

"Yes. Carter Duvall and his bastard goon. Cole Baker. The guy from the sketch." Before Pierce and Marco arrived, David had filled her in on what they'd learned about Bachman's cohort, Cole Baker. He'd also told her Riley was in the hospital in a medical coma because she'd overdosed while going undercover at Greenhaven.

Max blamed herself. She'd known Riley wanted to follow in her footsteps and Max hadn't impressed on her that she didn't have the experience yet and that she couldn't be responsible for her. Didn't want to be responsible. Max put herself at risk, but it was her life. She wouldn't ask others to do it.

But Max feared her guidance had been faulty, that she hadn't trained Riley properly, that maybe she'd even given her contradictory orders. Max may not have wanted responsibility for Riley, but the responsibility was nonetheless hers.

"Duvall was behind everything."

"Dr. Carter Duvall," Marco said bluntly.

She stared at him. "Yes," she repeated.

"We checked him out. Santini and I interviewed him yesterday. What's his motive?"

She looked over at Nick. He was standing apart from everyone, in the corner, watching the interview as if he were in another room. But he smiled at her, just a little smile, and nodded his head. She wished he hadn't seen her like this. What a disaster she'd been after her escape. She must have smelled worse than the garbage she'd hidden in.

Why was she even thinking about it? She'd fought back

and won. She would not let Duvall and Baker make her weak.

"I don't know why he targeted me," she said. "He thinks I slighted him or did something to him—I don't know what. I don't know him, never heard of him before this week. He knew everything about me. Everything."

"You can ID him?" Agent Pierce asked.

"Yes."

"You saw him," she repeated. "You stated that you were blindfolded until you fought with Baker."

"Yes, but I recognized his voice."

"So you met him before."

"Briefly. At Greenhaven on Wednesday."

"And you're certain."

"Yes, I'm certain!" She squeezed her eyes shut. "Duvall was the ringleader of the whole thing. Talk to Bachman. If you push it just right, he'll confess. He's the weakest link."

"Bachman's dead," Marco said. "He committed suicide Friday night."

She was stunned. She'd been completely out of it for three days. Why had Bachman killed himself?

Rose said, "Can you pick Duvall out of a lineup?"

She opened her mouth to say yes but couldn't. "I'd recognize his voice."

"You didn't see him."

She shook her head.

"Did you hear Baker call him by name?"

Again, she shook her head. "He only referred to him as 'doc.'"

"We'll talk to him," Pierce said.

"Arrest him," Max said.

"We'll talk to him," she repeated.

"He has an alibi, Max," Marco said.

"For all three days I was gone? Bullshit. He was there!"

"He has an alibi for when you were kidnapped, and for a large chunk of the time you were missing. But the FBI Evidence Response Unit is going through the entire warehouse. If his prints are there, they'll find them."

Max knew they wouldn't be. Duvall was a smart, crafty, manipulative bastard.

"I already told you it was Baker who kidnapped me."

"And you didn't recognize him from the sketch that"— Pierce checked her notes—"Melinda Sanchez approved?"

"He looked different. Had a hat. And it was dark. He was in a suit like all Horace's drivers wear."

"You saw what you expected to see."

Not very observant of her. "His tats were covered and he'd cut his hair short since Melinda saw him. I was tired and distracted. Get that bastard in a room and interrogate him."

"He's dead," Marco said. "Fleeing the scene, he pulled a gun and I shot him."

She caught his eye. This wasn't the first time Marco had killed in the line of duty, but Max had been there the first time and it had torn him up. Even though it was justified, even though he had no choice. She reached for his hand and squeezed, though she had little strength to impart.

"You talked to him?" she said. "To Duvall?"

"Santini and I went out to his house in Stamford. He was the keynote speaker at a conference in Boston. My office checked it out. He flew back Friday arriving at LaGuardia at ten in the morning."

"He could have been at the warehouse," she said. "I had no concept of time. Between the drugs and lack of windows, I didn't know if hours had passed or days."

"We're going through every minute of each day. If there are any holes, we will find them."

"You do believe me?"

He didn't say yes or no. He simply said, "Trust me. We

are running a full background on him and Baker. We'll find out why you were targeted. If there's any connection to Duvall, we'll find it."

"There's something I missed. I must have known him, or known of him, he had read all of my books, every article, he knew things about me that I implied but never spoke. He said he wanted to break me."

It was David who caught her eye. And he didn't have to say a word for her to know that he was her rock. She wouldn't care if everyone left, except for David. David would find the truth and that made her feel like everything was going to be okay, someday.

Agent Pierce watched the nonverbal exchange and said, "Mr. Kane, you need to let Agent Lopez and I handle this investigation."

"Yes, ma'am," he said.

"David," Marco snapped. "We're serious."

David didn't say anything. Max said, "Go talk to him. It was him. I know it, I heard his voice. I'll swear to that under oath."

"And you may be telling the truth—" Pierce began.

"*May* be telling the truth? I know what I heard. I'll find the connection and prove it!"

Her machines started beeping almost before she realized that her heart was racing and her hands were shaking. A nurse rushed in and said, "Everyone out *now*."

"I'm. Fine." Max barely got the words out. She knew she wasn't fine. Her heart was beating too fast and she couldn't breathe right. Was she still going to die? After all of that, after surviving and escaping, would she die?

"I'm staying," David said and sat down. Marco gave her a look, then left with Pierce, but Nick didn't leave with them. Immediately, Max began to relax, but those damn machines kept beeping.

The nurse injected something into her IV. "This is a

very mild sedative. We still don't know what he drugged you with, but this will help slow your heart rate."

Max nodded.

She turned her head and looked at Nick. She tried to smile. "So much for our weekend in bed."

He walked over, took her hand, and kissed it. "There's always next weekend."

"I'm going to hold you to that."

"You'd better. I'm going to go annoy the feds, ask some questions."

She smiled. The machines stopped their beeping and the nurse glared at Nick, but both of them ignored her. "That makes me feel better," she said. She wanted to say more, but it was a rare moment when words failed her. "Thank you for coming," she whispered, her voice cracking. God, she didn't want to get emotional. She didn't want to lose it again.

He winked, kissed her forehead, then left.

The nurse looked pointedly at David. "She needs to rest."

"I'll be quiet," he said.

The nurse didn't approve. "If her heart rate elevates, I will have you removed from the room."

"Understood," he said.

The nurse finally left and Max closed her eyes. She was so tired, but couldn't sleep. Whatever the nurse had put in her IV had taken the edge off the pain, and she was grateful, though she wanted to clean out her entire system. She wanted to go home, sleep in her own bed. But she could barely move.

"I'm sorry, David," she whispered.

He didn't say anything. A moment later, she felt a dip on the edge of her bed. She opened her eyes and David was sitting there, looking at her. "You didn't do anything wrong. Not this time." He tried to smile, but he couldn't, and neither could she. "I should have been there. I should have driven you home. We knew that Bachman had a partner—"

"Don't. This has nothing to do with you. I'm selfish, David. You know that. I'm grossly arrogant, a narcissist, and it came back to bite me in the ass."

"What did he do to you?"

"He told me the truth."

"Maxine, you know better than that."

"Riley is worse off than me, because she wanted to please me."

"Riley ran off on her own without telling anyone. That isn't on you."

"She kept asking me about my investigation in Florida, where Lois alerted me to the atrocities being committed at the senior care facility. I think Riley thought that I sent Lois in there, as if I'd send an octogenarian to do undercover work for me. Lois had no one—her family never visited, her friends were dying off one by one because of old age. I fell in love with her, David. I told Lois once that I wanted to be her when I grew up."

Max's eyes watered, but she refused to cry. She took a couple of deep breaths, calming her nerves.

"Riley asked me about going undercover at the women's prison, and so I told her about it," Max continued. "I was proud. Too prideful. She ran off and now she's in a coma. That's on me, David. I didn't train her properly. You warned me, and I didn't see."

"All I said was that she wasn't you and never could be. Max, you take risks, some I don't agree with, but you're smart about it. She wasn't. I hope she comes through— I really do. She's not a bad kid, she just needs to grow up. I talked to her father. He's torn up, but she has her family."

They sat in silence for a moment. Max closed her eyes again, but she saw Baker coming after her. She heard Duvall's voice in her head.

She whispered, "He knew everything, David. He knew things about me that I didn't think anyone knew."

"Do you really want to talk about this now?"

"I can't sleep. I'm exhausted, I know I need to rest, but right now I can't." She needed to talk even though she was so tired.

David said, "Baker quit Greenhaven two years ago and moved to New York. He hooked up with Bachman then, but he'd known him at Greenhaven. Both Baker and Bachman were patients of Duvall, but at different times. What happened two years ago?"

"I don't know. I started the show two years ago—the next show, in July, is our two-year anniversary. Six months before you came on board."

"The same month Baker quit."

She frowned. She couldn't remember which show aired then. "Ask Ben. Maybe you're right, and it had something to do with whatever investigation I was either working on or that aired around that time."

"Ben's already been working everyone around the clock."

"Ben's a good guy, even with all the shit I give him."

"I don't think it's about the show," David said.

"But you just said—"

"It's about your books. Bachman said you were required reading. We found all your books in Baker's apartment. During Marco's interview with Duvall, he said he'd read your books. He knew about Marco's career."

"What does that mean?"

"He knew Marco was a fifteen-year veteran of the FBI. He'd read the article on the *Maximum Exposure* Web site about Nick's investigation in Atherton."

Max wanted to forget almost as much as she wanted to remember everything Duvall said. "Things are fuzzy," she admitted. "Time was out of whack." She paused. "He said I took from him, so he'll take from me. He wanted to destroy my reputation, sue my estate—after I was dead. It sounded personal."

"That's what Arthur Ullman said. You're certain that Duvall's name isn't familiar?"

She shook her head, then winced.

"Didn't your fourth book come out after you started the show?"

Max had to think about it, because her memories were fuzzy, as if everything she thought came to her through a thick fog.

"I'd turned it in before I agreed to the show. It came out in November."

"The November after Baker quit."

"Yes. And we did a special on it, something Ben and my publisher worked out. Discounted orders through the *Maximum Exposure* Web site. A show with behind-the-scenes information that didn't make it into the book. Personal interviews." She smiled. "I interviewed Lois on the set. She'd never been to New York before." Then she frowned. "David, can you check on her?"

"Of course."

Max couldn't see any connection between Duvall and Lauren Smith, the brutal administrator who'd psychologically and physically tortured the elderly patients in her care. She couldn't see why that investigation would have anything to do with what was happening now. But she couldn't discount it.

"Then in January I covered the trial in Chicago."

"The one where Ben hired me because of the death threats."

It was a standard trial, something Max normally wouldn't have been interested in because it wasn't about a cold case. A woman allegedly killed her husband in cold blood, but Max thought she was innocent. There was something about the case that had been familiar, and she dug around and proved that the woman on trial wasn't guilty.

It had been the woman's sister. A case of envy and jealousy that had turned to violence and revenge.

But Max hadn't made a lot of friends. Even the woman who had her life back told Max she hated her. The only person who wanted Max involved at all had been the victim's mother.

Ultimately, the death threats hadn't come from that trial, but from something Max had written years before. David had saved her life then, and he'd saved her life now. He'd acted when others wouldn't have. He'd brought Nick and Marco in to help when Max didn't think he particularly liked either one.

"There's something I'm not remembering."

"Go to sleep," he told her. "I'm not leaving. I'll be here if you need me."

"David, I've never told you how much I appreciate you."

"You have."

"No. I haven't. Not what you mean to me." She felt the tears in the back of her eyes, but she didn't want to cry. She took a deep breath. "You're my rock, David. I've never loved anyone. I realize that now—I didn't think I was capable of it. I'm self-absorbed. I'm selfish. I'm independent. I love my family, but even that love is marginally conditional. It shouldn't be. I wish I was more trusting, less selfish, more . . . I don't know, *open*.

"I love you. I need you to know that. We're friends, but you're more family to me than I've ever had. When I thought I might die, the one thing I thought about, that I regretted, was that you would suffer for not knowing. That I knew you'd blame yourself, when you are blameless. I couldn't stand thinking about what you would go through. And knowing I'd never told you how I felt."

"Max." His voice cracked. "Max, you're stuck with me." He kissed her forehead. "Sleep."

She slept. Until the nightmares woke her.

Chapter Thirty

Nick sat in the backseat of the sedan and listened to Marco and Rose Pierce discuss Carter Duvall as they drove to Stamford. Pierce had already contacted Duvall about meeting at the local FBI headquarters, but he refused. They didn't have enough to arrest him, but they were hoping this conversation would give them something.

Nick wasn't holding his breath. Duvall was a psychiatrist. He was a smart guy. He wasn't going to trip himself up, not at this point. But sometimes, it was what the suspect didn't say—or didn't ask—that helped build a case.

"I know Ms. Revere is a friend of yours," Rose said to Marco, "but no U.S. attorney is going to indict based on voice recognition. Not without sufficient evidence to back it up."

"He's connected to two of the killers—Bachman and Baker."

"Weak, Marco. You verified his alibi yourself."

"Max said Baker kidnapped her. The dead driver was in the trunk of the Town Car he wrecked. We'll be able to tie him to that murder."

"The case against Baker is tight, I'm not arguing with you there," Pierce said.

"And," Marco continued, "O'Hara has been keeping me in the loop about Bachman's attorney—someone in the neighborhood ID'd Baker. They're still processing the scene but there are prints that aren't Warren's. His secretary said his briefcase is missing."

They were quiet for a while, then Marco said, "Max isn't flighty. She's sharp. If she says it was Duvall, it was him."

"She was drugged, tortured, dehydrated, and hallucinating. The doctors don't even know what was in her system. Our ERT unit is processing the warehouse and found numerous syringes and medical supplies. They'll put it together. But a good defense attorney will destroy her testimony. Hell, a bad defense attorney could destroy it."

"Prints. A witness. We'll build a case against him."

Nick asked from the back. "What's his motivation?"

"You don't believe her?" Marco said, glancing in the rearview mirror.

Nick wanted to challenge him then, because it was clear Marco planned to put a wedge between him and Max. Instead he said, "There's a reason he went after Maxine. Dr. Ullman said this setup felt personal. We need to find that connection."

"What do you mean by 'setup'?" Rose asked.

"Baker lived three blocks from where the Palazzolos were found. He could have easily known when Detective O'Hara found the sodium hydroxide container. It can't be a coincidence that the day after it was discovered, Bachman agreed to an interview that Max had been pushing to get for months."

"Bachman's only visitors were his mother and his lawyer," Marco said.

"And his lawyer was murdered. He could have passed information. He may not have understood the importance." Nick paused. "When Max has time to rest, she'll remember more."

"A lot of coincidences," Rose said. "And you're stretching believability. You're suggesting that these two men would somehow know Ms. Revere would be involved in the investigation in some way. That seems . . . implausible. Of all the reporters in New York City, she would be tasked with the Bachman case *and* the disappearance of the Palazzolos?"

"It's not implausible," Marco said. "Max is known for investigating cold cases—especially missing persons. She wrote an article about the Palazzolos only a few weeks after they disappeared."

"I saw that in her office," Nick said. "And she followed up three weeks ago, at the same time she pushed Detective O'Hara to look in the abandoned train tunnels."

"Okay," Rose said, "say I believe that Baker and Bachman knew that she was interested and laid out damn *bread crumbs* for her to find the bodies . . . why?"

"Bachman didn't think that she'd find the bodies—he implied that in her interview with him," Marco said. "And the interview keeps her interested and involved."

"Again, why?"

"Maybe so she doesn't leave town?" Nick suggested. "If she stays local, they have a greater chance of grabbing her." But even as he said it, he couldn't see that being the key factor.

"I'm getting a headache," Rose said. "And I'm going to repeat myself yet again. Why kidnap her? They keep her for three days but they don't kill her?"

"Max said Duvall wanted to break her. That he knew everything about her." Nick pondered the motivation. "It's a control thing for him, and Max is uncontrollable. She's pissed off a lot of people, there must have been something two years ago that set him off."

"That's presuming that Duvall was involved."

"He is," Marco and Nick said together. Nick caught Marco's eye in the mirror. They were on the same page here, they both believed Max. Proving it was going to be problematic. Nick recognized what they were up against; if they couldn't find forensic evidence connecting Carter Duvall to Max, they wouldn't be able to get a prosecutor to take the case to trial.

And Max would always be in danger.

It was nearly nine on Sunday night when they arrived at Duvall's house. Rose looked at her phone. "Bad news," she said. "We finished the analysis of Bachman's and Baker's medical records, but there's nothing in them that's useful."

"Did Ullman look at them?" Marco asked.

"Ullman isn't on staff anymore. We still have competent people."

Nick said, "But they confirm that Duvall was their psychiatrist."

"Yes, but Baker was there two years before Bachman as a patient. He was an employee at the same time as Bachman was a patient, but there's no record of Bachman returning after ninety days of treatment."

"We need a warrant for any drugs Duvall prescribed over the last year."

"Why?"

"Where did the drugs come from that they used on Max?" Marco asked. "If we can connect them with Duvall, that's a start."

Pierce considered it. "Thin, but when the ERT unit and Ms. Revere's doctors give us their lab reports, I'll take it to the A.U.S.A. and see what she can do with it."

Marco was as arrogant as Max, Nick realized, but he

also had a deep faith in her and her abilities. Max had long said there was something at Greenhaven about Bachman, and so far everything has proven her right. Nick didn't have the history that Marco had, and for the first time he felt a pang of jealousy. He didn't want to explore it, because he didn't really know what to do with it. He was the new kid on the block, he couldn't even call Max his girlfriend.

Marco had said Max always came back to him. Nick didn't want to get in the middle of something so volatile. He had a bitch of an ex-wife and a son he didn't see enough of. They were moving this summer, and he would have to find a job in another state just to be close to his son. He didn't need any more drama in his life.

Yet . . . the thought of not seeing Max again saddened him. He wasn't ready to walk away.

He might not have much of a choice. He was supposed to be back on duty Tuesday.

The three of them walked up to the front door and Marco rang the bell. It took several minutes before Duvall answered. He was in sweats and a T-shirt and blatantly irritated.

"I told you I wasn't talking to you on a Sunday night. I have to work early tomorrow morning."

Rose said, "We understand that it was inconvenient to meet us at FBI headquarters, so we thought you would be more comfortable in your own home."

"I don't have to talk to you," he said, indignant.

It was an act, Nick thought. The guy was too calculating, assessing all of them. But he focused specifically on Marco.

Marco said, "Cole Baker is dead."

Duvall looked confused. "Why do I care? I haven't seen the kid in nearly two years."

"May we come in?"

He hesitated. "It's late, as I said."

"This is a serious situation."

Nick saw the debate—a cunning calculation—crossing Duvall's face.

"A few minutes," he said and led them back to the living room they'd sat in before.

They sat again, in the same places, with Nick standing to the side and Rose next to Marco. Rose said, "Dr. Duvall, have you met Maxine Revere?"

"I thought you wanted to talk about Cole Baker."

"We have evidence that Mr. Baker killed Ms. Revere's driver, then kidnapped her. We have him on video surveillance."

"You have a video of him killing someone?"

"We have a video of him driving a car that was later determined to have been stolen. The car was recovered this morning, with the original driver dead in the trunk. Mr. Baker was shot and killed while firing on law enforcement from that car. So I ask again, have you met Ms. Revere?"

Rose Pierce wasn't bad. She gave Duvall the information he wanted, but then turned it back to what she wanted.

Duvall was briefly flustered. "Yes—Wednesday she came by Greenhaven with her assistant. Ostensibly because her assistant had a drug problem. The girl admitted herself into Greenhaven on Friday, then overdosed that night and was taken to the hospital."

"Did you meet Riley Butler, Ms. Revere's assistant?"

"No. I wasn't on duty Thursday and Friday because I had a conference in Boston."

"Which you returned from at ten on Friday morning," Marco said.

"If you say so."

"Where did you go after you landed at LaGuardia?"

"Home," he answered automatically.

They were still trying to build a solid time line of Duvall's whereabouts from the minute Max was kidnapped until Sunday morning, but there were holes—including several hours after he landed at LaGuardia and when they'd confirmed he was at his house at six because of a conference call he'd had with colleagues on the West Coast. One hour driving back means he could have been in that warehouse for seven hours.

But Marco didn't push him on that, because until they could catch him in a lie—such as finding him or his vehicle on surveillance tapes during the hours he said he was home—they didn't want to tip their hand.

Pierce continued. "You indicated to Agent Lopez yesterday that you were aware of Ms. Revere and had read her true crime books. Correct?"

"Yes."

"Are you aware that Mr. Baker had an obsession with Ms. Revere? That he had all her books, articles, photos of her in his apartment?"

"No. As you know, Mr. Baker quit two years ago from Greenhaven."

"Have you seen him since he quit?"

There was the slightest hesitation, and if Nick had been asking the questions, he might have missed it, but he was so focused on Duvall it was practically a warning bell. "As I already said, no."

Marco asked, "Have you seen Adam Bachman since he left Greenhaven?"

"No," Duvall said. He straightened. "I'm tired, I have to be up at five in the morning. I'm asking you to leave."

"One more thing," Marco said, leaning forward, "Did you drug and torture Maxine Revere?"

It was clear that Duvall hadn't been expecting the in-your-face accusation.

"Out," he said. "I don't know what that woman told you, but I have no idea what you're talking about."

"Did you leave your house yesterday after Detective Santini and I were here?"

"I do not have to answer your questions. I also plan on filing a complaint with your office, considering you have a personal relationship with the alleged victim. You have no authority or right to come in here and question me. You're completely biased." Duvall stood. "If you need to speak with me, call my lawyer."

They walked out. Immediately, Rose asked Marco, "Are you still involved with Maxine? Tell me you're not, Marco. You're going to fuck up this case."

Nick said, "He's not."

Rose looked from Marco to Nick and back again. "Well, shit. I wondered why a cop from California was tagging along. Detective, you cannot be involved in this investigation if you have a personal relationship with the victim."

"I wasn't asking any questions. But that guy is lying. You both know it."

"Knowing it isn't proving it," Rose muttered. She climbed into the car and immediately got on her phone.

Marco looked at Nick. "I want to nail this guy, Santini."

"So do I."

"And when this is over? I'm going to get Max back."

Nick bristled. Maybe he was too competitive, but Marco grated on him. "Go ahead and try."

Chapter Thirty-one

She was alone again.

She sucked on her finger, the one she'd burned when she put more wood into the stove, even though it had blistered and scabbed and only hurt a little. Her pretty blue watch told her that it was December 31, noon. Her mom had been gone for seven days. One whole week.

Today was her birthday. She was no longer five. But six didn't feel any different.

She wandered the big, cold house. She slept by the woodstove because that was the only real warm spot, even though she was too scared to put the big logs in. She fed the stove smaller pieces, and she figured out how to adjust the vent, but didn't know how to make the heat go everywhere. But the living room was warm. And she'd rather sleep in the big room than upstairs in the far corner where the wind blew the trees against the window, scratch, scratch, scratch, *as if a monster was clawing to get in.*

There had been a big storm the day her mom left. What if she got hurt in the storm and was stuck somewhere down the mountain? What if there was no one to help her? Max-

ine didn't have a phone to call anyone. The phone in the cabin didn't work, her mom said. Maxine had tried it. Her mom was right.

Maxine didn't want to leave—her mother told her not to leave—and it had taken them a whole seventy minutes to drive here from where they got gas in the small store down the road. Maxine knew, she'd timed it on her pretty blue watch. Her mom's last boyfriend had given it to her. Perry. Maxine liked Perry, but like all her mom's boyfriends, he left. Or her mom left. Maxine didn't understand grown-ups much, and she didn't really care to.

Perry had a boat and they'd spent three weeks on his boat, sailing all the way from Maine to Florida. Maxine had so much fun, she'd wanted to do it again. Perry had games and he played with her. He taught her how to play poker and blackjack and Yahtzee. He had books on the boat, lots of books, and he read to her, something her mom hated to do. Maxine could read herself, she was very good at it, but she liked Perry's voice. It was deep and dark, like his skin. Her mom had never had a black boyfriend before, and maybe that's why Maxine liked Perry so much. He was new and different and laughed all the time.

Her mom said that Perry was a blueblood, but Max didn't think black people had blue blood when hers was red. They were just different on the outside. She'd asked him, though, because she was curious. She'd always been curious.

He'd laughed, that deep laugh she loved, but she felt silly and didn't join in.

"Sweet girl," he'd said, "I have red blood, same as you. Martha means that I'm from an old, wealthy New England family. Old money, dear girl. Old money."

"Is old money the same as new money? Is it worth more? Like the old paintings at the museum are worth more than new paintings?"

"*Money is money,*" *he said.* "*A dollar is a dollar. New, old, black, white, doesn't matter to me.*"

"*Is that why you love my mommy? Because you don't care that she's white?*"

He flinched. "*I don't care that she's white, just like she doesn't care that I'm black. We're just having fun, Maxine.*"

Maxine didn't ask any more questions, because she knew what that meant. It meant when they got to Florida, Perry would leave, and Max would never see him again.

Max was right. On that last day Perry had given her the pretty blue watch. "*To remember me,*" *he'd said.* "*You're a good kid, Maxine.*"

She didn't ask if she would see him again, because she didn't want him to lie to her like all the other people her mother introduced her to. They made promises they never kept, or Martha wouldn't allow them to keep. Perry made no promises, told her no lies, and maybe that's why Max loved him most of all.

She'd given him a small stuffed bear she'd gotten in a Happy Meal a year ago. Because they traveled all the time, she couldn't keep much. And sometimes her mother just forgot to pack up before they left one place and Max had to start all over. This bear stayed in her backpack— the one thing she never went anywhere without because she didn't know what Martha was going to do next.

"*To remember me,*" *she said.*

"*Maxie—I can't take this.*"

Tears burned, but she didn't cry. Only babies cried. "*I don't want you to forget me.*"

He took the bear and kissed it. "*Sweet girl, I could never forget you.*"

That was six months ago. But that was also when Max started keeping her journal. She didn't want to forget Perry or anyone else. She didn't want to forget the places

she went or saw, the good and the bad. And she was start-
ing to forget.

And now, on her sixth birthday, she wrote:

> *I've been in this cabin for one whole week. Mommy*
> *might be hurt. I don't know what to do. I organized*
> *all the food in the pantry and if I am careful and*
> *don't eat a lot, I think I have enough food for forty-*
> *seven more days. But that means I have to eat the*
> *canned peas. I don't like canned vegetables, espe-*
> *cially canned peas. They're squishy and make my*
> *tongue feel slimy. I wish I had an apple. I love apples.*
> *They're my favoritest fruit.*

The memory, the dream memory, was bittersweet, and
Max was partly conscious. Something niggled at the back
of her memory, then she sank into sleep again.

Only now, her memory became a nightmare.

She had returned to the same Wyoming cabin, only now
she was an adult. And Carter Duvall was there.

She was strapped to a chair, far from the fire. She was
so cold, but her fingers were hot, burned. "You are alone.
Abandoned. Everyone leaves you, Maxine. Perry. Your
mother. Your BFF Karen. Do you think anyone is going
to stick around now? Nick? David? Why? What do you of-
fer them except sarcasm and suffering, you arrogant, te-
nacious bitch! If only I had more time with you. If only I
could kill you myself."

He ran at her, and suddenly she was a little girl again,
hiding in the closet with bars like the Mexican jail, the
scratch, scratch, scratch of the trees on the window, but
there was no window. It was the scratch of claws, of rats
as they tried to get to her, and Carter Duvall called out at
her with a singsong voice, "I will find you and take from
you what you took from me. . . ."

A thousand scorpions flooded the closet and she felt the prick of a thousand stingers . . .

"Max. Maxine, it's okay. You're awake."

She opened her eyes. Her heart was racing. The machines were beeping and the nurse rushed in.

Nick was standing at her side, his hands on her arms as if holding her down. "Max, it was a nightmare."

She took several deep breaths. The nurse was about to inject something else in her IV, but Max said, "No. No more. I need to clear my head. What time is it?"

"Five in the morning. I told David to take a break."

The nurse checked the machines, pressed a couple of buttons and they stopped beeping. She said, "You need to talk to the doctor. You're going through withdrawals from the drugs and we can give you something to help."

"No. It was only three days. I'm ready to go home."

"I'll have the doctor talk to you," she said as she left.

Nick sat on the edge of her bed. "Max, he pumped you up with some heavy-duty hallucinogens and narcotics. They tested all the syringes. The combination of drugs could have killed you."

"I'm tough."

"You are."

She didn't feel tough. She felt bruised and battered and scared. She did not want to be scared. She didn't want to feel like the lost six-year-old who sat alone on her birthday in the middle of nowhere singing "Happy Birthday" to herself.

"I want to go home."

"The doctors want to keep you for another day or two."

"No. Not even an hour. I need to get out of this bed and find out why Duvall did this to me."

She swung her legs over and felt dizzy.

The doctor walked in. "Ms. Revere, I'm Doctor Morris

Levin. I don't advise that you leave now. You're still feeling the effects of the drugs, and we've only just begun to regulate your bodily functions. I'd like you here for a minimum of twenty-four hours, and I'd like to run more tests."

"No. And no."

"Detective"—the doctor turned to Nick—"I hope you can convince Ms. Revere to stay."

Max said, "He can't. I need to be home. I'm not sick. I'm just tired and sore and I can't sleep here. I want my own bed. My own pillows. My stuff." She sounded like a whiny child, but she didn't care. She wanted to go home.

"I can give you something—"

"Hell no. I'm done. I can't think!"

Dr. Levin wasn't happy, but he said, "I'd like to draw some more blood, test your blood sugar, your fluids, and change the bandages on your foot. Can you give me two hours to get this done? And promise you'll return for a checkup this week?"

Nick said, "David's at your place. I'll have him bring you clothes."

"Okay," Max agreed. "Two hours."

It took nearly three hours before the doctor finished the tests. Max was surprised when David didn't drive her home, but handed Nick his car keys. "I'm meeting Sally and the team who processed Baker's apartment. I'll let you know if I learn anything."

Nick opened the passenger door for Max and she hated that she needed his help to sit. Every cell in her body ached. The doctor had given her pain medication—swore to her it was mild and wouldn't cause an adverse reaction—but she didn't want to take it.

She closed her eyes. She just wanted her bed. Her home. Her view. An unlimited supply of water. No bugs, no rats, no scorpions. No nightmares.

She woke up with a jolt. The car wasn't moving. She opened her eyes and it was dark. Her heart raced.

"You're home," Nick said.

Nick.

She breathed out a long sigh. She was in her parking garage.

"I don't want you seeing me like this," she whispered. Her voice was raw and she wanted to cry.

You don't cry. Man up, Maxine. You've been through worse.

But she hadn't. The Mexican jail was awful, and lasted longer, but somehow the last three days was worse than anything she'd suffered before. Duvall had not only exposed her fears, he'd exposed her soul. Everything that made her who she was had been dissected and analyzed and she didn't know if she would ever be whole again. She was nothing but a million shattered pieces.

Nick reached out and touched her cheek. She flinched, and that's when a tear slipped out. She squeezed her eyes shut.

"I don't know who I am," she whispered.

"I do," he said. He kissed her cheek, then got out of the car and opened her door. Getting out of the car was harder than getting in. "You shouldn't have left the hospital."

"I'm not going back."

"I know."

He did the protective cop thing, assessed their surroundings, checked the stairwell while waiting for the elevator door to open. But he wasn't David. There was another side to the protection, more intimate.

She didn't want him to worry.

"I'm okay," she said as they rode up the elevator to her top-floor apartment.

"You will be," he replied.

He led her into her apartment, then closed and bolted

the door. "Stay here," he told her, then searched the entire apartment. "It's clear," he said a moment later.

She crossed the living room to the kitchen and took a water bottle from her refrigerator. She drank half of it without taking a breath. It was so cold, so good, she almost cried out from pleasure.

Then Nick would *really* think she was crazy.

Crazy. Duvall was trying to twist her up, make her lose her mind. And he might have succeeded. Would he have? Would she have completely broken? She felt like she was . . . except that she'd escaped. But maybe that was just instinct. Maybe she really was broken and was too stubborn to accept it.

"You need to lie down," Nick said.

"I need a shower. And food. Real food." At the thought of eating, her stomach rebelled, even through the hunger pains. "Something light. Like the chicken noodle soup you fed me in California."

He smiled, his eyes almost sparkling at the memory. That relaxed her. Nick was exactly who she remembered. "Let me help you upstairs."

She didn't refuse his help, because she wasn't sure she could do it on her own with the damn boot on her foot.

"You could sleep downstairs with me," Nick said when they reached the top of the stairs.

"Why are you in the guest room?" Max asked.

"Someone beat me to your bed."

He said it casually enough, but there was an underlying hostility that Max didn't quite understand.

Until she saw Marco's overnight bag and an extra suit hanging on the outside of her closet door.

"Well, shit."

"We don't need to talk about this now."

"We don't need to talk about this *at all*."

Max strode—as much as she could in the boot—into

her bathroom. Marco's razor and other toiletries were neatly set up on the right. She put them all back in his shaving kit and zipped it up. She went back to her bedroom and put his shaving kit in his bag, grabbed his suit and stuffed it on top, zipped everything up, and limped to the staircase. She wanted to make a statement and take it to the guest room, but she couldn't muster the strength to walk downstairs. She dropped it, intending to leave it on the top step, but it tipped over and rolled down to where the staircase first curved around.

"You don't have to prove anything to me," Nick said.

She turned and stared at him. Six weeks. It had been six weeks since she'd first met Nick. Hardly enough time to foster a relationship, but she didn't want him to think she was keeping two men in the wings. Ten years ago? She would have. Even five years ago, because she and Marco had been on and off so many times it made her head spin.

But not now. She didn't think it was Nick who changed her, though he was part of it. She'd simply grown up. Marco was her past. Nick was her present. And she refused to think about the future.

"I was going to visit you this weekend," she said simply. "Not Marco."

"I know."

Nick was the opposite of Marco. If Marco had been the one to find another man's clothes in her bedroom while they were in the middle of something, he would have lost it. He would have yelled, tossed the clothes out, then they would have fought, and probably ended up in bed together. Marco was all fire, hot and Cuban and passionate. Passionate about everything.

Nick was calm. Cool and comfortable like an ocean breeze on a warm day when all you wanted to do was lie down and soak in some sun and sand. So calm that she couldn't read him. She wanted to. She wanted to understand what made him tick. What made him so levelheaded and in control. She wanted to know was he really mad about Marco's things or did he just not care?

Duvall was right. Maybe she was incapable of forming attachments to anyone. Maybe she masked her inner coldness and inability to express emotions because she feared there was nothing inside except the cold. The fear of being abandoned, of loss, of hopelessness. That she was inadequate. That she was only half a person because she didn't know who her father was.

Intellectually, she knew it didn't matter who her father was, that her mother was a wild child who'd dumped her. The first ten years of her life when she moved from place to place, no roots, no family, no friends because her mother couldn't—wouldn't—sit still. Living the life of princess and pauper in the span of weeks, over and over and over again.

She came from nothing and no one.

Then Nick was at her side and walking her over to the bed. "You need to sleep. I'll make some soup."

She sat heavily on the bed. Her head was spinning. Maybe it was the pain meds they'd given her in the hospital or her own suppressed emotions. She didn't know. She didn't want Nick to leave, but she hated that she didn't want him to leave. Did that make her weak? Was she using him like she'd used so many men in her life?

She wanted to tell Nick to run away because she would hurt him. It was inevitable. Look at her track record. But what came out of her mouth was something she didn't expect.

"Do you believe me?"

"Believe what?"

"I didn't see him. That bastard Baker didn't say his name. But Carter Duvall was there. He orchestrated the whole thing."

"I know."

"You do?"

"We'll prove it."

"How?"

"We'll find a way."

He kissed her on the lips. Once. Twice. She relaxed. She leaned back, closed her eyes, sinking into her sea of pillows. Her bed. Her home.

"Nick?"

"I'm here."

"Bring your stuff up from the guest room."

Then she was asleep.

Nick stood at the top of the stairs and watched Max sleep.

Someone had done a number on her.

He'd gone from worried to angry to worried again. He'd never seen her so vulnerable. The closest she'd come was the night she spent in jail in California when his colleague Beck had her arrested for obstruction, before Nick and her attorney got the charge tossed. He didn't know the whole story about the time she spent in a Mexican prison, but he knew it had been several days and Marco had gotten her out through some off-book quasi-military operation. That intel he'd learned from David.

Nick felt like the odd man out here. David was her closest friend, Marco was her lover.

Ex-lover.

Nick pulled a blanket over Max's pale body. The vibrant, cocky reporter was gone; he didn't like this version of Max. For weeks he'd wondered why he was getting involved with someone like her. They were opposites. He didn't like her methods. He didn't like her jump-with-both-feet mentality. She had no fear of repercussions. It was like anything went as long as she got the truth. If she got hurt, she put a Band-Aid over it. She didn't apologize, she didn't back down.

Yet all the things he thought would annoy him also enamored him. Reckless, but driven. She cared about injustice. She empathized with victims in a way that Nick had rarely seen. It wasn't fake, it wasn't sweet, it was simply authentic.

She was also sexy and beautiful and had an inner confidence that made her glow.

He feared he was going through some midlife crisis. *Glow. Right.*

He went downstairs and rummaged through the kitchen. She had many cooking supplies and basic ingredients, but few fresh foods. Not a surprise—she'd been planning on spending the weekend with him. He found a well-stocked freezer with containers marked in Max's large, sweeping block letters, with contents and dates. He found a gallon bag of frozen chicken noodle soup that had been made three months ago.

The soup had just started to simmer when David and Marco came in.

"I can't believe you let her leave," Marco said to Nick.

Nick decided to ignore the comment. "She's sleeping. What have you learned?"

"Pierce is working on a warrant to search Duvall's home and office. We think we can get it, based on Max's statement, but we need to be careful in the wording," Marco said. "The FBI's evidence response team are still at the warehouse. There's evidence that's where Bachman killed his five victims."

"Then why did Baker dump Max's phone off the Brooklyn Bridge?" David asked.

"To confuse us." Marco and Nick said simultaneously.

"They found plastic bags identical to the type used to

suffocate the five victims. They found trace DNA and are processing it, but there are multiple samples," Marco said.

"Duvall?"

"It'll take days to process all the evidence, weeks or months to get back anything on DNA, even if we rush it."

"What about the dead lawyer?"

"This is where it's interesting," Marco said. "We have a witness who recognized Baker's picture, saw him early Friday morning around six."

"Okay. Why interesting? We knew that."

"Because Rose and I talked to the witness again today, and she said that Baker wasn't alone. There was a young woman with him. The woman was in Warren's yard playing with the dog when the witness took out her garbage. The witness didn't really think much of it, even though she didn't recognize the girl. When she came back from the Dumpster, she saw Baker leaving with the girl."

"Six in the morning?" Nick said. "Sounds like maybe Warren let the dog out, Baker slipped in, stabbed him, left. There was nothing else disturbed in the house?"

"Nothing—except his briefcase is missing, with all his files and notes on the trial."

"Computer?"

"Warren didn't like computers."

Nick sighed. "So there was another killer hanging out with Baker and Bachman? Another accomplice?"

"Possible, or Baker has a girl on the side. Good news is the witness is sharp. She's working with a sketch artist, says she would recognize the girl if she saw her. She liked Warren because he used to watch her poodles when she went out of town. Said he was nicer to dogs than to people."

David said, "Baker has been watching Max for a long time."

He was upset and angry with himself.

"David," Nick began, but he brushed him off.

"On and off for nearly two years," David continued. "But for the last six weeks, since she got back from California, he's been tracking her daily. He knew what car service the station used, knew when she usually left work, a list of restaurants she liked. Here's the kicker—he knew she was at Fringe last week, and who she talked to."

Marco said, "We already put an agent on the place, and on Melinda Sanchez, the bartender who talked to Max."

"So this was the plan all along?" Nick said. "Why did he wait until Thursday?"

"Maybe for the trial to be over?" David suggested. "Though why, I don't know."

Nick turned off the soup and put a lid on it to keep it warm.

Marco said, "I'm going to check on Maxine and crash for a couple hours." He walked over to the staircase. He saw his bag at the bottom of the stairs. Whipping around, he glared at Nick. "What the hell?"

"Take it up with Max," Nick said with a straight face.

Marco glared at him. He grabbed his bag and brushed by Nick. Then he stopped, turned around, and said, "It won't last." He walked down the short hall to the guest room and firmly shut the door behind him.

David was sitting in the living room, looking out the window. Nick sat across from him. "Sorry about that."

David waved off the comment. Instead, he said, "I'm quitting."

"Max isn't going to let you quit."

"She really doesn't have a say. Ben hired me. And Ben was right the other day. I failed her in the worst way."

"David, I don't know you well, but it's clear that Max depends on you."

"More than she should. I think the problem is that I care too much. I need a level of disconnect, of impartiality, in order to be a good bodyguard."

"David, were you ever just a bodyguard?"

"Yes, when I was first hired."

"No, you weren't. Max uses you for everything. Research. Discourse. Security. But for her, security is last on her mind. If you leave, it will do more damage than Duvall did."

David looked out the window to the Hudson River and didn't say anything.

Nick added, "Besides, I doubt Max will let you quit. She's quite persuasive."

David smiled, just a bit. "She did good. She got out of there. I'm proud of her."

"She needs you now. I have to go back to California—I don't want to, and that I don't want to leave makes me uncomfortable. But I can promise I'll be back the first opportunity."

"Good." He winked. "Team Nick."

"Hey, all I need is you on my side instead of Marco's and I win."

Chapter Thirty-two

The words blended together. Words and words, flowing over the pages, ink from her pen spilling blood.

The claw of the monster at the window . . .

The sting of the scorpion . . .

The gnawing rats, eating the flesh of the dead, waiting for Max to succumb. Would they wait until she was dead or just unconscious before they feasted?

"*Do you even see? You go to all the places your mother took you. Searching for what? Answers? Answers you cannot possibly find. Everything is about you, isn't it? Everything is about you. You and your mother. What she did. When she left. How you felt. Selfish and spoiled.*"

Her mother had sounded so guilty after she'd left Max for nine days. When she returned, she promised never to do it again. And she hadn't.

But nothing had been the same.

Martha couldn't do the things she wanted to.

"*Max, how about if you stay with Mommy's friends for a few days so I can go skiing? You know you can't ski the big slopes yet.*"

Max just looked at her, and Martha said, "You're so

selfish. I just want some alone time. Why can't I have that? Why are you making me feel so guilty?"

Martha was the selfish one, but at the time Max didn't understand. Martha had told her Victor Tracy was her father, but he wasn't. She'd lied. Max never told anyone about how she confronted the man, what he'd said, how she felt . . .

She sat upright. Her head hurt. It was like her brain was playing catch-up.

But she knew how Carter Duvall learned about her past. Her journals.

She slowly pulled herself out of bed. Hobbled up the short stairs to her office. A walk-in closet, big enough to double as a small bedroom, housed her old files—things she didn't want to get rid of. Notes on every investigation she worked. Disks. And her journals.

She still wrote in a journal, though sporadically. She'd needed them more when she was younger than she did now. She used writing in an attempt to understand her world, learn who she was, where she fit in. She'd read and reread her oldest diaries, from the time before her mother left. She remembered confronting Victor Tracy when she was sixteen.

Max had never told anyone that her mother lied about her father's identity. It never came up, and it's not like people would ask. And it wasn't like Victor Tracy wanted to admit he had an affair while he was married.

But she'd written about it. Especially when she was in college and actively trying to figure out where she'd come from. Never for the public. Only for herself.

Her journals were all there, where she kept them, neatly lined up. Her grandmother had stately day planners with gold leaf lettering on leather covers that she wrote in every day without fail; Max's journals were small, some cheap, some expensive, a mishmash of sizes because when she was on the road with her mother, she took what she could get. The last few volumes were uniform but the older journals housed Max's secrets and fears.

The same secrets and fears that Carter Duvall had convinced her he'd learned through reading her books, as if he could read her mind.

I can read between the lines.

Bullshit. He'd been here. He'd read the raw material. He was a liar.

Nothing was missing, but he must have read these. When? How had he known about them? Had he been in her apartment? This was a secure building.

Secure, but not impossible to break into, especially when she was out of town more than half the year. What if he had a friend in the building? A relative? Tricked the doorman? Forged a work order from her?

Her home. Her sanctuary. And he'd been in here.

Anger flooded through her and she toddled down the stairs. Nick and David were sitting at her dining table, notes spread in front of them. "Carter Duvall has been in my apartment," she said.

They looked at her, skeptical.

"I've kept journals since I was five. He said he knew all about me because of what I'd written. That's true—but it wasn't my books. It was my journals."

"Are they missing?" Nick asked.

"No. They're all in a cabinet in my office. But it's the only way he could have known that I was looking for my father. My mother told me he was Victor Tracy."

Marco was standing in the kitchen. "Are we talking about Victor Tracy, the guy who's been investigated by the FBI a half-dozen times?"

She had never wanted to talk about this. With anyone. It had been a dark time in her life. But she had no choice.

She sat down because she was feeling dizzy. Marco handed her a bottle of water, which she drank greedily.

"I need to start at the beginning. But—this is difficult for me. I've never lied about it, but I never talk about it, either."

"You don't have to," David said.

"Yes, because Duvall knows things I never speak of." She sipped more, collected her thoughts. "He told me that I'd written about all the places my mother had taken me growing up. That in my books and articles, I mentioned I'd been to the town before when I was younger. I didn't consciously return to any one town—I lived in dozens of big cities and small towns across the country before my tenth birthday.

"But he knew about Jackson, Wyoming." She wasn't going to explain that, not with all three of them staring at her. "It was a particularly dark moment in my childhood and he asked about it. But he already knew everything, just like he knew my mother lied to me about who my father was."

"You've talked about not knowing who your father is," Marco said.

"Yes, but I never wrote about what I did except in my journals. You didn't know I thought Victor Tracy was my father, did you?"

Marco shook his head.

"My mother never wanted to talk about my father, but I kept pressing her. When I was eight, she got mad at my nagging and told me Victor Tracy was my dad, but he was going to end up in jail and she didn't want me around him. After she left me with my grandparents, I followed Victor in the press. He was the subject of investigations that never went anyplace. I was sixteen when I hopped a plane to New York. I knew he was still suspected of all sorts of illegal activities, but when you're a teenager and never knew your dad—well, you make up fantasies."

It was both simple and complex. She wanted to know if he'd known about her. She wanted to know why he didn't want to be part of her life. And mostly, she wanted to know who she was. Where she'd come from. Who'd given her half of her genes. It wasn't logical, maybe, but when she was a young girl it had seemed like the single most important question to answer: *Who am I?*

"Long story short"—and it was a long story, one she wasn't ready to completely share, especially in a group— "he denied it. It wasn't pretty, to say the least, but I stood my ground. He'd admitted that he'd been involved with my mother for a summer—but that she was already pregnant with me. He dumped her not just because she'd started showing, but because he was married and didn't want to leave his wife or raise another man's kid. Still, I threatened to go to the press and publicly announce that he was my father, so he took the paternity test. It was negative."

"Why didn't you tell me about him?" Marco demanded.

"Because you're an FBI agent and he's a suspected criminal. Really, Marco, is that so difficult?"

"Do you still talk to him?"

"Yes." She wouldn't say that she and Victor had become friends, but he'd been the only one in her life who was forthcoming about her mother. She learned more about Martha from Victor than anyone else. She knew he was a scam artist, but they didn't talk about that. "I'm done with this conversation. The point is that I have always said publicly that I don't know who my father is." She knew, in her heart, that she was waiting for the time when her real dad would see something she wrote and contact her.

"I didn't know you existed," he'd say in her fantasy. *"Forgive me."*

But that was a childish fairy tale, the one she'd believed until the paternity test proved Victor Tracy wasn't her dad. For years she'd believed a lie because the one person she should have trusted above all others had lied to her.

"That means," she continued, "Duvall read my diaries. He knew about the paternity test. Not in so many words, but he implied it. And he knew about the cabin in Wyoming."

"What cabin?"

"My mother—she left me once and I didn't know if she would return."

"Your mother walked out when you were ten," Marco said.

"This was before that."

"How long?" David asked.

"A week or so. There was a storm. She couldn't get back to the cabin." At least that's what Martha had told her. Max didn't know if that was the truth. She'd told so many lies. It was ironic that Max could tell when other people were lying, but not her own mother, the mistress of the lie.

"Duvall wanted me to tell him everything I remembered, how I felt, what I thought, and he played these psychological games. I see through him now. It's so clear. We need to prove he was here."

"I'll call for someone from the lab to come in and dust for prints," Marco said.

David said, "The building keeps security tapes for thirty days. I'll review them, but he could have come in anytime."

"It'll be when I was out of town," she said. "Both of us. It could have been two years ago. When all this started."

"How would he know you had the journals?" Nick asked.

"If he's read my books, he would know. I've talked about my journals. A couple years ago I wrote an article about journaling and mentioned I started my first diary when I was five."

"Five," Nick said with a half grin. "I'm not surprised." He got up and went into the kitchen. "I warmed some of the soup I found in your freezer."

"Thank you. I'm finally hungry."

"Did he give you any clue as to why he's doing this?" Marco said.

"I took from him so he takes from me," she said.

"He said that?"

She closed her eyes, put herself back in the hellhole.

"You took from me; I'll take from you."

She frowned.

"What?" David asked. Nick walked back in with a warm bowl of soup and put it in front of her.

"He also said he would sue my estate and take every last dime. What if this is just about money?"

"Does that mean something to you?"

"No." She scowled and looked down at her soup. "I will be so mad if this is about money."

"There's more to it than that," Nick said quietly.

They all looked at him.

"Adam Bachman killed five people. Cole Baker killed four people, possibly more. The lawyer's briefcase is missing, which means Baker must have thought Bachman said something about him or Duvall to the attorney. They both received psychiatric counseling at the same place with the same doctor. Did Duvall see psychopathic tendencies in these young men? Did he nurture it? Baker was violent, angry. Baker is the poster boy for teens who grow up to kill. Duvall must have known that, seen it, and used it."

"Duvall didn't want to watch," Max said. "He left. I made him angry."

"What happened?" David asked.

Max really didn't want to talk about it. Three days was a long time to think about her failures and fears. But they needed something. "The drugs had started to wear off and I started thinking somewhat clearly. I remembered who he was through his voice. I challenged him. He was angry that he hadn't left me a whimpering mass of jelly. I think that's why he said as much as he did, about destroying my legacy and making sure no one found my body."

Her voice cracked, and she really needed to get herself together. These three men were all watching her.

Marco said, "We need to go through your files."

"I promise you, his name isn't there."

"But maybe he was affected on the periphery by one of your investigations," Marco said. "If it's okay with you, I'd like Arthur Ullman to come over and interview you. He might be able to pull more information out, something that can help us narrow it down."

"Okay," Max agreed. "I want to see Riley."

"Are you sure you're up for the drive?" David asked.

"I need to see her," she repeated. "Please."

"I'll take you," he said. "Marco, go ahead and bring Arthur up here, get started. It'll be at least a four-hour round-trip with traffic." He glanced at his watch. "It's noon. The traffic won't be impossible coming back to the city, so expect us around five."

"I'm going to change. I'll be right down." She started for the stairs. She was getting used to the boot. At the bottom stair she turned and looked back at the table. "This all started after *Maximum Exposure* first aired. Duvall talked about my books, my articles, not the show—but Baker moved here two years ago. I've thought about those early programs and Duvall's name never came up. I never heard of him before this week."

"Then we start there and work backwards," Marco said.

"Money. Legacy. We're digging into his background. There's something there and we'll find it."

Max slept most of the ride to Hartford. Somehow, riding in the car with David, she didn't have any nightmares.

A family stood outside Riley's room, and Max knew they were Riley's parents and brothers. They stared at her with tired, worried eyes. Guilt crept up her spine. What had she been thinking coming here? Of course they blamed her. She blamed herself.

She walked as tall as she could over to the Butlers. "Doctor Butler, Lieutenant Butler, I'm Maxine Revere. I would have been here earlier, if I could."

Dr. Butler took her hand. She was a petite woman, with the same mass of black curls that Riley had, cut shorter. "David told us. How are you?"

Max didn't know how to take the honest concern in the woman's eyes. "Better," she said. "I wanted to see Riley."

"Of course. Her doctor asked us to leave for a minute, but she's going home today."

Relief flooded through her. "I'm glad."

"We're taking her to Boston," Lieutenant Butler said, underscoring the point that when they said home they meant with them.

"That'll be good for her."

They stood in an awkward silence. Max wanted to apologize, to tell these people that she was sorry. She should have seen the drive in Riley. It made sense now, in hindsight. All the hours she put in to sell herself to Ben. Always trying to go above and beyond because she thought David didn't like her. Riley had so much potential, and Max hoped she didn't give up.

"When she's ready to come back," Max said, "her job will still be there."

"We'll see," Lieutenant Butler said.

His wife glanced at him, exchanging one of those silent conversations that people long in love did so well. She then turned to Max and said, "Tell Riley that. She needs to hear it."

The doctor stepped out and was about to speak until he saw Max and David. Dr. Butler said, "Please, Doctor, you can speak freely."

"I'll sign her discharge papers as soon as I get the results of the last blood test," he said. "But she's ready to go. She's still having trouble with her memory, but that's due to the benzodiazepine she was injected with more than the heroin."

Max said, "Riley lost her memory?"

The doctor turned to her and hesitated, so Dr. Butler said, "It's a drug commonly used pre-op or for surgeries where the patient isn't put under general anesthesia. Variants are used in Rohyphol and similar drugs, but the primary side effect is retrograde amnesia. Riley can't remember anything from the day she was attacked. She doesn't remember why she was at Greenhaven, but she does remember visiting the facility with you."

Riley's doctor said, "I'll start the paperwork. She's over the worst of the withdrawal symptoms, but her system is weak and compromised. If she didn't have you at home, Doctor Butler, I would insist on keeping her here another couple of days."

"She'll do better at home," Dr. Butler said.

The doctor excused himself, and Max looked at Riley's parents.

"Go in," the lieutenant said gruffly. "But not long. She needs rest."

"I'll wait here," David said.

Max walked into Riley's hospital room alone. Riley was lying in the hospital bed, eyes closed, dark circles dominating her tan complexion. Her curly hair was limp and stringy and she'd lost weight.

"Hello, Riley," Max said.

Riley opened her eyes. It took her a moment to recognize Max, as if she hadn't been expecting her to walk in.

"Max," she said a moment later. "You're okay."

"Yes."

"What happened?"

"It's a long story."

Riley frowned. "I'm sorry."

"Don't apologize."

"I fucked up."

"You followed a lead. Yeah, it was stupid to go to Greenhaven without telling anyone, without having someone as backup, but your instincts were good."

"My dad is so mad. And—he's worried. I hate to worry my parents."

"Your mom's a rock."

Riley smiled. "Yeah. She's the only one who wanted me to take this job. She's always encouraged me to do what I wanted to do. But" — her smile faltered — "I can't remember who did this to me. I can't remember what I learned at Greenhaven. I don't even know if I found anything important."

"You must have, otherwise you wouldn't be here."

"I'm going back to Boston," she said.

"Your parents told me. But I want you to know, as soon as you feel ready, your job will be waiting for you."

Riley sighed and closed her eyes. "I don't know if I'm cut out for this."

"You are," Max said. "You're good. You needed a better teacher than me."

"You taught me so much." She looked at Max. "I just don't think I'm good enough. I never thought it was dangerous. I read all your books, all your articles, and you glossed over all that."

"Because whatever happens to me isn't important compared to what happened to the victims I write about. I've risked my life many times, and maybe I shouldn't have minimized those things."

"Did you ever regret anything?"

Max opened her mouth to say yes, but she couldn't. She didn't live her life in regrets. If she did, she wouldn't be able to get up in the morning. Instead, she said, "I've made a lot of mistakes, but I've never regretted exposing the truth to get justice for those who can't get it for themselves. I remember that if I hadn't gone to Mexico and exposed the human traffickers who'd let three dozen women and children die locked in a hot truck, their families would never have known what happened to them. They suffered far more than I did. If I hadn't exposed Lauren Smith and her group of wackos, innocent seniors would continue to die because of her greed and hate. I remember the successes. You have to as well." She paused. "Your dad understands this, because it's a lot like being a cop. They can't save everyone. But they do the job because they can save many."

"I'll think about it," Riley said a moment later.

"Call me. Whenever you want."

"I still made a mistake, Max. A big one. And I can't even remember what it was."

"But you did it for the right reasons, and that makes all the difference," Max said. "Is there anything you remember? Even if it doesn't make sense."

"I keep having this dream. I don't know if it's real."

"I'm listening."

"I'm at the courthouse and I run into this older guy. Not ancient, but older. And then I wake up."

"You spent a lot of time at the courthouse last week."

"And I think I really did run into someone. I was texting and walking in the hall. He teased me. That it was against the law to text and walk. And I think that's all real, but I don't know why I'm dreaming about it, or why I wake up scared."

Max took her hand. "Go home. Get better. Call me."

Chapter Thirty-three

Max woke up early Tuesday morning, before the sun rose, and looked at Nick sleeping next to her.

She'd fallen asleep on the couch in her office the night before while the six of them—Sally O'Hara had joined them shortly after Max got back from visiting Riley—went through Max's investigations. Arthur had talked to her extensively, asking questions about what she remembered, what Duvall asked, how he asked it. Her memory was good, but there were holes. Things she couldn't remember. She had a vague feeling of bugs on her skin, but she didn't know if that was real or the drugs. She had felt pinpricks on her feet, her arms, but were they even real? And the rats . . . certainly they had been a hallucination.

Marco was working with security at the courthouse to obtain a copy of all digital recordings for the week of Bachman's trial. He didn't find credence to Riley's half-dream/half-memory, but Max did. It was worth looking into.

The last thing she remembered Arthur saying before she dozed off was, "He's jealous. In a deep, subconscious way. He has a deep envy for Max that directly connects to something she has that he doesn't. It's likely a combination of money and status." He said more, but Max was exhausted, and she fell to sleep until Nick helped her down the half flight of stairs to her bedroom suite.

She hadn't dreamed all night, no nightmares, no memories. She was grateful, except that she woke at five in the morning and couldn't go to back to sleep. But five hours was more than she usually had, and dreamless hours were coveted.

"Hey," Nick said.

"I didn't mean to wake you." She rolled over to face him. "I heard you tell David you rearranged your schedule. Thank you."

"Don't thank me. I want to be here."

"When do you have to leave?"

"Tomorrow morning." He reached over and played with the ends of her hair. "Are you going to take some time off?"

She smiled. "Is that an invitation?"

"Always."

"I'll be there as soon as I can. I owe you."

"You owe me nothing."

"I'm surprised Marco let you work with him."

"He doesn't like me, but he respects me."

"What does that mean?"

Nick arched his eyebrows. "You're not that naïve, Maxine."

"You knew I had a history with him."

"Vaguely."

"I'll give you the full disclosure if you want."

He kissed her. "As long as it's in the past, I don't need any explanation."

"Of course he's the past. What did he tell you?"

"It's not what he said, it's what I know. He's in love with you."

She would have laughed, but it wasn't funny. "No, Nick. He's in love with who he wants me to be. Not with who I am."

"I guess I do have a question then. Why go back and forth with him for so long if there's nothing there?"

"You really want to do this?"

"Not if you don't want to. But I have a difficult ex-wife, a son, and I'm moving as soon as I find a job in whatever town Nancy settles in. She's changed it on me twice already. It's a common story, but complex at the same time. At least for me."

"I don't want to talk about Marco while I'm lying in bed with you. But I'll say this—we've been through a lot together, and I'll never forget that. I met him when I was twenty-two. He was the FBI agent in charge of Karen's murder investigation, because I got the FBI involved when the Miami police refused to do what needed to be done. I still blame them for her killer walking."

"I read your book."

She almost smiled. "So you know. Because of that year, Marco and I will always be connected. And there have been some other things we've gone through which means that any man in my life is going to have to accept that Marco will be part of my life in some way. But the intimacy is over. I can't—won't—be the person he wants." She paused. "He lied to me about something pretty big. It was related to an investigation we were both working. Different angles. I have a hard time with forgiveness."

"That *is* an understatement."

"I'm not an easy person, Nick."

"I knew that from the moment I met you. Maybe I need a little excitement in my life."

She reached over, put her hand around his neck, and pulled him in for a kiss. "I think I need a little excitement right now," she whispered.

* * *

Max almost felt like herself when she walked into the *Maximum Exposure* offices late Tuesday morning. Other than the fact that it was nearly noon and she usually arrived before eight.

David was at her side, which made the questions and well wishes easier to address.

Ben came up to her and spontaneously hugged her. It was a genuine emotion. He'd visited her briefly in the hospital, but she hadn't seen him since Sunday. Through David, Max knew that Ben was working himself and the entire staff hard, analyzing her *Maximum Exposure* shows and articles while also assigning their best researcher, C. J., to Carter Duvall himself.

"I have the main conference room set up," Ben said. "It's been a lot of work, but I'm impressed by our team and what we've accomplished."

Max followed Ben into the conference room. She agreed—the room had been transformed into a career summary of her life for the past two years.

Ben had brought in enough corkboard to cover three walls. A time line, similar to the time line in her home office that she used for each individual case, was labeled across the top, starting with July 10, two years ago, her first *Maximum Exposure* show. They'd covered active missing persons cases, leading with a case she'd investigated in Colorado Springs about a college student who disappeared while on a camping trip.

Each article she'd written or interview she'd done was attached to the corkboard with index cards as labels.

Directly under the time line were the facts related to the current situation—when Cole Baker quit Greenhaven, when he moved to New York, details from his journal on where he'd watched her and when. Max shivered as she realized he'd been watching her on and off for nearly two years.

Ben said, "We're focusing heavily on the first six months of *Maximum Exposure,* plus we've gone back to your last book, because we promoted it heavily in our opening show and in the release month. The articles on the left you wrote directly or indirectly related to the show; the articles on the right were independent."

"Ben, I don't know what to say. This is terrific."

"There's only one problem," Ben said. "Nothing jumps out at me that relates to any of these people. We've cross-referenced the names of anyone associated with these investigations to Duvall, Bachman, Baker, and Greenhaven itself—no crossovers. None. We're expanding it to include family and close friends, but that's harder to identify."

David held out a chair for her. "Off the foot, Max."

She sat. "Arthur Ullman said it's personal, and it sounded very personal when Duvall talked to me. I took something from him. Have you looked into my finances? The Sterling-Revere Trust? Did my family do anything to him?"

Ben sat down across from her. "Yes, the one thing I know better than television is money, so I had C. J. run Duvall's financials first. Other than his house, he doesn't have many assets. His salary is on par with others in the field, he receives a small supplement from royalties on his two books, he receives speaking fees several times a year."

"What did he do before Greenhaven that he could afford a house worth more than a million in Stamford?"

"Family house. It was his grandparents'. He and his sister inherited it."

"Where's his sister?" she asked.

"I don't know," Ben admitted. "His parents are divorced, both remarried, I don't know their status. His sister lives out of the area. We were focusing on more recent interests—the last two years."

"We should talk to his sister," Max said.

"I'll find the information," Ben said. "But you should know that everything we're getting on this we're also giving to the FBI. I agreed because Marco promised to share his information."

"And has he?" she asked. She was still irritated that he'd laid claim to her bed when he arrived. Though, she had to admit, he'd gone above and beyond in helping her. He always did, even when they weren't together.

"I believe so."

Marco stepped into the room. "Of course I have. And I have more." He dumped a thick file on the conference table. "This is everything we have on Duvall from the day he was born. It's all yours, Maxine. We've gone through it and nothing jumps out at us, so our analysts are digging into each section deeper. But you said something last night, that maybe because it's personal you'll see something that we might miss."

"Thank you," Max said. She opened the file, while Marco talked to Ben about the shows she covered during the first three months *Maximum Exposure* aired. She half listened to how Marco had gone through the records of the "Killer Nurse" case in Miami—since that was the subject of her last book and it had been published two years ago—and there was no connection to Duvall, Bachman, or Baker. He had questions about her other investigations, but Max blocked him out as she flipped through Duvall's background.

The FBI was thorough. Duvall and his younger sister Diana had been born in Stamford, Connecticut. He was forty-five, she was forty-one. Their parents divorced when he was seven. The FBI had copies of the court records. It had been contentious because while they'd started off with a lot of family money, they'd hit rough times—when most other people were doing so well. They overextended, and the money became the root of their conflict. Both ended up with very little, and they'd sold the family home. The mother, Faith Duvall, moved in with her parents, taking the kids with her. The father, Bruce Duvall, remarried almost immediately to a wealthy socialite from Virginia, where he relocated. There had been allegations of adultery, but they hadn't factored into the divorce settlement.

Carter Duvall graduated college in Connecticut, but there wasn't anything here about his high school years. "Where did Duvall live after his mother remarried?" she asked Marco. "In fact, there's nothing here about his mother's second marriage, but you said she'd remarried."

"Someone mentioned it," he said. "It should be easy to find."

Ben said, "I'll get C. J. on it. Connecticut?"

"And neighboring states," Max said.

"See something?" Marco sat down next to her when Ben left.

"No. But he was fixated on my past. What my mother did to me, how she lied to me, pulling things out from what I wrote in my journals, but wanting me to believe he figured me out from my books. There has to be a reason why he wanted to dredge up all that."

She skimmed his employment records. He'd spent most of his career at Greenhaven. He'd been employed as the staff psychiatrist at a juvenile detention facility in Staten Island prior to that, for seven years. The timing worked— college, medical school, Staten Island for seven years, then Greenhaven for nine years. There weren't any breaks in his employment, at least officially.

"You never talk about your early childhood," Marco said.

"I don't want to now."

"It explains a lot."

She turned to him. "Marco, do not try to analyze me.

am exactly what I appear to be. I've never lied about my mother or not knowing who my father is or that my mother dumped me when I was ten. Just because I don't talk about living like a nomad the first ten years of my life doesn't mean I've forgotten or lied about it."

"That's not what I mean."

"I know what you mean," she said. "You think you now have this insight into my personality that will somehow help you get me back into your bed. I haven't changed. I'm not going to."

"We've never just been about sex."

"You lied to me, Marco. It wasn't a lie of omission, it was a big fucking lie and I can't forgive that."

"I did it to protect you and protect my investigation."

"You did it to protect your criminal informant in order to get a bigger fish. Don't you *dare* say you lied to me to protect me. I don't want that kind of protection."

"Then let me *not* lie to you. Nick isn't going to stick around. He doesn't have the staying power. His family is in California. He has a son. His priority will never be you."

Though Max knew Marco was simply jealous, the comment still stung.

"I'm not competing with his son. And right now, I don't care about priorities or where I fall in some mythical range. Don't try to put a wedge between Nick and me because you think we're going to get back together. The chances are this thing with Nick won't work out—I don't have a great track record as you love to point out." She held up her hand to stop him from interrupting her. "But I still won't be calling *you.*"

He bristled and got up. Max hadn't meant to sound so mean, but he'd pushed her, and that made her mad.

She said, "I wish you would just accept my friendship and leave it at that."

She didn't know if he heard her because he was already

at the doorway. Then he turned around and said, "I wan more."

"I don't have more to give."

"Bullshit," he said and left.

Max stared out the lone window that hadn't been cov ered up by corkboard. She wished Marco could under stand. She wished she'd told him that she appreciated he' come here for her. That she respected him and cared abou him.

But he'd said it himself: he'd lied to protect her and hi case. And that would not stop. Max couldn't live like tha She shouldn't have to.

She held people to a high standard, and yes, it went bac to her mother. What didn't? Her mother had shaped he into being who Max was today. Her mother, who couldn' sit still. Who wasted money, going from princess to pau per in weeks, every single month for the first nine year and eleven months of Max's life. Who'd left her for day at a time with "friends" when Max didn't think her mothe ever really knew most of those people, not well. Wh hooked up with men like Perry and Victor for a month o two at a time, just because she was bored. Then she lef Max . . . without telling her why.

So yes, Max was who she was because of her pas Wasn't everyone?

Max realized she'd been looking at Duvall's backgroun check in the order it had been presented and, essentially fact-checking from when he started college. But there wer holes from his childhood. His mother's remarriage. Hi childhood after the divorce until he went to college. Wha happened in those years?

She got up and went down the hall to the research wing The team had individual cubicles where they could all spi their chairs around and sit in the center for brainstormin She liked the research team because they thought like sh did and, in some ways, more innovatively. And better, they knew how to get information as fast as—or faster than— he did.

C. J. was deep into reading a document when she interrupted him. "Sorry," she said.

"It's okay. I don't have anything new—at least nothing that's important."

"I need something very specific. I'd like his extended family. Aunts and uncles. Everything about his father's second wife and his mother's second husband."

"Do you know what you're looking for?"

"No. But he has a beef with me, and I think it goes back a long way. Maybe not me personally, but my family. And I can't discount that it's something completely benign, something he blew out of proportion."

C. J. looked up at her. "Nothing justifies what he's done."

Her cell phone rang. "Just feed me the information as you get it. Thanks."

She stepped out and answered the unfamiliar number.

"Maxine Revere."

"Hello, Ms. Revere?"

"Yes."

"This is Ava Raines. Do you remember me?"

"Of course. What can I do for you?"

"Um, I'm really confused right now. Ms. Golden told me what happened at the jail. That Adam Bachman killed himself. And I'm just . . . I don't know. It's like I don't have anything to do. And she said the jury has been disbanded. I don't even know if they would have kept him in jail." She paused. "I'm not making any sense, am I?"

"I understand. You don't have closure, and you want to put this behind you."

"Yeah. I guess."

"If you want my opinion, I think he was guilty, and his

guilt ate him up. It's likely the reason he killed himself
Either guilt or finally realizing he was going to spend the
rest of his life locked behind bars."

"You think so?"

"Yes, I do."

"Um, Ms. Golden said I can talk to you now, if I want
Do you still want to or do you not care anymore since it'
all over?"

"I care. Just because he's dead doesn't mean the victim
or their families can forget what happened. I can find tim
to talk to you." She stepped into her office and looked a
her calendar. Nick was leaving in the morning. David ha
scheduled him a 6:00 A.M. flight back. She had a lot o
work to do, but getting an interview with Ava Raines woul
be a coup. "How about nine tomorrow morning?"

"Tomorrow?" Her voice squeaked. "I guess."

"Is there something else?"

"No, not really. I'm just confused. There was a new
story last night that the police found the building wher
he killed everyone. Do you know if it's true?"

"I saw the same report."

"Then you heard the same thing, that there was some
one else there who might have killed people, and that th
police rescued a woman and killed the guy. And all I coul
think about was, what if it had been me?"

"It wasn't you."

Ava sounded lost and alone. Max asked, "Where's you
father? Do you have anyone who can stay with you to
night?"

"My dad's working this week, a job in Jersey. He's no
going to be home until this weekend. I just wanted to tal
to someone who knows what's going on. I'm sorry t
bother you."

Max looked at her watch. It was two. She had time, an
sitting around here waiting for information was going t

drive her crazy. "If you have time now, I can meet somewhere closer to you."

"I don't want to trouble you."

"Really, it's not. It might take me an hour or so to get out there, but I can do it."

"I'd like that—before we do a real interview or anything."

Max often met with her interviewees before the formal interview. It put them at ease in what could be an emotional situation. And what Ava Raines endured—being kidnapped, trapped, barely escaping, and now not getting justice because Adam Bachman took his own life—Max had more than sympathy for her. She knew exactly how she felt.

They'd both escaped death.

"Is there a coffee place you like near you?" Max asked.

"Um, you can just come to my house. If that's okay."

"Sure. Give me your address," Max said. She wrote it down, then said, "It'll be me and my assistant, but he'll give us space to talk."

"Thank you. Thank you so much, I already feel better. Like someone cares about me."

"I do," Max assured her and hung up.

David was standing in her doorway. "I'm glad you acknowledged that you were bringing your assistant," he said. "That would be me, correct?"

She smiled. "I promised I wouldn't leave without you. That was Ava Raines. She's confused and sounds a bit lost. Charlene gave her the party line, but the girl's been through the wringer of the trial and testifying and then the news reports about what the police uncovered at the warehouse." She hesitated. "How did you keep my name out of it?"

"That was all Sally. It may come out, but when it does, it shouldn't have as big an impact after the fact."

"I appreciate it." She hesitated. "It puts my job in a different perspective."

"Are you sure you're up to driving out to Long Island?"

She *was* tired. "I'm okay."

"After, straight back to your apartment."

"I won't argue. Let's leave as soon as I fill Ben in on the plan. I'm meeting Nick for dinner at seven, since it's his last night here."

Ten minutes later, as David pulled out of the parking garage, Max's cell phone beeped with incoming messages. "From C. J.," she said and skimmed them. "Holy shit."

"He found something?"

"Yeah . . . but I have no idea what it means." Max stared at the document he'd scanned. It was Faith Duvall's second marriage license. "Duvall's mother married Victor Tracy."

David glanced at her. "The guy you thought was your father? When?"

"Three years before I was born. Duvall would have been ten then, thirteen when I was born. Twenty-nine when I confronted Victor. But this has to be a coincidence. Victor *isn't* my father."

"It's the only connection we've found between you and Duvall."

"It's thin. And why, dammit? Why does he hate me so much that he planned to torture and kill me? Because his mother married a guy I *thought* was my dad? Because my mother had an affair with his mother's husband? That's ridiculous."

"The guy's a wack job, Max. I don't know that you can make sense of his reasons."

"No . . ." If Duvall's reasons had anything to do with Victor Tracy, it wasn't because of an affair. It made *no* sense.

"Talk it out," David said.

"I can't wrap my head around it." She thanked C. J. for the information and sent him a message asking for more information about Faith Duvall Tracy.

"Did you meet her?" he asked.

"Yes. She didn't know about my mother."

"How certain are you about that?"

"I didn't tell her. She didn't have any opinion about me, as far as I know." She paused, putting herself back into the past. "I was sixteen when I met Victor. We didn't hit it off, trust me on that. I manipulated him into the paternity test. But when I started classes at Columbia, I reached out to him again. I wanted to know more about my mother. I wasn't ready to hear it when I was sixteen. He's an interesting guy. I know all about his legal problems, and there's no doubt that he's a criminal, at least he had been. He ended up in prison for a short time—pled guilty on something and had his sentence reduced. It was a high-stakes game to him. Can people change? I don't know. But going to prison and having to pay restitution definitely impacted him. He's living a very quiet life now as a forensic accountant."

"Did he ever talk to you about his wife?"

"Not much. He said she was fragile. Delicate. He never talked about having two stepkids. But by the time I met Victor, Duvall would have been nearly thirty."

"It seems that if Duvall was this obsessed, it didn't come out of left field. He probably had issues growing up."

"Most killers do," Max said.

"Can you call Victor?"

"And say what?"

"That's up to you."

It was a good idea. They'd kept in touch, but nothing regular, and she hadn't spoken to him in more than a year. Nearly two years. He'd moved to Boston after serving his time in federal prison. She'd had dinner with him the night before he surrendered, and she'd visited him once in prison. That was the last time she'd seen him.

Before she could talk herself out of it, she looked up his number and pressed send.

He answered on the third ring. "Hello. Maxine?"

"Hello, Victor. How are you?"

"Surprised to hear from you. Is everything okay?"

"I'm fine. It's been a while, I know. I have a specific reason to call. Do you have a minute?"

"Of course."

"It's about Carter Duvall."

Silence.

"Victor?"

"I don't know what to tell you. I haven't seen him in years. What is this about?"

"He's your wife's son, from her first marriage, correct?"

"Yes. Is this official, Maxine?" He'd gone from friendly to confused to belligerent.

"Yes and no." What did she tell him? Vague was best. "Carter is the subject of a police investigation. He threatened me, the police are taking it seriously."

"What kind of threat?"

"He tried to kill me."

"Oh, God."

"I didn't know he was related to you until now, as we're going over his background. The police didn't know my connection to you, so they didn't even think to follow up."

"Did you tell them?"

"I just found out. What do you know? Victor, this is important."

"Faith is so delicate . . ."

"So you have said for years. Victor, do you know why Carter Duvall hates me so much that he wants me dead? He said I took from him and he'll take from me. What does that mean?"

"Are you positive it was Carter?"

"Yes. Why are you being evasive?"

"Faith has been in an assisted living facility for the past ten years."

"You never told me that."

"I don't tell many people. She had a nervous break-down. She's never recovered."

"Over what?"

"It's a mental illness. I don't think there was any one thing, it was a buildup. I care for her, but we never had a real marriage. I didn't realize, until later, that she knew about my affairs. She was so fragile, so sweet, but I didn't realize until we were married that there was something off about her. And I blame myself for making it worse.

"Remember the dinner we had before I went to prison?" he asked.

"Of course."

"I wasn't planning on surrendering. I knew the FBI had a fairly good case, and my lawyer had arranged a terrific plea agreement. But I wanted to run. My freedom meant something to me. But when I told you about the agreement, you were proud of me, and I felt ashamed. For what I'd done to strangers, for what I'd said to you, for what I'd done to my family. I didn't want to lie anymore. So I agreed to the plea deal and went to prison for four years.

"But I lost everything. Including the trust I'd set up to take care of Faith. Carter blamed me, and he took over paying for her care. It's expensive, especially in the place I had her. Now that I'm making a steady income, I offered to help, but he won't talk to me and won't take the money. He tried to stop me from seeing her, but I fought him on that. A few years ago he tried to legally end my marriage, but because I didn't want to and I wasn't receiving a finan-cial benefit from being married to Faith, the judge denied him."

"I had no idea."

"I didn't talk about it. You were only interested in finding out what happened to your mother. I didn't want to trouble you with my worries."

"I was selfish."

"You were young."

That didn't discount that she'd used Victor's knowledge and information without thinking to ask how he was doing.

"I'm sorry." And she meant it.

"Maxine, you were practically a child when you first came to me. I appreciate that you sent me letters while I was in prison, and that you were honest with me from the beginning. I wasn't as kind to you then, and I'm sorry about that."

"All this—it's about you and Carter. If he hurts me, he doesn't directly hurt you. We don't have that kind of relationship." Max's head was beginning to hurt trying to piece it together.

"I really don't—" he stopped.

"What do you remember?"

"There's one thing. When you moved to New York, when you were still in college, do you remember that we met once at the café near the Museum of Natural History? It was three months before I was arrested."

"I remember." Her great-grandmother had just died and left her one-fifth of her estate that would have gone to her mother. If Martha didn't show up within a year, the money went to Maxine. Max had been grieving and overwhelmed and Victor had given her a crash course on financial planning and trust management, starting at that lunch. "You saved my ass."

"I knew it was only a matter of time before the FBI finally gathered enough evidence against me, and I wanted to help while I could. And I felt bad for how I treated you when you first came to me. After that, Carter confronted me. He thought I was cheating on Faith again. I was angry, and told him to grow up. That you were far too young for me and we were just friends. He didn't believe me. And when the FBI came knocking, they said someone I was close to had turned state's evidence."

"Who?"

"I don't know. I didn't then, and the FBI never revealed the name of their informant when I pled. I suspect it was a bluff. But Carter thought it was you, that you'd seduced me to gain information to turn over to the feds."

"That's insane."

"I said as much. But Carter was angry. I knew Faith had married me for my money, and when things were going well, she was well. But when things got rough, that's when she fell apart. It wasn't normal, I see that now, but I blamed myself for her troubles. I didn't see that she had problems from the beginning. Well, maybe I did, and that's why I justified the affairs I had. I don't know. I've spent so much time trying to make things right, I've only made them worse. But I still don't see why Carter would try to kill you."

You took from me; I'll take from you.

It *was* about money.

"I think I'm beginning to understand," she said. "Did he have any troubles as a child?"

"Like what? He didn't kill animals or wet his bed, if that's what you're getting at."

Maybe she was, but she said, "No. Just—did he seem off to you?"

"He was distant. He didn't have close friends. He saw a therapist most of his childhood. Faith insisted on it, to help him deal with the divorce and her remarriage. I was stunned when he went into medicine and became a psychiatrist. He'd always been smart, but considering he spent half his childhood in therapy for no discernible reason I could see, I wondered why he chose that field."

"What about his sister, Diana?"

"Sweet kid, but she cut ties when I was first investigated. She'd always been closer to her father than her mother. She's married and living in Virginia, I think. I haven't been in contact with her in years, and she never visits her mother."

"I appreciate this, Victor."

"Are you going to tell me what's going on?"

"When it's over. Know that Carter is dangerous. You might want to avoid him for a while."

"Honestly? I haven't seen or heard from him since he tried to dissolve my marriage to his mother."

She thanked Victor and hung up. "Did you hear that?" she asked David.

"Most of it. Duvall is a nut job. Targeting you because he thought you had something to do with the stepfather he didn't like going to jail?"

"That's not it," she said. "It's not about Victor. It's about the perception that *I* took him down. And now it makes sense. He didn't know who I was, but he remembered me. So when he saw me on *Maximum Exposure* he made the connection. I was a reporter, I must have been involved in Victor's takedown which, by extension, hurt his mother who was dependent on Victor's money for her medical care. Carter had to take it over, which would be a huge drain on his finances."

"According to Marco, nothing jumped out as unusual on his finances."

"Maybe they weren't looking at the right place. Carter was raised by an expert in financial fraud. He probably learned a few tricks. *Someone* was paying for Baker's apartment in Queens, and I don't buy him getting by solely on odd jobs."

"Call Marco."

"We're nearly to Ava's. I'll send him a message and have him dig around more."

She typed fast, and hit send as soon as David pulled up in front of the Raines' property. It was an older house and had once been a charming Victorian, but had fallen into disrepair. But the bones of the house were solid.

It was nearly four. "One hour, tops," she said, "so I can get back to the city and say good-bye to Nick."

Marco walked into the conference room and was surprised to see Nick Santini standing there, reading the corkboards that Ben and his staff had erected.

"I thought you flew back to California," he said.

"Tomorrow morning." Nick turned around and faced him. Marco didn't want to like the detective, but he couldn't find fault with him. That made Marco grumpier, especially after his most recent conversation with Max.

"Max isn't here. She and David went to talk to one of Bachman's victims out in Long Island."

"I was getting restless in the apartment and took a walk here."

"Long walk."

"I had time to kill. Any news?"

"A loose connection to the criminal Maxine thought was her father. Duvall was his stepson and according to Victor Tracy, Duvall thought Tracy was having an affair with her when Max was in college. Three months later, Tracy goes to prison. He makes a plea deal that includes restitution and Duvall's mother loses everything."

"This is an elaborate plan for revenge of something that never happened."

"Duvall thinks Max turned Tracy into the feds and cost Tracy his fortune."

"Did she?"

"No. She wasn't even a reporter then. She was still in college. Says Tracy taught her to manage the money she'd inherited from her great-grandmother."

"Why would he do that?"

"Hell if I know. Unless he really *is* her father and somehow faked the paternity test."

"Do you really think that?"

Marco shook his head. "I have two agents going to the facility where Duvall's mother is."

"Back up—what facility?"

"She had a nervous breakdown when Tracy went to prison—" He stopped talking when he saw the expression of interest on Nick's face. "Shit, that would be a pretty good motivation, wouldn't it?"

Nick nodded. "If he thinks that Max had anything to do with his mother's nervous breakdown that might give him motivation to go after her. Though this plan of his is psychotic."

"The Farmington office in Connecticut interviewed Nanette Jackson about Duvall, and she's been cooperating," Marco said. "Once we waived the warrants around, she was more than happy to help. She doesn't have much to add, except we learned that the security at Greenhaven is lacking. Though all the doors are accessed by card code, it doesn't track *who* enters a building. Plus, there's external cameras, but no internal cameras. We ran through their security logs and tracked Riley Butler's whereabouts as best we could. We have her on camera crossing the courtyard and accessing the main building. That corresponds to a card key log. Another card key log enters her building about twenty minutes later."

"Riley returning?"

"No—because we see her exiting the main building five minutes *after* that and cross through the courtyard again

There's no camera on the dorm entrances, but a log has her entering about two minutes after she leaves the main building. She was carrying a small laptop in her hands, and that was not found in her possessions."

"Her attacker was waiting in her room."

"That's my guess," Marco said. "Friday night—early Saturday morning around two—it has to be Duvall or Baker. Duvall has access to the facilities, would know how to stay off camera, and has access to the drug cocktail that Riley was pumped up with. He wasn't on duty that day because of his trip to Boston, and someone else found her."

"He planned on killing her."

"And, barring that, injected her with a roofie so she'd forget everything about that night."

"You think Jackson is clean?"

Marco nodded. "We've been digging around her, and there's nothing there. But she's a nervous Nellie, and as we've been pushing on Duvall, she's come around to admitting that he has some unorthodox treatment techniques. Dr. Ullman is heading up there as a consultant to review Duvall's files."

Marco looked down at his phone. "Sally O'Hara just sent us a sketch of the girl seen with Baker the morning Warren was killed. Let me get this printed out and distribute it to NET staff."

Marco left the room and Nick had it to himself. He stared at the corkboards again, at what was essentially Max's life for the past two years. The woman didn't slow down.

He'd considered walking away now, before he became more invested in their relationship. As he'd told David, his life was complex, and Nancy didn't make it any easier. He'd even considered staying in Menlo Park when Nancy finally moved, because he wasn't doing his career any favors by following her around. And since it was so damn complicated, he didn't know if following her would make it worse.

Then he talked to his son Logan today. He'd said exactly what David had suggested. That he would have been there if he'd known.

"I know, Dad," Logan said. "I'll send you my schedule next year so you can put it in your calendar."

Logan was a good kid, and he deserved both parents, and if Nick's career had to take a backseat, so be it. He would still have a job, he would have a pension, and he would be able to go to Logan's baseball games. He wouldn't make captain, but he didn't much care. He liked what he did, and he was good at it. But he was more than his job.

He wondered if Max ever really relaxed. If she was more than what she did. If she ever did anything for herself. If she was even capable of it.

And yet, still, he was drawn to her.

Marco stepped back in with a small stack of paper. He handed one to Nick. "I've already given a stack to Ben to distribute to his people. The witness is confident this is the girl. ERT came back with crime scene forensics on Warren's place, and there are two sets of fingerprints other than Warren's—one we ID'd to Baker, and one that isn't in the criminal database. I'm betting they belong to this girl."

She was young, with blond hair and light eyes. She had a half smile on her face.

Marco said, "The witness said she was playing with the dog, smiling. And that was the only way it worked for the sketch. We're doing a limited distribution first, before we go wide through the media."

"Let me know what I can do."

"I appreciate it," Marco said, and Nick thought he really meant it.

Ben ran into the room with the NET crime reporter Ace Burley right behind him. "Ace knows this girl."

Marco and Nick both turned to him.

Ace said, "I sat in the courtroom for a day and a half. That's Ava Raines, Adam Bachman's would-be victim."

Chapter Thirty-four

When Max and David were seated at Ava Raines's dining-room table, Ava didn't seem to know what to do or say, so Max spent twenty minutes going through what she could expect from the interview tomorrow. How long it would take, the types of questions Max would ask, and Max's primary goal.

"I want you to be empowered," Max said. "You are not a victim. You escaped, you testified, you persevered. It's not easy—but you did it, you stood up and spoke for the victims who couldn't speak for themselves. You should be proud of yourself, whether or not you speak publicly."

"If I don't want to go on television, I don't have to?"

"No. You absolutely do not. I can interview you one-on-one and quote from the interview; I can interview you on camera but not show your face—only your voice. Or you can sit across from me and we can just talk. The tape will be edited, so if you get nervous or don't know what to say, we can cut those parts out."

"What happened to Adam Bachman? Ms. Golden really didn't tell me much. She said he killed himself Friday night."

Max nodded. "Like I said on the phone, guilt."

"How?"

"How what?"

"How do people kill themselves in prison? Aren't there guards watching them and stuff?"

"It happens. I was told he made a crude knife out of a toothbrush handle."

Ava didn't appear repulsed, but Max supposed knowing that Bachman planned on suffocating her might make her less emotional about his own demise.

"Do you have questions for me?"

Max glanced at David who was on his cell phone, texting someone. His posture changed, then he pocketed his phone.

"We need to go," he said, standing.

Normally, Max would question him, but after everything she'd been through this week she simply stood up.

"Okay," Ava said with a shrug. She didn't get up, but watched as David maneuvered Max outside.

"What's wrong?" Max asked as they walked briskly down the front walk. David was looking right and left.

"She knew Baker."

"Cole Baker?"

He nodded once. "In the car. Now."

David unlocked the car remotely and pushed Max into the passenger seat, slamming the door shut. He walked briskly around the front of the car to the driver's side, opened the door, then turned slightly, his hand on his gun.

It was too late. A gunshot echoed in the air, and David collapsed, half in, half out of the car.

Marco was driving while talking on both a radio and a cell phone. Nick was in the passenger seat juggling both for him, and giving him directions to Ava Raines's house on

Long Island. Local police were on their way, as well as federal agents.

"Her bodyguard said he was getting her out, but I haven't been able to reach either one of them for fifteen minutes," Marco was telling someone over the radio.

"Local units report two minutes ETA," the radio operator said.

"Shit," Marco muttered as he signed off. "God, I hate New York. I hate New York traffic. I hate the city. I hate all these damn people!"

Marco was driving an FBI Suburban with lights and sirens, but they were still moving slow. Nick was using the onboard GPS to help navigate.

"Forty-five minutes," Nick said.

"That's just stupid. Move it, people! I swear, New Yorkers think they own the damn country."

Marco's cell phone rang. He had it hooked up to the Bluetooth in the SUV and turned on the speaker. "S.S.A. Lopez."

"It's Pierce. I'm behind you, but just heard from the RA that they've arrived at the house and the car in question is not in the area."

"Have them approach the house with caution. Put SWAT on standby."

"Already done, waiting for a target address."

"Now just move these damn cars so I can get there. Where's Duvall?"

"He hasn't left his house."

"Get eyes on him. I don't like this."

"I'll call the team and get back to you."

Marco disconnected. "Kane is supposed to protect her."

"Trust them."

"I can't." He took a deep breath. "Maybe Maxine is right."

"She would say she always is."

"Yes, she would." Marco paused. "These risks she takes. It kills me, each and every time."

"I imagine it's what a spouse of a cop would feel."

"No. It's different. She's *not* a cop."

Nick understood what he meant, and he was partly right. They were trained for this. Max wasn't.

"She couldn't have possibly known that Ava Raines was involved with Cole Baker," Nick said. "Raines was the star witness for the prosecution. She'd almost been killed."

"And what was it? A setup? Was Bachman part of it? But that doesn't make any sense." Marco answered his own question. "None of this makes any fucking sense. And now I can't reach David or Max. How long?"

"Thirty-nine minutes."

Marco looked at the dashboard clock. "At least we're making faster progress than these damn—" He honked his horn and swerved onto the shoulder to avoid a collision. "I'm just going to stay here." He picked up speed driving along the narrow, bumpy shoulder. He sideswiped two cars and didn't blink.

Nick's cell phone rang. "It's Ben," he said to Marco and put the producer on speaker.

"Are you there?" Ben asked, anxious.

"Not yet."

"I called the D.A., Richard Milligan, and told him about Ava. He'd just heard from NYPD. He can't send me the files, but told me Ava Raines had an expunged juvenile record. We don't know why, or how long, but we know that she spent a year at a juvenile detention facility in Staten Island."

Marco slapped his hand on the dashboard. "When?"

"We don't know, but there's a high probability it overlapped with Duvall's employment there, based on her age."

"Didn't the D.A.'s office do a more extensive background on their star witness?" Nick asked.

"Yes and no. She was a victim. She really did go through paramedic training. Her friends' statements about that weekend all held up. There was no cause to dig into her juvenile years. She's been clean, no dings on her record since she turned eighteen."

"And no one knew she was associating with Cole Baker?" Nick asked.

"No one knew he was a threat until he kidnapped Max. No one knew he existed."

Nick corrected him. "You mean, no one knew he was a threat until Max started pursuing the idea that Adam Bachman had a partner."

"I've been trying to reach her and David," Ben said.

"We have, too."

"Richard will help anyway he can," Ben said. "A.D.A. Golden is on her way out there now. She has a photo from the courthouse surveillance with Duvall talking to Riley Butler, the first day of the trial."

"Riley can't remember what happened to her when she was drugged," Nick said, "but said she dreamed about someone at the courthouse."

Marco said, "The thing about memory-loss drugs is that they don't work predictably. But even though she recognized Duvall, she can't place him in her room at Greenhaven."

"But he was at the courthouse. He had no reason to be there," Ben said over the speaker.

"It's one more small nail in his coffin," Marco said. "If we can get to Ava Raines and get her to flip, maybe she'll be the final nail."

"Unless Duvall is already there," Nick said.

"Don't jinx it, Santini. Raines doesn't know we have a witness. We don't know why she lured Max to her house, but David is aware she's involved. He'll do everything he can to protect Maxine."

Ben asked, "Are you sure they're still at Ava Raines's house?"

Nick looked at the GPS tracker in his hand. "David's car is still there."

Marco disconnected from Ben and called Rose Pierce. "What's the status on Duvall?" he asked.

"I'm on the line with the team assigned to him. There's no answer at the door. They're searching the grounds."

"Shit, Rose! They let him slip away? When was the last time they saw him?"

"When he accepted a package delivery at twelve thirty this afternoon. His car is still there."

"Doesn't mean he can't get another. Find out where he went and when." He disconnected. "Twelve fucking thirty. That would give him more than enough time to drive to Long Island. Or that bitch could have been waiting for him, picked him up. Dammit!" He hit his steering wheel again.

Nick stared at the GPS map and willed Marco to go faster.

Max stared at Carter Duvall and felt nothing but hatred.

She didn't hate many people. She didn't like many people, either, but hate was a powerful emotion and she simply didn't want to give anyone that kind of power.

Max hated this man and wanted him to die. If that gave him power, so be it.

Maybe it was his own hatred of her that leached into her body, because when he looked at her now, all she saw was violence in his eyes. Like Adam Bachman during his trial, Carter Duvall was not the same man she'd met last week talking shop with his colleagues. He was wild and vengeful and desperate.

He had nothing to lose. And that made him more dangerous.

They were in the attic of Ava Raines's house. Max was

handcuffed to an old metal heater in front of a small window that overlooked the front yard. Duvall had positioned Max in that window so she could see everything below.

Including David's body.

David wasn't dead, but he was injured and possibly dying. She didn't know how bad, he was obscured from view by the car. She hadn't seen him run into the house, and prayed he wouldn't. Duvall had set some sort of crude trip wire over the doorways so anyone who entered the house would be maimed or killed.

"I'm willing to admit my mistakes," Duvall said to her. "I should never have let Cole take you. I'd thought you were selfish and self-absorbed and didn't care about anyone but yourself. And I still think that, except for one important fact: you do care about people. You're just a bitch. But if David Kane dies, you'll suffer. If Sally O'Hara dies, you'll suffer. If Marco Lopez dies, you'll suffer. Even that new guy from California—I think you'd be sad if he died. Sadder because you're the one who put the targets on their backs.

"I didn't see it before because I only saw *you* and my anger blinded me. It was my mistake, because everything was there in those pages."

"You read my journals."

"Yes, I did. Every last one." He smiled.

Max pushed away the overwhelming feeling of exposure in front of someone who despised her, who used her past against her. All her thoughts and secrets and fears were in those journals. They had given her peace as a child when her life had been full of surprises and upheavals, month after month.

"There's a pain deeper than death," he said. "And you will experience it today."

"They'll kill you."

"That's fine," Duvall said. And by the look in his eyes, he'd already accepted that he would die.

It didn't bother him. And that made him far more dangerous to Max and to everyone she cared about.

She glanced over at Ava who sat on a couch with her legs tucked under her, watching Max and Duvall as if it were a movie. She looked her part—a petite girl-next-door type who'd been the unfortunate victim of a serial killer.

Except she wasn't. How did that work?

Max remembered in the courtroom, the day Ava testified, how Adam Bachman became agitated. He'd lost his bravado from the interview earlier, and seemed to shrink. He'd said things to his lawyer that Max couldn't hear. Now she understood.

"You lied to him," Max said to Ava. "That's why Adam was so upset during your testimony. Because he realized he'd been set up."

"Yep," Ava said as if they were having a friendly conversation. "I was *so* his type. When he got out of line, the doc said time for plan B. I was plan B!"

Duvall walked over to her and smiled like she was his prize pupil. "You played your part brilliantly, Ava."

"He could have killed you," Max said. Maybe she just didn't get it because she didn't have a death wish.

"Cole was keeping an eye on me. It would never have gotten that far," Ava said.

"But why?" Max asked. "You risked your life. If Adam got out of line, so to speak, why not just kill him like Cole Baker did to the Palazzolos?"

"You mean what *we* did to the Palazzolos." Ava practically jumped off the couch in her giddiness. "It was *my* idea to use the tunnels and the chemicals. Adam didn't even know where they were. Cole told him everything—well, not *everything*. We didn't want Adam to know about me because I was plan B."

"You planned on setting him up the whole time?"

"No," Duvall said, "but it's always good to have a ringer."

"You shouldn't have killed Cole," Ava said. "I loved him." The way she said it made Max think they were words, nothing more. She had no love in her eyes, no rage, no real emotion at all. The tears, the breaking up, the hesitation on the stand—it was all an act. She behaved exactly how Charlene Golden and the jury expected a victim to behave.

"Did you coach her?" Max asked Duvall. "Because this girl has no feelings about anything."

Ava rolled her eyes.

Duvall said, "I recognized that Ava was a sociopath from the minute I met her. She was assigned to me at Staten Island Juvenile. But she was smarter than most of those kids. Many were ruthless and street-smart, but Ava had something special."

Ava grinned.

"I worked with her for two years. Taught her how to act like people expected her to act. Taught her how to dress, how to behave, how to show proper emotion."

Max said to Ava, "He's going to get you killed. You know that."

Ava faked a yawn.

Max glanced out the window. A police car rolled up. Then another. Two officers ran behind the car to where David was.

Duvall saw the same thing. He smiled, opened the window, and picked up a rifle that was propped against the wall, just out of Max's reach. He put Max in front of him, and leveled the rifle on the window ledge.

The two officers helped David up. David was okay, but he was unsteady. They were assisting him over to the cars.

Max knew exactly what Duvall was going to do.

"David!" she screamed. "Duck!"

Duvall fired the rifle, hitting one of the officers in the leg.

"Shit," he muttered. He fired three more times as the wounded officer was pulled away from the danger area. "It seems your friend had on a vest, otherwise he would have been dead. I'll go for the head shot next time."

He then hit her with the gun. She fell to her knees, her arm that was handcuffed to the radiator twisting painfully.

"Go ahead and warn them as much as you want. I like hitting you."

She seethed, but inside was relieved. David was safe. He was alive. He now knew Duvall was inside with a gun.

"All this because you were wrong."

"Wrong about how to hurt you."

"No. Wrong about what happened when Victor Tracy went to prison."

Duvall was visibly surprised at her statement. He stepped back. "How did you figure it out?"

"Because I'm good at what I do." She sat down, but Duvall pulled her back up. She cried out involuntarily at the pain in her shoulder.

"Hmm, looks like you dislocated your shoulder. I'll bet it hurts." He poked at it with the barrel of his rifle. "Too bad."

"You were wrong about me. I never had an affair with Victor. I thought he was my father."

"I've heard far sicker fantasies than girls who want to screw their dads."

"You probably have considering who you surround yourself with." She glared at Ava who was twisting her hair in her fingers.

"Ouch," Ava said.

Max was in a room with two insane people.

"I didn't turn Victor over to the authorities."

"You don't get it. Because you're so damn selfish."

"What? You want honesty? I'll tell you exactly what happened. My mother had an affair with Victor while he was married to your mother. I'm sorry. My mother was a liar. She lived her life how she wanted. I came along and I don't even think she knew who my father was. But she told me it was Victor, and I believed her. Until I forced him to take a paternity test."

"You forced him by threatening to tell my mother he'd had an affair!"

"I didn't tell her."

"She knew. It doesn't matter if it wasn't you. My mother is sweet, innocent, sickly her entire life. And Victor Tracy used her. He wanted her sweet innocence on his arm while he bilked millions from investors. He drove her to a nervous breakdown. And then, right after he met with *you*, he was arrested. And you didn't have anything to do with that?"

"I didn't."

"You did! Everything was perfect for my mom until *you* walked into Victor's life and *did not leave!*"

"You are so wrong I don't even know how to begin. You're as much a lunatic as your patients. Obviously, it runs in the family."

That was the wrong thing to say.

Duvall screamed and coldcocked her with the butt of the rifle. She collapsed to the floor, unconscious.

Ava Raines's house was surrounded, the residents on the street evacuated, and the street blocked off at both ends by the time Marco and Nick arrived. They were held back by the head of FBI SWAT.

"I'm Sam Shaw, SWAT team leader for Long Island. We have a situation, you'll have to stand back."

Marco showed his badge. "S.S.A. Lopez, this is Detective Santini. What's the status?"

"We have a witness, David Kane, who states that a female is being held hostage in the attic of the house. There are two suspects, a male and a female, who Mr. Kane identified as Doctor Carter Duvall and Ms. Ava Raines."

"Where is Kane?"

"He's being treated by a field medic. But we have an active shooter up there. He shot one of the first responders. An ambulance is on its way, but we can't bring the paramedics to the street. The shooter is in the attic and has a high, wide vantage point, which is why we're staging this far out."

"I need to talk to Kane. There's more information you need to know."

Shaw led Marco and Nick to a staging area outside of a direct line of sight to the house. David had no shirt on and a medic was bandaging his chest. He had a bandage on his arm and forehead as well.

The medic said, "He would have been dead if he wasn't wearing a vest."

David looked from Marco to Nick. "Duvall was hiding down the side of the house. Shot me as soon as I'd secured Max in the car and was about to get in the driver's side, otherwise he wouldn't have gotten to her. I went out."

"Head shot?"

"Hitting the concrete. The arm was just a graze. He was here the whole time. That bitch set us up."

"No one knew she was involved," Marco said. "She'd been seen as a victim. What's the plan, Shaw? Can we breach the house? Send in gas? What?"

"We're working through it. He hasn't made any demands and no one is answering the phone inside. Mr. Kane informed us that there may be explosives."

David said, "When I came to, I saw Ava setting up a

trip wire at the front door. We have to assume they set up similar devices at all entrances."

"What's his endgame?" Nick said. "Negotiate for Max's release?"

"He used Max as a shield when he fired on us," David said. "I was behind the car and couldn't move—didn't want to let him know I was only wounded."

"A cracked rib," the medic said.

"Could have been worse," David said. "We have to find a way to get inside."

Shaw said, "This is my operation. Agent Lopez, I appreciate any insight you can give me on the suspect and the hostage, but this is my team and my call."

"Understood," Marco said. He put his hand on David's shoulder. "You couldn't have known."

"I should have. As soon as you sent me the message, I should have assumed Duvall was there somewhere. My goal was to get Max out of the house."

"I assigned a team to sit on Duvall and he gave them the slip. They were watching an empty house. If I knew he wasn't there, I would have let you know."

"What does he want?" Shaw said. "If we know that, we can figure this out."

"He wants to hurt Max," Nick said. "And I think he figured out another way to do it since his first plan backfired."

"How's that?" Shaw asked.

"David would have been dead if he hadn't been wearing a vest. And now with Agent Lopez and I onsite, he's going to try to take one of us out."

"We won't give him that chance."

"He'll wait until he snaps and kills Max," Nick said.

"With her mouth, that will be sooner rather than later," Marco said. "Duvall is a psycho and he's already been party to more than a half-dozen murders. And what kind

of person puts themselves in front of a serial killer like Ava
Raines did? It was sheer luck the police arrested him with
her in the trunk."

"Unless it wasn't luck," David said. "It may have been
part of their plan."

Marco shook his head. "It's one big fucking game and
in the end, everyone dies."

Nick said, "I have an idea." He turned to Shaw. "With
your approval."

"Let me hear it."

Max's head ached. She turned, and the pain in her shoulder reminded her that it was dislocated, that her wrists
were raw from where she was handcuffed to a radiator, and
that two sociopaths wanted her dead.

"Get up," Duvall said, pulling her to her feet. "I need
you in the window so SWAT doesn't get any ideas."

"Your plan isn't going to work," she said, catching her
breath. She looked outside. There were more SWAT vehicles, though no one was visible except far down the street.
From this third-story window, Duvall had a vantage point
where he could see well. He'd at least thought this out.
"You're not an idiot," she continued. "You went through
medical school. You must have some intelligence."

"That's your fatal flaw," he said. "You presuppose that
everyone wants to survive."

"That's not what I was talking about," she said. "No one
is going to put themselves in the line of fire."

"I suppose not. But they will attempt to rescue you.
Which means they'll end up killing themselves and you
in the process."

She would have said, "And you, too," but she believed
for the first time that Duvall really didn't care what happened to him or to Ava. And Ava? She was unreachable.
She stared at Duvall as if he were the Second Coming of

Christ, and it was clear that she'd sacrifice herself or kill for him.

Max had seen it before. When she and Sally had rescued Jane, one of the girls was so far gone over to the Butchers's way of thinking that she preferred to die with them than return to her family. She might not have even known she had a family anymore. She was so brainwashed and manipulated, that she'd become just as dangerous as her abductors.

Ava wasn't here against her will, she'd been broken long ago, and Duvall had molded her into a better psychopath.

Was that what he'd done with Adam Bachman and Cole Baker? Seen their darkness and made it his own? Made them believe that they were normal, that they could and should act on their darkest impulses?

"What do you think will happen to your mother when you're dead?" Max said.

He flinched, just a bit. But he had his gun aimed out the window, waiting for a target.

"She's in that beautiful sanitarium now, but what about when you can't pay for it?"

"I have a trust set up for her. She'll be taken care of for the rest of her life."

"That trust will be tied up in legal fights from here to eternity."

"Hardly. I've been prepaying for her care for years." Duvall cocked his head, looked down the street as much as he could. He turned his gun and fired.

Max jumped, admonishing herself for reacting because it gave Duvall such pleasure.

"Winged him," Duvall said. "The nice thing about you standing here with me, Maxine, is that they're not going to shoot back.

From Max's angle, she couldn't see if he really did hit someone or not.

"So even though you now know I had nothing to do with turning Victor into the FBI, that I had nothing to do with him losing his money, that I had nothing to do with your mother's . . . fragility," she said cautiously, "you still want to punish me."

"But you had everything to do with it. If you hadn't come to Victor that day, my mother would never have found out about his affairs, she would never have tried to kill herself, she would never have lost her mind!"

Maybe it was true. Maybe Max unknowingly set up a chain of events that had far-reaching consequences. Her quest for the truth and everyone else be damned.

And in many other instances, Max would have believed that, because she did seek the truth, and she did believe that the truth was far better than a lie.

But this time . . . this was personal. This was her quest to find out who her father was. To find out what happened to her mother. To learn what happened when she was conceived, and why her mother roamed the country for ten years before leaving Max. That she'd gone to Victor wasn't to punish him for infidelity—though she certainly hadn't cared whether that truth was exposed. She'd gone to Victor to find the truth about herself and her mother.

All she'd uncovered were more of her mother's lies.

"Your mother was the innocent victim," Max said. "Do you think she's the only woman to have ever been cheated on?"

"You don't understand. She was delicate."

"That's exactly what Victor said, which is why I never told her. So if she found out, it wasn't on me."

"She found out *because* of you and the calls and letters to Victor. She told me how she was in physical pain because of the betrayal of her husband. How *could* he!"

"Why go after me? Why not go after him?"

"Because you were the catalyst. I've watched you for

two years being the noble, honest Maxine Revere, putting truth on a pedestal and condemning lies. Exposing secrets not because it's the right thing to do, but because you have the power to do it. Some secrets should never be revealed. Some lies are necessary to protect the people we care about. But you know everything, don't you? You wreck lives and walk away because you have money and a self-righteous stick up your ass.

"The truth kills, Maxine. And it's going to kill you."

Without turning his head, he said, "Ava, it's time. Good luck."

"Thank you for everything, Doc." Ava kissed his cheek, then left the attic.

"Time for what?"

"The catalyst so you can watch your friends die. They will come for you, and you'll suffer until your last breath."

Nick and Marco had donned SWAT gear and were working with Shaw and another guy, Bonner, to go in through the back of the house. They'd had to take the long way around to prevent Duvall from spotting their approach. But the layout of the house, and the lack of a window on the back side of the attic, enabled them to approach undetected.

"Have you confirmed there are trip wires in the doorways?" Shaw asked someone over his radio.

"Positive," was the response. "Garage and front door confirmed. You have eyes on the rear."

"Do you see the device?"

"Negative. Looks like a cylinder on both sides. Hold it—there's movement on the second floor."

Marco took out binoculars and looked up to the second floor of the ramshackle house. He didn't see anyone. He looked down to the back door. It was closed, but there was a thin wire going from one side to the other.

"There's a wire back here. I can't see a device, but it

it's sensitive, it'll detonate as soon as we open the door," Marco said. "Any confirmation on the windows?"

"So far we can see no devices hooked up to any of the windows in our sight, but we can't see into the house."

Another voice came over the comm. "Movement on the staircase going from two to one; I repeat, movement, appears to be a single figure, moving from floor two to floor one."

"ID?" Shaw asked.

"Negative. It's a shadow. However, we still have a visual on the hostage in the attic. There is a gun barrel visible next to her, and a hand of one of the suspects. Two confirmed in the attic; one confirmed on the first floor."

They waited. The windows in the back were covered and they couldn't see any movement. They waited for five minutes before Shaw asked for an update.

"We're ready," he said, "but I need to know where all three people are."

"We have heat signatures. The hostage and one suspect are in the attic; the second suspect appears to be in the basement, but the signature is fading. We've seen no movement on the first floor."

"It's now or never," Nick said.

"I hope this works," Marco said.

So did Nick.

Bonner and Marco crossed the small yard to the largest rear window. Marco stood watch while Bonner cut out the glass. It took several minutes. Then they had to carefully lower it so it didn't break and alert the suspects.

Shaw asked the status.

"We lost one of the heat signatures. It went underground, to the basement, which could be blocking it. I can adjust—"

"No—keep visual of the hostage at all times." Shaw glanced at Nick, then said to his team, "Widen the perimeter. One of them is going underground. Pull the maps, find out where."

"Roger."

"Duvall could be escaping," Nick said. "We need to be doubly careful. He could have this entire house rigged."

"Just what I was thinking."

Bonner gestured with a thumbs-up that they were ready to go in, then he moved his hands rapidly back and forth and he and Marco ran back to where Nick and Shaw waited.

"What's wrong?" Shaw demanded.

"Fire inside," Bonner said.

As soon as he said it, smoke started to drift out the cut window.

Shaw demanded a status and was told two individuals remained in the attic.

"He's burning the house down with Ava and Max in the attic?"

"No, he's not," Marco said and ran back to the window.

"Agent Lopez!" Shaw yelled.

Nick followed Marco.

Marco said, "You have a kid. I'll do this."

"We'll do it. You need backup."

Shaw and Bonner both followed them. "Lopez, this is a dumb move."

"He's going to kill her, and I'm not going to watch this house burn down with Max in it."

"Fire is on their way," Shaw said. "ETA six minutes."

"We don't have six minutes."

Nick boosted Marco up into the window, and Shaw helped Nick and Bonner up. He then hoisted himself through. "Watch all doorways."

The ground floor was quickly filling up with smoke; it was coming from the vents in the floor. This old house would burn fast. They didn't have a lot of time.

Shaw gestured toward the back door. Two cylinders were attached to a thin wire that went outside the door. "I'll defuse this door. Don't use any others. Get her down ASAP." He squatted and got to work.

Bonner stayed to protect Shaw while he worked, and Nick and Marco went as fast as they dared up the stairs toward the attic, looking carefully for trip wires or anything else that would kill them.

The smoke was rising, but no flames were visible. If the fire had been set in the basement, it would burn the foundation first, and then the supports, and the old house would collapse into itself.

They stopped at the attic door. There was a trip wire. Nick squatted to inspect it.

"Do you know what to do?" Marco whispered.

Nick leaned over and smelled the cylinders.

"It's rubbing alcohol with no trigger," he said. "They're good fakes, but they're fake."

"The rubbing alcohol will add fuel to the fire," Marco said.

"As if this house isn't fuel enough," Nick said.

A gunshot from the attic had Nick and Marco on their feet. Nick opened the door and Marco covered him. The narrow stairs went straight up; potentially, a deadly trap.

Another gunshot sounded.

"Cover me," Marco said to Nick.

"As soon as you reach the top, get away from the door," Nick said.

Marco nodded. It was a distraction technique and might not work, especially since they didn't know the layout of the attic. But they didn't have time to plan.

Nick trained his gun on the opening above as Marco quickly walked up the stairs. There was no being quiet now.

As soon as Marco got to the top, Nick started up. Then he paused and listened.

Marco put three fingers up. Then two. Then one. Nick nodded.

"Put the gun down," a voice behind them said.

Max's heart nearly stopped. It was Marco. He'd walked right into Duvall's trap.

Duvall turned slowly around, holding Max close. He'd put the rifle down, and now held a knife which he pressed into her side. He didn't seem surprised or concerned that the FBI was in the house.

Max smelled smoke.

"I told you, Maxine. Someone would come for you. Now we can all die together."

"You don't want to die," Marco said, his gun trained on Duvall. He walked toward them. The attic was dirty, but empty except for boxes stacked along the edges, and the old worn couch that Ava had been sitting in. "Put the knife down."

"I'm ready, Agent Lopez. I'm ready to die. I think Maxine here understands that now. And you're the lucky one who gets to join us."

Max was not going to stand here and watch anyone she cared about die. *She* wasn't ready to die.

She caught Marco's eye and mouthed, "Shoot him."

Duvall stepped aside half a foot and, using her as shield, threw the knife at Marco.

He tried to move out of the way, but Duvall's technique was flawless. The knife hit Marco in the leg and he crumbled. He couldn't shoot because Duvall held Maxine right in front of him.

Nick appeared in the doorway, gun on Duvall.

"Good," Duvall said, "we'll *all* die today. Too bad your friend David Kane couldn't join us."

Max didn't think, just kicked backward as hard as sh

ould into his groin, then dropped to her knees and held
er breath.

Gunfire erupted as bullets hit Duvall's body. She didn't
now if Marco or Nick or both had shot him, because she
vasn't watching, but he fell, dead, to the attic floor.

Nick strode over to Max and pulled her up. "We have
o—" he saw the handcuffs.

Marco reached into his pocket and tossed Nick his own
andcuff keys. Universal, Max thought, lucky for her. "Get
er out," he said.

"Like hell I'm going to let you play the martyr," Nick
aid as he unlocked the cuffs. He touched her face. "You're
leeding."

"I'm okay," she said. "I'm alive."

"And we're all going to stay that way."

The sound of sirens filled the air. The smoke was get-
ng thicker, and the house began to creak.

Into his radio, Marco said, "Suspect down, hostage safe,
e're coming out."

Over the radio, Shaw said, "Get out now. The building
going to collapse any minute into the basement."

Nick went over to Marco. He said, "This is going to
irt."

"Just do it."

Nick pulled out the knife. Marco winced and squeezed
s eyes shut.

Blood poured from the wound. "He hit an artery. You'll
eed out if I don't stop it."

"We don't have time," Marco said.

"Thirty seconds."

Nick pulled out a tourniquet from one of many pockets
d quickly tightened it around Marco's leg. He helped
m up.

"Get his other side," Nick told Max.

She complied.

Nick led the way down the smoke-filled stairs to the second-floor landing. The house creaked and groaned and shuddered as they walked down the hall to the stairs. They were all coughing, and Max's eyes burned. The boot on her foot slowed her down.

The stairs were on fire from the bottom up.

Nick turned them around and they walked to the back of the house. In the rear bedroom, Nick grabbed the nearest heavy object—a nightstand—and broke the window. Max pulled the comforter off the bed and tossed it over the windowsill.

Marco shouted into his comm, "We're jumping out of the second story into the back. Shaw, copy?"

"Roger."

The entire house sagged, dipped toward the center. Everything on the dresser crashed to the floor. Nick told Max, "Help Marco get over the ledge. It's about fourteen feet."

"I've jumped from higher," Marco said. "Get her out right behind me."

Marco jumped out of the window, cried out when he hit the ground. Max leaned out the window. The sides of the house were on fire at the base, smoke billowing up. Three men dressed in SWAT gear grabbed Marco and dragged him away.

"Go," Nick told her. "Now."

She climbed on to the ledge. The house groaned heavily and sagged, then didn't stop. It kept collapsing and she screamed, "Nick!" as she jumped. The heat was unbearable, and she fell heavily on the hard earth. The fire was so close she thought she was in the flames. Then arms picked her up.

"Nick!" she called through her scratchy throat.

He jumped from the window as the house dropped away behind him. Firefighters were running through the yard. Nick landed in a crouch and rolled, then jumped right back up. How'd he do that?

The earsplitting noise as the old Victorian collapsed into the basement made her heart skip a beat.

It had been close, much too close.

Nick caught up with the firefighter who carried her. "I got this," he said and took Max from the man. He settled her at the base of a tree in the neighbor's yard, and inspected her. "You are okay."

"How did you do that?"

"What?"

"Jump as if you jump from burning buildings all the time?"

"I was in the Marines. I've jumped from airplanes and helicopters and buildings. I usually had a parachute, but I know how to jump."

She spontaneously hugged him. And for once, she was at a loss for words.

Marco swore as the paramedics adjusted him on the gurney. "Watch the leg," he said.

One of the medics said, "That tourniquet saved your life."

He knew that. Marco didn't want to be grateful for the other man in Max's life, but he was. Not only for being competent—more than competent—but for being good to Max.

He saw David watching from the end of the gurney. Max's bodyguard had his own bandages over cracked ribs, but wasn't sitting down.

David smiled. He still looked dangerous, but Marco had done a complete background check on him when Max hired him. The man was a hero and never talked about his past. Marco doubted even Max knew much about David before he left the Rangers.

"I'm glad you'll live."

Marco grunted his response. He wanted to ask David to put in a good word for him with Max . . . or something. Maybe that's not what he really wanted. Hell, he didn' know what he wanted. Max's happiness. . . . but he wanted Max to be happy *with him*. And she wasn't.

Max was talking with Rose Pierce near the SWAT tac tical station. Santini was at her side.

"You know, Kane," he said, "I didn't want to like tha guy." Marco hadn't wanted to like David, either. What did that say about him? That any man in Max's life—gay o straight—was a threat?

"I know."

"I want her back."

"Not my place."

"I hear a *but* in your tone."

"Oil and water."

He wanted to argue, but David was right.

"We're ready to go," one of the medics said. He and his partner slid the gurney into the back of the ambulance.

Max saw Marco being loaded into the ambulance "Nick—give me a minute?"

He glanced over to where she was looking and nodded

She squeezed his hand and let it go. Her foot ached, and all she wanted was to sleep for two days. She limped over to the medics and said, "One minute?"

"One minute."

She climbed into the ambulance and sat next to Marco She took his hand. "I never thanked you for coming up here. David called, you came. You always have." This man had made her happy and made her miserable, but he wa dependable.

"I'll wait for you."

Tears burned behind her eyes. "Don't."

"It's not that simple."

"Marco . . . please . . ."

He squeezed her hand. "I know."

What was he talking about? Were they having two different conversations? Maybe it had always been that way
with them. "I haven't always been fair to you. But I appreciate you, and I don't think I've ever said that."

"You have. Maybe not in so many words . . ." He
winked. He was trying to make light of the emotional situation, and she was relieved.

"Good. I just want you to know that I'm sorry if I ever
took you for granted. I have never forgotten what you've
done for me since you investigated Karen's disappearance. And even when you don't want to, you always
came through for me." She kissed him lightly on the
lips. She didn't want to give him hope that there was going to be a future between them. But as she kissed him,
she remembered they had a past. And that past would
always bind them.

She pulled back.

"Um," she said, momentarily flustered and emotional,
"Rose Pierce was filling us in. Ava Raines was apprehended
at the end of a sewage tunnel, half a mile from here. She's
totally indifferent that Duvall is dead or her house is
destroyed. According to Pierce, she didn't even bat an eye
when she was arrested for kidnapping, perjury, arson, and
accessory to murder. Probably more—Pierce said they
have a lot to go through."

She paused, looked out the back of the ambulance to
where the collapsed house still smoked from the ground.
"She was a piece of work. I don't think I've ever met anyone like her before."

The medic said, "Ms. Revere, we have to go."

She nodded and allowed the medic to help her from th back. "See you, Marco."

"We'll talk later."

Max watched the ambulance leave, wishing she coul have said something more. Wishing she could be the per son Marco wanted.

But she couldn't.

She turned to look for Nick and found both he an David standing on the sidewalk, watching her. She limpe over to David and hugged him. "I'm so glad you're okay."

"Right back at you." He looked her over, then looked Nick. "Keep an eye on her tonight."

"I will."

Pierce came back over and said, "I have a few mor questions—"

Nick cut her off and put his arm around Max's shou ders. "They'll wait until tomorrow."

David said, "Agent Pierce, I need my gun back."

"Follow me. And Ms. Revere, we'll talk tomorrow."

They walked back to the tactical truck and Max leane into Nick. He sat her down on a short rock wall separa ing the sidewalk from a house.

Max looked up at Nick. "Thank you for that."

He touched her cheek. "I can't convince you to go t the hospital, can I?"

"No. I want my own bed."

"Let's go."

But she didn't move. "You risked everything for me."

"It's my job."

"This wasn't your job. Thank you."

"Don't."

"Don't thank you?"

"Don't say good-bye."

She was confused. Maybe it was the blow to her hea "I wasn't."

"Good." He kissed her. "Let's go have that dinner you
omised me."

"I'm not very presentable right now." Her stomach
owled. "But I'm starving."

He grinned, looking handsome even through all the dirt
d soot. "Good thing for you that I know how to cook."

Chapter Thirty-five

TWO DAYS LATER

David and Max walked along the Hudson River. Slowl
Max still wore the boot. David's ribs were still sore. The
were a pair. But they were alive.

And Max had to make sure everything was okay b
tween them.

"Nick said you were thinking about quitting."

"He shouldn't have told you that."

"We agreed that we couldn't have secrets. But, mo
than that, he knows how important you are to me." H
voice skipped and she didn't want to get emotional, but th
had been an emotional week. She wasn't used to it. Sh
was used to the indignant anger, justice, and pride in h
work. Now she was so sad, bordering on depressed, mc
of the bad guys were dead, and the deaths that precede
them seemed to have been for nothing.

She'd talked to all three Palazzolo children last night v
Skype. They were having a funeral next week in Ohio, ar
Max promised to attend. She wanted to—for herself, ar
for them—but the conversation had left her emotional
drained. Jim and Sandy were still dead, and there was r
ally no good reason *why*. Ava Raines was talking, b

Max hadn't pushed to read the transcripts. Soon, but not today.

"David?" she questioned.

"I thought about it, but I'm not leaving. I just need to work through a few things. I don't take failure well." He glanced at her. "I'm worse than you."

"You didn't fail anyone or anything."

"You."

"No."

"He should never have gotten to you a second time. The first time—I didn't see the threat. The second? I knew there was a threat, and I didn't act accordingly."

"The FBI was sitting on Duvall. He had this planned out to the last detail. He knew how to get out."

"And then Riley didn't come to me because she was scared of me. She didn't trust me, because I didn't like her and she knew it."

"David, if you're talking blame, I'm as culpable as anyone. More so. I didn't train her properly. I was enamored with the idea that I had a mini-me, someone to send into the field because I couldn't be in two places at once. I'm going back to an office assistant. I don't know if I'm ready for someone in the field, someone who isn't you."

She took his hand as they walked. "I'm glad you're staying. I need you. I don't like to admit it. If anything good has come from this last week, it's that I realize I have the best, most reliable, most loyal people in my life. People I haven't appreciated like I should. Even Ben surprised me."

"He surprised me, too."

She smiled. "We both need a break, before we go to Oregon. I already talked to Ben and he's going to send a research team before me."

"That's stunning."

"That Ben is giving me time off?"

"That you're giving up that control."

"We have a good team at *Maximum Exposure*. I see that now, the strengths and weaknesses. I am a control freak, I know that. I'm trying to delegate more. If I'm going to keep this show going, I can't do it all myself. I miss what I used to do. The undercover investigations. The research. The puzzle. And it's not like I'm giving up *all* control."

He smiled. "We'll see how far this goes."

"For now, it goes. I'm going to see Nick. He had to juggle shifts, so he doesn't have any time until July, but he's going to take a week off. We're going to Lake Tahoe and doing nothing."

"You? Do nothing?" He grinned.

"I want you and Emma to come."

"I don't think Nick wants a third wheel. Especially me."

"I'm renting a huge house, and Nick is bringing Logan. It's his week to have his son."

"Are you sure you're not inviting me because you want to keep distance between you and Nick?"

"What does that mean?"

"One week with one man, isolated? That's bordering on commitment."

"I need to start somewhere," she said. "Thinking about my mother's life for the ten years I knew her . . . the constant moving around. She said all the different people we stayed with were her friends, but they were freeloaders. She blew the equivalent of twenty-five thousand dollars a month, every month. She had different guys in different ports, so to speak. She might not even *know* who my father is."

They stopped walking and sat on a bench near the Hudson River Park Pier, looking out to the river. A warm wind whipped around them.

"I don't want to be her. Duvall said something that true."

David tensed. "You have got to get him out of your head, Maxine."

"I'm trying. But he was right in that I have a deep fear of being abandoned. I thought I had addressed that, that I recognized my flaws because of my mother. But I think it goes deeper than that. I need to battle it; I don't want to be alone for the rest of my life. I don't know if Nick is the one, but I need to put forth more of an effort than I have in the past. Does that make sense?"

"Yes. But maybe you've never put forth the effort because you never found the right person."

"Maybe."

"Marco still loves you."

"He thinks he does."

"He dropped everything when you disappeared."

"I appreciate everything he did." She frowned at him. "I thought you would be happy. You like Nick."

"My opinion is irrelevant."

"Hardly."

"You'll always have me, Maxine. I'm not going anywhere."

"Someday you'll find someone."

"I did. I lost him. End of story."

"It's never the end of the story." She put her head on her friend's shoulder and stared at the sparkling water. "You're my best friend, David. I've never said that because I was scared of what it meant. That if I acknowledged how important you are to me that you might leave. I knew in my heart about these fears, but now I can say it. I'm scared that my friends, that everyone I care about, will disappear."

David put his arm around her shoulders. They sat for several minutes staring at the water, lost in the past. Or maybe the future. But whatever it was, Max felt more at peace now than she had in a long time.

More at peace with herself, but more worried about her future. With Nick. With Marco. With her career. What she did and why she did it.

She had a lot of thinking to do, and taking time off would help.

David kissed the top of her head. "Emma and I will go to Lake Tahoe with you. But you tell Nick."

She smiled. "Deal."

Read on for an excerpt from
Allison Brennan's upcoming book

POISONOUS

Available in April 2016 in hardcover
from Minotaur Books

Dear Ms. Revere:

My name is Tommy Wallace and I live in Corte Madera, California. Last summer my stepsister, Ivy Lake, was killed and no one knows who did it.

I talked to the detective and she said she can't talk to me about what happened. She was nice and everything, but told me to talk to my dad. I thought she couldn't talk to me because I was too young, so when I turned eighteen last week, I went back to the police station and Detective Martin still wouldn't talk to me about what happened to Ivy.

I am writing to you because you help people. I've been watching your show and you find out what happened to people who died. I went to your Web site and read the article about how you found out what happened to an architect who was killed last year. That was in Atherton, which is not far from me at all! You said you wanted to find out what happened to him because his family deserved to know the truth and have closure. I don't really understand what closure means, but if it means knowing who hurt Ivy, that's what I want.

No one is like they were before Ivy died. My dad says that the police don't know who killed her or why. My stepmother gets mad all the time because the police haven't arrested anyone. My dad thinks that Ivy's boyfriend killed her. My sister thinks that Ivy's best friend killed her. My stepmother thinks that I killed her.

I would never, ever hurt anyone even if they were really mean to me. But now Paula won't let me come to the house to visit unless my dad is there, and he works so much he isn't home hardly at all. Austin says she's scared of me. He called her stupid. (I told him it wasn't nice to call people stupid. I don't like being called stupid.) I miss Bella and Austin so much sometimes I cry. (My mom says it's okay if boys cry sometimes, but my dad says I'm too old to cry.) I don't know why Paula thinks I would hurt Ivy. She wouldn't let me come to Bella's birthday party because my dad was out of town. I don't want Bella to think I don't like her anymore. My mom tried to make me feel better by taking me for an ice cream cone. I love ice cream more than any other food. I thought she was mad at me, but when my dad came back from his trip he came over and my mom yelled at him the same way she yelled at him when they were getting the divorce. My dad left and didn't say good-bye to me. I think he's mad at me, too.

I want everything to go back to the way it was before Ivy died, but Austin says that can't happen. He told me the only thing that will fix everything is if the police find out who really killed Ivy, and then Paula will know I didn't do it. But the police don't seem to be trying anymore. My dad says that we pay their salaries and they should be working harder. I don't have a job so I don't pay their salaries, is that why Detective Martin won't talk to me?

I don't want anyone to think I hurt Ivy. I don't want Austin to get in trouble for coming to see me when he's not supposed to. I want to go to Bella's birthday party in April when she turns six and give her a present. If you can just tell my stepmother I didn't do anything wrong, she'll have to believe you.

Thank you for reading my letter.

Sincerely, Tommy

Thomas Andrew Wallace

Chapter One

Maxine Revere and her right-hand everything, David Kane, flew into SFO on Labor Day. Max didn't like traveling on holidays, but she didn't have much of a choice with her hectic schedule. They took a shuttle to the car rental lot and David handled the paperwork while Max scanned her email for anything she needed to address immediately. A dozen messages down the inbox was an email from her lover, Detective Nick Santini.

I know you're angry that I cancelled our plans this weekend. I'll find time later this week to come up for a day. Let me know when you land.

Max didn't know why she was still so irritated at Nick. She'd planned on flying in a few days before her scheduled meeting with the detective in charge of the Ivy Lake homicide—thus avoiding flying on a holiday. But Nick called her Thursday night and cancelled. He said he had to swap shifts at the last minute. Something about his excuse didn't ring true, so she pressed him for the reason. Maybe what bothered Max the most was that she had to push him before he told her the truth. His ex-wife was fighting for sole custody of their son and he had a critical meeting with his lawyer. Max hadn't met Nancy Santini, but she doubted she'd like the woman who was attempting to prevent a good father like Nick from spending time with his own child. She was manipulative and vindictive, and why Nick couldn't see it, Max didn't know.

She dropped her smartphone into her purse without actually responding to Nick's message. What could she say? That she understood? She didn't, and she wasn't going to lie to Nick about how she felt. He didn't want her opinion on the matter, and she certainly wasn't going to tell him she would be waiting with intense anticipation for his unconfirmed arrival. If he drove the hour to Sausalito to see her, great. If not . . . well, she really didn't have much say in what he did or didn't do. He'd made that perfectly clear when she started asking questions about his custody battle.

David approached her, rental keys in hand. "Whose head did you bite off?"

She looked at David and raised an eyebrow. When she wore heels, she and David were eye-to-eye. "Excuse me?"

"When you're mad at someone, your eyes narrow and the lines in your forehead crease."

"You're telling me I have wrinkles. Terrific."

"It's Nick."

"If you know, why did you ask?"

David led the way to the rental car without responding. It was a rhetorical question, but Max wished David wouldn't act as if she were on the verge of dumping Nick. She was the first to admit she didn't do long-term—or long-distance—relationships well.

Nick was different. She wasn't being a romantic to think so; she wasn't a romantic at heart. Yet when he'd cancelled their weekend plans, her gut had twisted uncomfortably. She didn't want it to be over so soon.

David popped the trunk of the luxury sedan and ma-

neuvered his lone suitcase into the trunk alongside Max's
two large bags. Her laptop and overnight bag went into the
backseat. She sat in the passenger seat and slid the seat
back for comfort. After five and a half hours on a plane,
she wanted to stretch her long legs.

She could travel light if she had to, but she didn't know
how long she'd be investigating this case. She'd told Ben
she wanted ten days for the Ivy Lake investigation. He
scowled at her—it was the only word that fit his irritated-
with-Maxine expression. Then she told Laura, his admin,
not to schedule anything for two weeks. She'd almost
skipped town before Ben found out she'd blocked off so
much time, but he'd called her on the way to the airport
and whined at her. She'd already recorded the October
show—early, she reminded him—it wasn't like she had
to rush back. If she needed to do any retakes, they had a
sister studio in San Francisco.

*"You took a week off in Lake Tahoe, and now an inves-
tigation that shouldn't take more than a few days you're
taking two weeks?"*

*"Good-bye, Ben." She'd hung up on him. She wasn't go-
ing to explain herself. She knew what needed to be done
to keep her show running smoothly, and she'd do it.*

David pulled out of the parking space and merged into
the dense traffic that would take them through San Francisco and across the Golden Gate Bridge. Max stared out
the window. She liked San Francisco, but didn't have the
love affair with it like she did New York City. She'd never
once considered living here, though she grew up only
forty minutes south of the city. She couldn't put her finger
on why—maybe it was simply that San Francisco was too
close to her family.

"Why does he let her get away with it?" Max asked
after several minutes of silence.

"What are you talking about?"

"Nick's ex. The games she's playing."

"He's not letting her get away with anything," David said. "There's a process."

"She's trying to deny Nick the right to see his own son."

"No," David corrected, "she's seeking full custody so she can leave the state without violating the joint custody agreement."

"Why do you know more about this than I do?" She had mixed feelings about David's relationship with Nick. While it made her life easier that her closest friend actually liked the man she was sleeping with, she didn't particularly appreciate that Nick and David had conversations that she wasn't privy to. Lately, Nick had been talking to David more than her.

"This is an area I have more experience in than you," David said.

"Maybe I should have been a judge," she said.

David's spontaneous laughter didn't improve her mood.

"I would make a good judge," she added defensively. "I'm exceptionally good at weeding through fact and fiction."

"Perhaps in criminal court," he said and cleared his throat. "Not so in family court."

"I'd certainly put a stop to her blatant manipulation tactics. She's changed her mind three times about where she and her boyfriend are moving. And who is this boyfriend, anyway? First they're getting married, then they aren't, but are planning on moving in together? With Logan in the house? How can Nick put up with it? Doesn't he have a say in who his minor son shares a house with? This whole situation stinks, and it's not going to end well for anyone."

"You need to stay out of this, Max. Nick knows what he's doing, but it's sensitive."

"I don't understand."

"That's a first."

Max didn't respond. It was David's tone—what wasn't he telling her? Was there something else going on with Nick and his ex that David knew about but she didn't? Why would Nick hold back from her? They'd had a wonderful vacation together in Lake Tahoe six weeks ago—until it was cut short by Nick's ex-wife. Still, she'd been understanding. Mostly. Sort of.

Okay, she'd been a bitch after the fourth call from Nancy Santini demanding that Nick bring Logan back to town. Nick never told Max what their argument was about, but something Nancy said had Nick leaving the same day. Max detested these sorts of games, especially when children were involved.

Max had no children of her own and doubted she ever would. But she'd interviewed enough kids over the years and learned one important fact: kids picked up on lies faster than most adults. They knew what was going on in their family even if their parents tried to shelter them. How did that help them deal with the world? How did that help them grow into honest citizens? Never had Max found a lie better than the truth. Lies were expedient. They solved an immediate problem but created more problems in the future. And the only way to fix the situation was to keep telling lies until they exploded and everyone was stained from the deception.

Nick refused to say a negative word about Nancy in front of his son, and while Max could respect his position on the one hand, telling the truth was not being negative. The truth was neither good nor bad, it simply *was*, and Logan was smart enough to come to his own conclusions. What would he think about his father who remained silent in the face of Nancy's manipulations? How could he respect him? How would he handle his own relationships when he grew up if all he saw was Nancy's bad behavior, for which Nick remained silent—at least around his son?

"You're thinking quite loudly," David said.

"I haven't said a word."

"Sometimes you don't need to."

"Speaking of kids, will you be *allowed* to see Emma?" She winced at her tone. David didn't deserve her anger, though he seemed to be trying to irritate her. "I didn't mean it like that."

"Yes you did," David said. "I'm going to Brittany's tonight. She said we'd play it by ear."

"Another manipulative bitch," Max said under her breath.

"She is," David concurred, "but I want to see my daughter, so I deal with it. I have fewer rights than Nick because Brittany and I never married. I will not risk my time with Emma." He paused, then added, "Stay away from Brittany, Max."

David's tone had gone from normal to threatening in one sentence. A few months ago, Max would have pushed the conversation, but she'd realized over this last summer how deeply she valued David's friendship. She wasn't going to risk her relationship with her best friend and business partner by arguing with him about the mother of his daughter. So, as difficult as it was for her to remain silent, she kept her mouth shut.

Brittany treated David like garbage. She insulted him in front of Emma and refused to let David have more time with his daughter than the court mandated. The only consolation was that Emma was a smart kid. She'd be thirteen next week and adored her father. She was surprisingly well-adjusted considering her parents didn't get along. Brittany might be a bitch, but David got along with Brittany's parents and apparently they had a lot of clout over

Brittany. If it weren't for them, David said, he'd never have been part of Emma's life.

Max put David and Nick and their respective children out of her mind and spent the remainder of the drive responding to messages from her producer, Ben Lawson, and staff. Ben had wanted to send a small crew with Max because he sensed this case was going to be good—for Ben, "good" meant good for *Maximum Exposure* ratings. Max axed the idea of traveling with anyone but David. She needed time in the field without a cameraman or support staff. The interpersonal connections she made were important, but the nuances in tone, expression, and body language were lost when a camera was involved. Max had been a freelance reporter for years before agreeing to host *Maximum Exposure* for the cable network NET, and she still preferred to work a case alone, asking questions, pushing people to be truthful, proving or disproving evidence.

Though she'd be the first to admit she was happy to let the competent NET research team take over much of the grunt work. They'd compiled all the public information on the Ivy Lake investigation, including news clippings, profiles of Ivy's friends and family, and television coverage.

After going back and forth with Ben on the news crew until her irritation overflowed, she sent back a message:

I'll call in the crew when I see fit, but if I see a camera in Corte Madera before I'm ready I'll quit.

Ben just didn't know when to drop a subject, or how to give up control.

She could relate.

While Ivy's stepbrother's letter had affected her and prompted her to act, she'd grown even more curious after speaking to Tommy Wallace on the phone. He barely spoke. She tried to get him to talk about Ivy, about why he wrote

the letter, and his responses were simple and brief. Any
other case and she would have been suspicious and likely
dropped the matter altogether, but after reading the files
her staff put together, she realized from the media reports
that Tommy might be mentally handicapped.

Which made her wonder if he wrote the letter himself
or if someone helped him. And if so, why?

Max had spoken to Grace Martin, the detective in charge
of the Ivy Lake death investigation, when she received the
letter from Tommy Wallace two weeks ago. First to feel
out whether law enforcement was inclined to help or hin-
der her investigation, and then specifically to ask about
Tommy.

*"I spoke to Tommy Wallace several times," Grace had
said. "He's slow, not stupid."*

Grace seemed amenable to Max's involvement when
they spoke on the phone—the case was fourteen months
cold with no leads. She agreed to meet with Max in person, which was a big win for Max—too often she had to
fight with the local police for access.

Max had read Tommy's letter multiple times. Her
stomach twisted each time. There was an honesty of expression that surprised her, but what really hit her was the
lack of anger or grief. Maybe Tommy's "slowness" made
him less emotional. When people wrote to her, there was
always pain and anger. Rage on the page, Ben had once
said. Parents wanted answers about the murder of their
child. A spouse fighting with the police for more time and
resources because their betrothed had been murdered or
disappeared and there were no answers. But Tommy's letter was unlike any she'd read before. And while he might
have had help writing the letter, there was no doubt the
sentiments were true.

While Tommy's letter had her looking at Ivy Lake's
death, it was the circumstances themselves that propelled

Max to action. Ivy Lake had been seventeen when she'd been killed—pushed off a cliff, according to the forensics report. According to the police department, they had interviewed dozens of individuals, mostly minors, many who had reason to hate Ivy.

If the pen is mightier than the sword, the keyboard is mightier than the pen. And Ivy used her keyboard to expose the secrets of her schoolmates through social media—including one girl who'd committed suicide after bearing the brunt of Ivy's attacks. Ivy's murder had spun a web of stories in the local media about cyberbullying, but in the end, the stories stopped, the investigation hit a dead end, and life went on. Without a killer in custody. Without answers for the family. Without justice for Ivy.